Scythian Trilogy, Book 2: The Golden King

By Max Overton

Writers Exchange E-Publishing

http://www.writers-exchange.com

Scythian Trilogy Book 2: The Golden King
Copyright 2012, 2015, 2025 Max Overton
Writers Exchange E-Publishing
PO Box 372
ATHERTON QLD 4883

Cover Art by Julie Napier *www.julienapier.com*
from an original concept by Ariana Overton
Lion photograph by Julie Napier

Published by Writers Exchange E-Publishing
https://www.writers-exchange.com

ISBN **ebook**: 978-1-922066-85-5
Print: **978-1-925574-52-4** (WEE Assigned)

Contents

Prologue

A small body of Scythians rode fast toward a jutting outcrop of rock through the deepening gloom of sunset. Dense pine forest clung sullenly to rocky slopes, intensifying the shadows. A carpet of pine needles softened the sound of passage. The men, dressed in felt and leather tunics, jackets and leggings, sat astride wiry horses, thick felt blankets flapping against the horses' legs. Breath plumes of both men and mounts gusted whitely in the frosty air, ice coating beards and moustaches and flecking muzzles. They approached an outcrop and paused, pulling their mounts into a tight milling knot, searching the ground around them for the presence of others. The tallest of the men dismounted, slapping his arms and legs against the cold.

"Where in the Mother's name are they?" he growled.

A small man jumped down beside him, bowing obsequiously. "He will be here, my lord. He assured me..."

"Yes, yes, Scolices, I am sure he will be." The man scowled at the darkening sky and the clouds scudding overhead then turned his gaze to the surrounding rock. He pointed. "Make a fire, over there by the rocks." He watched as Scolices scurried off, calling to another rider to help him find

1

firewood and pinecones. Turning to the remaining men, now dismounted, the tall man beckoned one over. "Thoas, set a guard...a good one. I have no wish to be surprised."

"Yes, my lord Areipithes," Thoas replied.

"Two back down the trail, pairs off to each side and get someone on top of that rock." He pointed at the jutting outcrop of weathered sandstone. He stared at the man who stood waiting expectantly. "Now, Thoas, before we are discovered and have no need of guards," he added softly.

Thoas flushed and turned away, snapping his fingers at the men and shouting out orders.

Areipithes turned away with a sigh and trudged toward the beginning flickers of flame in the lee of the outcrop. He found a dry spot among the wind-strewn leaves and sat with his back to the rock, waiting, listening to the night sounds and the murmur of men and horses. He accepted a horn of wine from Scolices without comment, dismissing the man with an impatient gesture.

The fire burned down to flickering embers and a faint glow on the eastern horizon told of incipient moonrise. A shouted challenge and cries brought them all to their feet, weapons drawn. Riders emerged from the dark forest, pushing two men in front of them. Areipithes' men drew bows and readied arrows, covering the strangers.

A horseman detached from the group and rode to the fire. He stared down at the tall, burly figure of Areipithes for a few moments then grunted and slid off his horse. "If these guards are the best you have, you'll not keep your kingdom long."

Areipithes sheathed his sword and grinned. "May the dust demons take you, Parates; it has been too long." He waved a hand at his men. "Put your weapons up."

"Parates?" mused the man; "It is many years since I went by that name."

Areipithes raised an eyebrow. "Oh? And what do men call you now?"

The man shrugged. "I change my name as often as I need. In my line of work a fast horse and a new identity are my only friends." He grimaced and glanced around. "You can call me Scorpion for now."

Areipithes snorted. "Always fond of the dramatic weren't you my friend? Come to the fire. Warm yourself." He moved to one side and gestured.

Scorpion signalled to his men before nodding and moving to the fire. He spread his cloak over a large flat rock and sat down then accepted a horn of wine and sipped, eyes on the Scythian king.

Areipithes drank, staring at his erstwhile friend. The man who called himself Scorpion was tall and thin, his skin darker than the average Scythian horseman, tanned by nature as well as sun and weather. His clothing was rich, expensive-looking, despite the stains of travel, with the look of the southern lands of Persia rather than the cold northern steppes. Scorpion's eyes were a lustrous green, hooded, beneath dense black hair. His face was carefully neutral in appearance, giving nothing away as he waited for the other man to speak.

"You called me king," said Areipithes quietly. "News travels fast it seems."

Scorpion nodded. "Rumours fly faster than the North wind. They say you murdered your father and sister and have set yourself up as king of the Massegetae, doing away with the council of elders."

Areipithes glared at the man. "What else do they say?"

Scorpion shrugged. "That you rule with an iron fist and accept no advice." He drained his wine and expectantly held the horn out.

At a signal from the king, Scolices scurried forward with a wineskin and refilled the drinking horns before moving back out of earshot.

"Not what I would expect from a king's table," grinned Scorpion, "but passable on a cold night."

"Continue," growled Areipithes.

"Parricide is judged to be god-cursed, as is desecration of the Mother Goddess." Scorpion smiled wryly then leaned forward. "My friend, you walk a dangerous path. Already men say you rule without the consent of the gods and killing you would be a just action."

Areipithes snorted. "No man will challenge me for the leadership. They are cattle and will do my bidding." He thought a moment and inclined his head. "Unwillingly maybe, but follow me they will. I care not if men hate me as long as they obey me."

"Still, killing your father so openly was not prudent. Could you not have been more subtle?"

"He was a fool and a traitor," snarled Areipithes, "Besotted with that Greek, turning over his power to the enemy. I did what any true Scythian would do."

Scorpion raised an eyebrow but sat silently.

"The Greek was a spy from the south. He wormed his way into my father's heart and was plotting to take over the tribe--no doubt to hand it over to Alexander. He seduced my half-sister Tomyra, the priestess of the Goddess." Areipithes flung his horn to the ground, the wine splashing his leggings. "The penalty for that is death, for both man and priestess." He ground his teeth. "I care not for the bitch-slut but she could have brought the wrath of the Goddess upon us all. I was justified."

"If you say so, my friend," said Scorpion softly. He paused. "Will you take a piece of advice from me, if not from your elders?"

Areipithes picked up his drinking horn and brushed the dirt and pine needles from it. He signalled to the waiting Scolices to refill the horn. "Go on then," he growled.

"Show your actions to be just. Produce evidence that your father Spargises was planning to betray the tribe to the Greeks." Scorpion shrugged. "If you do not have the evidence, manufacture it. The same goes for your sister

Tomyra. Show everyone she dishonoured the Mother Goddess. Discredit your father, your sister and the Greek with evidence, not rantings."

Areipithes took a deep breath then exhaled noisily. "May the demons take them all. Why should I care what men think as long as they are all dead?"

"Because if you don't show yourself as a leader by right--not just by force--you will forever be defending yourself from plots and assassination attempts."

Areipithes scowled. "I will think on it."

"Are they in fact dead? I know your father is, but your sister and the Greek?"

"My sister..." Areipithes spat into the fire. "...is dead by now. Dimurthes took her with him. The fool desired her but will kill her when he sates his lust." He rose and paced. "I have no word of the Greek."

Scorpion leaned back against a boulder and watched the king stalking back and forth. "Nikometros, son of Leonnatos, cavalry captain of the Great King Alexander, son of Philip of Macedon, now known throughout your lands as Nikomayros, Lion of Scythia," Scorpion murmured. "He was alive three days ago."

Areipithes spun on his heel and stared at Scorpion. "Alive? Where? How do you know?"

Scorpion smiled. "You ask *me* how *I* know? Little goes on in the borders without coming to my attention."

"Where is he?"

"Out of your reach. He rode west and north into the territory of the Serratae." Scorpion cocked his head to one side. "From what you say, I would guess he follows Dimurthes and your sister." He grinned. "Interesting. He's prepared to risk his life for her."

Areipithes sat down and kept silent, thinking. Scorpion called Scolices over to refill his drinking horn then waited patiently for Areipithes' decision, sipping on the sour wine.

5

"I have thought on this matter already, in the hope that he lived still. He seeks Tomyra. He may find her," mused Areipithes in a soft voice. "He may even rescue her. He is resourceful and brave; even I will admit that. But what will he do then?"

Scorpion remained silent, knowing the question needed no answer.

"He won't return. His followers are scattered and will soon be dead. If I were he, I would return to my own people." Areipithes nodded. "Yes, he'll go south, to the army of the Great King."

"And if your sister is dead? Won't he seek revenge on you?"

Areipithes grinned savagely. "I hope so. If he returns I'll take delight in sending his ghost onward, after great pain and suffering." His grin faded. "If he goes south I won't have my revenge." He looked up, meeting Scorpion's gaze. "Then you will kill him for me."

"I?"

"Why else did I summon you? For the pleasure of your company?"

Scorpion's face went blank. "I did not realise I had been summoned," he said coldly. He rose quickly, unfolding with a reptilian grace. "I came for a friendship we once had. If that is past then I will depart."

Areipithes cursed. "You always were a short-tempered bastard. Sit down...please." He waited until Scorpion sat down then leaned over toward the other man. "A king can have no close friends. He can trust no one. You are the closest I have to a friend for I saved your life many years ago and there is a bond between us."

Scorpion sighed. "You remind me again of my debt. Is this your concept of friendship?"

Areipithes shrugged. "Nevertheless, the debt is there and I claim it."

"Tell me how I must repay you then."

"Kill the Greek for me if he should travel south into Persia."

Scorpion sat silent, staring at the fire. At length he stirred and put down the drinking horn he clutched. "If I do this, the debt is repaid?"

"Yes. Kill the Greek Nikomayros and my whore-sister Tomyra if she still lives. Then the debt is repaid."

Scorpion rose to his feet and stretched. He walked slowly round the fire toward the horses where his men waited.

"Well?" called Areipithes. "Will you do this for me?"

Scorpion turned and looked back at the Scythian king. He nodded. "Yes, but here our friendship, such as it is, ends. Do not look for me in your lands again." He strode to his horse and leapt onto its back. He kicked the horse into motion and, his men on his heels, disappeared into the blackness of the mountain forest.

Chapter 1

A solitary sparrow hawk hung effortlessly in the chill winter's wind, scanning the broken ground far beneath. Although early in the season, food was already scarce. Bodies of soldiers moved through the countryside, pillaging villages, burning or harvesting crops, slaughtering cattle and goats. For a time, their activity made hunting good. Small birds and rodents fled the disturbances and were easily killed by predators following in the wake of armed men. Lately, as winter set in, prey was harder to find. Larger raptors and the ever-present vultures found plenty of carrion in the aftermath of war but the smaller birds of prey hungered.

A gust caught the hawk and spilled air through its slotted wings, forcing the bird to fight to maintain its position. It hesitated then slipped into a long shallow dive to the west, crossing a line of low hills, away from the dense pine forests. The land grew barer beneath it, the vegetation sparser. A movement far below caught its yellow eyes and it watched for a few moments, searching. Then minute changes in its wings and tail feathers guided it into a slow descent toward the north, following the column of men on horses far below.

The column moved slowly but steadily along a vaguely delineated game trail in single file. Thirty horses made up the column, though leather and wicker panniers and bundles burdened a third of them. Twenty riders were mounted on lean horses that showed signs of heavy use in the recent past. Each of the riders was tightly muffled against the chill northerly wind that lifted dead leaves and rattled the branches of the scrubby willows on the barren hillside. Dank air smelled of snow coming; the leaden sky felt oppressive. Leather tunics and leggings creaked as the horses picked their way slowly over rocky ground, moving up and across the hillside. The riders were, with one exception, bearded and moustached, the only skin exposed to the wind was the weathered area around their deep-set brown eyes. Woollen cloaks with hoods swathed them, falling in loose folds across the rumps of their horses, flapping desultorily with the felt blankets draped over the horses' backs. Feet covered in leather boots hung low beside the small wiry horses or were tucked into leather straps girdling the bellies of their mounts. Swords and double-curved bows with bundles of arrows protruded from among leather and cloth sacks in front of and behind each rider.

Boredom was the predominant expression on the faces of the men. Days of traveling in familiar territory without the stimulus of an enemy or the immediate prospect of homecoming blunted their senses and perceptions. The steady movement of the horses and the monotonous view of the horse and rider in front through hours of travel produced a lassitude that even the biting air failed to dispel.

The man at the head of the column was tall and thin, even with the bundling effect of his voluminous cloak. His angular features gave him a predatory look and dark hair hung greasily over his shoulders, strands blowing across his face in the icy wind gusts. The hood of his cloak was turned down, allowing him a greater field of view at the cost of warmth. He was more alert than the men who followed him, his eyes roving forward along the trail and to each side. Every now and then he turned, swivelling his whole body to stare at the woman on the horse immediately behind him. When he did so, his face became contorted with emotion and his limbs took on a trembling rigidity that spoke of suppressed passion.

The woman slumped listlessly on the back of her mare, a fine roan animal that stood out from the lean, rangy horses of her companions. She shivered within her cloak, a green woollen one smeared with mud and torn in places. She pulled it closer about her, grateful for the heavy quality of its fabric. Beneath it, she wore only a lightweight shift of coarse linen and felt riding boots. Feeling hostile eyes upon her, she raised her head, meeting the glare of the man in front. With an effort, she held her bruised and bloodied face still, masking the fear and loathing boiling up inside her. She stared back until the man dropped his eyes and turned away. The young woman stared at the back of the man's head for a few moments before turning away and gazing listlessly at the monotonous vistas of stony hillside dotted with clumps of birch and alder, now nearly leafless.

Two women on horseback watched the column of men from a dense thicket of birch trees further up the slope of the hill. The taller of the two peered fiercely out from beneath dark locks of hair that fell in waves about her pale face. Clad in thick leather tunics, jackets and leggings with felted undergarments, the women looked indistinguishable from male Scythian warriors, save for their hairless faces. Any hints as to their gender lay hidden beneath voluminous clothing.

The taller woman turned to her companion with a savage grin. "Soon, Domra. They grow careless."

The other woman shivered, despite her thick leggings and cloak. She nervously fingered a small double-curved bow, checking every few moments that the quiver of arrows, slung about her slender waist, was still in place. "We are greatly outnumbered, Bithyia. It may be better to wait. Who knows what the Goddess will send?"

Bithyia raised her eyebrows in surprise. "Will you wait until those wolves tire of our lady and do away with her? You can see she is ill-used." The woman scowled, her hand gripping the hilt of the short sword in her belt. "We must take some action. If nothing else it will lift her spirits to know she is not forsaken. Besides," she added with a grin, "we can shorten the odds somewhat."

The horses stamped their feet and blew out great gusts of air, nickering softly to each other. Their breath wisped like smoke in the cold. Bithyia thought back over the last few days--how she had gathered a handful of warriors about her and tracked the beasts that held her mistress, the beloved priestess of the Mother Goddess.

Soon, if the gods are with us, we will free her.

Domra stared out over the barren hillside toward the slowly moving column. "What would you have us do?"

Bithyia grinned again, her eyes icy. "They think themselves safe in their own lands. See how their line is drawn out, and their lack of scouts? We shall take a straggler or two come nightfall, quietly, without alarming the rest. With good fortune we may learn something of their plans before we kill them."

"If we are caught, we are dead."

"All men...and women, die. Better our deaths now than to live on knowing we failed our lady. Remember we are 'Owls', Domra. We are the chosen warrior women of the Goddess, sworn to defend her priestess."

Domra shook her head, shivering again. "I would die for my lady, Bithyia, you know that. But I am no warrior. I am only a maidservant and untrained with weapons."

Bithyia glared at Domra for a moment then softened her fierce expression. "You came, Domra, because your love for our lady was greater than your love of safety. You will do your duty, I know. Now come, let us rejoin the others."

The riders pulled their horses' heads around and walked them slowly through the birch grove until they were out of any possible sight of the column of Scythian men. They kicked their mounts into a reluctant trot, back down the hillside toward six other women huddled in the lee of a rocky outcrop.

The horses disturbed a lark that burst upward in panic, meeting death in the rushing talons of the patient sparrow hawk. The tiny raptor crouched over the cooling body of the lark for several minutes, its fierce yellow eyes blazing defiance in the direction of the disappearing horses. When silence reigned once more on the frozen hillside, the hawk bent its head and started to feed, tearing into the breast of its prey. The first snowflakes fell.

Chapter 2

D imurthes roared in anger, his fist gripping the leather jerkin of his deputy. "What do you mean...missing?" He lifted the man bodily from the ground then flung him down and stood over him. "How can three men go missing?" he hissed.

"My...my lord," stammered the man, fingering his throat. "When we made camp tonight three men did not report in. No one can recall seeing them since just before nightfall."

"And where did they last see these men?"

"Er, it seems Rhitores stopped to relieve himself and his brother stayed with him," said the deputy, struggling onto his hands and knees. He looked up at Dimurthes apprehensively. "Just after we crossed the stream on the other side of the forest. No one can recall having seen them since."

Dimurthes wrinkled his face in disgust. He strode to the tent entrance and lifted the flap, startling the guard outside. He hawked and spat, narrowly missing the guard, before turning back to his grovelling deputy.

"Get up, Taraxes, you look ridiculous," snarled Dimurthes. He waited until the man scrambled to his feet before continuing. "And the third man?"

Taraxes shrugged. "Nerraces. He was at the rear. Nobody saw him leave or stop. He just wasn't there when we camped. Nor have Rhitores or his brother shown up," he added hurriedly.

"Have you thought to send anyone to look for them?" inquired Dimurthes.

Taraxes flushed. "No, my lord. I thought..."

"Then do so." Dimurthes stood and looked at the other man who continued to look expectantly at his leader. "Now, you fool!"

Taraxes stepped back and gave a sketchy salute. "Yes, my lord, at once." He turned and hurried across to the tent flap.

"Taraxes." Dimurthes spoke softly. When the man turned, Dimurthes went on, "Send at least five men. If those fools have not got themselves lost or hurt then we must allow for the possibility of hostile action."

Taraxes saluted again and ducked out of the tent, letting another flurry of cold air past him.

Dimurthes pulled his woollen cloak tighter about him and turned back to the interior of the tent. He eyed his surroundings with distaste, longing for the comforts of his base camp. Only the barest necessities could be brought on field expeditions. The tent linings themselves were made of thick felt, dyed a deep red with inlaid designs of men and horses. These were, however, the only things approaching luxury in otherwise Spartan surroundings. The floor was bare earth or naturally carpeted in drifts of damp, dead leaves. In the far corner burned an oil lamp, giving out a plume of black smoke from its badly trimmed wick and a small brazier, struggling to dispel the cold and damp.

A faded carpet, replete with bare patches and tears, lay in one corner, with a pile of furs and a few battered cushions. Dimurthes walked over to the pile of bedding and snatched back the bearskin lying on top. A woman, her long black hair matted and dirty, hugged her torn green cloak to her and sat up, glaring at the man. She edged away as Dimurthes advanced on her with a smile.

"Come, Tomyra." Dimurthes smirked. "It is time for you to repay my hospitality again." He reached out and gripped Tomyra by the shoulder.

"Get away from me, you animal," she hissed. She wrenched her shoulder free and struggled upright. Her cloak fell open briefly, revealing a ripped linen shift, through which a pale breast swelled.

Dimurthes licked his lips and moved forward, removing his jacket as he did so. "Come, my dear," he breathed. "A little cooperation and we can both enjoy this."

"Bastard son of a Serratae whore," snarled Tomyra. "I would rather rut with a pig."

Dimurthes chuckled. "I assure you there are no whores in *my* tribe, Tomyra. Can you say the same of your Massegetae?" He moved closer and reached for the girl. Tomyra slashed at his hand, scoring a deep furrow across the back of it with a nail. Dimurthes swore and snatched his hand back. He licked the wound then smiled.

"How is it you hold your virtue so highly, woman?" Dimurthes stared at the girl standing against the felt wall of the tent, defiance blazing from her eyes. "I could understand if you were still a priestess of the Mother Goddess." He dropped his hand in an unconscious motion, palm down, as he spoke the Holy Name. "But priestesses are virgins and you whored with that Greek warrior, the one they call the Lion of Scythia. Now you are nothing more than a common slut, to be used by the strongest." Dimurthes grinned again. "And I am the strongest, woman. Make no mistake about that."

Dimurthes leapt forward and grabbed Tomyra, pinioning her with his strong arms. Tomyra struggled silently, knowing it was useless to cry out. She raised her knee swiftly, striking at his groin but he shifted as she did so and the blow fell on his thigh. He grunted then pulled her head back violently and kissed her on the mouth.

Tomyra turned her head as far as she could, pressing her lips together. She worked an arm free and lashed out at his face with her nails, seeking his eyes.

Dimurthes cursed and fell back, though retaining a grip on the young girl. He drove his fist into the side of Tomyra's head and she collapsed with a small cry of pain.

Swiftly, the man dropped to his knees and loosened his heavy trousers. He pulled her cloak to one side and forced her shift above her waist.

Tomyra groaned, forcing herself back to consciousness. She clamped her legs together and rolled away from him. His breath coming fast, he forced her onto her back again then slammed his fist into her belly. Tomyra cried out in agony, clutching herself then screamed as the man forced himself between her legs.

Tomyra continued to writhe beneath the man as he went through the perverted motions of love, his excitement building until he collapsed exhausted on top of her. A moment later he swiftly rose to his feet, easily avoiding a weak kick from the girl.

Dimurthes grinned and readjusted his clothing. He looked down at Tomyra as she pulled her ragged shift and cloak about her, grimacing at the look of hatred on her face. "Really, woman. You do take it so personally. Enjoy it while it lasts. I ought to kill you as your brother requested, but I may set you free when I tire of you." He refastened his jacket and adjusted his cloak. "If you continue to resist me I could just give you to my men. You would find them less considerate than I."

"Bastard!" gritted Tomyra. She furiously willed away the tears of rage and shame that threatened to spill from her eyes. The pain from her renewed violation made her grimace as she moved, sitting up. "I promise you, in the Mother's name, you will die for this."

"You call on the Mother still?" asked Dimurthes in an amused tone. "I doubt she will answer the prayers of a whore."

"She will answer the prayers of a violated priestess."

"I have not violated you, woman, merely used you. You forfeited any rights when you whored with the barbarian."

"As I have told you, I am still a priestess of the Mother Goddess. You abuse me at your peril."

Dimurthes laughed. "I don't see anything to be afraid of."

"My Nikomayros will kill you himself, if I do not."

"Nikomayros? Oh, you mean that Greek barbarian, the Lion." Dimurthes laughed out loud again. "Do not look for him, woman. Your brother Areipithes is now king of the Massegetae and he will have killed your Greek by now."

Tomyra shook her head. "He lives and he will find me."

"And will he want you when he finds you?" Dimurthes grinned. "Even if he were to follow..." He broke off, his smile fading. Dimurthes nodded slowly. "So, he is the one who follows..." He turned and strode to the tent flap, calling to the guard. He stepped outside and spoke urgently. A few minutes later two horsemen galloped off in pursuit of Taraxes.

Dimurthes re-entered the tent and moved across to where a small iron pot sat cooling beside the sputtering brazier. He lifted the lid and sniffed then ladled out a thin mutton stew onto two wooden platters. He held one out to Tomyra, who sat huddled in her cloak. She ignored it and Dimurthes shrugged, setting it down on the bare ground within reach.

He sat on the pile of cushions and picked at his food with his fingers, chewing on the gristly meat. "You should eat something," he observed. "You are already too thin." He leered at the young woman. "I prefer my women with a bit of meat on their bones." Dimurthes turned back to his meal and swiftly finished off the meat, licking the juices from the platter before tossing it casually into a corner. He wiped his hands on a cushion then pulled out his dagger and a piece of carved bone. He turned it over, examining the design carefully before picking at it with the point of his dagger, scraping away thin slivers, moulding the form of the running deer already outlined on it.

Time passed, the man slowly expressing himself artistically, the woman huddling into the furs, fighting her fear and despair. She kept her eyes fixed on the man, glaring her hatred and praying softly to the Goddess. From time to time, Dimurthes glanced up at Tomyra. If the looks of hatred disturbed him, he gave no sign.

The guard outside coughed softly and called out, "My Lord?"

Dimurthes stretched and tucked the carving back into his tunic. He sheathed his dagger and brushed the thin shavings of bone from his lap before rising fluidly to his feet. "Yes!" he barked.

The guard pushed through the tent flap, his eyes flicking from the figure of his chief to that of the woman with great interest. "Taraxes returns, my Lord. Shall I admit him?"

Dimurthes nodded and dismissed the guard with a gesture. Taraxes entered a few moments later, his hair dishevelled and cloak wrapped tightly about him. A gust of cold wind swirled in with him, carrying dead leaves into the far corners of the tent. He ran a hand over his moustache and beard, tugging at it gently as he faced his chief.

"We found Nerraces, my Lord. Just this side of the ford. No trace of Rhitores or his brother Parmes though. We searched the trail back as far as..." he fell silent as Dimurthes scowled and gestured.

"And what does Nerraces have to say for himself?"

Taraxes blanched and stammered. "N...nothing, my Lord. He was dead. His throat was cut and he had an arrow in his back. A Massegetae arrow."

Dimurthes turned away, his teeth clenching in rage. "What else did you find?" he ground out.

"Horse tracks, my Lord, but we could not follow them in the dark."

"How many?"

Taraxes shrugged. "A few. Perhaps five or six."

Dimurthes looked thoughtful then waved Taraxes away. "Double the guards tonight. I must think on this." He started pacing then stopped and stared at Tomyra.

"So, your Lion comes for you after all. He is braver...or more foolhardy than I thought. I must arrange a proper welcome for him." Dimurthes smiled savagely then spun on his heel and strode from the tent.

Chapter 3

Five horses stamped and blew impatiently in the chill wind that gusted from the low mountain peaks to the north. Three men sat astride their mounts, wrapped in woollen cloaks as they watched a tall golden-haired man and a shorter, stockier, dark-haired man bending over the trail. The dark man squatted and pointed to faint hoof marks in the packed earth.

"See, there...and there. Her horse leaves quite distinct tracks."

"How far behind are we?" queried the fair man.

"A day, perhaps two." The dark man stood up and scanned the trail ahead of them, noting the direction it took across the hillside. "They are heading for Zarmet, the winter quarters of the Serratae."

"How far away is that?"

The dark man shrugged. "If they travel no faster than they do now, perhaps five days." He turned to face the fair-haired man. "Nikomayros, if they reach Zarmet she is lost to you." His voice, like that of most Scythians, slurred and slipped around the fair man's name. Nikomayros was the best pronunciation he could manage for Nikometros, son of Leonnatos of Macedon.

"Then we must hurry, Parasades." Nikometros turned to his horse and grasping its mane, vaulted onto its back.

Parasades stared at the tall man astride his great golden stallion. "It is nearly nightfall, Nikomayros. We must wait until tomorrow to follow the trail."

Nikometros scowled and jerked the reins of his horse, making it rear. "They follow this trail and have done for two days now. We can follow the path in the dark. We must close the gap."

"And if they leave the trail we could lose them completely."

One of the other riders edged his horse alongside the stallion. He was a stocky man, bearded and garbed like the Scythians, though his skin was lighter. When he spoke, he used the rough patois of the Macedonian army.

"It makes sense, Niko. If they leave the trail in the night we could lose them."

Nikometros scowled at the man alongside him. "We must take the chance, Timon. I fear for her in the hands of these bandits."

Parasades swung himself onto his small, wiry steed and pulled it alongside Nikometros on his other side. "I understand your concern, Nikomayros," he said softly. "But they have kept her alive so far. I believe they will take her to Zarmet."

"Then they will keep to the trail and we can follow through the night," responded Nikometros.

The other two horsemen approached. One, a slight young man with a broken nose set askew drawled his opinion. "Unless they tire of her first, of course. No doubt they will have used her..."

A look of fury swept across Nikometros' face. He rounded on the young man with a deadly look. "Mind your tongue or I will cut it from you. She is your priestess."

The man paled and pulled his horse back. "I...I am sorry, my lord. I did not mean to give..."

The older rider with him reached over and cuffed the young man sharply across the head. "A plague on you, Certes. When will you learn to think before you speak?"

Certes drew back to avoid another blow, his hand dropping to the short sword in his belt. "You have no right to lay a hand on me, Agarus. You are not a warrior; you are but a servant."

"Enough!" snapped Parasades. "Already I regret bringing either of you. Agarus, apologise for hitting Certes. He is a warrior and you had no right to lay a hand on him. Certes, beg forgiveness of the lord Nikomayros for your unruly tongue. Do it!" he hissed as the two men hesitated.

Surly expressions on their faces, both men apologised. They drew apart and ignored one another, making a show of examining their equipment or looking out over the darkening hillside.

Parasades sighed and turned back to Nikometros. "Very well. We shall follow the trail tonight. If it forks we camp until first light. We must not risk taking the wrong path. Agreed?"

Nikometros nodded impatiently and kicked his stallion forward. Timon fell into place behind him, followed by Parasades and Certes. Agarus brought up the rear, grumbling quietly to himself.

The path wound slowly downhill into sparse woodland. The light diminished as the sun disappeared, the pace of the horses slowing accordingly. The five horses settled into a slow plodding walk, picking their way carefully over rough ground. Nikometros found his thoughts wandering, despite his fears, lulled by the monotony. He glanced back over his shoulder at Timon.

Good, honest Timon, he thought. *A proper Macedonian soldier, forthright and loyal. He has proven himself a true friend.* He remembered back to the days when Timon was just another soldier in his small command. *Was it only a year ago?*

Nikometros' promising career had been cut short by a wound--a head wound sustained in a minor skirmish against the Sogdians. As a junior officer in Alexander's own Companion cavalry, just starting to distinguish himself in battle, Nikometros could see only a glittering future ahead of him. The Macedonian army had shattered the barbarian Persians, mopped up all resistance and was advancing on to India, China and encircling Ocean to bring the whole world under Greek hegemony. Sogdiana was a minor province to be subjugated on the way, but they were fierce fighters. Then disaster--an incapacitating wound and a drawn-out recovery found Nikometros left behind by the army as part of a local garrison.

Nikometros shrugged his cloak to one side and reached for his skin of watered wine. He sipped, grimacing at the thin, sour taste. *As thin and sour as my prospects of advancement away from the main army,* he thought.

Fighting depression, he had sought to further his career within the limited confines of local government, riding out to quell disturbances, hunting down bandits. On one such expedition his force was all but wiped out in an ambush. Scythians captured the three survivors, Nikometros, Timon and a young Persian recruit named Mardes. Their very lives had hung on the thread of superstition. Nikometros wore an antique armband of gold, plated over heavy iron, a gift from his mother. The band depicted a serpent-bodied woman, the unusual design catching the eye of the leader of the Scythian raiders, who identified it as the embodiment of the Mother Goddess, the titular deity of the roving tribes. It had bought Nikometros and his two surviving companions a brief respite.

A low call from behind him stopped the column. Parasades pushed his horse up alongside Nikometros, indicating a gap in the trees off to one side. "A path. We should camp now."

Already? thought Nikometros. "We have made no gain, Parasades. At least let us look for tracks before we stop." He gestured to Agarus. "Get your flint out, Agarus. See if you can light a torch."

Once lit, the fitful light of the sputtering torch revealed hoof prints on both tracks. Nikometros felt his spirits sink. "Can you not distinguish Tomyra's horse?" he asked dully.

Parasades shook his head. "We will have to wait until morning." He sat back on his heels and looked down both trails. He rose and handed Certes the torch. "Go down this side path. Tell me what you find." The man nodded and dismounted, moving off down the path with torch held high.

Timon looked puzzled. "What do you hope to find?"

Parasades did not reply but stood staring after the faint light bobbing down the path. After a few moments the torch moved first to one side then the other, dipping and rising. Shortly, Certes stood before them again, a grin on his face.

"You were right, my lord Parasades. They camped."

"Was there a path beyond the camp?"

"No, my lord."

Parasades turned to Nikometros with a smile. "As I suspected. They camped here for the night before resuming their journey along this path." He heaved himself up onto his horse. "Now we can make up some real time."

The pursuit resumed. At first, Nikometros was buoyed by the thought that they were catching up, but after several stadia he settled back into a reverie, remembering.

Brought back to the winter quarters of the Massegetae tribe, the Scythian town of Urul, their safe passage had come to an end. Despite the armband, or perhaps because of it, they were to be sacrificed to the Mother Goddess. Nikometros fingered the place on his left arm where the armband had so recently been. The bright iron had gleamed through the gold when he handed it to Tirses just five days before, a result of a sword cut. The sword would have ended his life in the single combat of sacrifice had not the armband blocked it.

The Massegetae took it as a sign of the Mother's favour, urged on by the young priestess, Tomyra, and her father Spargises, the powerful chief of the tribe. Made blood-brother to Spargises, Nikometros, and his men, had risen swiftly within the ranks of the Scythians.

That first battle did it, he thought. Eschewing the usual Scythian tactics of inflicting light casualties through fast but indecisive attacks, he had led his men and a group of young tribesmen in a cavalry charge that shattered the enemy, despite their numerical superiority. After that, he had become known as the Lion of Scythia, named for the lion emblem on his shield.

The path left the forested slopes and angled westward again, dipping into the undulating grasslands that covered much of Scythia. The air grew colder away from the protecting shelter of the trees. The moon rose, casting yellow rays fitfully through the clouds, dimly illuminating the path ahead of them. Timon pushed his horse up alongside Nikometros.

"We will find her, Niko," he murmured.

Nikometros smiled briefly and nodded his head in agreement. "Yes. For the first time I feel we are catching up."

Timon edged his horse closer and glanced back at the others. "Niko..." He hesitated then dropped into the coarse language of the Macedonian army, thickening his Greek accent. "Niko, can you trust the others?" he asked quietly. "Agarus follows you and is loyal. Even if he wasn't, he is no warrior and no threat. But I don't trust that fox Parasades. Why is he even here?"

Nikometros turned and looked at his friend before answering in the guttural speech of the common Macedonian soldiers. "I have wondered that myself, Timon. He has been a friend but he is undoubtedly hungry for power. Why is he here with me instead of gathering an army to oppose Areipithes?"

"The army would follow you, Niko. You have proved yourself in battle. And the lady Tomyra. Perhaps he wants to be sure of both."

"I'm not sure they would follow me. I'm Greek still in their eyes. They will follow Areipithes, despite his crimes...or Parasades." Nikometros fell silent for a few paces. "They might follow Tomyra. The Massegetae love their priestess."

Nikometros' heart surged at the thought of her. As a consecrated virgin priestess of the Mother Goddess and daughter of the chief, her person was sacrosanct. Yet he had felt an immediate bond, an attraction that grew and finally blossomed into love.

Despite their better judgments they had become lovers, his personal honour guard, the Lions, turning a blind eye even as her personal guard, the Owls, gave in to their mistress' desires.

Not all Massegetae were as understanding, however. Spargises, chief and father to Tomyra and brother in blood to Nikometros, would have killed them both if he had known of their acts. *And died of a broken heart later*, thought Nikometros. The chief's son, Areipithes, was another, though he would have taken great delight in their deaths. Half-brother to Tomyra, jealousy and rage ruled him. He hated Tomyra because his father loved her and he hated Nikometros because his father turned increasingly to the Greek for advice and trust. No longer sure of his place as heir, he had resolved to precipitate events. Calling in the help of the Serratae, a Scythian tribe to the west of the Oxus River, he had murdered his own father and banished his sister, to rule as chief of the Massegetae.

A few days ago, I was war-leader of the Massegetae, loved and trusted by all...by most, he amended. *Now what am I? I lead but four men and I cannot be certain of the loyalty of three of them.*

Nikometros glanced across at Timon, riding silently beside him. "We shall find her, Timon. I know it."

"Aye, sir," muttered Timon. "Maybe we shall also find others."

A look of agony and comprehension swept over Nikometros' face. "Gods, I am sorry, old friend. In my own loss I was forgetting yours." He remembered the love that blossomed between the old Macedonian soldier and the young warrior-woman in Tomyra's guard. "Bithyia is safe, my friend. She is a worthy warrior and will have found others of the Owls."

Timon grunted and slowed his horse, dropping back, losing himself in his own thoughts.

The moon rose higher, smoky-gold through the dark clouds on the eastern horizon. As it rose, the colour changed, softening and lightening, casting a pale glow over the rippling grasslands. The path ahead of them stood out as a dark ribbon of earth, disappearing into the distance. The land rose and fell slightly, undulating gently. It reminded Nikometros of the narrow strip of sea that the army crossed when first they invaded Asia. That was the only time he had been on a ship and it had terrified him, even as the wonder of it flooded his senses. Now he was crossing a vaster ocean, one of grass. The wonder was still there but the terror had been replaced by a fear, not for him, but for the woman he loved. Somewhere ahead of him, Tomyra was being carried off to an unknown fate...if she was still alive. Nikometros' mind shied away from the thought, returning instead to the heady days when he knew his love for the young girl was reciprocated.

Death was the penalty for taking the priestess, yet they revelled in their illicit love, cautious at first then becoming more daring. There was no hope of hiding the affair from their respective guards and, despite efforts to weed out any whose loyalty was suspect, others came to know of it. Areipithes, the chief's son, used the information to precipitate his revolt. Parasades, too, had known. Nikometros was unsure still why the man had kept their secret. He was a friend but he also made no secret of his views about Nikometros. Only Scythians ruled Scythians.

As if reading his thoughts, Parasades urged his horse alongside Nikometros' and looked up at him. "What is your intention when we catch up with Tomyra?" he asked quietly.

"Rescue her. Beyond that I haven't given the matter much thought."

"Then I suggest you do so. We're in hostile territory, trailing a group of over twenty men who, though they are only Serratae dogs, are still warriors."

Nikometros sighed. "I know, Parasades. But what plans can I make? Our actions will depend on when and where we catch up with them."

Parasades regarded the tall Greek on his towering stallion for several minutes, his expression hidden in the shadows cast by his hooded coat. "Do you seek merely to rescue the priestess or do you desire vengeance?"

"I will be content to bring her away...unless they have harmed her." Nikometros' voice hardened. "If she has been hurt I will kill for it."

"Remember we are only five and they number over twenty."

"I will remember," growled Nikometros. "If you have not the stomach for it, Timon and I will continue alone."

"You would not find her," stated Parasades flatly. "Do you think these lands uninhabited because we have seen no one since we started? Villages lie ahead of us and the winter quarters of the Serratae. You and your man could not pass for Scythians. You would die quickly."

Nikometros drew back on his reins, bringing his horse to a stop. He glared at the other man. "Just why are you here, Parasades? Why aren't you back at the Oxus gathering support to oppose Areipithes?"

Parasades smiled, his teeth showing as he turned his horse. "I'm your friend, Nikomayros. Perhaps your only one. I would see you reunited with your woman."

"Horse turds!" snapped Nikometros. "You have more in common with Areipithes than with me. What are you planning?"

Parasades' smile slipped. "Be careful, my friend. You're close to insulting me. Isn't it enough that I'm here, helping you find your woman?"

Nikometros stared at him, his anger fading. "You're right. If I offend you, I apologise."

"Then let us move onward." Parasades pointed out over the waving grass. "If we press on we can reach the next line of hills by daybreak."

Chapter 4

After a night spent in fitful unease, Dimurthes' camp burst into frenzied activity an hour before dawn. Within minutes, fires were extinguished and the chief's tent struck and packed onto horses. Tomyra was hustled unceremoniously onto her horse, where she sat shivering in the cold pre-dawn wind.

Dimurthes strode among his men, barking out a series of orders, gesticulating and scowling fiercely at anyone who hesitated. The column formed up, though in a different formation from the last three days.

Tomyra found herself in the midst of a small group of riders with drawn weapons. Her hands were tied and a noose settled around her neck.

Dimurthes looked up at her. "I think we shall remove a threat today," he said softly. "Your Greek has obviously caught up with us and will attempt your rescue. If you cry out or try to ride to him you will be killed immediately. My men don't need to seek my permission to kill you. They have their orders." Dimurthes smiled. "If you wish to live to enjoy my companionship another night, I would advise silence." He laughed and turned on his heel.

Dimurthes leapt onto his horse and drew his bow, tucking several arrows into the cloth pack in front of him. His eyes flicked quickly over the men forming up behind him, noting their weapons and judging their demeanour. He nodded in satisfaction and signalled, following the small knot of riders around Tomyra as they set off down the trail in the slowly strengthening light. His men followed, alert and ready, scanning the hills around them as the features of the countryside emerged from the night.

The path wound slowly through the foothills, narrow and rocky, often forcing the column into single file. When this occurred, three of Tomyra's guards rode ahead of her and two behind. The man immediately behind her kept a firm hand on the rope around her neck, tugging her back if her horse moved too far ahead.

The light strengthened, though day arrived not with a flash of golden fire from a welcome sun, but rather as a slow seeping of greyness washing over the world. A heavy overcast with steely skies ahead of them presaged snow. The north wind picked up, scattering dead leaves and making the horses snort and sidestep.

A rider urged his horse up the line from the rear, jostling the other horses that whickered and nipped at the flanks of the horse. He leaned over and murmured in his chief's ear.

"We are being watched, my lord."

"Where?"

"In the trees upslope. Something moves, man-sized and purposeful."

"Very well. Return to your place and watch for my signal."

The rider slowed his horse, waiting as the column passed him. Dimurthes forced himself to casually scan the slopes around him, his eyes passing over the tree line on the slope above him, hesitating a moment before moving on. He saw nothing but he trusted in his man's abilities. If he saw something, something was there. Now they only had to catch it.

The path dipped into a shallow valley, crossing a tiny rivulet of icy water tumbling over small boulders. A short expanse of frost-browned turf led up from the stream to the next low hill, the path passing into a line of heavier pine forest some fifty horse lengths above. Dimurthes smiled and nodded to himself. He rode to one side as the column crossed the stream then followed his men up the slope and into the trees.

Within the shelter of the pine forest, he halted and called softly to his men. At once, they turned their horses and gathered around their leader. The guard around Tomyra ushered her to one side and drew their daggers in readiness, one pressing the point of his blade to her throat.

Dimurthes sat silently and watched the trees on the other side of the valley. For a long while, nothing happened. The wind soughed softly in the pine leaves and the distant burble of the stream came intermittently to their ears. Behind them, in the depths of the forest, came the staccato drum of a woodpecker searching out a meal. The horses blew impatiently and stamped their feet, their riders fidgeting as they waited.

Then a figure appeared in the tree line on the far hillside. It emerged, holding the reins of a horse and stood looking out across the valley. Soon, it turned and waved, whereupon four other figures pushed out from the cover of the trees, leading their horses. One of them pointed back at the trees, gesticulating violently. The first figure stood firm, pointing down the hillside. For a few moments it appeared as if the confrontation might erupt into violence then the figure in front vaulted onto its mount, urging it down the slope. The others wavered then scrambled onto their mounts and rode swiftly down the slope to the stream.

The waiting Serratae warriors fitted arrows to their bows, drawing back the strings. Each face was taut with tension.

"Wait," hissed Dimurthes. "On my signal." He leaned forward, scanning the riders as they rode their horses carefully across the slippery boulders. They started up the slope, their horses' hooves silent on the turf. Dimurthes chopped his hand down and with a whisper; a flight of arrows flew from the forest. A second followed before the first arrows fell among the riders and horses, and, as the third volley rose, Dimurthes, sword in hand, plunged from cover, his men screaming behind him.

The riders milled in confusion near the stream, one already fallen, transfixed by three arrows, another screaming in agony from a wound in the stomach. Dimurthes burst into the group, a slash from his sword silencing the cries of the wounded rider. A blade flashed toward him. He contemptuously knocked it aside, his eyes darting over his adversaries, seeking the face of the Greek.

These are all boys, Dimurthes thought. *Not a bearded warrior among them.*

A javelin whiffled past him then the three surviving riders fled, pursued over the stream by his warriors. The Serratae surrounded another rider on the far side of the stream and cut him down quickly. Another fell as they fled for the cover of the trees on the far side of the valley. Only a single rider made it back to the dubious safety of the woodlands. Dimurthes gave a shout, recalling his men. They rode back, dragging the corpses of the fallen riders behind them.

Dimurthes leapt off his horse and stretched, wiping his sword on the turf and sheathing it. He walked over to the body of the rider he had killed and kicked the arm away from where it covered the face. He stared down at the smooth and hairless face in its mask of bright blood for a moment then bent and ran his hand quickly over the body.

"A woman?" he muttered softly. Straightening, he crossed to the other three corpses then ripped their tunics open. Dimurthes shook his head in wonder; his men gathering round with grins and ribald comments. One man bent and pulled the leggings of one of the corpses down amid laughter.

Dimurthes stood and watched as his men took their pleasures then called Taraxes to him.

"Remove their heads, leave their bodies for the carrion-eaters." He vaulted back onto his horse and waited as Taraxes and two other men completed their grisly work. Taraxes soon approached, bearing their grisly trophies. Leaning down, Dimurthes grasped the matted locks of the bloody heads. He turned his horse and rode back up to the pine forest, keeping his hand with its dreadful contents behind him. His horse shied as the heads bumped its flanks and he jerked its head savagely, kicking his heels into its sides.

Tomyra had heard the distant shouts and screams, knowing she was helpless to aid her Niko. She strained against the noose, feeling blood trickling from the sharp pain in her throat as the dagger dug deeper. Her eyes moved restlessly and she moaned softly, numb to the pain in her throat as she strained toward the sounds of battle. A wash of despair came over her as the sounds died away. Soon, the sound of a single horse, its hooves muffled by the thick carpet of pine needles, roused her. She looked up, hope disintegrating as she recognised her tormentor.

Dimurthes rode up close to her shying horse and stared dispassionately at the woman. He jerked his head and his men backed off, though keeping their weapons in a state of readiness. He tossed the heads at the foot of Tomyra's horse, which shied and reared, forcing her to cling to its neck. The heads rolled to a stop, presenting blood-spattered faces smeared and covered with dirt and pine needles.

Tomyra gasped and went white. She reeled and almost fell then with an obvious effort, steadied herself, breathing hard. With anguish in her eyes, she stared down at the head closest to her. "Domra...," she whispered. She tore her eyes away to look at the other heads but long matted hair obscured their features. Tomyra looked back to Domra's head resting against a tree root, its features distorted by death agony. "Oh, Domra," she breathed. "What made you come? You were always so gentle."

"I am amazed women should be following us," sneered Dimurthes. "Is your Greek so cowardly that he sends women to do his work? Or is it that the only real men among the Massegetae have nothing between their legs?"

Dimurthes' question drew appreciative chuckles from the guards. Tomyra glared at the Serratae chief. "Do not think to judge others by your own shortcomings," she hissed. "You will know the difference when my Nikomayros finds me. You will pray to the Mother Goddess for an easy death but She will not hear you."

The smiles disappeared from the faces of her guards as she spoke, and some made warding signs, holding their hands low by their sides. Dimurthes' grin also slipped, his hand twitching in an automatic response before he caught himself.

"Perhaps I should leave your lovely head here on a spike to greet him then," he grated. He edged his horse alongside Tomyra's and drew his sword. Raising it slowly, he laid it alongside the girl's neck. Tomyra flinched momentarily as the steel touched her but then her eyes flashed defiance and she straightened her back, glaring at Dimurthes.

For a long moment they sat and stared, the woman rigid and unsmiling, the man fighting to control his urge to kill her. His arm muscles trembled before he blinked and turned away, sheathing his sword. He moved his horse a few paces then looked back. "I really would like to see your face when I bring you his head, though."

Dimurthes touched his heels to his horse, guiding it back onto the path. "Come," he said. "We shall ride for the village of Turkul." His men reformed around Tomyra and, rejoining the other warriors, turned westward once more.

Silence descended on the pine forest, broken only by the wind in the trees and the distant tapping of the woodpecker. Long afterward, as the sun slipped toward the western horizon, a pine marten, foraging for mice and insects, happened upon the stiffening remains of the maidens. It sniffed, its bright eyes suspicious of the smells and unfamiliar shapes. It edged forward, whiskers twitching, circling the head that had been Domra's before ambling off into the depths of the forest.

Chapter 5

Bithyia sat relaxed and at ease astride her mare as it picked its way slowly across the bare hillside. Her spirits were high, her mind freed from the concerns of the last few days while tracking her mistress' abductors across the frozen land of the Serratae. She idly gazed at her two companions riding ahead, talking quietly but animatedly to each other. They seemed like different people. No longer tense and absorbed in their duties, the young women's cheerful natures had reasserted themselves.

I must make sure we can all have a break from our duties, she thought.

Bithyia reached out to stroke the ruffled feathers of the brace of chickens dangling across her mare's back. They were lucky to stumble across a small farm in their foraging expedition. A couple of chickens gratefully liberated and a small sack of some non-descript and mouldy roots would provide a welcome change from the half-cooked squirrel meat and berries that was their recent fare.

Bithyia grimaced briefly as she recalled the indignation of the farmer and his two sons when the armed women descended upon his hut. Serratae women were generally downtrodden and they never used weapons. By the time the men recovered from their shock, they were disarmed and could do no more than splutter in rage as Bithyia and her companions took what they needed. It was a poor farm, eking out an existence from the thin soil and truth be told, the loss of even a chicken or two and roots fit only for cattle would bring hardship in its wake.

Still, reasoned Bithyia, *our need is greater.* She shrugged. *Call it a tax for the service of the Great Goddess and her priestess.*

The tiny campsite was empty and desolate when they reached it. The only signs of recent occupation were mounds of horse dung, cold but not yet frozen and the scuffmarks in the lee of a pile of rocks where people had huddled from the bitter wind. Bithyia looked around then dismounted and ran quickly up the slope. She peered cautiously over the lip of the rise toward the main track below and the encampment of the Serratae tribesmen.

"Gone. Domra follows them," she muttered to herself. Bithyia rose and ran back down to her waiting companions. "Come, we must hurry. Our foe has moved on and Domra leads our companions after them." She swung up onto her mare and kicked it into motion, up over the lip of the small depression and down the hillside, following the tracks of her friends.

Glancing up at a leaden sky, Bithyia noted the direction of the wind. *Snow coming.* She sat up straighter and called to her companions to ready themselves. She pointed down the slope to their right, at the track that wound around the hill toward the woods.

"Prithia, Sarmatia, be on your guard. We do not know how far ahead the others will be."

The two young women nodded their assent and unshouldered their small double-curved bows, slipping an arrow from their quivers into the rolled cloth across their horses' necks. The horses turned from the rough goat track they were on and cut downhill to the main track, their hooves slipping in the loose soil and rocks.

Bithyia stopped when she reached the trail and bent down, scanning the ground. She noted the presence of many hooves then grunted and smiled as she recognised the distinctive hoof print of Tomyra's horse. She twitched the reins and urged her mare along the path.

An hour later they found the tracks of several horses that left the main path, angling across the shoulder of the hill and disappearing into the sparse woods. Bithyia examined the path again then pointed to an unobtrusive pair of stones, sitting one atop the other.

"Domra led them to one side," she said. Bithyia scanned the hillside, judging the route of the main path and the direction taken by Domra's group. "She seeks to close with our enemies and keep them in sight. She is brave but she is not trained as a warrior. I hope she realises the dangers."

"The others will advise her, help her," said Sarmatia.

Bithyia nodded and pointed along the main path. "We must catch up. It will be faster to follow our prey rather than have to track our friends." She kicked her mare into a slow gallop along the muddy path. As she rode, her eyes moved restlessly over the path in front and the tree line above them, seeking any sign of their companions.

The path crested a small rise before dropping down into a shallow valley with a rocky stream. Bithyia abruptly reined in her horse and slid from its back, pulling it back over the crest as Sarmatia and Prithia joined her. Leaving Prithia with the horses, she crept back up the trail with Sarmatia and stared down into the valley.

Sarmatia nudged Bithyia and pointed downstream toward a pile of rocks. "Bodies," she murmured. "There was a battle."

Bithyia shaded her eyes and squinted. "Can you see who they are?"

Sarmatia shook her head. "They are dressed as warriors, but then, so are we." She turned her head to the other young woman. "What do we do?"

Bithyia carefully examined the far hillside, watching the margins of the pine forest for any sign of activity. There was no movement anywhere, save for the swaying of the treetops and the wheeling flight of carrion crows. She turned her head, searching the path in front of her before moving cautiously over the rise and down to a pile of horse dung. She stuck her finger into it and held it there for a moment before wiping it on the ground and retracing her steps.

Bithyia dropped down beside Sarmatia. "The centre of the dung is faintly warm. They passed here but an hour or two ago."

"If it was indeed them and not some itinerant peddler or farmer," muttered Sarmatia.

"A well-off merchant perhaps, or else warriors. That horse had fed on grain." Bithyia chewed her lip then edged back from the crest and stood up. "We must know who lies below, but I will not risk us all. Wait here. If it is a trap then leave me and follow our priestess as best you can, Sarmatia." She swung onto her mare without waiting for a reply and trotted over the crest and down into the valley.

The girl kept her eyes fixed on the pine forest ahead, her shoulders braced unconsciously for the impact of a killing arrow. None came, and as she drew near to the stream she saw a squirrel run along a branch of a tall pine then leap to the ground. Bithyia grinned, her shoulders slumping slightly in relief. No squirrel would leave a tree if there were anyone near.

She urged her mare through the shallow ford then turned her downstream toward the bodies. Two crows flew up from the nearest body as she approached, cawing loudly in protest. One perched on a nearby rock, gulping a thin ribbon of flesh, staring disapprovingly at the intruder.

Bithyia scanned her surroundings once more then slipped to the ground. She walked around the corpse, her face blanching at the savage hack marks on the neck. She dropped to her knees and examined the body more closely, her face flushing with anger as she saw the ripped tunic and leggings. Small breasts pointed coldly at the sky, sullied with bloody handprints. Bithyia pulled the tunic about the young girl's body then rose and strode over to the others, rearranging their clothing and covering their ravaged shoulders with cloths from her horse.

She signalled for Sarmatia and Prithia to join her.

"Who...?" asked Prithia in a stricken voice.

"This one is Tarmia," choked Bithyia. "I recognise the tattoo on her shoulder." She shuddered and looked away. "I cannot be sure of the others; they were stripped of their jewellery and...violated."

Sarmatia squatted beside the body of Tarmia and picked up her cold hand. "What manner of beast would violate a corpse?" she grated.

"Were...were they dead...when...?" quavered Prithia.

Bithyia pointed at one of the other bodies. "She was. There are three arrows in her." She turned and stared at Prithia. "Servants of the Mother do not allow any man to take them unbidden. You know that. Would you be forced or would you die first?"

Prithia blinked. "I...I would choose death, lady."

"Just so. As did our sisters. Now let us protect their bodies from the carrion eaters before we ride to find their killers." Bithyia turned to the streambed and picked up a large smooth rock then laying it beside the headless body of Tarmia.

"There are but four bodies here, Bithyia," said Sarmatia. "Where is our other sister?"

Bithyia pointed to scuffmarks and blood on the far bank of the stream. "The dead were brought here for...for their violation. Our sister survives but she will be far from here, else she would have seen us. We cannot waste time looking for her."

Prithia looked horrified. "How can we not search for her? She may be wounded."

"It grieves me," whispered Bithyia, putting her hand on the shoulder of her companion. "But we dare not drop behind our enemy. Our Lady is our only concern."

"I could go and look..."

"No, Prithia. I will not divide our group again. I erred and as a result, four of our sisters lie dead. I am responsible for all of you." Bithyia thrust away her bitter anger and replaced it with an iron determination. "Now help me do what little we can for our companions." She bent to lift another stone. The others joined in and a cairn of rocks swiftly rose above the four young women.

At last, Bithyia stepped back. She lifted her eyes to the sky and the circling crows then down to the earth beneath her feet. "Take your servants to your bosom, Mother. They served you well in life. We shall make a blood sacrifice for their spirits in due course." She lifted a hand, joining Sarmatia and Prithia in a last farewell. "Be safe with the Mother, beloved sisters. Until we meet again in death."

The three women mounted their horses and rode slowly back to the muddy track then up the hill and into the silent pine forest without looking back.

Chapter 6

The village of Turkul nestled comfortably in the lee of a small hill just beyond the rolling expanses of pine forest. Sheltered from the cold northerly winds, the dozen or so timber houses huddled together as if in mutual defence against the hostile world beyond its boundaries. An imposing two-story structure in the centre of the village doubled as an inn and the home of the village elder. An open space in front of it harboured a stone-lipped well and a few rough trestles sparsely covered with the miserable offerings of local farmers and hunters. Smoke coiled from soot-stained holes in the roofs of several houses, adding the sour smell of wood smoke to the stench of open middens and animal dung.

Dimurthes rode into the open space at the head of his men, his hand on the pommel of his sword as he looked keenly around. Traders and their customers glanced at the column of Scythian warriors with interest, noting the armed readiness of the men. They quickly avoided eye contact before averting their heads and busying themselves with their trades or hurrying off as if suddenly remembering an urgent appointment elsewhere. Women gathered children away from the stalls into the relative security of their homes.

Taraxes led the men, with Tomyra still bound on her horse, toward the inn, while Dimurthes dismounted at the well. He drew up a hide bucket of water and scrubbed dried blood from his hands before splashing his head and face with cold water. Tossing back his sodden hair, he strode over to a nearby midden and relieved himself with a great sigh of contentment in full view of the remaining villagers. He fastened his leggings back around his waist and walked over to the inn, snatching a loaf of coarse unleavened bread from a stall as he passed. The trader opened his mouth to protest then obviously thought better of it and turned away.

Approaching the inn, Dimurthes was accosted by a tall, thin man dressed in patched and grubby clothing. Despite the grime and stench of wood smoke and food in his clothes, the man carried himself with an air of authority. Accompanying the man were two burly men carrying spears and short swords. They wore expressions of sullen indifference as they stood silently a few paces behind the thin man. With a glance at his companions as if for reassurance, the man deliberately stepped into the Serratae chieftain's path.

"Your business?" he grated.

Dimurthes slowly looked the man up and down before answering. "My business is my own."

The tall man flushed. "I am the Elder here. All that happens in Turkul is my concern."

Dimurthes turned his attention to the two men with the Elder. He caught a movement from his own men as they stood off to one side of the inn's entrance, tending to their horses. As Taraxes stepped forward, Dimurthes waved him back and turned to the Elder once more.

"I did not know that Turkul warranted an Elder. It seems a miserable collection of huts but it will suffice for my needs. Be so good as to see that my men are fed. We will not be staying long." He moved to push past the man.

The Elder gave an inarticulate cry of outrage and shouted to his bodyguards. One of them clumsily pushed his spear toward Dimurthes as the other yanked his sword from his belt. Dimurthes moved quickly to one side, grasping the spear shaft as it probed past him. He tugged on the shaft then rammed it hard into the belly of the guard. The end of the shaft caught the man just under the ribcage, expelling the air from his lungs and doubling him over in agony. Before the first guard could collapse to the ground, Dimurthes snatched the spear from his hands and thrust it at the second guard who had just freed his sword. The spear point stopped an inch from the man's throat. The guard's eyes bulged and his sword slipped from his hand.

"Shall we reconsider your welcome?" asked Dimurthes softly.

The Elder looked at his two guards, at Dimurthes with the spear held rock-steady at the man's throat, and at the other Scythian warriors now ringing the small group. He paled, his throat working convulsively as he fought for words.

"I...I bid you w...welcome, my Lord," he stammered. "I am happy to provide food for you and your men."

Dimurthes smiled. "A sensible decision." He tossed the spear to one of his men and gestured to the Elder to precede him into the inn.

The elder bowed obsequiously. "May I enquire as to your name, my Lord?" he asked.

"I am Dimurthes, chief of the Serratae. My people are at Zarmet, just three days from here." Dimurthes smiled pleasantly at the man. "Would you like me to bring them here to meet you?"

The man paled further. "N...no, my Lord Dimurthes. My apologies. I did not know." He bowed again, sweeping his hand toward his house. "Please enter and refresh yourself. My name is Portrax, Elder of this village. My wife has not been well, but she is a good cook." He kicked the fallen guard as he passed. "These fools mistook my purpose, my Lord," babbled Portrax. "I will see they are punished..."

Dimurthes scowled. "If I desired to know your name I would ask but I care not. Just feed my men and myself and your pitiful village will be your own again by nightfall."

"Of course, my Lord, forgive me." Portrax hurried ahead of Dimurthes, pushing the wooden door aside and ducking to enter through the low doorway. He started shouting to his wife and a serving girl to fetch food and drink, cursing as he knocked over a stool.

Dimurthes moved swiftly through the doorway on the heels of the other man, whirling to scan the room, with his hand on his sword. The room was large, occupying most of the ground floor of the house. Rickety stairs on one side led upward to the darkness of the top floor, which Dimurthes guessed were the living quarters of the Elder and his wife. At the far end of the room were two doors, covered with thick hides that flapped in the wind, pushing cold draughts of air gusting inward. Odours carried on the gusts told of the function of the open areas beyond the hides. The smell of baking bread and roasted meats wafted from the one and the stench of the eventual voiding of that same food carried to him from the midden behind the other.

Dimurthes noted a large fire in the middle of the room, giving off welcome pulses of heat, the smoke billowing upward to exit through a hole in the ceiling above. Daylight showed through the hole, indicating the upper floor was considerably smaller than the lower one. Rough wooden tables with benches and stools were ranged around the fire, with several men at one of them and two old women at another.

Taraxes and the other men entered noisily and ousted the diners from their table, pushing them to a corner of the room then calling loudly for food and drink. The serving girl hurried forward with platters of freshly baked bread and skins of sour beer. After a few slaps and pinches of the girl's ample assets, they fell on the food with gusto, calling for more bread and for meat.

Dimurthes ushered Tomyra to another table and pushed her down onto a stool. He took his dagger and cut her bonds before thrusting a plate of bread and a cup of beer toward her.

"Eat," he said. "We will not be staying long."

Tomyra picked at the loaf and sipped at the sour beer. Despite her hunger, grief and anger constricted her throat. She stared at the rough-hewn table in front of her and tried to ignore the babble of voices filling the smoky room.

Mother Goddess, she prayed silently. *If you hold me yet in your favour, help me avenge my sisters who have died this day.*

She thought back to happier times, when in the first flush of her love for her handsome Greek lover, her honour guard of young warrior women had truly seemed like fleshly sisters, not just Sisters serving the Goddess.

A rising tide of anger in a voice near her brought Tomyra back to her present sufferings. Dimurthes glowered up at a frail old woman standing beside the table. Another slightly less ancient woman stood a few paces back, a worried expression on her face, her thin, bony hands clasped in front of her chest.

"A plague on you, old woman," snarled Dimurthes. "I told you this woman is a captive and no business of yours. Now get out of here before I have you thrown out."

The old woman calmly stared at the angry man. "You would dare to lay hands on a consecrated priestess of the Mother Goddess?" she softly enquired.

Dimurthes pushed back his stool, rising to his feet. He leaned over the table and glared at the old woman, his face suffused with rage. "How in the name of all the gods of the Underworld...?" He took a deep breath. "I don't know what tales you were told, old hag, but this woman is no longer a priestess. She took a barbarian as a lover and is under sentence of death." He dragged his eyes off the old woman and stared at his men, still eating hungrily at the other table. "Which of you loose-tongued jackals has been spreading tales?" he shouted.

"I was not speaking of the girl," the old woman calmly went on, as if the enraged man was still sitting quietly in front of her. "I am Atrullia, priestess of the Mother Goddess in Her Aspect of the Huntress. Do not seek to anger Her."

Dimurthes whirled back to stare at the old woman again. His flush of anger faded to pallor and his brow wrinkled in perplexity. "What did you say? You are..." his voice trailed off. With an effort, Dimurthes collected his wits and drew himself upright, throwing his unruly locks of hair back from his face. "My apologies, Lady," he grated. "I am Dimurthes, chief of the Serratae and these are my men. I am taking this woman back to Zarmet to face her just execution for her crimes."

Atrullia nodded. "I defer, of course, to the authority of your position in all matters pertaining to tribal law," she agreed. "I was merely concerned that this girl has obviously been abused. I wished to offer my assistance." A troubled expression settled on her wrinkled brown face. "But you say this girl is, or was, a priestess. If this is so then no matter what her offence, I must intervene."

The old priestess sat down on a stool and, assisted by the other old woman, drew it close to Tomyra. "Thank you, Solma." Atrullia squeezed the other woman's hand before turning to face Tomyra. She looked into the young girl's eyes for a few moments then her gaze slowly travelled over the rest of her, taking in her dirty, dishevelled appearance and her torn cloak and shift. "Is there truth in what this man says, my dear?" she asked quietly.

Tomyra closed her eyes for a moment then opened them again and nodded. "Yes, Lady. But there is more to it."

Atrullia sighed. "There always is." She waited for a moment then as Tomyra continued to sit in silence, prompted her. "Go on, child. In what way is this man correct and in what way is he false?"

"Enough of this," interrupted Dimurthes. "I have been more than patient with you, Lady. This matter is now a secular one and will be dealt with by me at Zarmet."

"If this girl was a consecrated priestess then the offence, if there really was one, is of concern to the Mother Goddess," observed Atrullia. Her voice sharpened in tone. "I will examine her story now and will brook no further interruptions."

"No. She is mine. I warn you..." grated Dimurthes.

Atrullia rose to her feet and, despite the fact that the top of her head came only to the man's chest, stared him down. Her stature seemed to swell in the flickering firelight and she threw back her cloak to reveal a rich green woollen dress stitched with gold thread. On it, a huntress drew a bow at a leaping stag. "You warn *me*?" she icily inquired. "Remember who I am. The Mother Goddess rules us all, men and women alike. She was there at your birth, at your naming, at your ascension to chieftainship and at every ceremony or formal occasion you attended with your tribe. She will be there at your death. If you have any hope of the afterlife or of rebirth then you will behave with civility and courtesy to Her chosen ones. Do I make myself clear?"

The conversation and laughter at the other tables died away when Atrullia spoke and her last question cracked like a whip in the silence. Dimurthes flushed and stepped back, knocking over his stool.

Atrullia continued in a softer voice. "Go and sit with your men. I will question this girl." She waited until Dimurthes sat down at one of the other tables across the fire. The old priestess reseated herself with Solma's help and turned back to Tomyra.

"Thank you, my Lady," smiled Tomyra. "It gladdens my heart to see that man..."

A sharp gesture from Atrullia cut off Tomyra's thanks. "Do not think that was done for you, child. If you have truly sinned against the Mother then you will feel her wrath, both in this world and the next." She looked at Tomyra's stricken face and continued in a gentler voice. "Compose yourself, child, and tell me who you are and where you come from."

"Yes, Mother," Tomyra whispered while smoothing her unruly hair with one hand. She collected her thoughts for a moment. "My name is Tomyra. I am the daughter of Spargises, chief of the Massegetae and Starissa, priestess of the Sauromantians."

Atrullia leaned forward. "How can that be? Do not Sauromantian priestesses consecrate their virginity to the Goddess? Or did your father rape her?"

Tomyra shook her head. "My mother was captured in a time of war by the Triboi and sold in slavery. Eventually, my father bought her but he did not force her, even though it was his right. He married her and held her in honour."

"I see. Go on, child."

"My mother died when I was twelve. By then she had instructed me in the ways of the Great Mother and I consecrated myself to her service. Two years ago the old priestess died and I became the path of the Mother's goodness for my people."

"And this Greek lover he refers to?" asked Atrullia, jerking her head toward Dimurthes, who sat glowering in the firelight.

Tomyra's eyes softened and a gentle smile curved her lips. "Nikomayros, son of Leonnatos of Macedon. Last year he led a patrol into our lands under the orders of his king, Alexander. You have heard of Alexander, the Great King of the West?"

Atrullia nodded.

"He, Nikomayros, was captured and was to be sacrificed to the Great Goddess. The Mother saved him though." Tomyra smiled.

"Saved him? A barbarian? How?" The old woman frowned down at the young girl.

"Though unarmed, he overcame my champion and killed him with his own sword. Further, the champion's blow was turned by an old iron armband worn by Nikomayros." Tomyra leaned forward as she eagerly recounted the event. "It was an ancient armband of the Mother, serpent-bodied and gilded, and passed down from mother to daughter in his family. His mother passed it to him when he left home." Tomyra sat back and shook her head. "It was a sign. Then later, at the ceremony of brotherhood..."

"Brotherhood?" gasped Atrullia. "What in heaven are you talking about, child? Barbarians are not made brothers of the True People."

Tomyra picked up a morsel of bread from the table and rolled it between her fingers before she spoke. "I have never heard of it before," she admitted. "After my vision, though, my father greatly desired it. I could not refuse him. Especially as the Mother willed it."

"What vision was this?" asked Atrullia sharply. "Tell me!"

"It...it was strange, Mother. I have had visions sent by the Great Goddess before, of course, but this was strong, so strong." Tomyra shivered and lapsed into silence. She drew her cloak about her despite the warmth of the room. Her eyes became unfocused as she remembered and when she spoke again it was in a quiet, remote voice.

"The Mother Sea. A tribe without a head. A king. Conquest. Change."

Atrullia leaned forward, her dark bright eyes searching Tomyra's face as the young girl spoke.

"From the blood of kings comes a warrior of the People. Great glory. A Golden King lies in his future. Death, and..." Tomyra broke off, her face flushing.

"And?" enquired Atrullia softly. "Those were words of prophesy, child. I could tell, even hearing them repeated in this place. What else did the Goddess say that you fear to say to me now?"

Tomyra coughed as a billow of smoke swept across the table, the hide covering of the door flapping violently in a gust of wind. "Fear? Once I feared, Mother." She shook her head and stared back at the old woman. "The Goddess told me I would love a man from the West and that he would take me away from my people and I would bear his children." The young girl smiled and pushed her long black hair away from her face. "Nikomayros the Greek is my lover and I will go where he leads. The Goddess wills it."

Atrullia leaned back with a look of shock on her face. "You take too much upon yourself," she hissed. "The Great Mother does not give Her daughters to be the lovers of men. You have sinned, child. Do not pretend to have the blessing of the Goddess."

Tomyra drew herself up and stared back at the old priestess. "I tell no lie, Mother. The Goddess herself guides me."

The old woman sighed, fanning smoke away from her face with one hand. "Child...Tomyra. Priestesses are virgins. The Great Mother would not allow one of Her consecrated virgins to be taken by a man and still remain a priestess. You were deceived, either by your heart or by some evil spirit." Atrullia made a warding sign. "Admit your folly child, and I will do what I can to mitigate your fate." She reached across and took Tomyra's hand in her wrinkled one.

Atrullia's brow creased and a look of puzzlement crept over her face, followed by astonishment. "What is this?" she cried in a thin voice. "The Goddess speaks through you!" She snatched her hand back and stared at Tomyra with wide eyes. "Power resides within you child," she whispered. "Your consecration is intact, despite..." She turned and looked across the room at Dimurthes in horror. "What has he done to you?"

Tomyra turned her head and shot Dimurthes a venomous stare. "What has he not done?" she grated. "He helped my brother kill my beloved father and betray my people. When my brother told him to kill me, he took me captive and repeatedly raped me. I wish him dead in a most horrible way."

Atrullia rose to her feet and tottered toward the fire. Solma hurried to her side and supported her as she stood in front of Dimurthes. She took several deep breaths to calm herself, coughing slightly in the smoky air. "Dimurthes of the Serratae, your captive accuses you of rape. What do you say?"

The room quieted, the Scythian warriors looking up from their beer with interest.

Dimurthes snorted and looked beyond the two old women to where Tomyra sat staring at him. "What of it? She is a captive, a spoil of war. What I choose to do with her is my concern only. She is nothing and has no rights in this."

"She is also a consecrated priestess of the Great Goddess," hissed Atrullia.

"Was, old woman, was," sneered Dimurthes, rising to his feet. "Now, if you have no further questions for the girl, we will depart from this lice-infested village."

Atrullia pointed a bony finger at the chief. "She is a priestess still. I can feel her power within her."

"Impossible. She has lain with a man even before I..." Dimurthes' voice trailed off. "She cannot be," he finished, his voice flat and emotionless.

"Do you doubt my word?" asked Atrullia.

Dimurthes shook his head then shrugged. "No, Lady. Yet it cannot be so. She has deceived you somehow."

"Then we must find the truth of it. You and the girl will accompany me back to the sanctuary of the Goddess on Mount Mora. There she will be put to the question." Atrullia nodded to herself in satisfaction. "Yes," she muttered. "It is possible for even a priestess to be deceived, but no mortal can deceive the Goddess Herself."

"Lady, I cannot. I must rejoin my army in Zarmet. I appreciate your concern but I will hand the girl over to my tribe's priestess when we get there." Dimurthes turned and called across to Taraxes, who stood gawking with the other men. "Come, we ride for Zarmet at once." He pushed past the old women and gripped Tomyra by the arm, pulling her to her feet.

"Stay!" Atrullia's voice crackled with power. The warriors stopped and turned toward her. "You have no choice in the matter. You have been accused of raping this girl. If she is indeed a holy priestess then you may yet die for that action. Come with me and find the truth of the matter. If you refuse you will find your people turned against you on your return to Zarmet."

Dimurthes paled. His mouth opened but no words came out. Several of his men held their hands low, palm downward and muttered brief invocations to the gods.

Atrullia smiled coldly. "If you are afraid, you may bring three men with you. No more." The old woman, accompanied by an anxious-looking Solma, walked imperiously to the doorway of the inn and pushed through the hide hangings.

Chapter 7

"Rider coming...fast." Parasades held up a hand and listened intently. After a moment he nodded. "One horse." He snapped his fingers and pointed to one side of the track at the low cover of some medium-sized boulders. "Certes, get ready to take him." Turning to the other riders, Parasades smiled briefly. "My lord, if you would be so kind as to move off the path."

Nikometros nodded and turned his stallion's head up the slope. Timon and Agarus followed, their horses picking their way carefully in the loose stony soil. When they reached the low boulders they slid off their mounts and crouched low, though the horses remained in full view should anyone look that way. Certes strung his bow and fitted an arrow after sticking two others into the dirt in front of him. He took aim at a point in the path just a few feet in front of Parasades.

Parasades sat relaxed on his horse in the middle of the hill path, facing the now generally audible sounds of approach. He stroked his moustache gently with one hand while keeping the other on the hilt of his short sword. The reins hung loose over his horse's neck, tiny movements of the man's feet and legs keeping the restless mount from turning toward its fellows on the hillside.

The drumming of hooves came louder. Around the shoulder of the hill burst a lone rider, crouched low over the neck of a lathered horse as it came at a full gallop toward Parasades. At the last moment the rider caught side of the man and with a low, inarticulate cry, dragged back on the reins, attempting to turn the horse's headlong rush. The horse went down on its haunches in a shower of pebbles and dust before struggling to its feet again. The rider half fell awkwardly to one side, desperately clinging to the back of the horse as an arrow thrummed through the space the rider's body had occupied a moment before.

Parasades leapt to the ground and ran to the struggling horse. He reached up and dragged the rider down, cracking him across the head with the flat of his sword. The rider collapsed in a heap while the horse staggered a few paces then stood, its flanks heaving and legs trembling.

Parasades reached down and turned the fallen rider over, keeping his sword ready. He stared at the hairless face for a moment, taking in the clothing and bow still strung across one shoulder. "Diratha?" he muttered. "What are you doing here?" He looked up as the others scrambled down to the path, leading their horses.

Nikometros bent over the figure with interest. "A woman?" he asked. "Who is she?"

"I think I recognise her, sir," said Timon. "Though I don't know her name. She is an 'Owl', one of your lady's warriors."

"Diratha is her name, and yes, she is a Massegetae warrior-woman," Parasades said slowly. "What I would like to know is what she is doing here, and coming from enemy land."

"Then we must ask her, if you haven't killed her," commented Nikometros. "Timon, see if you can revive her." He glanced up at Diratha's trembling horse. "No horse should be abused like that. Agarus, would you please attend to it."

Timon knelt beside the young woman and probed her dark hair with his fingers. He glanced up at Parasades with a disapproving look. "You couldn't have been a touch more gentle with her?" His fingers came away with blood on them.

Parasades snorted. "If I had known she was a woman before I struck her then yes, Timon." He beckoned to Certes. "Ride up the way she came a ways," he said. "See if she is pursued." Certes nodded and turned to his horse. "Certes," added Parasades quietly. "Do not engage the enemy alone. Come back and warn us." He watched until the young man rode out of sight around the hill.

Timon took the skin flask from his belt and trickled the thin sour wine over the wound. He soaked a cloth with the liquid and dabbed the woman's face until she moaned. Diratha opened her eyes and stared up at the faces uncomprehendingly for a moment. Then she gasped and tried to shield herself with her arms.

Parasades leaned down and grasped one of her arms, dragging it aside. He stared at the woman with a fierce expression for a few moments before nodding and pursing his lips. "Be at ease, Diratha. You are among friends." He released the young woman's arm and gestured around at the others. "See, here is your mistress' champion, Nikomayros the Lion. Also Timon, his friend. You remember them, do you not?"

Diratha lowered her arms slowly and looked around. She nodded, wincing from the pain in her scalp. "Yes, my lord," she whispered.

"What are you doing here, Diratha?" asked Parasades. "I certainly did not look to see a Massegetae woman riding out of Serratae lands."

"My lord, I came to look for my mistress, the lady Tomyra."

"Alone? You are either brave or very foolish."

"No, my lord. The lady Bithyia led us..."

"Bithyia!" broke in Timon. "She is here? Where is she now?" He grabbed the young woman's shoulder and turned her to face him.

"I do not know, sir, she was not with us when the enemy struck."

"Why not? Where did she go?" yelled Timon.

"What enemy is this, Diratha?" Parasades asked. "Do you mean Dimurthes?"

"She went...I do not know who...we followed the lady Tomyra..." Diratha looked from one to the other of her interrogators then burst into tears.

"Gods!" exploded Nikometros. "Have you no regard for this girl's troubles? She has fled the enemy only to be set upon by those she would consider friends. Let her gather her wits." He knelt beside the distraught young woman and rubbed her hands in his. "Diratha, you are safe now. We will protect you. We need only to know what lies up ahead." Nikometros smiled encouragingly at her. "Take your time and tell us from the beginning."

A clatter of hooves on the stony ground made Nikometros look up. Certes pulled his horse up abruptly and slid to the ground. He looked at Parasades and shook his head. "No sign of pursuit," Certes said quietly.

"There, Diratha," smiled Nikometros. "Certes says there is no one nearby. You are safe."

Diratha sniffled and wiped her nose on her sleeve. She struggled into a sitting position and looked at the men's faces slowly. "We followed the trail of our mistress from the Oxus River, leading west and north. We knew it was her we followed as we recognised the mark of her mare. We followed into the hills then across the grassland then..."

"Just a moment, Diratha," broke in Nikometros. "Who do you mean when you say 'we'?"

"Bithyia led us, my lord. Also Sarmatia, her deputy and Domra, though she was no warrior." Diratha thought for a moment. "Prithia, Tarmia, Stallias, and Portas also. And myself of course."

Nikometros nodded and smiled. "Thank you, Diratha. Now continue, please. You followed until today?"

"Yes, my lord. Before daybreak, while our enemies still lay encamped below us, Bithyia took two others to forage for food. She left Domra in charge with strict instructions to wait on their return and not to take any actions that might endanger the others. But at daybreak our enemies moved on and Domra decided to follow instead of waiting for Bithyia." Diratha paused and passed a dirty hand over her face. "We should have overruled her, my lord, but as she only meant to follow we left signs for Bithyia and went with her." She looked up at the men with a trembling lip. "If we had obeyed, we would all be alive."

Nikometros looked around at the others with a troubled expression. He made no comment and raised a hand to stop a question from Timon. Diratha took a ragged breath and continued.

"We came to a wide valley with a stream. There was no cover but we could see no sign of the enemy. Domra wanted to cross immediately but Tarmia argued that we should wait there for the others. Domra rode into the valley and we followed. We could not let her ride out alone, my lord." Diratha sighed. "It was an ambush. Tarmia was the first to die under the arrows, then Domra. We fought but it was hopeless, we were three against a dozen. Portas and I fled but Portas' horse was lame. I heard her die behind me." Tears trickled down Diratha's cheeks. "Her death bought me time and I escaped."

The men stood and knelt silently round the crying girl, anger and distress warring within them. Diratha's sobs grew louder. "I should have stayed and died with my sisters. Instead, I fled in shame. I deserve to die."

"No, Diratha," said Nikometros gently. "You could do nothing. You are safe now."

Parasades stepped forward and put a hand on Nikometros' shoulder, squeezing it firmly. "Yes, Diratha," he said grimly. "You fled the battle and left your companions to die. You deserve to die too." He drew his dagger from his belt and held it out hilt-first to the girl. "Does your guilt prompt you to take your own life?"

Nikometros twisted round to stare up at Parasades in astonishment. Timon shifted uncomfortably and looked down at the ground. Certes and Agarus watched with interest as Diratha stifled her sobs and stretched out a trembling hand toward the dagger.

As the girl touched the dagger, Parasades drew it back sharply. "Or will you rather seek to revenge yourself by helping us find the killers of your sisters?" he asked softly. He waited while Diratha hesitated, emotions contorting her features. "If you wish to die I will not stop you but do not waste your death, woman. Help us first."

The young woman stared up at Parasades for several minutes then sighed again and struggled to her feet. "I will help you, my lord. I will seek to avenge my sisters before I die."

Chapter 8

"We cannot just ride into the village."

"Why not?" inquired Prithia. "Nobody knows us here. They are only ignorant peasants."

"For the most part, yes," conceded Sarmatia. "But we do not know if our mistress and those we pursue are still down there. They know of our presence now and will be on guard."

Bithyia turned from her scrutiny of the several paths that merged in front of them. The paths, now almost a road, bore the signs of wheeled carts and many horses. Only close examination revealed one or two prints of Tomyra's distinctive mare in the hard packed soil.

"We won't enter the village," she stated flatly. "We'll ride around and see whether there are other roads leading out of here." She remounted her horse and pointed off to her left.

The three women urged their horses off the converging paths and into the trackless pine forests. They picked their way carefully across the rocky ground made slippery by a thick covering of pine needles. The trees shielded them from the bitter winds that blew down from the low mountains around them, the mournful sigh of the gusts in the foliage rising and falling.

By noon they had completed a circuit of the village, finding only three other paths. None of these showed any sign of recent usage and indeed, seemed scarcely capable of sustaining much traffic.

Bithyia examined the crossroads again and nodded in satisfaction. "Good. They are still in the village. We'll wait for them to come out." She looked around, scrutinising the cover critically before choosing a small densely vegetated hillock some distance from the road. Leading the group to it, she dismounted and pushed through the bushes into a small clearing. "This will do. Prithia, attend to the horses please. Sarmatia, perhaps some food?" Bithyia wet her finger and held it up. She grunted and nodded. "The wind, such as it is, blows from the road to us. I think we can risk cooking those chickens now. Keep the fire small and the smoke will lose itself quickly in the trees."

While Prithia groomed and fed the horses with a few handfuls of grain and water from a depleted skin container, Sarmatia started a small, almost smokeless fire of pinecones and twigs on a bare patch of rocky soil. When it burnt down to red coals she gutted the birds and placed them carefully on the embers. The feathers crackled and emitted a stink and a cloud of smoke curled up into the treetops. Presently, the skin of the chickens started to char and the bodies hissed gently, juices leaking out into the fire as they cooked. The stink of burning feathers was replaced by the pleasant odours of cooking meat.

A faint noise carried to Bithyia as she lay beneath the dense bushes of the hillock, scanning the distant crossroads. She signalled behind her with one hand, silencing the muttered conversation of the other two women. Bithyia listened intently then hissed a warning.

"Horses coming. Cover the fire. Quickly!"

Prithia quickly lifted the almost-cooked chickens from the embers and laid them onto fresh green pine needles. Sarmatia scooped earth over the fire, dampening down the nearly smokeless ashes. The two women scrambled to the edge of the copse and lay alongside Bithyia, staring through the trees at the road.

Minutes passed, through which the faint clop of horse's hooves came and went with the breeze. At last, a figure appeared on the road leading up from the village, followed by a column of men on horseback.

"Yes. It's our quarry," whispered Bithyia in satisfaction. "But I cannot see our mistress."

"There." Sarmatia pointed near the front of the column. "See, she wears a different cloak."

"Then who is that that rides beside her?" asked Prithia in a low voice. She stared hard at the apparent figure of another woman alongside her mistress. "And there, too. See, further back. Another woman."

Bithyia shook her head. "What are they doing picking up other women?"

"Wives, maybe? Or village girls for their pleasure?"

"They are not young," said Sarmatia. "Even on an easy path they ride slowly and with care."

The column passed slowly, the men gesturing and laughing together, relaxed and careless. At the rear rode the single figure of a man. Though the women were too far away to see his face, the way he sat astride his horse and the carriage of his shoulders told them he was tense and alert. Abruptly, he reined in his horse and stared around at the pine forest stretching away on all sides. He raised his head and wafted air toward him with one hand. The man turned his head and looked back down the road to the village then at the forest again.

Bithyia glanced at the extinguished fire anxiously then sniffed the air. A faint odour of wood smoke and cooked chicken drifted on the cold air. *Surely he cannot smell the fire at that distance,* she thought. *And against the wind...*With horror she realised the wind had changed, the odours of their campsite now carrying toward the road.

The man kicked his horse gently and twitched the reins, urging it off the path and in the general direction of the wooded hillock. Bithyia edged backward cautiously and scrambled to her horse. Hastily stringing her bow and grabbing a handful of arrows, she slithered back into position. *Mother Goddess,* she prayed. *Please not. To kill him here would betray our presence.*

The man rode slowly toward them. Bithyia carefully selected a straight arrow and checked the feathers. She set it in place and drew back on the sinew, holding the bow flat and parallel to the ground. Sighting the arrow, Bithyia prepared to kill the man.

Unaware of the threat of his imminent demise, Dimurthes brought his horse to a halt less than twenty paces from the hidden women. He sniffed audibly and looked back toward the road and the village. He shrugged and muttered "Just the village," then turned his horse back to the road.

Bithyia waited with bow drawn and arrow trained until the man disappeared from sight before relaxing. "Thank you, Great Mother," she whispered.

"You should have killed him while you had the chance," grumbled Prithia. "One less of the murdering swine."

"He would be missed too easily and his death would alert them to our presence," said Sarmatia reprovingly.

The women returned to their horses and repacked their meagre gear. Prithia picked up the cooling chickens and tore off a leg. She bit into it and grinned as the hot juices ran down her chin. "Gods, that tastes good." She divided one of the birds and handed the pieces to the others then wrapped the other one in a cloth and tucked it into a bag slung across the neck of her mare.

"Eat quickly," said Bithyia. "We must keep close to them now. We are getting near Zarmet and no doubt there will be other villages. If we are to rescue Tomyra, it must be soon."

Flinging the bones and fragments of uneaten flesh to the ground; they wiped the grease off their hands with handfuls of fallen pine needles then mounted their horses.

The road used by the column of men with Tomyra and the two old women branched off the old path to the south and east only a few yards back. The new road wound to the south and west, rising slowly to follow the increasing elevation of the mountains. The road was stony and hard-packed, the hooves of the many horses leaving only faint tracks.

Bithyia forced the pace, catching up to their quarry as quickly as possible. Once almost within earshot of the column, she became more circumspect. Each twist in the road was approached with caution, each new stretch viewed carefully from cover before moving swiftly to the next clump of trees or rocky outcrop. The landscape itself prevented the women from following under cover of the thinning forest. Steep ravines with rushing streams bisected the rocky slopes and loose shale slipped beneath their horses as they guided them as best they could along the edges of the narrow road.

The loose stones of the steep hillside that threatened their safety ultimately proved a blessing. A clattering of rocks from around the shoulder of the hill sent them scrambling for the nearest cover behind a massive boulder perched precariously amid recently crushed shrubs. Peering around the edges, the three women saw the column of men milling around a branch in the road as the party broke into two unequal groups. Orders were shouted and several spare horses were ushered by the larger group toward the main road. One of the old women pointed at Tomyra then at the mountains above her. The man that had nearly discovered Bithyia and her companions shrugged and snapped out an order. Tomyra was ordered off her mare and remounted on one of the smaller, wiry hill horses. The mare was led to the larger group.

The old woman signalled and guided her horse toward a narrow but well-worn path leading up the slope. Tomyra followed, together with the other old woman and three men. The man giving the orders nodded to the main group and waved them on before turning his own horse up the mountain. The large group of a dozen men and the spare horses clattered off down the main road.

"Now what is the reason for that?" mused Bithyia from her cover behind the boulder.

"Does it matter?" asked Prithia. "There are now only four men guarding our mistress. We can take them now and free her."

"That is true," urged Sarmatia. "We may never have a better opportunity."

"Look upward," Bithyia said softly. "We yet have a problem."

The two women turned to look up the slope of the mountain to where the small party of men and women followed the rough path upward. Only a short ride above them the last of the thinning scrub died away completely, leaving expanses of bare rock and loose scree slopes stretching across the mountain.

"There is no cover," said Sarmatia in horror.

Chapter 9

At about the time that Bithyia and her companions watched the small group of riders moving away across the bare slopes of the mountain, Nikometros and his men approached the village of Turkul. They too, noted the faint marks of Tomyra's horse in the stony ground of the crossroads, leading both into the village and back out of it.

"They rode back the way we came?" puzzled Timon. "Surely we would have seen them?"

Nikometros shook his head. "Obviously they took one of the other roads. We must look carefully." He turned his horse Diomede back toward one of the other paths, followed by Timon.

Parasades halted and sat looking at Nikometros until the Greek turned inquiringly toward him. "We need provisions, Nikomayros. The village can provide those and information too."

Nikometros thought for a moment then tossed his head in assent. "Very well. Let us ride into the village." He turned his stallion.

Parasades smiled. "There may be soldiers stationed here. What do you think their reaction would be toward a fair-haired stranger and an armed woman?" He shook his head. "No, Certes and I will go down. You must remain here with the others. We will return soon." He kicked his horse into motion and trotted down the road into the village with Certes at his heels.

"Who in Hades does he think he is?" muttered Timon. "Ordering you around like that, sir. I have a good mind..."

Nikometros grimaced sourly at the disappearing Scythians then shrugged. "He's a powerful Scythian lord, Timon, in a land that he knows well. We're at a disadvantage for the time being." He turned his horse off the road, looking for a suitable place to wait for their companions' return. Only one place looked to provide sufficient cover from casual scrutiny of any passers-by; a small wooded hillock a hundred paces from the crossroads. "Over there, I think."

The three men and a woman pushed through the undergrowth into the small clearing on the summit of the hillock. Agarus slid off his gelding and limped across to a heap of scuffed dirt. He squatted beside it and raked the soil back, digging his gnarled fingers into what lay beneath.

"There has been a fire here," he said. "Recently, too. The ashes are still warm."

"Aye, and horses." Timon bent down and picked up a few grains of feed. "Somebody stayed here long enough to rest and feed their horses. Three, I'd say, from the signs."

"It must be Bithyia," exclaimed Diratha. "With Prithia and Sarmatia. We must ride after them."

"Be patient, Diratha," said Nikometros. "We must wait for the others to get back from the village. Besides, if Bithyia is only a few hours ahead of us then so are the ones they follow. We do not want to ride into them unawares." He dismounted and stretched. "Get some rest. I will take the first watch."

Agarus and Timon unloaded the horses and rubbed them down, giving them a drink of water and a handful of dried grass from an almost-empty sack. Diratha sat with her back to a large pine tree and drew her sword from its sheath. Spitting on a small piece of worn sandstone, she started honing the blade with careful strokes. She sang beneath her breath as she worked, the words indistinct. Her eyes glittered with unshed tears as she sang.

Timon jerked his head at the young woman. "What is she singing, Agarus?" he asked. "I thought I knew most of the campfire songs but I haven't heard this one before."

Agarus hawked and spat. "It's a death song, my friend. A warrior sings it before he goes into battle, knowing he'll be killed." He grimaced. "I've never heard a woman sing it though."

Timon sat down under another tree across the small glade from Diratha, watching the young woman as she honed her blade and sang her welcome to death. He turned his mind to his own woman, Bithyia. Although not a consecrated virgin like her mistress Tomyra, her dedication to the service of the priestess of the Great Goddess had kept her away from the attentions of men. By custom rather than law, the female companions of the priestess were also viewed as sacrosanct. Falling in love for the first time with Timon, Bithyia's passion had raged uncontrollably. Their affair had no doubt deflected attention from the forbidden love of the priestess for her Greek champion.

Timon grinned, remembering the nights of love beneath the summer stars and the thrill of the chase, pursuing deer through the thickets by the riverbanks. Bithyia, like most Scythians, seemed as if she had been born on horseback. She could hunt with the most skilled of the men, hold her own with arrow and sword and even wrestle many young men to a draw. Despite her slight body, her courage and determination drove her to excel in traditionally manly pursuits. Only with Timon had she surrendered, after a suitable time, willingly allowing the Macedonian soldier to claim the prize of her own body.

A low cough brought Timon back from his memories. He saw that Agarus lay curled up over the dirt-covered ashes of the old fire, extracting a last remnant of heat. Diratha had ceased her efforts to sharpen her weapon and leaned back against the pine bark. Her eyes were open but unfocused. Timon looked around and saw Nikometros beckoning to him. He crawled over and looked toward the road, in time to see a man on horseback disappearing at a fast trot away from the village.

"Parasades?" he asked.

"No. A soldier though. I hope they haven't run into trouble." Nikometros glanced round at Agarus and Diratha. "Get everyone ready to move. I think we should move closer to the village in case they need assistance."

Nikometros and his companions moved cautiously back to the road then along it toward the village. At a bend in the road, at the point where it dropped over a low ridge, they left the road and worked their way slowly along the crest. From this vantage point they could see down into the village, making out some of the marketplace and square over the roofs of the houses.

"I don't see them," muttered Timon.

"There are a lot of people down there, though I don't see any soldiers," remarked Nikometros. "The activity seems to be centred around that large house there."

"Probably the inn," said Agarus, licking his lips. "By the dust demons, I could do with a beer right now. Perhaps my lord Parasades will bring some back with him," he added hopefully.

"There." Nikometros pointed. "See, at the door of the...inn. I'm sure that is Certes." The figure of a man rapidly crossed the open space, disappearing behind one of the intervening buildings. A few moments later he reappeared, leading two horses.

The unmistakable figure of Parasades exited the inn, together with a tall, thin man and a burly man--a soldier--armed with a spear. Parasades and the thin man stood, apparently in argument, with much waving of hands and pointing. The armed man stood stolidly to one side, watching them. Certes pushed past the group into the inn, reemerging a few moments later with two bags that he slung over the backs of the horses.

Parasades clapped the man on the shoulder and turned toward his horse. He and Certes mounted and kicked their horses into a walk, disappearing among the houses.

Nikometros pulled the reins of his stallion back toward the road, the others following. They reached the bend just as Parasades and Certes clattered up. Parasades checked his horse momentarily as he caught sight of Nikometros then came up alongside him.

"Nikomayros, you startled me," he said. "I had thought to see you farther from the village."

"We were concerned when we saw the soldier ride past."

Parasades hesitated. "He did not see you?"

"No. What happened down there in the village? Did you find out anything?" enquired Nikometros.

"Did you bring any beer?" Agarus asked.

Certes grinned. "No beer, cripple. We sampled it, though. They make a good brew hereabouts."

Agarus scowled and turned away, muttering imprecations under his breath.

"Tomyra was here," stated Parasades. "They are no more than two hours ahead of us. The headman was most forthcoming."

Nikometros grinned. "Then we shall find them by nightfall."

"If the gods so wish it, my friend Nikomayros. There is a complication or two to my tale though." Parasades frowned. "The headman tells me there was an altercation in the inn and the local priestess now rides with Dimurthes to her sanctuary on Mount Mora. The argument concerned Tomyra. Further, there is a patrol of Serratae hereabouts. We must be cautious."

Nikometros looked puzzled. "Dimurthes is no longer going to Zarmet?"

Parasades shrugged. "The headman was unclear on that point. Dimurthes has undertaken to bring the old priestess and her servant to her mountain sanctuary, but whether he will do so himself or assign his men is uncertain."

"So, we must still follow as before," frowned Nikometros. "Well, let us away while there is still light."

The sound of hooves on the hard packed road intruded on the conversation. Parasades pointed off the road and spurred his horse into the forest. They reached the shelter of the first trees, though still in view of any who might turn their heads, before the lone rider thundered up from the village and past them.

"The soldier," muttered Timon. "Where is he off to in such a hurry?"

Parasades turned and looked at Timon. "The soldier? You have seen him before?"

"In the doorway of the inn," replied Timon. "We saw him through the trees when you talked to the headman."

The Scythian frowned then nodded. "Come," he said. "As the lord Nikomayros says, we must make the most of the light." He walked his horse back down to the road.

Timon caught Nikometros by the arm as he rode past him. "My lord," he whispered. "There is something wrong, I can feel it." He grimaced at Nikometros' questioning look. "He looked alarmed when I said I had seen the soldier, just for a moment. There's something else he's not telling us."

Chapter 10

G orinax cursed under his breath as he forced his horse into a gallop, thrashing it across its rump with a willow wand. Despite the cold late afternoon air he sweated, the odours of his fear and apprehension mingling with the unwashed stench of his body. His eyes darted nervously over the rocky hillsides and gullies with their sparse coverings of scrubby vegetation. Somewhere out here, he knew, was the enemy.

A pox on that bastard son of a fornicating goat, he thought savagely. *Sending me out alone with the gods only knew what dangers.* Gorinax pulled his horse to a halt on the crest of a low rise and looked about him, searching his memory for a landmark. "May a demon take Portrax and use his guts..." he muttered. *Ah! There it is.* He scrutinised the massive table of rock jutting out from the ridge far above him then looked back down the road toward Turkul. *I should be home with my woman and a good hot meal inside me.* He hawked and spat, the action sending a spasm of pain through his bruised chest and belly. *Gods curse all fornicating horse-warriors,* he thought sourly, remembering the agony as the spear haft had thudded into him earlier that day. *And now that fornicating Portrax wants me to find that fornicating Serratae patrol.*

He jerked his horse's head, urging it off the road and up the line of the ridge. It balked at the loose stony ground and he slashed it with his willow branch. Reluctantly, the horse started forward, picking its way carefully uphill.

The sun dipped below the horizon before he reached the flat rock. He moved past it to stare over the ridge into the next valley, straining to make out the road far below in the deepening shadows. Already, Gorinax regretted taking this shortcut, though he knew it would cut many miles off his journey. The passage down into the darkened valley before him would be fraught with dangers from the icy, loose rock. At least those cursed Massegetae warriors reported to be hereabouts would be keeping close to the forest roads.

An hour later, the soldier reached the road, having been thrown no more than twice. He turned north, toward Zarmet, riding down through the foothills toward the plains of grass that stretched out to the northern snows. As night fell he slowed his horse to a walk, letting the animal pick its way cautiously along the faint glimmer of the path. *Hours yet to moonrise,* he thought. *Not that a waning moon will be much use.* He shivered and drew his patched cloak close about him.

A faint smudge of ruddy light drew his attention. Off to his left and down in a wooded gully, the glow flickered and danced. Gorinax stopped and rubbed his eyes. *Ah, those fornicating Serratae,* he thought. *Or the Massegetae? No, they would not dare a fire.* He glanced back the way he had come then urged his horse off the track toward the glowing light. The glow grew larger and brighter as he approached and the smell of wood smoke assailed his nostrils.

A faint clatter of pebbles sounded from his left and Gorinax turned quickly, his hand moving toward the sword at his waist. He gave a muffled cry as hands reached out from the darkness behind him, drawing him swiftly to the ground. He felt hands over his mouth and nose, suffocating him, and cold steel at his throat.

"Bind him," muttered a voice. "Bring him to the fire."

Rough hands fumbled at Gorinax's back, tying his hands with a leather rope. The hand over his face eased and he drew a noisy breath. A voice with a wash of breath redolent of meat and herbs, whispered in his ear.

"You feel my blade?"

Gorinax nodded, his eyes bulging.

"Then remember it," the voice went on. "And keep silent."

The hand withdrew and Gorinax drew a quavering breath. Hands reached out and hauled him to his feet, pushing him toward the fire. Gorinax stumbled and fell to his knees in the orange light. He looked around at a number of bearded and moustached men, clad in Scythian leathers. A man detached himself from the circle of onlookers and walked around the fire toward Gorinax, fingering a short dagger as he approached.

"Who are you?" the man grated. "Why were you trying to spy on us?"

One of his captors guffawed. "He was as quiet and subtle as a stallion at rut."

The man glanced up at the grinning faces and frowned. The laughter died, the men looking down at the ground or staring stonily at their prisoner.

"Who are you?" the man repeated.

"G...G...Gorinax. I am a soldier at Turkul."

"What are you doing here, Gorinax?"

Gorinax looked around the circle of faces and licked his lips. "I...I seek warriors of the Serratae. I was told there was a patrol here." He looked up at the man standing over him, dagger in hand. "Are...are you Serratae?" he quavered.

"Why do you seek the Serratae?" asked the man, ignoring the question.

"Portrax sent me. A stranger came to Turkul today, asking questions. He..."

"And who in the seven levels of Hades is Portrax?"

"He is Elder of our village, the Headman. He said to tell you about the stranger."

The man yawned and picked at his nails with the tip of his dagger. "I am getting bored with this conversation." He looked over Gorinax's head at the men standing behind him. "Take this sorry fool into the bushes and kill him."

Gorinax let out a high-pitched scream as hands hauled him to his feet. "My lord, no! Please, my lord, Massegetae are here...Portrax said I should find you...the Lion...nooo!" The words tailed off into an inarticulate scream as the men dragged him out of the circle of firelight. Steam rose from his leggings as his bladder let go, the stench of urine mixing with smoke in the cold night air.

"Wait!" The command halted the Scythian warriors. The man crossed swiftly to the little group and stared into Gorinax's tear-streaked face. "Massegetae are here?"

"Yes, lord," sobbed Gorinax. "Please don't kill me, lord. I was only bringing a message from Portrax. He said...the stranger said..."

The man flicked his dagger across the face of the crying figure in front of him, a look of disgust curving his mouth downward. "Be quiet." He waited for the sobs to die down before he continued. "Think carefully before you speak. If you babble I will kill you. Now tell me in as few words as possible about the Massegetae."

Gorinax gulped and licked his lips. "He...they..." He gave a low sob and drew a quavering breath. "T...two men came to Turkul today. They were Massegetae warriors with one they called the Lion of Scythia. They hunt the Lord Dimurthes."

The man stared at Gorinax for a moment. He nodded to the men holding the soldier. "Bring him to the fire." To Gorinax he added, "You have bought yourself a few minutes more of life." The man strode back to the fire and seated himself on a large boulder. He grimaced as Gorinax was thrust at his feet. "Not so close," he growled. "He stinks."

The man held out a hand to one side. "Perisces," he said softly. "Bring me koumiss." He waited until a hide flask was thrust into his hand. He took a long drink and belched softly, an odour of fermenting milk wafting over his prisoner. "Now, Gorinax, soldier of Turkul," he said. "Tell me about this Lion of Scythia."

Gorinax trembled and shuffled on his knees, the stony soil digging into his flesh. "I do not know about this Lion, my lord. I only know what the stranger told my headman, Portrax."

"And what was that?"

"He said five Massegetae, including one called the Lion, followed the lord Dimurthes and a woman captive of his. They left Turkul just before sunset. Portrax told Lodas to find and warn my lord Dimurthes and sent me to find you." Gorinax looked into the man's face in doubt. "You *are* Serratae, my lord?" he asked tremulously.

"Indeed, I am," mused the man. He inclined his head a fraction. "I am Sparses, advisor and deputy to Dimurthes." The man stroked his beard thoughtfully. "Where is Dimurthes now?"

"He left with his men and the old priestess of Mount Mora. He was to escort the old woman to her sanctuary but whether he meant to go there himself or send his men, I know not."

"So either way he takes the Zarmet road via the Holy Mountain? And the Massegetae follow him, you say?"

"Yes lord. And there are but five of them."

"How many men does the lord Dimurthes have?" asked Sparses.

Gorinax shrugged. "A dozen or so, my lord."

"Then they are in no immediate danger." Sparses turned to his men and beckoned one of them forward. "Lorcus, how long until moonrise?"

Lorcus shrugged. "Three hours, my lord. Perhaps four. Without the stars it is hard to be certain."

Sparses nodded. "Then get some rest. We ride at moonrise."

"What of this one?" asked Lorcus, indicating the kneeling figure of Gorinax.

"Cut him loose and let him dry himself by the fire," sneered Sparses. "Then feed him and guard him. He rides with us."

Lorcus gestured and barked out a string of orders before turning back to Sparses. He lowered his voice. "Who is this Lion he mentioned?"

Sparses gave a savage grin. "A Greek invader of the Persians to the south of our lands. He has grown in power among the Massegetae and now desires to be known as the Lion of Scythia." He laughed. "I have greatly desired to meet this man in battle and kill him. I rejoice that he is near. I will find him and take his life."

Chapter 11

The small party of three women and four men trudged uphill, the horses' hooves slipping in the loose rock. The old servant of the priestess, Solma, rode in the lead, followed by the priestess Atrullia herself then Dimurthes and Tomyra. The three Scythian guards brought up the rear. As they rode, the men cast apprehensive looks about them in the gathering twilight, staring with distrust at the long, steep slopes of unstable rock devoid of all vegetation.

Tomyra felt the first faint stirrings of hope. She was aware, still, of the undercurrents of power that stemmed from the Mother, but had wondered these last few days whether perhaps this was just her imaginings. Now the old priestess had reaffirmed her status, staring at her in the inn with her bird-bright eyes, Atrullia's gnarled and ancient hands gripping hers. She felt her spirits surge for an instant before the backwash of despair clutched at her heart again. *Domra*, she recalled. *Domra and the others...* A tear formed at the corner of one eye and she brushed it away angrily. *I will mourn later*, she thought. *I have so many to mourn for now--my father, Domra, the others who tried to rescue me...my Niko?*

O, Mother Goddess, she prayed. *Keep him safe.* She refused to believe the Goddess would put him in her life without a purpose. That purpose must surely still be unfulfilled. *Surely?*

Tomyra looked up as one of the guards pushed past her, causing her own scrawny mount to shy and slip on the narrow path. The man called softly to Dimurthes and she strained to hear what was said.

"My Lord," the guard said. "We are followed still."

Dimurthes turned and looked back down the mountainside, his eyes following the path downward as it zigzagged across the open slopes. He grunted and pulled his horse to a stop, his cloak flapping in the biting wind. The other riders slowed and stopped also, turning to look enquiringly at Dimurthes before staring back the way they had come.

"Three riders," Dimurthes muttered. "They are not my men. They look like boys." He whipped round to confront Tomyra. "More of your confounded women playing at warrior?" He ground his teeth, staring at the young woman. "Well, they'll find the same reward for their play as the others." Dimurthes barked out a laugh and raised his voice to call to the other women waiting up the path ahead of him. "How far to this sanctuary of yours, holy mother?"

"Not far," answered Atrullia crisply. "But we must be off this path by nightfall."

Dimurthes glanced up at the heavy overcast and at the black shadows oozing across the mountains. He shrugged. "Let them follow then, for the moment." He urged his horse forward, waving the others on.

The path ceased its upward course and followed the contours of the mountain, easing around the shoulder of a great ridge, bare with loose rock. In the lee of the ridge the wind dropped, the distant rushing of mountain streams now impinging on their senses. The path dropped into a steep-sided gully--the horses scrabbled for a foothold. At the top of the next rise, the path disappeared into the gloom of night. Tomyra glanced back across the gully and thought she could barely make out a movement on the ridge behind her.

"There," said Atrullia. "And not a moment too soon." The old priestess pointed down into the next valley. A path wound down into a flat valley crowded with vegetation. After the bare slopes of the mountain all about them, the densely wooded valley looked unreal and distant. Too little light filtered down from the last shards of the day for Tomyra to make out any colours, but the valley looked warm and inviting after the cold ride across the rocky bones of the ranges.

The horses whinnied and pushed forward, hurrying down the path as fast as they dared in the poor light. As they descended, Tomyra felt a warm humidity wash across her, unexpected in the cold aridity of the Scythian steppes.

Atrullia looked back at Tomyra as if she had heard her unspoken thoughts. "Hot springs, child. The Mother blesses us here in Her valley."

As the first scrubby beginnings of vegetation rose about them, willow and alder, Atrullia called a halt and turned to face Dimurthes. "We are about to cross into the sanctuary of the Great Goddess. None may enter here unless they are called." She glanced at Tomyra. "The Goddess bids you enter, child."

The old priestess turned back to Dimurthes, her face hidden in the darkness, her voice flat and expressionless. "Dimurthes, lord of the Serratae. You are accused of raping a priestess of the Mother. You may enter to plead your case before the Goddess."

Dimurthes ignored the sharp intake of breath from his men. "And if I choose not to?"

"Then your guilt will be evident. The Mother will turn her face from you. No man or woman will aid you. You will exist out of law until death, and the Mother will not welcome you into the kingdoms of the dead. Choose."

Dimurthes was silent for a space, his horse stamping and fidgeting beneath him. "I will enter and plead my case," he said quietly. "I have done only what any warrior would do to defend his people."

"You enter willingly?" asked Atrullia.

"I have said so, yes."

"Then enter into the holy place of the Mother."

Dimurthes kicked his horse into motion, passing close to the dark figures that were the three women. As his men moved forward after their chief, Atrullia's voice snapped out.

"Hold! You are not invited."

The men reined in their horses abruptly, milling on the narrow path. Dimurthes leaned forward, close to the old priestess. "My men accompany me," he said. "They are needed to guard me and the girl."

"Are you afraid of the presence of women, my lord?" asked Atrullia, a hint of amusement in her voice.

"No," grated Dimurthes. "But the girl may try to use this place to escape me. When I have proved myself before the Goddess she will want to escape her just punishment."

"Just as none may enter save with Her permission, none may leave without the Goddess' consent. Besides, there is but one path, my lord. If your men wait here, she would have to pass by them."

Dimurthes swore under his breath. "Very well." He snapped out an order to his men. "Wait here and guard the path. Remember, too, we are followed." His teeth flashed in the dark as he grinned. "Three women follow. Amuse yourselves until I return."

Atrullia urged her horse forward into the path of the warriors. "Do not enter the forest, do not cut wood. Only burn that which has fallen." She leaned forward and whispered in a low voice. "The Mother gives and sustains life, but she can also kill. Death comes silently from the dark. Remember that and be respectful." She turned her horse and kicked it into a walk. As she passed Tomyra she smiled. "Come, child. The Mother awaits."

The four riders moved on into the inky blackness beneath the trees. The horses of the old priestess and her companion moved slowly but steadily along the nearly invisible path, the sound of their hooves dulled by drifting windrows of fallen leaves. The other horses followed closely, stumbling and shying at shadows, at the furtive scrabbling of unseen creatures. Dimurthes wrapped his cloak tightly about him, his body tense and expectant.

Tomyra felt herself relaxing for the first time in days. Even the presence of the hateful Serratae chieftain failed to impinge on the lassitude that drifted over her. The silence of their travel, the gentle susurration of wind and fallen foliage, the monotonous movement of her horse as it grew used to the darkness, lulled her. She drifted in and out of sleep, remembering childhood travels in her father's wagon, rumbling across the open steppes. The smell of the horses in the cold night air brought memories of riding with her father, balanced astride his horse, held firmly by his strong arms. Tomyra felt the warmth of her mother's love in the hut at night and heard her voice whispering to her in the darkness. *Tomyra, I was captured yet found love in a distant land. Trust in me, your destiny lies elsewhere. I will not abandon you.* The voice of her mother became fainter and merged into the sigh of the wind.

"Mother!" Tomyra cried out, jerking awake. She looked around her and found that the horses had stopped beside a small stream. The water gurgled and riffled through moss-covered boulders, wisps of steam rising into a low, surging layer of mist. Starlight lit the opening in the forest with a dim light. The old priestess was looking curiously at Tomyra.

"We have arrived, child." She stared at Tomyra for a moment longer then shook her head and turned to Dimurthes. The chief shifted uneasily, staring around him at the silent forest and deepening mist. He looked up at the now cloudless sky, ablaze with cold stars, with an expression of awe.

"Arrived where?" he muttered. His hand moved unconsciously in a placating gesture, palm downward.

"At the sanctuary of the Great Goddess, of course," said Atrullia. "We walk from here." She slid to the ground and handed the reins of her horse to the already dismounted Solma.

"Why must we walk?" asked Dimurthes, not moving from his horse.

"It is holy ground. Only Her chosen and invited may enter." Atrullia shook out her cloak and caught Tomyra's hand as the young woman joined her on the ground. "The horses will be cared for here. You will leave your weapons here too," she added.

Dimurthes leapt from his horses back, his bow in his left hand and his right hand on the hilt of his sword. "My arms do not leave me," he grated.

"You must do as the priestess bids you," interjected Solma, taking the reins of his horse.

Dimurthes scowled and set his shoulders squarely. "I will not be disarmed," he stated flatly.

Atrullia sighed. "There are no weapons in the sanctuary, not even a knife for eating. Since none can harm you, what need have you of weapons? Further, if the Mother set Herself against you, could mortal arms defeat the Goddess?"

Dimurthes stood silently then handed his bow and sword to Solma. The old woman took the weapons gingerly and slid them into a hide sack.

"You have a dagger for eating?" asked Atrullia.

"Yes."

Atrullia stood patiently. Dimurthes shrugged and tossed it at the feet of the old priestess.

"Any other weapons?"

"No," replied Dimurthes quickly, his hand jerking slightly.

"It is folly to try to deceive the Mother," observed the priestess quietly. "She is everywhere within Her sanctuary...see! Even now she comes." Atrullia pointed into the shadows across the stream.

The mist swirled, rising and falling in the direction of her outstretched finger. Dimly within the vapour a figure moved, silently and smoothly, flitting between the trees, moving ever closer.

Dimurthes blanched and a cry gurgled in his throat. His hand rose in a warding gesture then dropped to his boot and extracted a long thin blade, flinging it to the turf. "Great Goddess forgive me," he muttered. He fell to his knees and bowed his head, tearing his eyes away from the approaching terror.

Silence fell over the group, Tomyra staring open-mouthed at the swirling mist and the figure within it. The cowled and cloaked figure of a woman in a long richly embroidered dress stepped from the mist onto the stream bank and bobbed in a curtsey to Atrullia.

"Ah, Tallia. We have guests," the old priestess said. "You have brought a torch?"

"Yes, lady." The figure brought out an earthenware pot from under her cloak and thrust a brand into it. The torch flared within the pot and, on taking it out, cast a ruddy, blood red glow over the figures by the stream.

Dimurthes opened his eyes and looked about fearfully. "Where...?" he whispered.

"As I said, She is everywhere. Tallia has come to greet us in the Mother's Name. Come now, cross the stream."

Atrullia lifted her skirts and hopped spryly across the stream, steadied by the woman Tallia. Tomyra followed, and then Dimurthes stepped across, his eyes still darting around the clearing. Solma pulled on the reins of the horses and led them downstream.

Tallia held the torch high, sending an orange glow through the pearly mist. She moved off between the trees followed by Atrullia and Tomyra. Dimurthes spun on his heel, surveying the clearing, his hand dropping to clutch vainly for his relinquished sword. He swore beneath his breath and hurried after the figures of the women.

Chapter 12

Nikometros scowled up at the overcast sky with the last remnants of a scarlet sunset fading from the lowering clouds. He slid from the back of his stallion, Diomede, and stared at the dusty road in the fading light. A narrow but well-used path broke from the road and soared toward the mountaintops.

"Which way did they go?" he asked.

Parasades glanced up from where he squatted in the road, one finger tracing in the dirt. "Oh, both ways I think. See," he pointed to hoof prints, "They split up." He rose to his feet and dusted his hands off on the sides of his leggings. "For one who was brought up among horses, Nikomayros, you know little about tracking them."

Nikometros gave the other man a black look before grating out, "Which way did Tomyra go?"

"To Zarmet, my friend," replied Parasades equably. "A group of some half dozen broke off up that mountain path, but her horse continues toward Zarmet. No doubt the priestess is returning to her holy place with an escort provided by the redoubtable Dimurthes."

"And can you tell how long ago they passed by here?"

Parasades shrugged. "They left the village a few hours ahead of us and travelled slowly, whereas we made good time. The tracks are fresh and undisturbed by wind or rain. I would guess perhaps an hour, maybe less."

"Then we must hurry." Nikometros grabbed the reins of his horse and swung it around to face down the road to Zarmet.

"It is dark already," said Parasades quietly. "We should at least wait for the moon's light."

Agarus nodded. "My lord Parasades is right, my lord. We cannot track them at night."

Nikometros glared up at his servant. "I do not ask you to come. I will go by myself if no other will follow." He vaulted onto his stallion's back.

"I will follow you, Niko," said Timon softly.

"And I, my lord." Diratha edged her horse alongside the stallion. "It is why I came."

Agarus flushed beneath his beard. "Of course I will come. You are my lord. I only meant..." His voice trailed off and he shrugged and kicked his horse into motion.

Parasades smiled gently and stroked his beard and moustache contemplatively. "Well, it appears that Certes and I must bow to the inevitable." He gave a short laugh and spurred his horse, making it leap forward. Within moments the others joined him, strung out in a line as they galloped down the Zarmet road to the plains.

By the time the party reached the flat roads at the start of the plains, full night had fallen. They slowed their progress as the darkness all but obscured the road. Timon glanced across at the shadowy outline of his friend Nikometros. His features remained in shadow but the slow grind of his jaw told of his anger and frustration.

The pace of the horses dropped to a walk. Timon coughed gently and leaned closer to Nikometros. "Niko, this is madness. We could walk right past and not see them." His friend remained silent. Timon sighed and tried again. "We need only stop until moonrise. Even the waning moon will give us light."

"It is hours to moonrise, Timon," Nikometros growled. "I have delayed enough. I intend to find my Tomyra tonight."

"And I, my Bithyia," agreed Timon. "But see, even now the moon rises." He pointed off to their left at a faint yellow glow.

Everyone stopped and stared at the faint light limning a grassy ridge in the inky blackness off the road.

"If that is the moon then we are traveling south," said Nikometros slowly.

"It is not the moon," stated Parasades. "It will rise behind us and not for some time. That is a fire." He turned to Nikometros, his features hidden by the darkness. "It seems we have found our quarry. What will you do now?"

Nikometros sat silent for several moments. "First, let us be certain." He dismounted, signalling to the others to do so too. Together, they walked off the road into the long prairie grasses. "Agarus, Diratha, wait here with the horses."

"My lord," Diratha said. "I came to fight not tend horses. Let the cripple do so and let me kill men."

"You will have your chance to avenge your sisters. For now, hold the horses and keep them quiet while we reconnoitre."

Without waiting for a reply, Nikometros started off at a fast walk toward the low swell of the grassy ridge, followed by Parasades, Timon and Certes. As they approached, the light of the campfire grew stronger and the sound of raucous voices reached them on the gusting breeze. Crouching on hands and knees, the four men eased themselves to the edge of the ridge and peered over.

A large fire burned at the bottom of a shallow gully. The remains of an old pine tree, from whence the fuel for the fire came, leaned precariously from the near side of the depression, partly blocking their view. Sparks showered upward in the gusts of wind, sputtering into extinction in the damp grass or drifting skyward into oblivion. Smoke clouded the air, urged first this way then that by fitful eddies. Several men lay or sat around the fire, drinking from skin bottles or munching on hard unleavened bread. To the left of the watchers milled the horses, legs hobbled and halters joined, huddling against the cold in the shadows on the edge of the firelight.

Parasades squeezed Nikometros' arm and pointed off to his left, near the horses, and held up two fingers.

Nikometros stared into the darkness, shielding his face from the glare of the fire. After a long moment he nodded and whispered, "Two guards only?"

Certes pointed to the right at another figure leaning on a spear, staring with bored fixity into the darkness beyond the fire.

Nikometros continued to scrutinise the surroundings and at length was rewarded by a small movement some twenty paces below them in the shadow of the old pine. He pointed, eliciting a nod from the others.

"I do not see the lady Tomyra," breathed Timon.

"Nor I," said Parasades. "Yet her mare is here."

Tomyra's fine roan mare, one of her favourite mounts, and the one with the distinctive hoof print, indeed lay beneath them, milling with the other horses.

"She may be beneath us, near the dead tree," said Nikometros. "I do not see any man who looks like a war chief either."

Parasades gestured a withdrawal and the four eased themselves back from the edge of the hollow. Withdrawing several yards into the darkness, they discussed their plans.

"I counted eleven men," whispered Parasades. "Four on guard, seven around the fire."

Certes nodded his agreement then added, "Count in the chief Dimurthes and we are outnumbered three to one."

Timon grunted. "Long odds in battle but not where surprise and fear aid us."

"Exactly," agreed Nikometros. "I say we remove the four guards first, by stealth, also reducing the odds considerably. Then we can take our time, get close, and be among them before they know we are there."

"I suggest we allow the girl Diratha to help us," said Parasades. "She can employ her bow to good effect in the initial attack."

"Very well then. Certes, fetch the girl. We will wait."

Certes disappeared into the blackness, reappearing a few minutes later with Diratha. Nikometros hurriedly explained the plan to her then motioned for them all to return to the grassy lip. He pointed out the four guards. "Parasades, Certes. Take the horse guards. Timon, the one by the tree. I will silence the other." He turned to look at the young girl, searching her face for signs of fear or doubt. Satisfied, he went on. "When I wave my sword, fire into the men. Be sure your first arrow kills, but thereafter shoot as fast as you can. Fear will be our ally. Only be sure of your man, all of you. Remember the lady Tomyra is down there somewhere." He looked around at the shadowy figures. "Any who harms her will answer to me."

The figures melted into the darkness and in a moment, Diratha found herself alone. She crept to the ridge and peered over, selecting a spot that gave her good visibility of the fire and the enemy. She laid several arrows on the grass beside her, within easy reach, and fitted another to her bow. From her vantage point she could see the outline of the guard by the old pine tree and the one standing out to the right, but not the horse guards. The laughter and revelry by the campfire died down, men tending to their equipment and weapons. Already one or two were settling down for the night.

Far to the left a horse nickered and stamped its feet in the shadows then was answered by another. One of the men by the fire raised himself on his elbow and called out an enquiry. A few moments later a rough voice called back something that was unintelligible to Diratha but appeared to satisfy the Serratae men below.

A movement far to the right caught her eye. Despite the darkness of the night, Diratha could just make out the shape of a man creeping from tussock to tussock, toward the guard. Nikometros was approaching from above, working himself into a favourable position for a swift strike.

Below her, a shadow detached itself from the dead tree and glided forward. A brief flicker of metal told of the weapon drawn for use. The guard turned and the shadow that was Timon froze, merging back with the tree. The guard advanced a few paces then, lifting his tunic, fiddled with his leggings and directed a stream of urine onto the stump, the liquid steaming in the frosty air.

Timon held his breath as urine splashed over the tree trunk only inches from him. He waited, his lungs aching, as the man refastened his clothing and stretched, yawning widely. The guard started to turn away and Timon gently released his breath. The puff of water vapour blew whitely against the blackened tree and the guard stopped short in his turn. With an oath starting on his lips, his eyes opening wide in shock, the man swung his spear around.

Timon lunged with his dagger and the guard, his spear swinging, caught the blade on the haft and turned it aside. The spear continued its sideways motion and glanced off Timon's arm, throwing him off balance. He stumbled and fell, rolling as he hit the ground. He groped his way upright again. The guard let out an incoherent shout and stabbed with his spear in the general direction of the intruder. The spear point passed under Timon's arm and Timon threw himself onto the man, his knife stabbing downward.

Shouts from the camp made Timon desperate and he forgot the knife he held, instead hammering his fist into the man's head. His blows seemed to have no effect and he felt the guard's knee thud into his belly. Fingers reached for his throat and Timon struck the man on the side of his head again. The man desperately grasped Timon's throat and tightened his grip, his knee again seeking Timon's groin. Timon could feel himself sliding into darkness, wondering why his own blows were unfelt. He remembered the knife in his hand and, with the last of his strength, struck sideways.

A rush of hot blood fountained up into Timon's face. The man tensed beneath him and gave a gurgling cry, his fingers loosening. Breath rushed into Timon's lungs and he rolled sideways, coughing and spluttering. Beside him, the body of the guard shuddered into death.

～⁓∽ᆖ⁓～

Nikometros heard the cry and the answering shouts from the camp. The man in front of him at once broke from his bored reverie and turned back toward the fire, drawing his sword. Nikometros rose from the tussock grasses, sword in hand and charged at the man, now only some twenty steps from him.

The man whirled toward Nikometros, sword rising in defence against the shadow hurtling out of the night. His blade was knocked aside and he felt a heavy blow to his shoulder. The guard struggled to raise his blade again but could not. He swayed, looking down with a detached expression at the sword at his feet, a hand and arm still gripping the hilt. His mouth opened to shout but only air gusted out as another crushing blow ripped into his ribcage.

93

Nikometros did not pause in his downhill rush. His last slash at the guard unbalanced him and he almost fell. He realised all elements of surprise were lost as the camp below him erupted into a frenzy of activity. He ran down, leaping over the tussocks and waving his sword over his head, shouting a paean to the gods. Blood spattered in a fine rain over his head and shoulders. Ahead of him, men milled in the firelight, weapons glinting crimson.

⌇⌇⌇⌇

Beside the horse corral, itself nothing more complex than roughly piled branches, lay two bodies. Parasades and Certes crouched over the bodies of the guards, stripping them of their weapons and gold ornaments. Parasades grunted in satisfaction and clapped the younger man lightly on the shoulder.

"Well done, Certes," he whispered.

Taking advantage of the cover provided by the piled undergrowth and branches, Parasades and Certes had risen like wraiths at the feet of the unsuspecting guards. Throats gushed warmly in the cold air at the same moment and bodies were eased to the ground together. Only a branch breaking beneath one guard as he collapsed marred a perfect attack. The shout of inquiry from the camp was answered by a single gruff word of explanation from Parasades in the Serratae patois. It had been accepted without further question.

Beckoning to Certes, the older man moved around the horses that snorted and stamped at the smell of fresh blood on the men. As they edged toward the camp, a sudden shout sent them diving for the sparse cover of the tussocks. A babble of cries arose ahead of them. Parasades looked at his companion and shrugged. He rose to his feet and started running toward the flickering light of the fire.

Parasades and Certes burst out of the shadows and into the turmoil of battle. A man lay sprawled across the fire, an arrow jutting upward from his neck. Black smoke roiled around him and the smell of charring flesh hit their nostrils.

Parasades jerked his gaze back to the men jostling in the small clearing. Two had swords out and were hacking savagely at a figure pressed against the old dead tree. Another lay on his back across the clearing, blood pooling beneath a great rent in his side. Astride his body, stood Nikometros, blood matted in his long blond hair and soaking his upper body. He furiously parried the blows of three men in front of him, shouting some incoherent song Parasades assumed must be Macedonian.

Parasades pointed at Timon, fighting for his life beside the tree and Certes grinned, drawing his sword. He raced across the sandy floor of the gully and swung at the nearer of the two men. The man turned and defended himself with a cry.

Parasades ran to where Nikometros fought silently now, his breath coming in harried gasps as he slowly retreated before the onslaught. Parasades stood for a moment behind the Serratae warriors, sizing up the opposition then casually selecting a spearman, stepped up behind him and slid his blade into the man's side. Between the thrust forward of his spear and the pull back, the man died. Collapsing onto the sandy ground, the arm of the already dead man brushed against the leg of one of his companions. Startled, the man glanced around, into the smiling face of the Massegetae warrior.

With an oath, the Serratan whipped around, his sword swinging. Parasades pushed the blade aside and slashed at the man's face. The man stepped back and swung again, the tip of his sword ripping through Parasades' tunic. The smile slipping from his face, to be replaced by a grimmer expression, Parasades moved forward, blade flashing.

Nikometros' breath came hard, his arm numb from the repeated blows of his adversaries. Then, without warning, the pressure eased. His eyes flickered momentarily, taking in the dead man falling and the sudden appearance of his Massegetae companion diverting the attentions of one of his foes. His opponent's sword flashed across his inattention and he stepped sideways, narrowly avoiding a stroke to the head.

Nikometros thrust, felt his sword parried and fell to one knee. His sword rasped along the blade of his opponent's then fell free. He swung low and heard a howl of pain. The man in front of him staggered back, clutching a wound that bloomed redly on his thigh. He tripped over the corpse lying on the sand and fell flat on his back. Nikometros regained his feet and leapt after him.

Timon's face glowed with his exertions as he grasped his sword in both hands, hammering his opponent. Freed from the necessity of holding himself back to prevent an enemy getting around behind him, he gave a great bellow of rage and leapt to the attack. He smashed the Serratae warrior's sword aside and swept his own sword downward, scarcely noticing the shock as metal met bone. He stood panting, looking around him for his opponent, ignorant of the red ruin lying at his feet.

Certes smiled as he fought, confident in his youth and training. He smoothly blocked and parried the other man's blows; thrusting energetically forward, forcing the man back to the fire. At last, the man could retreat no further, the embers burning his feet as he fought. He glanced down involuntarily, as Certes knew he would, and looked up again just in time to see a glint of steel and feel the cold slide of death into his throat. The man fell back into the fire with a gurgling cry, his blood hissing angrily when it gushed over the flames.

Certes looked around at the carnage. He nodded appreciatively toward Timon, standing bemusedly over the wreckage of his opponent then at Parasades, who still fought with his.

Parasades slowly worked his man back into the clearing, content to parry the other's blows, making no real effort to kill the man. As his opponent stepped back into the full light, Parasades withdrew two paces and waved his sword above his head.

The warrior in front of him slowly lowered his sword, a puzzled expression crossing his face. Something whispered behind him and his puzzlement was replaced by shock then pain. He fell to his knees, his sword slipping from suddenly numb fingers. The Serratae warrior swayed and looked up at the smiling Parasades then another blow shook his frame and he tumbled forward, two arrows buried deep in his back.

The last survivor scrambled frantically backward on hands and knees, followed by Nikometros. The man turned, sitting on the sandy soil in the flickering firelight and stared up at the advancing apparition in its mask of blood. The warrior raised his sword, the tip trembling as he faced his death. Nikometros kicked the sword aside and dropped to his knees on the man, forcing him onto his back. He raised his sword, pointing it down at the man's eyes.

"Where is she?" shouted Nikometros. "Where is Tomyra?"

The man gabbled and cried, his fingers scrabbling in the sand.

Timon moved across, his sword hanging by his side. "No sign of her my lord. She is not here."

"Where is she?" repeated Nikometros in fury, pushing the tip of his sword downward. "Tell me or by the gods above and below I will..." A hand caught his arm and Nikometros swung round angrily.

"My friend," Parasades quietly said. "Perhaps if you asked in his tongue. I fear he does not understand Macedonian." He released Nikometros' arm and patted him on his shoulder. "I will ask him if you like."

Nikometros scowled then eased off the man, rising to his feet. "Tell him I will kill him if he doesn't answer."

Parasades nodded then squatted beside the man. He spoke rapidly in a tongue that had similarities to the Massegetae language, but also many differences. He listened to the hesitant reply then fired off another string of questions. At last, he nodded and got to his feet.

"Well?" asked Nikometros.

"Dimurthes has taken both the old priestess and Tomyra to the Mount Mora sanctuary."

"Why would he do that? And without his men?"

Parasades hesitated. "He is unclear on that point but it seems Dimurthes may have angered the Goddess."

Nikometros swore violently then flung his sword to the ground and looked up at the black sky. He took several deep breaths then ran his fingers through his matted and sticky hair. He stared down at the slime and blood coating his body as if seeing it for the first time. Closing his eyes, he groaned softly before looking up at Parasades. "Have any taken hurt?" Nikometros enquired softly.

Parasades shook his head. "Nothing beyond a cut or two. These are only Serratae cattle," he sneered. "They were not warriors."

Nikometros nodded slowly, looking at the Serratae man kneeling abjectly before him. "So we must go to Mount Mora, it seems," he said quietly.

"It would seem so," agreed Parasades, "But in the morning." He held up a hand as Nikometros turned to him. "We cannot ride mountain trails at night and we could all do with a good meal and a warm night's sleep."

"What of him?" asked Timon, gesturing at the fallen enemy with his bloody sword. "We cannot leave him behind."

"Kill him," said Parasades, drawing his dagger.

"No." Nikometros moved forward and caught the Scythian warrior's arm. "I gave him my word."

Parasades stared up at the fair man in surprise. "I heard no such promise. You swore only to kill him if he did not answer."

"Even so. I have my answer and I say he may live."

Parasades shrugged. "As you will, my friend." He gestured to Certes. "Bind him well or we may wake to find our throats cut." The warrior laughed out loud then turned and called to where Agarus and Diratha led their horses down into the gully. "We camp here tonight, my friends. See what you can find in their supplies, this fighting has given me an appetite."

Chapter 13

D imurthes squatted beneath a misshapen birch, in a stand of trees that gathered on the slope like sentinels, digging furiously in the wiry turf with a stick. Above him, the weak winter sun filtered down through a sparse canopy of leaves, still green and healthy, despite the bare branches of their kin on the surrounding slopes. There was little warmth in the sunlight, though he had loosened his leather tunic well before noon in response to the heat battening upward from the floor of the valley.

Throwing the stick away from him, Dimurthes rose and started pacing along the strip of flattened grass between the grove of trees and the stream. The air grew warmer as he neared the brook, with wisps of steam arising from the tepid waters. Far above him, lost from sight amid the rocky hillside, the waters burst boiling from the Goddess-given hot springs. Gusts of air carried sulfurous fumes to his nostrils, prickling his skin with superstitious dread.

Earlier that morning he tried to force the issue, to join the priestess and Tomyra in the small stone temple nestled under the crags of black rock. Several young women turned him away, gently but firmly. Dimurthes' face flushed as he remembered the shame of his failure. He had pushed his way through the women, shouting for the priestess. For a moment it seemed as if he would succeed in forcing his way to the temple then his muscles cramped and a wave of nausea swept over him. Groaning, he was led to the grove of trees and left to recover on warm turf.

Across the stream, Dimurthes saw the young women patiently sitting outside the temple entrance, watching him but making no further move to restrain him. *Bitches*, he thought sourly. *They must have fed me something last night.*

When Atrullia and Tallia, the young woman sent to guide them in the previous night, had reached the small stone village, Dimurthes was separated from his erstwhile prisoner, Tomyra, and housed in comparative luxury. The stone house was dry and warm, with a crackling fire to ward off any stray night chills that might invade the valley. Several young women attended to his needs, bringing heated water and soap root. A meal was served, plain but wholesome, followed by a flask of wine. Dimurthes cast his eye about him, weighing up the young women speculatively, noting with approval a tilted breast here and a firm buttock there.

The dishes were removed and the young women disappeared with them, replaced by an old crone with a squint who turned down the furs on his bed, baring her gums at him in a toothless grin. With a shrug and a scowl he pushed her away and shut the rickety wooden door as she hobbled out into the night, cackling to herself.

Morning found Dimurthes tired and apprehensive, despite his apparently unbroken sleep. He used the midden and washed his face before breaking his fast on fresh-baked bread and a pitcher of cold water. Moving out into the crisp morning air, he saw Atrullia and Tomyra walking slowly up the valley toward the stone temple, accompanied by several other richly dressed women. With a shout, Dimurthes raced after them, only to be ignominiously hustled away before he could get near.

Several hours passed. Dimurthes paced, wearing a flattened path in the tough grass, seething with anger. As the day slowly grew older, his anger abated and worry took its place.

What is that bitch Tomyra saying?

He removed his jacket and threw himself down on the turf beneath the trees. He dozed fitfully, his mind conjuring frightening visions that sent him starting up and panting. Wandering downstream, he found a shallow backwater where the brook had cooled and splashed his face and head, feeling the water trickling refreshingly down his linen undershirt.

He walked back to the grove and sat down on the grass, looking across at the silent temple. *What is going on in there?* The words of the old priestess worried him, he was forced to admit. Despite his air of bravado and lifestyle as a tough and battle-hardened Scythian warrior, Dimurthes was as superstitious as most of his fellows. The power of the Mother Goddess was very real and one slighted Her at one's peril. *But I have done nothing wrong!*

Dimurthes chewed his lip and cast his mind back. Areipithes, war-leader of the Massegetae had approached Dimurthes through intermediaries and invited the Serratae to help him overthrow his father, chief of the Massegetae. Areipithes intended to kill his sister, the priestess Tomyra, at the same time and some troublesome Greek who had wormed his way into the tribe.

Why in Hades would Scythians adopt a Greek?

This Greek apparently violated the priestess, though it seemed she sinned willingly enough. *An attractive wench,* Dimurthes thought, *and fiery.* He asked for and had been given her as prize from her brother. Her rape and degradation thrilled him to his core, though she disappointingly refused to beg for mercy, despite his efforts to break her.

*Such spirit! Under other circumstances...*Dimurthes grinned then forced his mind back to his problem.

The girl Tomyra is no longer a priestess but a legitimate spoil of war and as such, is mine to do with as I please.

His forehead creased as he remembered the words of the old priestess Atrullia. *She is priestess still...*That was impossible, no matter what the old woman said. The teachings of the Goddess were clear on that point. A priestess was virgin...always. Her body was sacrosanct and death followed for any man who violated her. Death also for the priestess if she gave herself willingly.

She gave herself to the Greek! It is common knowledge. She cannot be a priestess still.

Dimurthes rose to his feet in agitation and tore a branch from the tree above him. He stripped off the twigs and leaves, crushing them in his hands then throwing them down violently.

"She cannot be," he hissed between clenched teeth. He turned and hurled the branch across the stream at the silent women sitting below the temple entrance. "She cannot be!" he shouted.

A young girl hurried down to the edge of the stream and retrieved the broken branch, carrying it up to the sitting women. She placed it reverently at their feet then ran back down to the stream. Facing Dimurthes across the shallow water, she spoke softly to him. "You must not damage the sacred trees, my lord."

"Where is my prisoner, bitch?"

"You must not damage the sacred trees," the girl repeated. "It is forbidden."

"Then answer me or I will do more than just damage them," spat out Dimurthes. He wheeled and strode to the nearest tree, firmly grasping one of the branches. He pulled down hard, making the tree bend and sway. The bough creaked and groaned, the silvery bark splitting.

"Hold!"

Dimurthes looked over his shoulder and saw the women around the temple entrance running toward him. He grinned and released the branch, making the tree whip wildly. He turned and looked expectantly at the women clustered on the far bank.

"The priestess Atrullia will see you now, my lord Dimurthes," said one of the women. "Please accompany us without showing further disrespect."

Dimurthes nodded and leapt across the stream, pushing through the knot of young women. He half expected them to resist and block his progress but they moved aside, following him as he strode up the slope toward the dark entrance of the stone temple. He hesitated at the doorway, searching the dim interior for some sign of life.

"If you would follow me, my lord," said a voice at his side. He turned to see the old woman, Solma, the companion of the priestess. She gestured into the temple then scurried on ahead, leaving Dimurthes to hurry after her.

The interior of the temple was dark and cool after the bright sunlight of the valley. Dimurthes halted just inside and looked around, allowing his eyes to adjust to the dimness. His hand groped ineffectually at his belt for his sword before he remembered he was unarmed. He swore softly then shrugged.

"My lord?" came Solma's voice from the twilight ahead of him. Dimurthes made out her figure and strode toward her, following as she turned and hobbled deeper into the temple.

The walls of the temple closed in around them and after a few paces, Dimurthes was in a passage of dressed stone, lit only by infrequent oil lamps glimmering in small niches in the walls. Their faint yellow light served to accentuate the darkness rather than light their way. Gradually, the passage narrowed, the walls becoming rougher and the floor and ceiling uneven.

"Where are we, old woman?" His voice threw back harsh echoes, overlain by a rustling noise that slowly died away.

"Hush," whispered Solma. "You are on holy ground. Do not profane the sanctuary with your noise."

Dimurthes held his hand out flat, low to the ground in a placatory gesture. "Where are we?" he whispered back. "This cannot be the temple, we have come too far."

"That was but the entrance, my lord. The true sanctuary lies within the living rock of the mountain. You are..." Solma hesitated. "...honoured indeed. Few men are invited into the presence of the Mother Goddess."

Dimurthes stopped, his hand pressed against the rock wall. "The presence of the Goddess?" He swallowed and made the sign again. He barked out a quick laugh. "You mean the priestess, of course." Exhaling loudly, Dimurthes gestured to Solma. "Lead on then, old woman."

The passage dipped, plunging deeper into the mountainside. The rock walls grew warmer to the touch then, as the passage angled upward again, cooled. The dim yellow light of the oil lamps gradually faded and was replaced by a misty white radiance that increased until Dimurthes could plainly see the figure of the old woman in front of him. Then, between one step and the next, he found himself staring up at a shaft of light angling down through particulate air, plunging from a vaulted rock ceiling far above into a cavern that faded into darkness all around him. Tiny motes danced in the light as if alive, reminding him of mayflies swarming above the rivers of his youth, far to the north.

Dimurthes gasped in awe, the sound sending whispers cascading around the cavern. He dragged his eyes down from the glory of the light to the cavern itself, to find he was alone. A faint noise from the darkness ahead indicated the direction of Solma's path. Moving forward, Dimurthes called out. "Woman! Where are...?" Echoes crashed back at him from the walls of the cavern, together with a rising tide of angry rustlings that quickly faded. He swallowed and called out again in a hoarse whisper. "Where are you?"

Rustling echoes died into nothingness and silence beat down upon him for the space of several minutes. Then from the air around him, silence curdled, a whisper formed around the thudding of his heart in his ears. Words coagulated from the sibilance. "I am here, mortal man. Why do you seek me?"

Dimurthes' hair prickled and his hand jerked placatingly downward. "I...You...I was sent for," he stuttered.

Echoes of his reply died into silence. Dimurthes cautiously looked around. He stepped forward, moving stiffly, the muscles in his neck betraying his tension.

"Stay!" cracked the voice. "You do not have my permission to move!"

Dimurthes gasped, his heart racing. He felt a tiny trickle of warmth in his groin as fear gripped him. With an effort, he mastered himself and sank slowly to his knees on the rock floor of the chamber. Despite a lifetime of danger and battle, Dimurthes, for the first time in his life, felt terror. He had heard the power in the voice and felt awe and superstitious dread beating at his mind. The old stories of the Mother Goddess in all Her savage majesty, told in whispers around the fireside, returned. He waited, trembling.

"Why do you come...man?"

"I was sent for," Dimurthes whispered without looking up. "I wish to defend myself against an accusation of raping a priestess."

Silence bore down on the cave like a suffocating hand.

"My...my lady, Mother Goddess. I honour you. I would not..."

"You forced her?" the voice hissed.

"Yes, but she was not a priestess." Dimurthes looked up, his eyes searching the shadows in front of him. Beads of sweat stood out on his forehead, despite the cool air. "She was under sentence of death..."

"You are chief of your tribe, the Serratae?"

"Yes. I am Dimurthes, son of Sartes, of the Serratae."

"You worship the Mother?"

"Yes, lady."

"How are my priestesses called?"

Dimurthes knelt silently for a moment then..."I do not know, lady. I suppose they are chosen by you...by the Mother."

"I make myself known to them."

Silence descended around the man once more. White light from the vault far above slowly became golden, shifting as the day wore on. Dimurthes shifted on his knees, easing the pain where the rock dug into his flesh.

The whispers built again.

"You knew she was my priestess?"

"She said so, lady, but she was not a virgin. Everyone knew she violated her oath."

"An oath that stands between me and my priestess, no one else." After a pause, the whisper continued. "You deny me my priestess?"

"No, lady, of course not."

"No man can take what is mine from me, but I can freely give. Do you understand?"

Dimurthes shook his head, his sweat flying out to darken the rocky floor. "No, lady."

The whispers rose in volume and the voice deepened. "I, through my priestesses, say when an oath is broken. Not you, Dimurthes, son of Sartes, nor any man. I have not withdrawn my power from Tomyra, daughter of Starissa. You have forced my holy one and the sentence on you is your death."

"Lady, no!" Dimurthes threw himself forward, his hands groping in supplication. "I did not know. Have mercy, lady."

"Neither Goddess nor woman in this place will claim your life, Dimurthes, son of Sartes. Arise and approach me."

Dimurthes craned his neck, looking around at the shadows. He rose slowly to his knees then got to his feet, tentatively brushing the dust off his clothing.

He moved hesitantly forward, peering into the gloom. Ahead of him, a small yellow flicker of light appeared. As he approached, he could make out a low table with an oil lamp burning brightly, casting a pool of golden light over the surroundings. By the lamp lay a dagger, its blade glinting.

A figure moved in the darkness beyond the lamp glow. Dimurthes trembled, his hand pressing downward in superstitious terror as the figure approached, resolving slowly into that of a woman clad in a long robe. The woman came closer, her bare feet stepping calmly beneath the woollen folds of the robe that hung richly green to the rocky floor. Her head was bowed on her chest, her long black hair sweeping over her shoulders. Grasped in her slim white hands, held out in front of her, was an ornate silver cup, worked with enamel and gold. The woman stopped in front of Dimurthes and raised her head, looking straight into the shocked man's eyes.

"You," he breathed. "Tomyra, I did not..." His voice trailed off into silence.

The air rustled around the man and woman and the voice returned. "Dimurthes, son of Sartes. Drink from the cup."

Dimurthes dragged his gaze from Tomyra's face and stared at the cup. He reached out for it then snatched his hand back. His features grimaced in a mixture of fear and anger. "Why must I drink from it? You seek to poison me."

Dry laughter swept around the chamber. "I do not seek to poison you. See, my priestess will drink first."

Tomyra, her face still and expressionless, lifted the cup to her lips and tilted it. She swallowed several times before lowering the cup. A thin dribble of blood-red wine trickled from the corner of her mouth. She held out the cup to Dimurthes.

"Drink from the cup," repeated the voice.

Dimurthes took the cup, his fingers brushing the girl's as he did so. He lifted the cup and sniffed gently then sipped, holding the wine in his mouth for a few moments before swallowing. He waited a few moments then drank again, more deeply, setting the cup on the table when he finished. "What now?" he rasped.

"Look at the lamp."

Dimurthes shrugged, his fear lifting from him as he did so. *The Mother speaks only truth. Though I am guilty She will let me live. 'Neither goddess nor woman...' She said.*

The flame on the wick burned golden, flickering gently in the almost motionless air of the cavern. The glow surrounding it expanded and contracted as he looked, pulsing in time to his heartbeat. Colours paled as the glow grew, shedding light further into the chamber. In the periphery of his vision, Dimurthes became aware of other figures, standing motionless around him. He tried to look up at them but the flame held his attention. It fascinated him and he moved closer.

"Dimurthes," said the voice. "Look at my priestess."

He tore his eyes obediently from the lamp glow and stared at the face of the robed figure before him. His forehead wrinkled and he squinted, cocking his head to one side.

"That is not..." he muttered. Dimurthes looked in confusion at the figure in the long green robe. He noticed with shock the thick beard and moustache set above dark eyes set in a pallid, sweating complexion. *Who is that? I have seen him before somewhere.* Memories of polished bronze and still waters floated past and recognition flooded over him.

"It cannot be, I stand here myself," breathed Dimurthes. His eyes widened and his hand flew to his mouth as he heard a woman's voice issuing from his throat. His hand met soft lips, a smooth chin and finely sculpted jaw. He looked down at his hand, small and delicate, and at the woollen robe swathing the body beneath him. Across from him a man wearing familiar features stared back, hands plucking distractedly at the waistband of dusty leather leggings.

This man has wronged me greatly, he thought. *This man has forced himself...*With a great cry of anguish Dimurthes swept the dagger from the table and hurled himself at the figure, burying the blade in the man's belly just below the ribs.

A wash of pain swept over Dimurthes and the cavern darkened, the lamp glow once more illuminating just the table. He looked down at his fist, clutching the hilt of the dagger. A puzzled expression flitted across his face and he dropped to his knees. He pulled the dagger, groaning with pain as it came out in a flood of blood, rapidly soaking his undershirt and leggings.

Dimurthes stared up at Tomyra, his eyes wandering over her face. He groaned and bent over, one hand steadying him, the other clutching his abdomen. Lifting his head once more, he opened his mouth to speak but fell before he could do so, his breath escaping as a gasp. Dimurthes rolled onto his back and lay still.

Tomyra stood in silence looking down at the body of her captor and tormentor. She extended her foot from beneath her robes and nudged the body. It shifted slightly but otherwise showed no signs of life.

"He is dead," Tomyra said softly. "I wish it had been at my hand but this will suffice. May his spirit never find rest."

"Even one such as he, is with the Mother," answered a dry voice from the shadows.

Tomyra turned as oil lamps flared around her, revealing the presence of a dozen robed women standing in a circle. One moved forward, hobbling painfully on arthritic joints, supported on each side by a young girl.

"Lady Atrullia." Tomyra inclined her head toward the old woman. "I pray you are wrong about his spirit."

Atrullia shook her head. "You are young, Tomyra, and young people are quick to judge. Despite the grievous wrong he did you, he was a good leader of his people and much loved by all accounts." She shook off the young girls and moved closer to Tomyra. "Yes, he deserved death for violating you but a case could have been made for his ignorance of the Mother's wishes. He chose instead to take his own life. The Great Goddess guided his hand. It was imperative that his blood not be on your hands."

"I have killed men before, my lady. In my own tribe I ride out with the patrols. The blood of this one would have brought me much joy."

Atrullia gripped Tomyra's arm with a strength that surprised the girl. "One day you will have to tell your daughter of her father. You will at least be free of his death."

Tomyra opened her mouth then closed it, her eyes growing large. "My daughter?" she whispered.

"Yes, child. Your daughter grows within you."

"How can that be, my lady? I had my moon but...ten days ago. I have not lain with my man since..." A horrified expression swept over Tomyra's face as the realisation came upon her. "I bear *his* child?" Anger formed in her eyes and her throat worked convulsively. "I cannot," she whispered. "I must find the necessary herbs and...."

"You will do no such thing, Tomyra," snapped Atrullia. "The Mother Goddess forbids such an action."

Tomyra shook her head. "He *raped* me, my lady. I must be rid of his...his *thing*. Other women do so, with less cause. Surely I can too?" she asked weakly.

"Do you question the Mother? Is her order too much for her priestess to obey? Speak now, girl, and perhaps you can yet be dismissed from her service." Atrullia sniffed loudly. "No doubt we can find you a position as a serving girl or slut in one of the villages nearby."

Tomyra lowered her head into her hands and sobbed softly. After a few moments she wiped her face with the back of her hands and raised her head. "I will obey the Mother in all things," she whispered.

Chapter 14

Parasades woke when the eastern sky paled. He stretched and looked about him at the remnants of the smouldering campfire. Several bodies lay wrapped in blankets near the embers, huddled against the chill night air. In a parody of his companions' efforts to keep warm, the corpses of the Serratae warriors they'd ambushed the night before lay piled on the edge of the clearing. Their tangled limbs and pale upturned faces, streaked and splotched with dark gore, bore a mute testimony to the chilling finality of death.

Looking across at the stump of the old pine tree, Parasades could make out the form of the Serratae prisoner and, a few paces beyond him, the outline of Certes. The young man paced in the dawn light, shivering beneath the folds of his woollen cloak. His breath gusted white in the cold air.

Parasades rose to his feet, wincing at the stabs of pain in his muscles. He flexed his arms and legs and ran his fingers through his long black hair. He hawked and spat on the ground then walked over to the prisoner who sat, head on chest, against the tree stump. Squatting beside the man, Parasades nudged him in the shoulder. The prisoner at once raised his head and glowered at his captor.

Parasades drew his dagger, fingering the point absently as he examined the bound man. "What should I do with you?" he mused.

The prisoner sat silent, staring up at Parasades with hate in his eyes.

"What would you do if I set you free?" asked Parasades in a low voice. He waited a moment then continued. "Not going to answer me? No matter. There are only two options available to you. If you are a coward you could run and hide, but if you wanted revenge for the deaths of your companions, you would gather your fellow tribesmen and return quickly." Parasades smiled coldly, tapping his teeth with the point of his dagger. "Of course, you have no way of knowing that a Serratae patrol is no more than three hours from here on the Plains road." He sighed and looked over at the campfire.

"It will be light soon. If you were to escape it would have to be now." Parasades slipped his dagger between the ropes around the prisoner's legs. "You will need a horse. The grey gelding stands ready." Parasades turned the man and sliced through his wrist bonds. "Run and hide, fellow."

The prisoner got to his feet slowly, rubbing his wrists. He glanced over at Certes, who stared back at him, spear in hand. Parasades gestured, waving Certes away, and the prisoner, with a puzzled look, took to his heels in the direction of the horses. A few minutes later, the two men heard the muffled sounds of a single horse dissolve into the silence of the grasslands.

Certes turned to his chief. "My lord?" he queried.

"Keep silent, my friend," grinned Parasades. "You were on guard on the other side of the camp when he escaped."

The warrior inclined his head. "As you command." He turned and walked away.

Parasades watched Certes moving away then stretched and walked back to the fire. He stirred the embers with a stick and threw on more wood. The crackle of the flames soon intruded on the silence of the streambed camp. A wave of warmth emanated from the fire and Parasades sat, with hands outstretched to the flames, deep in thought.

The dawn light strengthened and a chill breeze blew from the direction of the mountains. Certes moved over to the fire and stood in its warmth, looking at his lord with troubled eyes.

Nikometros sat up and yawned then reached over and shook Timon's shoulder. He arose and stretched, nodding at Parasades. Other yawns and grunts emanated from Agarus and Diratha on either side of him. Diratha mumbled something indistinctly then got up and moved rapidly in the direction of the horses.

"Morning, Parasades," greeted Nikometros. "You slept well?"

"Too well, it seems," replied Parasades quietly. "Our prisoner has escaped."

"What?" Nikometros spun round and stared at the tree stump and the ropes lying at its base. "How in Hades did that happen? Who was on watch?"

Parasades shrugged. "Certes. I have already questioned him. He heard a noise and investigated. When he returned, the prisoner was gone. He then woke me."

"And you did nothing?"

"What could I do?" asked Parasades. "We searched the surroundings. He took a horse. We could not track him at night."

Timon scowled. "Something stinks, sir. When I passed over the watch to Certes, the prisoner was secure. I checked his bonds myself." He strode over to the ropes and picked them up. "They have been cut! He was helped to escape."

"Or else you missed a knife when you tied him," observed Parasades dryly.

"I searched him. He had no knife, I would swear to it," spat Timon.

"Then someone aided him," said Parasades quietly. "Tell me, Macedonian, who do you accuse?"

Timon glowered at the Scythian lord but said nothing.

"Perhaps you accuse me, or Certes? Of course, we have been fighting the Serratae since we first bore arms. We have no reason to aid an enemy." Parasades put his hands on his hips and smiled at Timon. "If you remember, I wanted to kill him last night. Only the intervention of my lord Nikomayros," he inclined his head, "Saved him then." He stabbed out an arm at Agarus, still seated by the fire. "Perhaps the cripple, or the woman?" He looked around. "Where is she, by the way?"

"Here my lord," replied Diratha. The Scythian woman walked out from behind the low hillock by the horse lines, refastening her tunic as she came. "What has happened? There is a horse missing."

"The prisoner escaped," said Parasades. "Our Macedonian companions think one of us let him escape."

"That is nonsense!" exclaimed Diratha. She flushed then continued. "With respect, my lord Nikomayros. No Massegetae warrior would allow a Serratae dog to live, save by your command."

"Well, if it was not one of us then he must have used a hidden knife." Parasades turned to Timon with a blank face. "Unless my lord Nikomayros helped him to escape?"

Timon dropped his gaze, a flush of anger reddening his features. "Maybe he had a knife hidden," he ground out.

Nikometros clapped Timon on the shoulder. "It is past, my friend. At least we were not knifed in our beds." He looked thoughtfully at the dawn sky. "We shall have to find him though, and quickly."

"My thoughts too, my lord," agreed Parasades. "I feel a measure of responsibility over the affair. After all, he escaped while my man was on watch." He glanced quickly at Certes, who stared at the ground. "I will take Certes and search for him. He cannot have got far."

Nikometros nodded. "Thank you, my lord. We will be ready to move out when you return."

Parasades snapped his fingers at Certes and shouldered his way past Timon. The two men trotted over toward the horse lines, picking up their bags as they went. A few minutes later, as the first rays of the sun broke through the ragged cloud on the horizon, the sound of hooves drumming on the earth died away.

The two riders broke out of the dewy grassland onto the narrow dirt road. Parasades brought his horse to an abrupt halt and swivelled in his seat, looking about him.

Certes reined his horse in further down the road then walked it back to the other man. "My lord?" he enquired. "Are we not to look for the prisoner?"

Parasades ignored his question and pointed to a small stand of pines several hundred paces further down the road. "That looks satisfactory," he said. "Come." He kicked his horse into motion and led Certes down the road and into the cover of the trees. The men dismounted and tied the reins of their horses to a small sapling on the far side of the stand within reach of the grass. Parasades cleared a patch of ground of fallen branches and stones and settled himself comfortably. Certes squatted beside him, peering out through the foliage at the road and the swell of grassland where their companions camped.

"I don't understand, my lord," said Certes. "First you release the Serratae then you say he escaped and will fetch him back. Now we sit and do nothing."

Parasades picked at his teeth with a broken twig. "What do you know of our Greek, the lord Nikomayros?" he asked.

Certes shrugged. "Only what most men know. He is a good fighter and nearly as good a horseman as any man of the plains."

"Would you follow him into battle?"

"No," replied Certes after a moment. "He can lead men bravely, but..." His voice trailed into silence.

"But what?"

"My lord, I know he is your friend but I am unsure of his intentions."

Parasades glanced up at the other man. "What do you mean?"

Certes got up and walked over to the edge of the pine grove. He stared out at the road and the dew-soaked grass sparkling in the weak rays of the winter sun. "He is not of the People, my lord."

"That makes a difference?"

"May I speak freely, lord, without fear?"

"Of course."

"Then, yes, it does make a difference. I would follow you, my lord, or any worthy Massegetae warrior into any battle, regardless of the odds." Certes swung round and faced his lord, his sword arm tensing as he spoke. "Forgive me, my lord, but I would rather follow the traitor Areipithes than the Greek."

Parasades' mouth gave a quick, jerky smile. "Do others think as you do, Certes?"

"Yes." Certes waved his hand dismissively. "Oh, there are a number of young men, the ones who shave and like to call themselves his 'lions', who would follow him anywhere. But most men distrust him. They followed as long as Spargises supported him, but now?" He shrugged. "Many would look to a true-born son of the Massegetae to lead them. If Areipithes is the only leader then they will follow him."

"Then I shall have to give them another leader."

Certes grinned. "Aye, lord. Many would follow you if you gave the sign. But what of the Greek?"

"I spoke truly when I told the prisoner of the Serratae patrol on the Plains road. The headman of Turkul will have sent word to them already. It only remains for our freed prisoner to guide them to their prey."

Certes' mouth dropped open. "You would betray the Greeks...and our own tribesmen with them?"

"Certainly," laughed Parasades. "A crippled servant and a woman. I regret their deaths but their sacrifice will rid our People of a troublesome man."

Certes shook his head uncertainly. "Then what has this all been about?" he asked, waving his hand in the general direction of the mountains. "Why did you not let the Greek ride to his death alone? Why this pretence?"

"The girl is important. Whether or not she is still a priestess is immaterial. The people love her and she is a daughter of Spargises. I need her support if I am to make a bid for the throne."

"Throne, my lord?" gaped Certes. "The Massegetae are a strong tribe and Spargises was a redoubtable warrior chief but he never claimed to be a king."

"He never saw what was plain to others. The Jartai, the Dahai and the Dumae recognise the authority of the Massegetae. Others will follow. There is a kingdom waiting to be claimed. You can be sure Areipithes has seen the potential."

"Will the priestess support you if you have let her champion die? Some say he was even her lover."

"He was, and she must never know. There are no certainties this far into enemy lands. He fell by some chance encounter with superior forces. We escaped to rescue her as the lord Nikomayros wished."

Certes nodded slowly. "Then we continue to search for the priestess?"

"Indeed. Dimurthes has no more than two or three men with him now. I dare say we can free her of his clutches." Parasades patted the ground beside him. "Wait until the patrol has done its work and we can be on our way."

Certes sat against the bole of a pine tree, his arms wrapped around his hunched knees, looking out toward the road. Parasades lay back and closed his eyes, listening to the soft sighing of the wind above them.

Time passed slowly, the sun creeping higher in the sky as they watched and waited. Twice, a tiny figure appeared briefly on the road near the camp. It shaded its eyes against the low sun and searched the road and surrounding plains for a few minutes before hobbling back out of sight. Certes woke his master and pointed.

"The cripple," observed Certes. "They grow impatient for our return."

Parasades nodded. "That is the one thing that concerns me. If they decide not to wait for us they may yet escape the patrol. Ah, see there!" He pointed at movement far up the road.

The movement, vague and unformed, swiftly resolved itself into a body of horsemen approaching at a fast pace. As they grew closer, Parasades thought he could make out a familiar grey gelding and nodded in satisfaction. The riders slowed then divided, fanning out over the undulating grasslands in a thin line, encircling the as yet unseen campsite. At a signal the horsemen turned and moved inward, bows drawn and ready. They disappeared behind the ridges and once more the plains became silent and empty.

"How long do we wait, my lord?"

Parasades pursed his lips. "How long to kill three men and a woman? A few minutes, unless they seek revenge." He shrugged. "No doubt they will give their comrades at least some sort of burial, gather up the horses and gear. We will be on our way within the hour."

They sat silently, wrapped in their own thoughts, as the morning grew older. A thin wisp of smoke appeared over the grassland and several kites could be seen, circling far above, drawn by the presence of men. At last, the smoke dissipated, and shortly after, a body of horses emerged onto the road. Parasades and Certes leapt to their feet and pushed through the screen of pines cautiously.

Four riders set off along the road toward the village of Turkul, each trailing a long rope with several horses in train. The others, perhaps a dozen or more, turned in the other direction, their main concern being the three figures bound to the backs of the horses in their midst.

"They did not kill them all," exclaimed Certes. "I can see three prisoners there. But who?" He screwed up his eyes and stared at the party of men moving off to the northwest. "I cannot make them out, though that big one at the rear could be Timon."

"The tall one is the Greek, I am sure. So, they did not kill him immediately. I wonder why not?" Parasades chewed his lip, his brow furrowed in concentration. "They take the road to Zarmet at least. He will die there for certain." He exhaled loudly and turned back to the horses. "No matter. We must find Tomyra and rescue her, my friend. It is time to move on."

Chapter 15

B athed and rested, a good hot meal in her belly and thick woollen robes protecting her from the chill morning air, Tomyra rode out of the sanctuary of Mount Mora, her mood buoyant but her mind troubled.

The events of the previous day were hazy, the edges of memory clouded by the withdrawal of the Goddess' spirit. Last night, the clarity of her perceptions had startled and delighted her. The unfolding of the Great Goddess' purpose was apparent and breathtaking. This morning, her awareness of this purpose had waned, dissipating even as the drugged smoke and ritualised chanting dissolved with the dancing shadows in the cave of the Mother.

The bright light of the winter's morning brought forth a whole new array of possibilities but brought with them the realisation of what had happened to her. Tomyra's hand strayed toward her belly and for a moment she felt the warmth of future motherhood before she thrust it firmly from her. This was no child she could love, but rather a growth that had been thrust into her by a hated enemy. *Oh, Great Mother, how could you do this to me?*

"Do not fight it, child." The quiet voice at Tomyra's side startled her and she looked round, wide-eyed.

"Lady Atrullia," she gasped. "You startled...fight what, lady?"

Atrullia smiled and urged her mare closed to Tomyra's. "Your thoughts are open for anyone to see, my child."

The two women walked their horses through the shallow stream and encouraged them up the steep bank on the far side. They passed into the leafless birch and alder forest of the valley edges, the sunlight streaming through the bare branches warming them despite the cold breeze from the mountains. Twigs and dry leaves crackled beneath the hooves of their mounts.

"Have you already forgotten the Mother's purpose, child?" Atrullia spoke softly, as if addressing her mare, but her words clearly carried in the crisp air. "You hate the unborn one inside you for no other reason than your hatred of her father. Beware of your hatred, Tomyra. Turn against your daughter and you turn against the Mother."

"You need not fear," snapped Tomyra. "I will obey you as I have sworn to do. The child will be unharmed."

"Only unharmed? Unloved too, I fear."

"You ask me to love this...this thing I carry?" Tomyra shook her head. "I will not get rid of it as I long to do, but you cannot ask me to love it."

"*I* do not ask it, my child. The Great Goddess who rules us all, from the bellies of our mothers to our graves, asks it of you." Atrullia reached out a hand and grasped Tomyra firmly. "Learn to love your daughter, Tomyra."

Tomyra drew back on the reins of her mare and turned to face the old woman. She stared grimly at her for a few moments then dropped her eyes. "It is hard," she breathed.

She shook herself and looked around her at the bare forest. "What is to happen when I leave the sanctuary, my lady?" she asked in a small voice. "His men are waiting for me."

"I did warn them, did I not?" said Atrullia dryly.

"What do you mean?"

"The sanctuary of the Mother is not a good place for men to come with violence in their hearts," chuckled the old priestess. "It seems they were visited by the women who were following us when we arrived. I regret they did not survive the encounter."

"They are my women?"

"So I am told. Come, let us ride to meet them."

Tomyra pushed her mare on eagerly through the thinning forest toward the boundary of the valley sanctuary. Atrullia followed more sedately, a smile on her wrinkled face. As the trees gave way to bare scrubby willow and bush alder, a woman stepped out of the cover, a drawn bow in hand. For a moment, the look on the dirty unkempt face of the woman was one of pure astonishment, followed by one of intense joy.

"My lady? Oh, Great Mother! It is you." The woman turned and gesticulated wildly at the scrub. "Sarmatia, Prithia! It is our lady. Come quickly!" She turned back to Tomyra who was sliding off her mare and threw down her bow. "My lady," she cried again, tears running down her cheeks. "We have found you at last."

Tomyra ran toward the woman, her thick woollen robes flapping. "Bithyia! My dearest Bithyia! I feared you were dead." Tears coursed down her face as she clung to the woman dressed in warrior leathers, hugging and kissing her.

Sarmatia and Prithia ran from the cover of the willows, discarding their bows as they came. They hesitated a moment then dropped on their knees, clasping the folds of Tomyra's cloak.

"Lady," breathed Prithia.

"My lady," added Sarmatia. "We are here to serve you."

Tomyra looked down at the two of them and brushed her tears away, her lips quivering in a smile. "Faithful Sarmatia, and Prithia too. I dared not hope you were still alive. When I saw what they did to Domra..."

Bithyia's face clouded. "Domra, yes, and others. That man will answer for it when I find him."

"He has already, Bithyia. Dimurthes..." Tomyra spat his name out, "...died by his own hand in the Mother's sanctuary. Domra is avenged." She paused then in a quiet voice, "You said others? Who?"

"Tarmia, Stallias..."

"Not gentle Stallias?"

"...and Portas, my lady." Bithyia hung her head, fresh tears staining her cheeks. "I failed them, sending them to their deaths. I have failed you too."

Tomyra reached out her hand and raised Bithyia's face, brushing away the streaked grime with her sleeve. "What happened, Bithyia?"

"Her only fault is one of trust, my lady," said Sarmatia grimly. "We needed food. Rather than send us out alone to forage in enemy lands, she led us, leaving Domra in charge."

"Enough, Sarmatia," Bithyia said dully. "I was commander, the fault is mine."

"No, it is not," interrupted Sarmatia. "Forgive me, my lady, but Domra was left in charge of our sisters and Domra led them into a trap by disobeying her commander."

Tomyra looked at Sarmatia then at Prithia, who nodded her head in agreement. She sighed and turned back to Bithyia. "Sister, my dearest friend, you forget I know you too well. I mourn the deaths of our sisters but I know you and I know my Owls." Tomyra put her hands on the other woman's shoulders and gazed into her dark eyes. "Your sisters are loyal but honest, Bithyia. If they say you are not at fault then you are not." Her look hardened. "Put it behind you. I have need of your experience, my friend."

Bithyia drew a shuddering breath. "Aye, lady. I am yours to command, as always." Her eyes darted over Tomyra's shoulders and her hand flew to the sword at her side. "Someone comes," she hissed.

Tomyra turned quickly and spread her arms out protectively as Atrullia's mare ambled out of the forest. "Put your weapons up, sisters. This is the lady Atrullia, priestess of the sanctuary of Mount Mora."

Sarmatia and Prithia stepped back quickly, heads bowed. Bithyia sheathed her sword and bowed low. "Forgive me, lady," she said boldly.

Atrullia inclined her head toward the woman warriors. "My women informed me of your presence...and of the deeds you performed on the portals of our sanctuary." She glanced about her. "I trust that you have given them at least a token burial."

"Aye, lady, though such as they deserve no rest." Bithyia smiled coldly. "They lie under rocks in a small ravine over there." She gestured off the track in the direction of the mountains.

Atrullia nodded. "I will see they have the proper rites." The old woman tossed her head, dismissing the slain men from her thoughts. She turned to Tomyra, holding out a short, carved staff. "Tomyra, go with the blessing of the Great Goddess. You will need to ride fast for your own lands, for once the news of Dimurthes' death is revealed, there will be many who would seek to do you harm, priestess or not."

"Are the Serratae so ungodly that they would knowingly harm a priestess of the Mother?" hissed Sarmatia.

"Perhaps not," observed Atrullia quietly. "Yet he was much loved and respected among his people. Some will seek vengeance, if not upon Tomyra herself then upon her companions."

"We will go quickly, my lady," said Tomyra. "I long to see my homeland and my Niko." She grinned. "There is nothing to keep us here." Tomyra gestured toward her woman companions. "Come, it is time." Prithia disappeared into the shrubbery and emerged a few minutes later, leading several horses.

"Ours, and a few others we acquired," she grinned.

Atrullia held out her short staff again. "Take this, my child. It is known as a symbol of the power of the Mother. It may provide you with safety if all else fails you."

Tomyra took the short staff and ran her hands over the smooth dark wood, feeling the ornate carvings and the warmth of the wood, despite the chill air. "Thank you, my lady. I will honour it." She leaned over to the old woman with a smile. "Thank you too for saving my life."

Atrullia shrugged. "Thank our Great Mother, and remember the charge she puts upon you." The old woman gripped Tomyra's arm tightly. "Go in peace, my child. Both of you," she added softly.

Bithyia shot Tomyra a questioning look but said nothing. She leapt up onto her horse and gathered the reins of one of the spare horses. Sarmatia and Prithia followed suit. Tomyra turned back to the old priestess.

"Farewell, my lady Atrullia. May the Great Goddess bless you," she intoned formally. Tomyra flashed a warm smile at her and added, "I will always remember your kindness." She wheeled her mare and urged it after her companions, up the narrow trail that led out of the valley.

Tomyra looked back into the valley as she crested the ridge. Below her the winter landscape of the rocky mountainside merged into the forests of the sanctuary. There was no sign of Atrullia but Tomyra raised her hand in salutation anyway before allowing her mare its head as it picked its way carefully down the far side of the ridge.

The group of women forded the shallow rushing stream in the gully and scrambled up the far side. The wind tugged at their cloaks as they wound their way down the mountain, heading for the thin ribbon of the road far below them. Tomyra sat astride her mare in silence, thinking her own thoughts. The women kept quiet too, respecting their mistress' privacy, concentrating on the trail in front of them.

They emerged onto the road by late morning and turned toward the east and the town of Turkul. Tomyra reined her mare in and sat staring in turn along the road in either direction.

"My lady?" enquired Bithyia. "Our way lies to the east." She pointed along the road.

"You saw no sign of my lord Nikomayros?" asked Tomyra.

"No, lady." Bithyia hesitated then added, "He knew of your capture and is certain to be looking for you, but we have not seen him."

"He would come for me, I know it. I fear something has happened to him, Bithyia."

"Perhaps he looks for you elsewhere. We were fortunate to come across your trail early. I am sure we will find him when we return to our people, my lady."

"What sort of welcome will we get there?" asked Tomyra with a bite in her voice. "My father lays dead and my brother rules in..."

"Horses," hissed Sarmatia, pointing to the west. "I can hear horses coming."

Bithyia listened for a moment then signalled the party off into the scrub beside the road. She ushered Tomyra ahead of her, impatient with her mistress' obvious reluctance to move into cover. She dismounted and, drawing her bow, joined Sarmatia and Prithia at the edge of the scrub. The noise of the horses' hooves grew rapidly louder then slowed to a stop at the junction with the mountain trail to Mount Mora.

Bithyia peered out, sighting her arrow on the nearer of the two horsemen. "Hold," she whispered. "Only kill them if we are discovered."

Beside her, Prithia gave a squeak of excitement and lowered her bow. "Certes!" she cried.

The horsemen swung round at the sound of her voice, their hands sweeping their swords from their belts. Sarmatia released her arrow. It flashed toward the more muscular rider, tugging at his cloak. The man gave a roar of anger and leaned low over his horse's neck, spurring it toward the women.

Prithia screamed and pulled at her companion's arm. "It is Certes, do not kill him!"

Bithyia swore as she recognised the men. She stepped out with her hands raised above her head into the path of the charging rider. "My lord Parasades!" A moment later she dived to her right, scrambling to avoid the downward slash of his sword.

Parasades pulled back on his horse's head with an oath, the animal slipping and skidding in the loose scree as it turned. His eyes swept over the figures standing before him then he grunted and shoved his sword back into his belt.

"I know you," he grated. "You are one of Tomyra's women."

"Bithyia, my lord. I, and these others, came in search of our lady."

"And they found me."

Parasades whipped round at the sound of Tomyra's voice. He stared at the slim woman dressed in fine robes of Serratae design pushing her way out of the willow scrub then grinned. "Tomyra, by the gods. We came to rescue you but it seems your own women were enough."

Tomyra looked up at the mounted horseman, her eyes searching his face. "We?" She looked over at Certes, who had leapt off his horse and was embracing Prithia. "Just the two of you?"

Parasades pursed his lips. "No," he said slowly. "My lady, I bear ill tidings."

Tomyra sucked in her breath, forcing herself to control her suddenly trembling lips. "What tidings?"

"The lord Nikomayros, my lady." Parasades beckoned to Bithyia. "Attend to your mistress," he snapped. When Bithyia put her arm around Tomyra, a look of intense concern on her face, Parasades continued in a low voice.

"There were five of us, my lady. We were ambushed out on the plains. The lord Nikomayros is dead, together with his man Timon and his crippled servant."

Tomyra gave a small cry and collapsed against Bithyia. The other woman stared up at Parasades with tears in her eyes, a soft moan of anguish escaping her lips. Her arms cradled the trembling Tomyra.

"You are certain of this?" Bithyia asked in a small voice.

Parasades nodded. "It brings me much sorrow to bear such news, ladies." He hesitated and looked around him. "It is imperative that we ride on immediately. There will be enemy riders out looking for us."

Tomyra wiped her face with the sleeves of her cloak and drew a ragged breath. "How is it that you and Certes survived this ambush?" She glanced over at Certes who was in animated conversation with Prithia. "I see no wounds or evidence of battle."

"We were at some distance from the others when it happened, my lady," said Parasades smoothly. "A large patrol happened upon them and overwhelmed them before we could ride to their aid." He shrugged. "I thought it foolish to throw away our lives when we still sought you."

Sarmatia had been listening to the conversation. She approached, putting her arm around Tomyra, supporting her from the other side. "Where are their bodies? Can we at least give them the rites of burial?"

"They took the bodies and rode toward Zarmet." Parasades leaned toward the women. "My lady, I must stress the danger of our situation. We should leave here immediately."

Tomyra gazed up at the horseman listlessly. "How can I leave my beloved Niko in the hands of his enemies? He should..." Her voice broke. "He should at least have the rites."

Bithyia nodded through her own tears. "I would rather die than leave my Timon dishonoured."

Parasades swore under his breath, controlling his sudden urge to strike the women. "My lady, the lord Nikomayros and Timon sacrificed their lives to rescue you and bring you home to the tribe. Will you make their efforts valueless? For their sakes, if not for mine, come with me. Now."

Tomyra clutched Bithyia to her and bowed her head. "Mother Goddess," she muttered. "Where is your purpose in this? Why did you send him to me only to snatch him from me?" She raised her head, wiping her tear-streaked face with the back of her hands. "You are right, my lord Parasades. Though it tears my heart apart to leave my beloved, we must do as he wished." She hugged Bithyia and Sarmatia then turned away to where the horses were tethered.

Sarmatia helped her mistress onto the back of her mare, adjusting the folds of her cloak, making sure that as little as possible of her skin was exposed to the biting wind. She looked up as Prithia approached, arm in arm with Certes. The look of intense sorrow on her face vanished, replaced by a growing anger at the smiling young woman.

"Have you no thought for the feelings of our lady?" she hissed.

Prithia stopped dead, the smile giving way to concern. "I did not mean to make light of her grief, Sarmatia. It just seemed to me that the situation is not hopeless. Certes told..."

"Are you a fool, girl, or just heartless?" interrupted Bithyia. "The lord Nikomayros and...and my Timon are dead, lying cold in this hateful land without even the rites of burial and you say the situation is not hopeless? Ahhh!" She turned away with a look of disgust. "Go, get ready. We ride for the Oxus immediately."

Prithia paled, her voice stammering. "B...but they are not dead. At le...least not yet. Surely if they are captive there must be hope?"

Parasades pushed his horse closer to the group, a thunderous expression on his face. He opened his mouth to speak then thought better of it, closing his mouth with a snap.

"Captive?" asked Tomyra, her eyes wide. "What do you mean? They are dead."

"No, my lady." Prithia shook her head. "Certes here says they were captured and led off toward Zarmet unharmed." The young woman wrung her hands. "Oh, my lady, they will surely die unless we go to their aid." She swung round and grabbed Bithyia's sleeve. "How can we just ride off and leave them to die?"

Tomyra looked across at the glowering Scythian warlord. "Parasades," she asked quietly, "Is this true?"

Parasades stared down at Certes, who blanched and stepped back. The warlord's face twisted in anger as he wrenched his gaze up to the young priestess. "This young man is a fool," he hissed. He fought for control of his anger and continued in a more even tone. "I thought to spare you the anguish of a hopeless situation. If they are not dead yet, they will be as soon as they reach Zarmet. Dimurthes will put them to death immediately."

"But they were alive when you saw them last?"

"Yes, lady," said Parasades impatiently. "But they will be killed as soon as they arrive at Zarmet. Dimurthes will see to that."

"Dimurthes is dead."

"Dead? How?"

Tomyra shook her head. "It is enough that he is dead." She pursed her lips and thought for a few moments. "There will be uncertainty at Zarmet for at least a day, until the news arrives. That may give us time."

Parasades' eyes widened. "My lady, don't even consider it. We cannot rescue them from Zarmet. We would all be killed and I cannot allow our priestess to die."

"Then you'll have to make sure I remain alive," Tomyra said grimly. "For I tell you now, I'm not leaving unless my beloved Niko comes with me."

Chapter 16

Timon sniffed the air and stared up at the rapidly clouding sky. "Snow," he muttered. "And soon." He turned his attention back to the man at his side, swaying awkwardly on the back of a small Scythian horse. A look of concern came over his face and he edged his horse closer. "My lord," he whispered.

Nikometros paid no attention. His eyes remained closed and only the involuntary clenching of his hands on the reins and the largely automatic flexing of strong thigh muscles in response to the horse's movements showed signs of continuing life within him. A spreading red stain over his left shoulder and chest told of an injury that drained him of life.

Timon called softly to Agarus who rode a few paces back. "Agarus, we must stop. Nikometros' wound needs attention. Tell the guards we must stop or he will die."

Agarus nodded wearily. "I will try, lord, but I fear we will all be dead very soon." The crippled servant at once began to talk to the men around him, quietly, as if talking unconcernedly about mundane affairs.

Timon listened, his ears catching the occasional familiar word or phrase. He cursed his own difficulty with languages, his eyes flicking from man to man, hoping to see some concern or hope.

At length the leader of the Serratae war patrol rode back down the column and ended the argument with an angry outburst. He pulled his horse alongside Nikometros' and prodded the wounded man with the tip of his bow. He grunted and looked across at Timon. "He live," he said in passable Massegetae dialect. "At least for now. Soon, maybe not." The man roared with laughter and spurred his horse back to the front of the column. Timon swore colourfully in Macedonian patois at the man's retreating back.

"That's my Timon," came a whisper from beside him. "I'm glad to hear you are still a Macedonian at heart."

Timon whipped round, nearly overbalancing in his haste. "My lord!" he cried.

"Easy, Timon. Do not let them see us talking."

"Gods, Nikos, I thought you were dying on me."

"I may yet, my friend," grated Nikometros through clenched teeth. "This arrowhead must come out soon. Already I can feel it burning within me."

The effort of the few words brought perspiration to Nikometros' forehead, despite the chill air. He opened his eyes, the pale blue of his irises staring unfocussed at the man riding in front of him. "Where are they taking us, Timon, do you know?"

"Zarmet. I gather we'll be there by sunset."

Nikometros shook his head gently, grimacing with pain. "It seems we've done this before, Timon." He chuckled weakly and coughed. After a few moments of silence he went on. "No doubt we'll be offered up as sacrifice but this time there'll be no beautiful priestess to save us."

"Parasades is out there somewhere. Maybe he'll rescue us."

"You don't sound very confident of that, my friend," whispered Nikometros.

"I'm not, my lord," Timon growled. "I don't trust the man. It seems odd that after the prisoner escaped on his watch that he should go in search of him, only to avoid capture when the prisoner returns with this patrol. If it weren't that he desires the finding of his priestess, I would swear he betrayed us."

"Ah, Tomyra. What's to become of her, Timon?"

"The Goddess will look after her, my lord. Even Dimurthes will come to his senses and set her free. All the tribes honour the Mother Goddess and her priestesses."

"I pray you're right..." breathed Nikometros. "I'm sorry, Timon, I must..." He slumped forward over his horse's neck, almost falling.

One of the Serratae guards shouted and brought the column to a halt. Slipping off his horse, the guard moved up and secured Nikometros to his horse with a leather strap passed under the horse's belly and another round the horse's neck. With a laugh he remounted and, taking Nikometros' reins in hand, waved for the others to proceed.

The column of horsemen rode slowly north and west, following the road across the rolling plains of grass. The bright morning sky clouded over, darkening, and the wind veered to the north. The sun sank toward its western home, the light dimming, as the riders came to the edge of a river bluff. Below them the land dropped steeply away to a flat riverbed and a broad expanse of water glistening in the last rays of the setting sun.

On the far side, in the shadows of the opposite bluffs, lay a sprawling collection of tents and wooden structures. Campfires flickered in the open spaces and lanterns and oil lamps glowed behind curtains in the dwellings. Outside the rough wooden palisade atop an earthen rampart that surrounded the town, milled vast herds of horses and cattle. Riders could be distinguished, guiding the herds out toward the pastures and back in again to the relative security of the town.

Timon looked down at the scene with a sour expression on his face. He leaned toward one of the Scythian guards and asked what the town was in the Massegetae tongue, hoping that the question in his voice would overcome the differences in language.

The guard grunted. "Zarmet," he said, adding a string of other phrases to his answer. Timon could make little of the words except one that possibly meant 'food'. He hoped so.

The column edged over the bluff, working its way down a steep path. As they descended, the first large flakes of snow fell. By the time they reached the valley floor, a thin covering of white muted the outlines of rocks and the bare scrubby trees along the river's edge. The riders splashed into the shallow river, a rim of ice crackling beneath them. The water proved to be no more than waist deep and Timon's legs were the only part of him to feel the icy current. Despite this, he was grateful when they emerged onto the far bank, into the lee of the hills. The snow fell faster, straight down; rapidly obscuring the town that now lay close in front of them.

A challenge rang out and a body of men, arms at the ready, galloped up to them. After a brief exchange of words, the patrol fell into place alongside the column and escorted them into Zarmet. Crowds of men and women flocked around the warriors as they rode through the crooked streets. Children raced alongside, darting between the horses, leaping up to touch the prisoners. They screamed and shouted, laughing and pointing at the strange sight of the fair-headed barbarian reeling on his horse.

The cavalcade came to a halt outside a large, richly decorated house in the centre of the town. The horsemen pushed the crowding populace back with good-natured shoving and ribald jests, clearing a space around their three prisoners. The leader of the patrol leapt off his horse and strode up to a group of men waiting outside the house and loudly started to speak.

Timon supported Nikometros with one arm and strained to hear but could not make sense of the diatribe. He turned to a despondent-looking Agarus beside him. "What is he saying?"

"He says that he, Sparses of the Serratae, has captured the renowned Lion of Scythia, scourge of the East," muttered Agarus grimly. "When Dimurthes, their chief, returns, he will personally send the barbarians...that's you, Timon, and my lord Nikomayros..."

"Thank you, Agarus, I gathered that," growled Timon.

"...to their ancestors with much pain. The Massegetae warrior...that's me...will merely die at the hands of their champion as a sacrifice to the Mother Goddess," went on Agarus. "He calls for rejoicing and for messengers to be sent out to find Dimurthes."

Abruptly, the crowd erupted into cheers. Sparses grinned and raised his arms above his head, looking very pleased with himself. The men around him crowded round and drew him into the warmly lit interior of the house.

The warriors of the patrol dismounted and dragged the prisoners from their horses, jeering at the stifled groans of pain forced from a barely conscious Nikometros. Timon struggled to his side and half-supported him as the guards pushed and jostled the trio toward an imposing stone structure at the far end of the central open space. The crowd followed, calling out insults and pelting the prisoners with dirt clods and frozen lumps of horse dung.

The guards opened a heavy timber door and led the way inside, holding aloft a burning brand. The flickering light showed a large stonewalled room lined with thick tapestries. A rough wooden trestle table with accompanying benches and stools sat squarely in front of a small fireplace, in which crackled a small fire. Several guards immediately set to, building up the fire and preparing a meal from stores stacked along one wall. Others hustled

Nikometros, Timon and Agarus toward another door, pushing them through into a cold, dank unfurnished cell. One of the Serratae men stood in the doorway and slowly let his eyes drift over the frost-rimed walls of the room.

"Hey, Lorcus," yelled one of the guards, "lock them in and be done with it. There is a cold draught coming in."

Lorcus grunted and growled a response without turning. "I will come when I am satisfied. Sparses will have our heads if these barbarians escape his wrath." He finished his inspection and turned to the three prisoners. "Be quiet and give us no trouble and you may be fed later." He turned to leave.

Timon nudged Agarus sharply and ordered him to translate what he said. He gestured at Nikometros' blood-soaked tunic. "We must have help or he will die. He has an arrow still within him."

Lorcus turned back and stared at Nikometros in the flickering light that came through the open door. He drew his sword and stepped forward cautiously. Holding the blade at Timon's throat, he roughly tore away the sodden cloth from Nikometros' shoulder. His nose wrinkled as he caught a faint whiff of putrefaction. Lorcus stepped back and shook his head. "He's dead anyway. It would be a kindness to let him die now rather than tomorrow." He stepped backward through the opening and slammed the door shut, bolting it securely.

Agarus stood morosely in the darkness, feeling the chill of the room seep into him. "It seems Diratha was the lucky one," he muttered. "At least she died swiftly under the arrows. Our deaths will be slower and infinitely more painful."

Chapter 17

Tomyra peered through the swirling snow clouds at the distant lights of Zarmet. Bithyia and Sarmatia lay beside her on the bluff overlooking the river valley, the chill damp of the ground seeping into their clothes. Parasades crouched beside them, staring at the town and sucking the hoarfrost from his moustache. Prithia and Certes remained some distance behind them, guarding the horses: Prithia because she was good with horses, Certes because Parasades refused to have him anywhere near him.

Tomyra got to her feet and brushed the snow from her robe. "So, we are none the wiser. We must assume Nikometros and Timon are in Zarmet, but I can think of no easy way to get them out."

"They must be there," said Sarmatia. "We followed the tracks of the patrol."

"We do not even know where they are being held in Zarmet," commented Bithyia. "It could make all the difference."

"They may even be dead already. All right, all right!" Parasades held up his hands defensively as Tomyra and Bithyia rounded on him. "I have to say it, my lady. I'm a trained warrior chief of the Massegetae, which you women seem to be forgetting. I know these people, I've been fighting them all my life." He dropped his arms and held them out toward the women in a placatory gesture. "Be reasonable, my lady. You can see how large Zarmet is and how many men defend it. How can six of us invade the enemy stronghold?"

"I have told you already," said Tomyra stubbornly. "I will not leave without my Nikometros."

"Nor I without my Timon."

Parasades sighed. "Think then of your people. Would you deprive them in their hour of need of their priestess and one of their foremost warriors?"

"If you are afraid of the enemy, my lord Parasades..."

Parasades stiffened. "You dare to say that?" He clenched his fist and stepped toward Tomyra. Bithyia interposed herself and Sarmatia's hand slipped to the sword at her side. "If you were not priestess, I would have your life for that," he hissed.

"My lord, no insult was intended," said Tomyra softly. "If you took offence at my words then I offer my apology freely. We are six among the vastness of the enemy lands and people, there should be no quarrel between us." Tomyra put her hands out to gently push the women aside, standing alone within range of the man's fists. "I say only that I and my women mean to enter Zarmet and attempt the rescue of our men. If you wish to leave us and return to the lands of the Massegetae, you have my permission."

Parasades stood, the colour rising in his cheeks and his hands clenching and unclenching as his anger fed upon itself. "Gods save us from women who think themselves warriors!" he roared. "Do as you please, you fools. It is obvious I cannot save you from your fate." He turned on his heel and took several deep breaths of cold air, his exhalations white and swirling in the storm. His hunched shoulders slowly relaxed. "I don't need your permission to leave, Tomyra," he grated. "If I choose to leave, I will. As it happens, I choose not to. I'll join you in your mad quest for death. It may be that I can yet save you."

"Thank you, Parasades." Tomyra stepped closer and put one slim hand on the man's shoulder. "We have need of your strength, knowledge and skills." Turning to the others she said briskly, "Come, let us return to the shelter of the brush. We must make our plans."

The women walked back, shielding their faces from the icy storm, leaving Parasades to follow, cursing under his breath.

Chapter 18

"Identify yourself!" The challenge rang out. Figures moved obscurely in the darkness, muffled by the swirling clouds of snow, backlit by the sputtering orange glow of a watch fire. The figures resolved into three men, spears held at the ready, who moved into the path of the three riders. "Dismount and identify yourselves!" shouted the man in the lead once more.

Tomyra took a deep breath and forced some measure of calm into her voice, hoping her racing heart was not as loud as it sounded to her. "The Mother Goddess seeks an audience with the chief of the Serratae," she called. In a whisper she added to Bithyia, "With any luck the absence of Dimurthes will make them uncertain."

The men made a quick placatory gesture toward the ground. "The Mother Goddess? What do you mean?" They peered at the three riders as if expecting to see a deity come to earth. "Who are you?"

"I am a holy one of the Mother and these are my servants," called out Tomyra. Silence met her, dragging out in the howling wind that whipped at their cloaks and stung their bare skin. "Do you mean to show disrespect for the Goddess or are you just foolish men?"

The men muttered then reluctantly stepped aside. The leader gestured with his spear. "If you would accompany us into the shelter of the gate, we can decide this out of the storm."

"Could be awkward," whispered Bithyia as they urged their horses forward between the guards. She slipped her hand toward the hilt of her sword. "Perhaps we should take them?"

"No. Stay calm and aloof. I am the priestess and you are my guardian maidens. Keep to the plan."

The guards ushered the three riders through the gate and into a small enclosure out of the direct blast of the storm. Brushing down his cloak, the leader gestured for the riders to dismount. Several other men appeared from a lean-to by the palisade, dragging spears with them.

Tomyra slid from her mare and drawing herself up, stood firmly in front of the guard leader. "I am Tomyra, priestess of the Great Goddess and these," she gestured toward Bithyia and Sarmatia, "Are my maidens. I have business with Dimurthes, chief of the Serratae. On what authority do you deny me passage?"

"I do not deny you passage, lady," said the leader equably. "But these are troubled times. I wish merely to be sure of any who come calling in the night."

Tomyra held out Atrullia's staff. "You recognise this symbol of my authority?"

The leader knuckled his brow respectfully. "Of course, lady." He hesitated. "It is my duty to assess any threat to the safety of this town."

"And you see a threat in three women?"

The man stared at Tomyra then at the other two women standing by their horses. "Your women carry bows and swords, lady. Why?"

"As you say, these are troubled times. Would you have priestesses wander the land unescorted and unprotected?"

The man grunted. "Why do you want to see Dimurthes?"

"That is between him and the Goddess." Tomyra smiled. "Are you perhaps Dimurthes, paramount chief of the Serratae?"

One of the men guffawed and the leader rounded on him, silencing him with a gesture. "No, lady, I am not." He came to a decision and beckoned two of his men over. "These men will escort you to the chief's house."

"I would not want to trouble you further on such a cold night," said Tomyra. "Just point us in the right direction and we will find our own way."

The man wrinkled his brow and cocked his head to one side. "I have not seen you before in Zarmet, lady. It would be best if you were escorted." Turning to one of the two men he barked. "Thysis, you will escort this lady and her two companions to Dimurthes' house. See that no harm comes to them." He paused briefly. "See too that they go straight there and wait to see that they are admitted." He bowed to Tomyra. "My lady."

Tomyra inclined her head graciously. "Thank you...May I know your name?" she enquired. "I would commend Dimurthes on the zeal of his men."

"Myres." He grinned then nodded to Thysis and his companion. "Go quickly, my lady, the storm worsens."

Tomyra remounted her mare and with Bithyia and Sarmatia on either side of her, walked her horse into the streets of Zarmet. Thysis and the other man walked ahead of them, holding a burning brand aloft. The howling wind scattered sparks that died quickly in the driving snow, the fitful glare rapidly dampened by the gloom. After what seemed an interminable time, winding through the crooked streets, the space between the wooden houses and tents opened out into a space in which the snow gusted into drifts.

Thysis pointed ahead. "There is Dimurthes' house, my lady. Pallos, carry word of our arrival." The other man scurried away. He pushed aside the heavy entrance flap, letting a slab of golden light fall over the piled snow, and disappeared inside. A few moments later he reappeared with several other men.

Thysis brought Tomyra's mare to a halt in the light cast by the open flap, holding the bridle in one hand. "A priestess of the Great Goddess come to see Dimurthes," he said importantly.

"Thank you, Thysis," replied a heavyset man. "Welcome, my lady," he added, turning to Tomyra. "May I offer you the hospitality of my humble dwelling?"

Tomyra dismounted and waited until Bithyia and Sarmatia joined her. She inclined her head toward the man. "May the Mother bless you for your hospitality."

The man stepped aside and ushered the three women into the house. The interior was warm and draught-free when the heavy flap closed behind them. Several braziers poured out a fierce heat and burning brands supplied a warmly welcome glow. Cushions and rugs covered the floor around a long trestle table in the centre of the circular room. The smell of cooking meats and fresh baked bread made Tomyra's mouth water. Seated at the table, looking at the women with great interest, were at least a dozen men, eating and drinking. Several hounds lay scratching and picking at scraps under the table. One of the dogs ran over to the women, growling, only to be kicked aside by a guard.

Tomyra threw back the hood of her cloak and brushed the snow from her hair. She turned to face the heavyset man who had followed them in, together with several men. "I thank you again, in the Mother's Name, for your hospitality." She held her face expressionless and asked carefully, "I have a message from the Goddess for Dimurthes, chief of the Serratae. Are you he?"

"No, lady," replied the man. "I am Sparses, his deputy. My lord Dimurthes is expected to return shortly." His eyes raked over Tomyra then over the other two women. "I have not seen you before. What is your name?"

Tomyra inclined her head and smiled. "I am Tomyra, priestess of the Great Goddess. These are my guardian maidens."

Sparses narrowed his eyes. "Tomyra? I have heard that name before somewhere. Where are you from?"

"From the east," she replied, waving her hand vaguely. "A small village, but loyal to the worship of the Mother." Tomyra looked around the room and smiled at the men. "If I may impose on your hospitality further, we have ridden some distance today..."

Several men at once got up from the table and gestured for the women to seat themselves. Platters, piled high with smoking meats and bread, were pushed in front of them and cups of wine poured. Bithyia and Sarmatia immediately started to eat, making an effort to hide how hungry they felt. Tomyra sipped her wine and picked at a piece of bread. She continued to smile at the men around her, thanking them for each proffered morsel.

"East of here you say?" asked Sparses softly. "Your robes are like those of the Mount Mora priestesses, yet the leather garments of your maidens are like those of the Massegetae." He advanced to the end of the table and put his hands on the wood, staring down at Tomyra. "Please explain this, my lady."

Tomyra put down her wine and swallowed before turning to face Sparses. "I had business with the lady Atrullia at Mount Mora," she replied calmly. "She gave me these robes as my own were inadequate for this storm. As for my maidens," she gestured at Bithyia and laughed softly. "A warrior maiden must be chaste and ready to defend her priestess at all times. The garb of the Massegetae women warriors seemed suitable."

Sparses grunted and turned away from the table. He gestured to one of the men standing around the table and whispered in his ear. The man hurried out into the cold. Sparses returned to the table and, ousting one of the seated men, took his place at the far end.

"So, you have come from Mount Mora today?" he asked.

"Yes."

"And you saw the lady Atrullia there?"

"I have said so, yes."

"Yet you did not see the lord Dimurthes?" Sparses picked up a dagger and began picking at the tabletop with the point. "I find that strange, my lady, as he took the lady Atrullia back to her sanctuary yesterday."

"Oh?" Tomyra fought to keep her voice even. "I was already there when she arrived. Perhaps he left again immediately. I did not see him."

Tomyra returned to her eating amid a general silence. Sparses sat and continued to pick at the wood with his dagger, his men standing around awkwardly, unsure of what was happening.

"And this message for my lord Dimurthes?" Sparses asked at length.

"Is for his ears only."

The entrance flap parted, sending a gust of cold air into the room. The man sent out some minutes before returned and hurried over to Sparses. He bent over and whispered to the chief then, at a flick of Sparses' hand, withdrew to the edge of the room. Sparses tapped the blade of his dagger on the fingers of his other hand.

"Tomyra, daughter of Spargises, chief of the Massegetae," he stated flatly. He nodded and steel whispered behind the three women. Bithyia pushed herself upright, only to be hurled back down, a sword at her throat. Sparses pushed his seat back and strode around the table. He gripped Tomyra's long hair in one hand and pulled her head back savagely. "I knew I had heard your name before."

"My lord Sparses," whispered Tomyra, tears starting in her eyes from the pain. "You lay hands on a priestess of the Goddess at your peril."

Sparses bent low, thrusting his face close to Tomyra's, his dagger pricking her throat. "I don't believe you are a priestess, bitch. I think you came here to kill our chief."

Tomyra swallowed painfully. "Then test me. Bring your own priestess, she will attest to the power of the Goddess in me."

The point of Sparses' dagger bit deeper and a trickle of crimson blood-streaked Tomyra's throat. One of the men holding a sword on the other women coughed nervously. "My lord, she may...she may be telling the truth. We should test..." His voice trailed off as Sparses glared at him.

"We risk the anger of the Mother, my lord," added another man. "Send for Rhynna."

Sparses uttered a cry of frustration and slammed Tomyra's head forward onto the table. He whirled and barked out an order to a guard standing by the entrance. "Go to the priestess' tent. Tell her...no, ask her to attend on me immediately. Escort her here." He turned back to the men around the table. "Stand back from them but keep your weapons ready." Sparses strode back to his seat at the table. He picked up a slab of beef and began worrying at it with his teeth, the meat juices running down into his beard.

Several minutes passed. Tomyra gave Bithyia and Sarmatia a covert sign to keep calm and silent then straightened her clothing and used a crust of bread to stem the blood still oozing from the nick in her throat. She tossed it to the floor where a hound snapped it up and retreated back under the table.

A rush of cold air and a flurry of snow signalled the arrival of the priestess. A short, plump, middle-aged woman dressed in voluminous robes and a thick woollen cloak bustled into the hut. She brushed the snow from her cloak and threw back her hood then hurried over to the nearest brazier, rubbing her hands.

"Well, Sparses," she said over her shoulder. "What was it you wanted that could not wait?"

"I need your ability to find the Goddess if She is present," said Sparses, getting to his feet. "This woman claims to be a priestess but I know her only as an enemy and the daughter of an enemy. Examine her Rhynna. Tell me if I can kill her."

Rhynna looked at the three women seated at the table with interest. "A priestess, you say? Which one...no, do not tell me, let me see if I can find her." She walked slowly over to the table, a smile on her lips and her dark eyes twinkling. "Hmm, two dressed as warrior maidens." She touched Sarmatia gently on the shoulder then Bithyia. "No, no powers here save those of bravery and loyalty." Rhynna continued round the table to Tomyra. She reached out and fingered her brown robes. "She is dressed as befits a priestess of Mount Mora. Look at me, woman."

Tomyra raised her head and stared at the rather plain features of the woman standing beside her. She lifted her hand toward Rhynna, smiling as the other woman touched her.

Rhynna's eyes widened and she dropped Tomyra's hand as if bitten. "Holy Mother!" she whispered. She turned on her heel and stared at Sparses. "I have seldom felt such power flow from one of the Mother's chosen," she gasped. "This is indeed a priestess of the Great Goddess. Treat her with courtesy, my lord."

Sparses ground his teeth and slammed his fist on the table, sending a plate of meat toppling to the floor. At once a savage dogfight erupted as the hounds hurled themselves on the unexpected bounty, snarling and yelping. With loud cries and blows the men restored order, sending the dogs whimpering into the shadows.

"You are certain of this?" grated Sparses. "She could not fool you?"

"Of course not!" snapped Rhynna. "A woman...any woman, could fool a man, but no woman can deceive the power of the Goddess. She is who she says she is."

Colour bloomed in Sparses' face as he rose to his feet and stalked around the table to Tomyra. "My apologies, lady," he snarled. "It seems I was mistaken."

"No matter," said Tomyra, with a dismissive gesture. "Perhaps you could arrange suitable accommodations for my maidens and myself while we await the return of your chief?"

"Very well." Sparses nodded and snapped out an order to one of the men. "Arrange it." He cleared his throat and hesitated a moment before continuing. "I am still curious to know why a priestess of the Massegetae travels into Serratae lands to converse with our chief. Do you not know our peoples are at war?"

"I know only too well," replied Tomyra in an expressionless voice. "I seek news of one called Nikomayros, sometimes known as the Lion of Scythia."

A hiss of hatred echoed through the room. Sparses bared his teeth in a snarl. "You ask after that one? Why?"

"The word is you have him here in Zarmet."

Sparses stared into Tomyra's eyes. "My men hold him in custody. He cannot escape and he will die tomorrow."

Tomyra paled slightly but held Sparses' eyes unwaveringly. "It matters not to me. He fled the Massegetae with a sacred object and I wish its return."

Sparses raised his eyebrows. "I had heard that you and he were enamoured of each other."

Tomyra shrugged. "The power of the Goddess would not be in me if that were true. However, he used his position to get close to me then stole something from the tribe."

"What?"

"A scroll, with sacred writings."

Sparses shook his head. "I saw nothing like that. He had only weapons and a small amount of food when captured."

"Perhaps he might have hidden it when you attacked. I would question your men."

"All of them? That will take time."

"I can ask them all at once, my lord. If you would take me to them I can deal with this matter immediately." Tomyra hesitated then smiled. "I can also question your prisoner."

Sparses shook his head. "No, by the gods! No one questions him until he dies tomorrow. Maybe then, lady, if your question is still unanswered." He thought for a moment. "Many of my men have dispersed through the town but others are guarding my prisoner. You will not go to the guardhouse. I will not allow anyone close to my prisoner. The men can come here. I will send for them."

"However, you see fit to arrange it my lord." Tomyra smoothed her robes and seated herself at the table again. "Bithyia, pour me some wine while we wait."

Sparses rapped out a series of orders and bowed as the priestess Rhynna was ushered out. He spoke quietly to some of the other men, who put down the food they were still eating and wiped their greasy hands on their trousers before leaving.

The sound of many feet outside the house signalled the arrival of Sparses' patrol. A great deal of cold air entered as the men slowly trooped in and stood in a semi-circle around the table. They eyed the three women curiously, looking toward Sparses for enlightenment.

Sparses nodded toward them. "Lorcus," he asked. "Are the prisoners secure?"

Lorcus bowed. "Yes, my lord. The captain of the watch is with them."

"Very well." Sparses turned to Tomyra. "My lady, you may ask your question."

"Thank you, my lord." Tomyra arose and walked toward the men, slowly passing along the front rank, looking into their faces. "You men captured the man known as the Lion of Scythia?" she asked.

The men looked at each other in silence.

"You may answer singly or all at once," encouraged Tomyra with a smile.

"Answer the priestess, you fools," snarled Sparses.

"Er, yes, lady," muttered one of them.

Tomyra turned to the one who had spoken. "When you first saw him, did he have a scroll with him?"

"A scroll, lady?"

"A roll of parchment, with writing on it."

The man shrugged, looking around him perplexedly.

Sparses sighed. "The fool does not know what writing is." He strode over to a chest by the wall and threw open the lid. He rummaged inside it and drew out a battered scroll. "Here, Tyrax," he exclaimed, holding it out. "This is a scroll. See the markings on it? That is writing."

"So, Tyrax," asked Tomyra again. "Did the man have a scroll with him when you caught him?"

Tyrax grinned, showing a mouthful of bad teeth. "No, lady. How could he? It was in that chest over there." Several of the men laughed.

Tomyra smiled and waited for the laughter to die down. "Not that scroll, Tyrax, another one." She looked round at the other men. "Anyone else? Did anyone see him with a scroll like that one?"

"No, lady," said one man. "No," said another. A few others shook their heads.

"Could he have hidden it between you attacking and capturing him? Buried perhaps, or under a log?"

Lorcus laughed shortly. "With an arrow in him he was not about to go hiding things."

Tomyra sucked in her breath then forced herself to calmness. "He was wounded?"

Lorcus flashed a look at his leader then nodded. "If he is lucky he will survive until we kill him tomorrow." He laughed as the other men grinned in appreciation.

"What of the others with him? Could they have the scroll?"

"Lady," interposed Sparses impatiently. "My men have denied seeing the scroll. They have their duties to attend to, so if you have finished..."

"A moment more, my lord. What of the others with this man? Could one of them have the scroll?"

"If they did, they have it no longer," rasped Sparses. "The woman is dead and no doubt in the bellies of crows by now, together with anything she may have carried. The men were searched. They carried only weapons." He nodded to Lorcus. "Take your men and return to your duties."

Lorcus saluted and turned toward the entrance, as the hangings were swept aside. A guard stumbled into the room, sword in hand.

"My lord Sparses," the man stammered. "The prisoners! They are escaping!"

Sparses moved fluidly across the intervening space and gripped the guard's tunic in a powerful hand. "What? What do you mean, escaping?"

"My lord," choked the guard. "The captain of the guard sent out for more wine. When we returned with it..."

Sparses shoved the man from him, sending him reeling through the doorway into the storm. "Out!" he screamed at his men. "Out! Find them!" He whirled and grasped the shoulders of two men as they shoved past him. "You two stay here. Guard the priestess closely until I return." He flashed a vicious look at Tomyra then whirled and ran out into the night.

Chapter 19

It was easier than they thought to gain entrance to Zarmet. Parasades, Certes and Prithia approached one of the smaller gates at much the same time as Tomyra was being challenged at the main gate. The ferocity of the storm and the biting wind had driven the token guards into shelters just inside the palisade. Swirling snow and darkness hid the trio as they slipped through the entrance on foot and into the town beyond.

"Where to?" yelled Certes, struggling to make himself heard above the howling wind.

Parasades shrugged. "How in Hades should I know? We will have to ask somebody I suppose." He looked around the deserted streets then put his head down and started pushing himself toward the centre of the town. His cloak cracked and tugged at him, ice rapidly forming on his beard and eyebrows. Certes and Prithia clasped hands to help each other and staggered after him.

They worked their way steadily into the town, searching for some sign of life. The tents along the edges of the streets were securely fastened and the doors of the houses bolted. Glints of light showed through chinks and cracks, reminding them of the warmth that lay so close at hand. At length, they turned down a narrow street and saw an open door. A heavy hide flapped across the entrance, letting shafts of light flash intermittently across the drifts of snow in the street. Raucous laughter and the sound of singing rose and fell on the wind.

Parasades pushed through the entrance with the others close on his heels. The laughter and talk died away as they entered, some twenty pairs of eyes turning to regard the strangers standing by the door. Parasades casually brushed the snow from his cloak and swaggered to a nearby table. Certes followed, guiding Prithia ahead of him. The girl kept her hood over her long hair, hiding her hairless face.

A boy scampered up and set a hide flask on the table, together with three rather dirty wooden cups. The sour smell of koumiss rose from the flask, mingling with the stronger odours of wood smoke and sweat. Parasades tossed the boy a coin that he caught adroitly before trotting back to his station.

Certes unstoppered the flask and poured a generous amount of the milky brown liquid into each cup. He sipped and smacked his lips appreciatively, savouring the sour, slightly nutty taste of the fermented milk. He grinned around at the other drinkers in the room, who turned away and slowly resumed their talking. Prithia took a cup in her slim hand and sipped, keeping her head down and the hood of her cloak tipped forward.

Parasades drank, his eyes drifting over the men around them. He settled on a pair of men in a corner throwing dice. He got up and wandered over, cup in hand. One of the men, a bald overweight man, looked up as Parasades approached. He gave him a cursory examination then turned back to his game. He threw his dice onto the table and cursed. Parasades watched as the other man claimed a few coins.

"Any chance of a few throws myself?"

The fat man turned with a scowl. "And who might you be?" He leaned back against the wall and stared at Parasades. "I have not seen you here before."

"I am from the north, friend. I have just arrived in Zarmet."

"You are not Serratae," stated the other man quietly. "Where in the north?"

"No, indeed, though I hope for a welcome," said Parasades. "My tribe is the Marsae, a small one but with fierce fighters. I heard there was a war brewing in the east and hoped for some sport."

The man shook his head. "Never heard of them." He gave Parasades a considering look. "A warrior, you say? We might have some work for you. I am Sarrates, third deputy of the Black Division. Sit down and talk." He turned back to the fat man. "Make yourself scarce Phallax. Come back when you have some more money to lose."

Phallax flushed and heaved himself to his feet. He flashed Parasades a vicious look and waddled off, shouting for the serving boy. Sarrates gestured to the vacated chair.

"So, what is your name?" asked Sarrates.

"Portos," replied Parasades. He leaned closer to the man. "Is there really a war coming?"

Sarrates nodded. "In the spring. The Massegetae have overthrown their old chief and are ripe for the taking." He held out the dice. "You wanted a few throws? If you have money."

Parasades grinned and pulled out a small purse. He slid a coin into the middle of the table. "Throw then." The man threw, the dice clattering across the uneven wooden surface. "The Massegetae, eh? They have rich lands." Parasades picked up the dice himself. "But I have heard tales they have a new war-leader, a foreigner by all accounts." He threw the dice, shrugged and passed the coin over to Sarrates.

Sarrates smiled and picked up the dice again. "Another throw?" He waited until Parasades produced another coin then tossed the dice down. "Ha, beat that, fellow!" He watched as Parasades shook the dice. "The Greek, you mean? No worry there, he lies captive right here in Zarmet."

Parasades threw. "Mine, I think." He accepted a coin from the other man and slipped it into his purse. "Here, in Zarmet? I would like to see him. A great bear of a man, I am told."

Sarrates snorted. "Not so fierce now. He is tall, but thin, no meat on his bones." He laughed and slapped his belly. "Nice horse, too. A great golden stallion. Naturally he is being kept for Dimurthes." Sarrates grinned and shook his head. "Spoils of war. Anyway, the Greek will die tomorrow even if he survives the night. Again?" Sarrates pushed another coin forward.

Parasades threw and gave a cry of disgust. His opponent cast and pocketed the coins then threw again. "He is wounded? Well, no matter. One barbarian less to kill." Parasades threw and passed over another coin. "I would still like to say I had seen him though."

"Not likely. You might see his stallion or the men captured with him."

"What do I care about his men? Or his horse for that matter. No, I want to see this fearsome Greek."

"Pity. The horse is easy to see. It is on display to the people in the great square. The Greek himself, though? Hmm, well, perhaps you will be lucky. He is to be sacrificed to the Great Goddess at noon tomorrow. As a foreigner yourself you will not be allowed to witness his death, but there may be another way." Sarrates threw the dice again. One fell to the floor and the man bent to pick it up. As he did so, Parasades reached across and quickly changed the low score on one of them to 'star'. Sarrates straightened and threw the single die again then raised his eyebrows. "Star and cup?" he exclaimed. "I thought I had two cups. And another star now!" He laughed and slapped his thigh. "You will have trouble beating that."

Parasades smiled ruefully and scattered the dice. He shook his head and passed over another coin, peering into his purse. "Running short," he commented. "But I can play another. You say there might be a way I can see the barbarian?"

"Be there when he is brought out of his cell. You will at least be able to tell people you saw him. Yes! Stars again!"

"Hardly worth throwing, my friend. So, where is this cell?" Parasades tossed the dice down and sighed. "Not my night it seems."

"Up this street then right and right again. Then cross the great square. You cannot miss it, it is the only stone building in Zarmet."

"I will be there tomorrow. I thank you, Sarrates, though not for taking my money." Parasades laughed. "I will not be eating as well tonight as I thought." He pushed his stool back and stood up.

Sarrates leaned back and nodded in farewell. "Come and see me when you have found lodgings, Portos of the Marsae. I can always use a handy fighter. Ask anyone for directions, the Black Division is renowned."

Parasades nodded and walked away. He tapped Certes on the shoulder. "Come, time is short." The others stood and started for the exit. As they pushed through the throng of men, one grabbed at Prithia's cloak, exclaiming as her hood fell back.

"A pretty one!" the man leered. "Such soft skin, almost like a girl's." He roared with laughter, displaying a mouthful of rotting teeth. "Come, give us a kiss, my pretty." He clutched at Prithia, pulling her close.

Certes rounded on the man, his hand on his sword hilt. Parasades pushed him aside and tapped the leering man on the arm. "I would advise you to let my son alone," he said softly.

"Son?" laughed the man. "Daughter, more like."

"Son," repeated Parasades coolly. "And he has killed more men than you, I am sure. I taught him well."

The man let go of Prithia and turned to face Parasades. "What have we here then? Father of a pretty boy?" He poked Parasades in the chest with a grimy finger.

Parasades instantly reached up with his left hand and bent the man's finger back until it cracked. As the man let out a surprised howl of pain, Parasades stabbed the fingers of his right hand forward into the man's face. The man screamed, clutching his eyes, and staggered back. Parasades grabbed Certes and Prithia and pushed them through the doorway into the night, following on their heels. "Quickly, up the street," he hissed.

They ran into the storm. Behind them they heard shouting and some laughter, the bright light from the tavern door quickly extinguished as the men decided it was not worth the effort to follow them.

Parasades ran up the street and cut to the right between two large houses, followed by Certes and Prithia. He turned right again then burst into an open space and stopped dead. "There." He pointed at a low stone building at the far side of opening. "He is in there." He looked around carefully then led the others across the bare ground until they stood in the lee of the stone building.

"No guards?" said Certes softly. "There must be some. Where are they?"

"Perhaps this is not the right place," commented Prithia, looking around nervously.

"He said it was the only stone building in Zarmet." Parasades looked around. "He said too, his horse was in the great square. I do not see it."

"Does it matter?" asked Certes. "We are here for Nikomayros, not his horse."

Parasades shrugged. "It would be a pity to leave such a good piece of horseflesh for the Serratae. Still, no great matter." He beckoned them along the side of the building. "There will be guards inside but not outside on a night like this. Look for a window, or some other door besides the one opening onto the public square."

They cautiously circumnavigated the building but there was no other way in. Prithia slumped against the icy wall. "What do we do now? We have no idea how many guards are in there."

Certes nodded. "She is right, my lord. It would be foolish to attack an unknown force."

Parasades wrapped his cloak tighter about him and hunkered down out of the wind. "We wait. Tomyra said she would provide a diversion. If she has not by dawn then we go back empty-handed. This was a foolish enterprise from the start."

"My lord," whispered Prithia. "You said you would rescue the lord Nikomayros."

"And so I shall if the gods allow. But I will not throw our lives away," he added. "Now wait."

Time passed slowly, the wind falling and rising, swirling gusts of snow driving into their faces, chilling them. Two men crossed the great square and disappeared into a wooden shed. A broad swathe of yellow light poured out as the door swung open. A horse whinnied loudly and the timbers of the shed crashed as angry hooves connected with wooden walls.

"I think we may have found Nikomayros' horse," whispered Certes.

"Yes, and I think we may have found something else too," Parasades murmured while watching frantic activity across from where they hid.

A man came out of a richly appointed house nearby and disappeared into the gloom. A few minutes later he reappeared, ushering in a woman. Minutes dragged by then the man and woman came out again and vanished into the storm. Shortly after, another man slipped out and ran into the night. At length the sound of muffled feet approached and Parasades arose and flattened himself against the wall.

Three spearmen marched up to the prison building and rapped on the door. A chink of light appeared and words were exchanged, though Parasades was unable to make them out above the howling wind. The men entered the building and the door closed.

"Maybe the guard is changing," said Certes hopefully.

The door opened again and about ten men emerged, huddled in cloaks and grumbling at the cold. They moved in a group across to the house and disappeared inside.

"The three men who entered were not among them," said Parasades. "They must be the replacement guards. We will not have a better opportunity." He drew his sword and strode around the corner to the wooden door. Making sure his companions were ready he rapped on the door with the pommel of his sword.

The door creaked open and a surprised face peered out. "Finished already?" The man stared at the unfamiliar face and the upraised sword. His mouth fell open, a gnawed chicken leg falling from it as he stepped backward croaking an alarm.

Parasades pulled the door open and stepped forward. The croak turned to a choking scream as Parasades plunged the sword into the man's belly and leaped inside the room. Wrenching his blade free he swept his eyes around the room.

Two men squatted by a roaring fire with cups in their hands. Another sat on a bench by a small table, picking over a platter of meats. They looked up in surprise then leapt to their feet and reached for weapons. The man at the table flung a dagger at Parasades and without waiting to see its effect, picked up a stool and hurled himself toward the intruder with a roar of rage.

One of the men by the fire grabbed a spear standing against a wall and lashed out with it, swinging it in an arc as Certes rushed in, only to stumble over the corpse by the door. He landed painfully on his knees, the spear haft whistling just above his head. Before he recovered from the blow, Prithia jumped forward and slashed the man in the arm with her sword. He dropped the spear with a curse and fumbled for the sword at his waist with his other hand. Certes stabbed up from a kneeling position and took the man under the ribcage. The guard fell with a groan and a clatter.

The other guard meantime drew his sword and leapt clear of the fighting. As his companion dropped he stepped forward and brought his blade down sharply on Certes' sword, following it with a numbing kick to the young man's side. Certes rolled sideways, gasping with pain, fighting to retain control of his sword. Prithia pushed between her fallen friend and the guard. She blocked the guard's next blow then the next, but felt herself forced backward. Certes struggled to his feet and awkwardly slashed at the man. The guard pushed Prithia back savagely and turned to face Certes again.

Certes thrust forward, almost overbalancing. The guard swept the blade aside, hacking at Certes then thrust in turn. Certes spun to the side, appalled at how close the sword blade came to his chest. He stepped back again then again as the man's sword probed for his body. The wall thudded into his back as he retreated and the man grinned, redoubling his efforts. Certes flicked his eyes desperately toward Prithia, only to see her still standing dazed in the far corner. Certes blocked another blow and slashed back. The man contemptuously knocked his sword aside and moved forward, his blade glinting as it came for Certes' life. The realisation of his death crowded in upon the young man as the point of the guard's sword seemed to creep toward him.

The guard staggered, his eyes widening and his mouth opened, the sword wavering downward. A glint of metal appeared in the centre of his chest, growing rapidly. Blood sprayed out, spattering Certes' face. The man dropped to his knees, his face working in agony then fell forward, a spear quivering between his shoulder blades. Certes looked up to see Prithia staring wide-eyed from the far side of the room.

A crash whipped the young man's attention from the girl, to see Parasades rolling around the floor with a howling man. Parasades' teeth sank into the man's hand and his own right hand, gripping his dagger, hammered at the man's side. Certes stepped forward, his sword at the ready, looking for an opening. The man's cries abruptly choked off and blood soaked his tunic.

Parasades rolled off the man and clambered to his feet. He hawked and spat, smearing the blood running into his beard with the back of his hand, a hand already red with blood. He kicked the corpse and turned to look at his companions. Nodding at them, he grinned and pointed to the other door. "Prithia, keep watch! Certes, get that door open. Hurry!" he barked out.

Prithia immediately shut the swinging outer door, putting her eye to a chink. Certes hauled back on the bolt of the inner door, pushing it open. He stepped into the darkened cell and almost fell as a fist glanced off his head. He gave a shout of surprise and grappled with the man. Parasades grabbed a burning brand and thrust it high above him as he entered, his sword ready.

"Certes, Timon, stop fighting." He watched with a smile on his face as both men slowly came to a realisation of the identity of their opponent. "We do not have time for this." His eyes swept the bare cell. "Agarus," he nodded, "...and, oh fornicating demons, what has happened to him?" Parasades dropped to his knees beside the unconscious body of Nikometros lying on the frozen earth floor of the cell. His hands probed the torn clothing on the Macedonian's chest, feeling the fever-hot wound and his icy limbs.

Nikometros stirred and groaned. "Tomyra?" he muttered. "Is that you?"

"We cannot take him," stated Parasades, rising to his feet. "He would hold us back." He gestured to Timon and Agarus. "Come, if we hurry we may yet get out of here."

Timon stared back at Parasades. "I'm not leaving without him."

"Nor I," affirmed Agarus. "It would be better to die than to leave my lord alone among these savages."

Parasades cursed long and loud. "Look at him," he pleaded. "Feel his wound. He is dead, or will be by morning whether he stays or comes."

"I will not leave him," growled Timon.

"He cannot even walk. How are we supposed to evade a town full of warriors if we have to literally drag him along?"

"I can carry him."

"I am sure you can, Timon," agreed Parasades. "But can you run and fight at the same time? If you fall behind, I will leave you. I will not put these others in my care at risk."

"I can help carry him," said Certes quietly. "No man deserves to die in a stone cell. If he must die, let him do so in freedom, with his friends around him."

"I cannot carry him, but give me a weapon and I will fight to the death for my lord." Agarus drew himself up and stared into Parasades' blood-smeared face.

"You are all mad," muttered Parasades. "And I can see I will die with you."

"My lord!" came an urgent whisper from the next room. "Two men are coming this way!"

Parasades flashed a look at the men standing around the cell. "Decide now, and follow." He ran out into the guardroom and eased his eye to a crack in the outer door. He grunted and tightened his grip on his sword. "When they reach the door," he whispered. "Take the one on the right, Prithia." The girl nodded and hefted a spear in her hand. Parasades glanced behind him and groaned when he saw Timon cradling the unconscious Nikometros in his burly arms. Agarus had armed himself with a spear and stood behind Timon. Certes hovered uncertainly between Timon and the door.

Footsteps crunched in the snow outside the door. A gruff voice called out. "Open, we have wine!"

Parasades nodded and threw his shoulder against the door, slamming it open. He leapt out, his sword stabbing. The man he targeted fell without a sound, the wineskins in his hands bursting purple over the snow. The man on the right took the full force of the door and staggered backward and fell, the spear launched by Prithia whistling over his head. With a cry he scrambled to his feet and ran, screaming a warning.

Chapter 20

Bithyia stared at the entrance of the hut, the hangings still swinging from the violent egress of Sparses and his men. She walked over to her mistress and leaned close to her, whispering.

"My lady, we must leave immediately." She edged around so that the two guards standing by the doorway could not see her face. "We can take these men." Her hand moved slowly to her sword hilt.

Tomyra held Bithyia's gaze then barely shook her head. "We leave, but not with bloodshed unless we are forced to it," she answered softly. Aloud, she spoke matter-of-factly to Sarmatia. "Gather some food together, Sarmatia. We shall retire for the night." Tomyra pushed past Bithyia and walked casually up to one of the guards. "Take us to our lodgings, please."

"Eh?" The guard looked perplexed and turned to his companion. The other man raised his eyebrows. "What do you mean? You are to wait here for my lord Sparses."

"Take us to our lodgings," repeated Tomyra, with a gentle smile on her face. "You heard the lord Sparses. He agreed to arrange accommodations for my ladies and me. Please take us there now."

"He said nothing about that." The guard shook his head and gripped his spear harder. "We were to wait here and guard you. Guard you means preventing you from escaping."

"What need have we of escape, soldier?" asked Tomyra. "What man of the Serratae would lift a hand to a priestess of the Great Goddess? Sparses said for you to guard us and protect us until his return. With armed men apparently roaming Zarmet, he could be gone some while." She smiled encouragingly at the other man. "I wish merely to rest in some greater comfort than that provided by this place."

The other guard shuffled his feet. "Yes, lady. But he said nothing..."

"You will be able to guard us just as well in our lodgings." Tomyra leaned close to the guard and dropped her voice. "To tell the truth I would feel safer with you guarding me in a place further from the prison. If that Greek knew I was here he might seek to avenge himself."

"I suppose we could," said one of the guards slowly. "But where would we take her?"

The other man thought for a moment. "The merchant Urax has rooms. They could wait there until we find out what is to happen." The guard looked sourly at the three women. "I suppose these others," he indicated Bithyia and Sarmatia, "Must come too?" He nodded, reaching a decision. "Very well then, lady. You will accompany us."

The man lifted one of the sputtering torches from the iron stand near the entrance and swept it back and forth to fan the flames before tossing it to his companion. Taking another torch, he pulled the entrance hangings back and motioned for the women to follow him out into the night.

Outside, the guard waited until his companion joined him then pointed across the open space. He shielded his torch from the gusting storm and shouted above the creak of ropes and the flapping of hide tents. "Over there!

Keep close and do not become separated." The man turned away, lowering his head into the driving snow.

Tomyra grabbed his arm. "My horse?" she inquired. "I must have my bags. Where is it?"

"It will be brought to you. Come." The man pulled his arm free and walked away.

"No." Tomyra stopped, Bithyia and Sarmatia standing firmly beside her. She waited until the man returned, cursing under his breath. "I have need of my bags. No doubt my companions also need theirs. We will wait here until you fetch our horses."

"Follow me mistress and I will send for your bags once we have reached your accommodation."

"I wish for our horses too. I would make certain they are well stabled and fed." Tomyra stared at the guard adamantly. "I will not move from here until you show some respect for me as priestess. Fetch our horses."

The guard cursed out loud and looked around for some help in the situation. The other man looked down, avoiding his companion's eyes. After a few moments the guard slammed the butt of his spear into the frozen ground in exasperation. "Fetch their horses, Anapses," he grated. "And hurry, before we freeze."

The other man ran off around the side of the house, disappearing into the swirling blackness. Tomyra waited, her cloak wrapped warmly about her as she studied the armed man in front of her. She noted the growing unease in the man, the way he continually looked toward the lights of the town. Distant shouts came to them fitfully on the gusting storm. The guard's hands clenched his spear and several times he started to lower the point toward them, only to draw it back once more. When his eyes moved across the women, Tomyra was sure they held suspicion.

"Be ready," Tomyra murmured.

The horses were almost on them by the time they heard them, the deepening snow muffling the sound of their hooves. The man walked backward awkwardly, holding the reins of the beasts as they pulled and plunged, shying from the wavering torch brand in the man's hand.

"Help him, Sarmatia," called out Tomyra. As the girl hurried across to grasp the reins, she nudged Bithyia and nodded at the man Anapses. "Take him," she said flatly.

In a fluid movement, Tomyra stepped across the intervening space toward the spearman. The man's mouth opened in surprise and his spear started its downward course toward the advancing woman. Tomyra stepped inside the spear, pushing it to one side and thrusting her other arm forward. A glint of metal winked in the light from the torch held in the man's other hand for a moment then was gone as the dagger in Tomyra's hand buried itself in his throat.

The guard gave a gurgling cry as he staggered back, dropping both spear and brand. His hands scrabbled ineffectually at his sword. Blood gushed out into his beard and spattered the snow. Tomyra closed with the man and wrenched her dagger free before dragging the sharp blade across the man's throat. Blood sprayed into Tomyra's face then the man collapsed into a heap at her feet. She bent and wiped her blade on his clothing, rubbing a handful of clean snow quickly across her face.

Bithyia called from the darkness behind her. "My lady, it is done."

Tomyra turned and grasped the reins of her horse as Bithyia and Sarmatia ran up to her. She grasped the mane and swung up onto its back. She waited, calming the animal as it shied at the body on the ground. When the other women were mounted she nodded and smiled grimly. "Now if we can just find our way out of Zarmet."

Bithyia looked around at the swirling storm, the muffled lights of the town and the flickering motion of hand-held torches moving through the darkness toward them. "I think we had best be leaving, my lady...but which way?"

"The wind is from the west, so...this way." Tomyra kicked her horse into a reluctant walk into the teeth of the gale, moving across the open space. Rapidly the three women faded into the night, leaving behind them the first flares of alarm as the bodies of the two guards were discovered.

Sarmatia and Bithyia closed with Tomyra, urging their horses closer together. There was a measure of protection from the storm once they entered the warren of streets leading off the central open meeting place. The wind gusted and swirled, deflected by a building then howling in fury down a narrow lane, lifting the snow and driving it in a stinging blast. The streets were dark and silent, save for the wind and the cracking and flapping of hides and cloth window coverings.

The riders stopped at the junction of two larger streets. Tomyra peered down each then pointed up the left one. "That way, I think." She turned her head and coaxed it over the icy ground, staying in the lee of the buildings.

The street twisted and curved, smaller lanes and alleys branching off in all directions. The darkness surrounded them, leaving them to move in a cold shell of driving white, the horses picking their way carefully over the uneven surface.

"A light, my lady," yelled Sarmatia, over the noise of the storm. "There, to our left."

Tomyra squinted into the darkness, wiping the icy crust from her eyelids. "Yes, I see it. Let us hope it is the gatehouse." She turned her horse toward the light.

The glow ahead of them came stronger and resolved into several points of light, moving and swaying. The buildings fell away on either side and

Tomyra pulled her horse to a frantic stop in the open ground. "We are back where we started," she groaned.

A shout came from the lights in front of her then a challenge, and the muffled sound of running feet. Tomyra pulled her horse round sharply, colliding with Sarmatia's mare. The horses squealed and shied before being kicked into motion again. The three women pushed their horses back into the dark streets, rapidly leaving the running men behind.

They pushed their mounts as fast as they dared in the icy conditions, back the way they came. Arriving at the junction again, Bithyia urged her horse down the right-hand fork, followed by the others.

"Do you remember the wind direction when we came in?" screamed Tomyra, above the howl of the wind.

"I think it was behind and to the left," yelled Bithyia in reply.

"No," shouted Sarmatia, "It...It was behind us at the start, but to our left only w...when we came out in the open space."

"I think you are right, Sarmatia, about the direction when we arrived." Tomyra pulled her horse to a halt and rescued her cloak that had flapped free. "But I remember it more to our right when we came to the gate."

Sarmatia shrugged, her teeth chattering. "S...so, wh...which way now?"

"Into the wind, but keep it to our left."

Bithyia nodded and led the way down the street. She turned into a side street that rapidly narrowed, forcing them into single file. The wind direction swirled and gusted, blowing first one direction then abruptly changing. They struggled on for several more minutes before pulling their horses into the shelter of a large wooden house.

"This is madness, my lady," said Bithyia, pitching her voice over the moaning of the wind. "We could wander all night."

Tomyra nodded. "We have no option, we must ask for directions."

"Ask?" Sarmatia gaped at her mistress. "They will kill us or at the very least raise the alarm."

"Maybe. We must pray the Mother is with us." Tomyra slid off her horse and, handing the reins to Sarmatia, strode to the door of the wooden house. She pounded on the door with her fist, waited a few moments, and pounded again. Movements came from within the structure, followed by a muffled voice.

"Who is it?"

"Your priestess, Rhynna. Open in the name of the Mother."

Silence followed then voices could be heard in argument. Tomyra pounded on the door again. "Open. The Mother demands it."

The door rattled and then creaked open a hand width. A bearded face peered out.

"My lady, what is it you...? You are not Rhynna." The man started to close the door again.

"Of course I am not Rhynna, you fool," screamed Tomyra at the closing door. "I am sent by Rhynna. She requires your urgent assistance."

The door creaked open again. The man peered out suspiciously, eyeing the two other women standing by the horses. "How do I know you are sent by the priestess?"

Tomyra groaned softly then dug into the soft hide bag at her waist. She pulled out Atrullia's short carved staff and held it out. "Do you recognise this? It is my authority as a priestess."

The man's eyes widened and he bobbed his head, opening the door wider. "Yes, my lady. All men recognise the authority of Mount Mora." He backed away from the door, waving his arm toward the inside of the room. "Enter, my lady. Be at ease."

"Wait here with the horses, Sarmatia. I will be quick." Tomyra stepped over the threshold and threw back the hood of her cloak. Bithyia entered after her, darting her eyes quickly around the room. Her hand rested on her short sword beneath her cloak.

"Please, my lady, will you take refreshment? My wife and I..."

Tomyra forced a smile. "Thank you, no. I merely wish directions."

The man scratched his hairy chest and looked at his wife. The woman, a short fat woman of indeterminate age, shrugged and tucked her long skirts about her. She scowled at Bithyia, standing by the open door, and at the drifts of snow blowing in, but said nothing.

"Directions, lady?" The man looked puzzled. "Directions to where?"

"The south gate."

"Why would you want to go there?" asked the man, darting another look at his wife.

"Surely it is enough that your priestess wishes it," burst out Bithyia. "What business is it of yours?"

"Gently, Bithyia," interposed Tomyra. Turning back to the man, she smiled. "I must get back to Mount Mora at once. The Mother demands it of me and I must obey. Will you help me?"

The man nodded glumly and scratched his chest again. "Go down the street of the cloth merchants then turn into the street of the tanners. You will see it ahead of you."

Tomyra shook her head. "I am a stranger here; else I would not need your help. Will you show me?"

The old woman clucked her tongue in annoyance and stamped off across the room, pushing some hangings aside and disappearing from view. The man looked after her then picked up a felt jacket from a bench near the door. He shrugged into it, and sat to pull on leather boots. "Very well, my lady." He grabbed a cloak and pushed past Bithyia into the frigid night.

The man waited until the women were mounted once more then beckoned and led the way down the street. After a while he turned into an alley that looked no different from any other and pointed. "See, the lights of the guard house."

Tomyra peered into the night and nodded. She smiled down at the man. "May the Mother guard you and bless you in these troubled times." The man flashed a quick smile, bobbed his head and disappeared into the night.

Tomyra walked her horse on toward the gate, the others on either side of her. The snow muffled the sound of the horse's hooves, the wind carrying away the soft creak of their leather tack. The distance to the guardhouse closed steadily, the light of the fires growing stronger. Voices rose and fell on the wind gusts, the guards laughing and joking as they huddled in their shelter. The women came alongside the guardhouse, staring straight ahead, afraid that even to look at the guards would draw their attention. They rode past, into the darkness between the earthen ramparts, to the gate. It was closed.

Chapter 21

"Out! Hurry!" yelled Parasades. He ran a few paces and spun on his heel in the deepening snow, searching for signs of trouble, his sword at the ready. He ground his teeth at the slowness with which Timon staggered from the prison, Nikometros cradled protectively in his arms. Certes and Prithia stood ready, with swords drawn on either side of the door and Agarus hovered behind them, a long spear gripped in his gnarled hands.

"Which way?" grunted Timon. "I cannot remember the way we were brought in."

Parasades pointed across the open area to the darkness of the town. "Over there." He ran back to the others. "I will lead the way. Timon, follow with your master. Agarus, stay with him and keep up. Certes, you and Prithia are our rearguard. Move fast." He stared at Timon for a moment, noting the lolling blond head of Nikometros then shrugged and turned away. "Come." He ran off into the night.

The others followed more slowly, limited by the pace of the burdened Timon. They were barely in the middle of the open space when shouts from behind made Timon stop and turn his head. A flare of light cast long shadows over the frozen ground. The door of the house beside the prison gaped wide and men streamed from the building, some bearing blazing torches and all armed.

Timon cursed softly and turned away, staggering forward again. Certes moved up alongside him, urging him onward. Prithia turned and backed after them, her sword ready for anything. Agarus snarled savagely and levelled his spear, backing away alongside her.

The wind picked up as they stumbled across the open area, out of the meagre protection afforded by the buildings around the prison. Swirling snow obliterated the glow of the torches around the prison door, though not before Prithia caught a glimpse of several men following their tracks in the snow.

"They follow," she called urgently. Prithia turned and sprinted to catch up with Certes and Timon. "They found our tracks." Her voice shook and she glanced back at the blackness behind.

Certes gripped her arm firmly. "Courage, Prithia. They are only Serratae after all." He grinned at her then tapped Timon on the shoulder. "Let me take him, Timon." He held out his sword to the old Macedonian. "Here, you might enjoy using this."

Timon gave Certes a sharp look then set Nikometros' feet down, still supporting the half-conscious man. When Certes relieved him of the weight, he grasped the proffered sword. "With pleasure," he growled. Certes bent and hoisted Nikometros over his shoulder and broke into a slow run.

Timon turned to Prithia and Agarus as he joined them. The moving glow behind them resolved into two running men with torches held high. The warriors came on with eyes cast down, following the rapidly disappearing tracks in the snow. Timon pointed left then right, sending Prithia and Agarus off a few paces. "This will indeed be a pleasure," he snarled.

The Serratae burst out of the snowstorm and saw the three figures waiting for them. The first man abruptly stopped then staggered forward when the man behind collided with him. Agarus threw his spear. It missed the first man as he fell but impaled the second man in the leg. He fell back with a scream, dropping his torch, which sizzled and went out in the deep drifts. Timon ran forward and chopped down at the warrior struggling to get up. The blade caught the man on the side of the head, dropping him again.

Prithia joined him and pursued the man wounded by Agarus' spear. She stabbed at him and missed, the man scrabbling backward, bellowing at the top of his voice. Other figures appeared out of the darkness, their torches held high and their swords glinting. Prithia engaged one with a clash of metal, forcing the man back. Timon took on another one, hacking and slashing, battering down the man's defences.

The man slipped in the snow and Timon gave a roar of triumph and plunged his sword into the man's chest, twisting it as the man went down. He turned to see Prithia fighting furiously, blocking and parrying the warrior's blows. Timon's feet crunched in the snow as he ran up behind them. The warrior turned his head quickly and Prithia saw her advantage. She stepped forward, gripped the man's wrist and pushed it aside a fraction, pivoting as she closed with him, her sword slicing across his belly. The man gave an agonised cry and dropped his sword, clutching his abdomen. Timon ran him through from behind. The pristine white snow was now splattered with blood.

Timon nodded to Prithia and pointed back. "There will be others here soon enough and we can't cover this up." They turned and ran. Agarus limped out of the night beside them, clutching his spear in one hand and a bloody sword in the other.

"Got the fornicator with his own sword," he grinned. Timon grinned back and slapped him on the shoulder before resuming his headlong run after Certes and Parasades.

Certes leaned against a rough wooden building on the far side of the great square, catching his breath. His burden, Nikometros, stood slumped against him, conscious now but muttering incoherently.

Three figures loomed out of the darkness and Certes tensed then let his sword point fall as he recognised his companions. "What in Hades kept you?" he rasped.

"Our right to leave was disputed," grinned Timon. "We persuaded them to reconsider." He looked around. "Where is Parasades?"

Certes cursed softly. "I don't know. He wasn't here when I arrived."

"I'm here," came a laconic voice from the darkness. A figure moved out of the night, followed by a towering shadow. "I could not, in conscience, leave this beast behind."

The great form of Nikometros' stallion loomed out of the night. It caught sight of Nikometros slumped against Certes and pushed its muzzle into the man's face, snorting softly. Nikometros struggled to focus his eyes, a painful smile on his face.

"Diomede," he whispered.

The great golden stallion rubbed his soft nose against Nikometros, blowing warm air into his face and neck.

"Excellent thought, my lord," grinned Certes. "Nikomayros can ride." He and Timon hoisted Nikometros onto Diomede's broad back and steadied him. Nikometros wound his fingers into the stallion's white mane and slumped forward over its neck.

Parasades grunted. "Try and keep up." He turned and taking the bridle, pulled the stallion down the alley, not looking back to see if the others followed. Timon ran alongside, keeping a hand on his friend, steadying him. Agarus joined him, supporting his master on the other side. Certes touched Prithia on the arm and peered at her in the dark, feeling her tremble beneath his touch.

"Be strong, Prithia. We all have need of each other."

The girl nodded. "I am all right," she said shakily. "I have never killed a man before tonight."

Certes stared at her for a moment then nodded. He put his arm around her and coaxed her into the alley.

The others were waiting at the far end of the lane. Parasades pointed to his right. "The gate lies that way," he said. "To get to it we must pass the street of taverns. We risk all if we are stopped, but it would take too long to find our way around. We will be pursued."

"We cannot delay," said Timon. "Niko will die unless we can get him to shelter soon."

"I agree, my lord." Certes nodded vigorously. "We must take the risk and go by the route we know."

"God-cursed fools," breathed Parasades, his words whipped away by the gale. "You will get us all killed for the sake of a man already dying. Come then," he raised his voice. "Keep close together. We are a party of friends returning to our lodging after a drinking party. At least our friend here," he indicated Nikometros leaning heavily on Diomede's neck, "Already looks the part." He sheathed his sword, wrapped his cloak tighter about him and plodded off down the street.

The others hurried after Parasades then fell into a tight grouping behind him, their weapons out of sight except for Agarus' spear, which he used as a staff. They reached the end of the street and turned into another, narrower one.

Certes, who was bringing up the rear, tapped Parasades on the shoulder and shouted hoarsely at him. "Men, coming up behind us." They stopped and listened. Behind them, in the night, footsteps crunched in the snow and presently the glow of torch brands became apparent.

"We must run," hissed Prithia, taking a few steps forward.

Parasades grabbed her arm. "Too late. Quick! To the side of the street, against the buildings. Hurry!" He pulled her across and thrust her down into the snow against a wooden wall. The others hurried after them, pulling the stallion into the deepest shadows. Timon put his hand on the horse's muzzle, calming it. They reached the building just as the first of their pursuers came into sight.

A dozen men loped steadily down the street, the faces of all but the leading man cowled against the storm. The man in front darted looks to either side as he ran, a burning brand sputtering in his left hand and a sword in his right. His gaze swept over the obscure huddled shapes by the building and moved on. For the barest fraction of a moment he faltered and half turned his head back then he resumed his running.

The running men turned down the street of taverns and darkness returned. Parasades held up a hand to restrain Certes from moving out from the wall. Minutes passed, with the only sound the howling of the wind. Impenetrable blackness enveloped them. At last, Parasades relaxed. "Let us go. Keep to the sides of the street." He moved on cautiously.

They reached the street of taverns and peered down it. No longer was the street in darkness and quiet. Several doors let out slabs of golden light as men hurried to and fro between the buildings. Arguments and shouting erupted from one or two of the taverns, together with some coarse laughter.

Parasades nodded and moved on down the street, keeping to the shadows as much as possible, his cloak and hood obscuring his features. The others followed on his heels, with Nikometros muttering on the stallion's back. They passed an open door, the light from within briefly illuminating them then another. A man hurrying across the street nearly collided with them, muttered an apology and entered one of the taverns.

They reached the midpoint of the street, where shafts of light broke unevenly across the whole expanse. Keeping their heads low they strode across the lit area, trying to appear unhurried. Several faces looked up as they passed and one man called after them. Without pausing, they walked on.

A man's voice came again, more insistent. Parasades cursed softly and turned. "Carry on to the end of the street then left," he muttered to Timon, handing him the reins of the horse. "Wait for me there." He walked back to the man standing in the street, just beyond the well of light thrown by the open tavern door. "What is the problem?" he asked casually.

The man peered around Parasades at the figures disappearing into the night. "Who are you and what is your business?" asked the man. "Have you not heard that everyone is ordered off the streets until they are found?"

Parasades nodded, standing half turned away, his face in deep shadow. "Aye, something about an escape I was told. My companions and I were out drinking. We are in a hurry to get back to our lodgings."

The man looked at Parasades, his brow wrinkling in suspicion. "Who are you? You are not Serratae."

"Indeed, I am not," replied Parasades. "I am Marsae, from the north. I have lodgings with my companions." He turned a waved toward the now-empty street. "I must catch up with them or I will not be able to find my way."

"Portos? Of the Marsae?" A rough voice spoke from the doorway. Parasades turned and saw Sarrates, third deputy of the Black Division, leaning against the doorpost, with arms folded across his wide chest. "What are you doing here?"

"Ah, Sarrates," Parasades slowly replied, edging more into the shadows. "I found lodgings with men of the city and I have been out drinking with them. I was returning home but this fellow accosted me."

"I am glad you found lodging so easily, my friend. But I thought you said you had no money to eat, let alone to drink?"

Parasades snorted with laughter. "My hosts were generous."

Sarrates lifted an eyebrow. "Indeed? May I know their names? Such generosity is worth cultivating."

Parasades hesitated, searching for a Serratae name. "Sparses...Sparses was one, I think. I cannot remember the names of his companions."

"Sparses? Deputy to our chief?" Sarrates pushed himself away from the doorpost and stepped out into the snow. "He was here but a few moments ago with his men. He did not say he had been drinking."

Parasades shrugged, edging away from the Serratae warrior. "Perhaps it was another name or another man of the same name. Either way I must hurry after him or else I will lose my way."

"Why did he not wait for you?" Sarrates moved after Parasades. "Portos. Stand still. Something is not right here." He drew his sword with a rasp. "You." He turned to the other man standing nearby. "Tell my men in there," he jerked his thumb toward the open doorway, "to get out here immediately."

Parasades leapt at the bystander, his sword whispering from its sheath. The man uttered a brief startled cry before staggering back with blood pouring from his chest. Parasades spun back toward the doorway and barely managed to block a slash from Sarrates' sword. The force of the blow forced him down on one knee. He rolled to the side, narrowly avoiding another hack downward. He scrambled to his feet and readied himself, crouching.

Sarrates circled, his gaze probing into his opponent's face. "Get out here!" he yelled. "Tamates, Rortaxes, to me!"

The howl of the wind blew his words away into the night. The shaft of light from the tavern entrance remained unsullied by the figures of reinforcements. Parasades feinted, then again. Sarrates' blade weaved slowly in front of him, the warrior not reacting to Parasades' ploys. Parasades tried again and Sarrates moved forward fluidly, within his opponent's guard, his sword stabbing. The blade sliced cleanly through Parasades' tunic, barely missing the flesh. Parasades quickly stepped back, his free hand checking the damage.

Sarrates grinned and advanced. "Come, Portos of the Marsae. You said your people were fierce fighters. Show me." He lunged but his blade was deflected at the last moment. He continued to circle, his sword point weaving hypnotically in front of him.

Parasades parried the man's blow and flicked a glance down the dark street. He saw nobody and barely jerked his eyes back again in time to fling his body aside from another fluid rush. Parasades collided heavily with the wall of the building. A sword swept by his face and bit into the wood with a resounding crash, sending splinters flying. A shouted query came from inside the tavern and the sound of tables and chairs being pushed back carried to the fighters.

Sarrates grinned again. Parasades flung his sword at the other man. Sarrates lifted his own sword to block the missile, involuntarily ducking as he did so. Parasades leapt forward and rammed his head into the warrior's face.

Sarrates howled with agony and staggered back to fall in the snow. Parasades glanced at the shapes of men appearing in the doorway then swept up his fallen sword and took to his heels down the street.

Shouts rose behind him but Parasades did not look back. He ran until, rounding the corner at the end of the street, a blast of wind knocked him off his feet and into a drift of snow. He lay, his chest heaving, as icy air stabbed its way into his lungs. Groaning deeply, Parasades rolled over onto his knees. Hands grasped his arms and hauled him upright. He struggled weakly, trying to wrest himself from the clutches of his captors.

"For love of the Mother, Parasades," spoke a voice from the darkness. "We found the gate. Even now, Timon and Agarus are carrying their lord to safety. Come, we must hurry."

Certes began pulling him along. Parasades sheathed his sword and stumbled after him, trying to brush the caked ice and snow from his cloak. "You came back for me? Good man." Then, after a pause, he added, "You met with no opposition?"

"We met none, though we saw armed searchers twice," replied Certes. The sound of shouts and running feet induced them to shrink back into deep shadows, the weak flickering light and dancing shadows of handheld brands hiding more than they illuminated. They watched the men disappear down the street. "Truly the gods are with us tonight, my lord."

"More like the Goddess," reprimanded Prithia sharply.

"You could be right, girl, though it seems to me that She does not command the weather," Parasades gruffly responded. "Still, remind me to make proper sacrifices when we return home."

They met no further search parties inside Zarmet. The three fugitives slipped through the gate and into the wide expanse of empty land sloping down to the river. Ahead of them, they could just make out the footprints of the others, now rapidly disappearing in driving snow. They hurried down to the riverbank. The river itself, still ice free despite intense cold, stood out as a dark slash across the snowdrifts. In the dim light, reflected back off the ghostly white landscape, Parasades could just make out the dark clump of willow scrub where they earlier hid their horses.

Stumbling through deep snow, they reached the refuge. The wind dropped within the shelter of scrub brush where the horses stood in a tight group, their breath blowing white about them. Huddled close to the horses were Timon and Agarus, desperately trying to glean some warmth from the shivering animals.

Timon looked up as the others stumbled into the refuge. His dark eyes were screwed up in misery. "We must find shelter," he demanded. "Niko will die unless we can get him warm."

"There is a herder's hut an hour's ride from here," said Certes. "The others will meet us there." He gripped the old Macedonian's shoulder. "If the gods allow, we shall yet save his life."

Chapter 22

Bithyia dismounted and ran her hands over the heavy timbers of the gate. She pushed against the solid crossbeam holding the halves of the gate shut. It stirred, the wood creaking loudly as it did so.

"Help me, Sarmatia, quickly!" said Bithyia.

Sarmatia joined her sister Owl at the gate and heaved at the crossbeam. It shifted slightly then refused to move any further. "Something is stopping it." She peered into the darkness of the gate well then moved along the crossbeam, searching with her hands. "Ah!" she cried. "Here, a rope holds it."

Sarmatia struggled with the rope then stood aside to let Bithyia wrestle with the frozen knot around the beam. "It is too tight," complained Bithyia, her voice breaking with frustration. "We will never get it undone."

"So cut the rope and be done with it," said Tomyra impatiently.

"Of course. I should have thought of that, my lady." Bithyia drew her dagger and began to saw at the thick hemp rope.

Tomyra looked back toward the guardhouse, edging her mare deeper into the shadows by the gate. Beyond the subdued babble from the guards she heard another noise rising above the whine of the wind. She strained to hear and at last made out the sound of feet and hoarse angry shouts. Doors slammed further up the street and light flared, cutting through the storm.

"Hurry!" Tomyra called softly to Bithyia. "They are searching this street."

Sarmatia ran to Tomyra's side, holding the reins of the other horses and peered toward the guardhouse. The torches of the searchers grew brighter and the noise of their coming grew louder. Tomyra and Sarmatia drew back into the shadows and drew their swords. Bithyia stopped sawing through the tough rope and joined them.

"Show them your priestess stick, my lady," whispered Sarmatia. "They will respect that and let us go."

"Unless they have discovered the two guards we killed," replied Bithyia dryly. "I do not imagine they will forgive murder easily."

"Hush. Wait and listen."

The three women strained to hear the shouted voices as they carried through the storm's noise. The hubbub from the guardhouse died away and figures appeared at the entrance, lifting aloft blazing brands to discover the reason for the outcry. Two men ran out of the night with weapons drawn and accosted the guards. Tomyra recognised one of the men as Sparses. She stepped forward, to the very edge of the shadow to listen.

"Ho, fellow! Why all the noise?" The guard suddenly realised who stood before him and gulped. "My...my lord Sparses. We did not expect you..."

"Has anyone passed this way tonight?"

"Th...this way, my lord?" stammered the guard. "Er, yes, my lord. We let in several farmers just before nightfall and..."

"Has anyone left Zarmet, you fool? I am not interested in farmers entering."

"Left Zarmet, my lord? Who would want to leave tonight?" He smiled weakly and drew his cloak about him.

"The so-called priestess and her murdering bitches. You let them in, Myres. Have you let them out?"

Myres paled and stepped back, shaking his head vigorously. "No. No, my lord. No one has passed this way. The gate is barred and secure. See for yourself my lord."

Tomyra hissed softly and drew back as far as she could, holding the muzzle of her mare to keep it calm and quiet. "Great Goddess, protect us," she whispered.

Sparses glanced toward the gate hidden in the shadows of the gate well. He grunted. "Leave two men here and bring the rest of your squad. I will search the whole of Zarmet if I must. The Greek prisoner has escaped and that Massegetae whore posing as a priestess helped him do so, somehow." He turned on his heel and strode back to his men who were noisily searching houses further up the street, their shouts mingling with the loud objections of the house owners.

Myres told two men to watch the gate and led the rest of his guard squad up the street at a run. Gradually the sound of the search died as the men worked their way into the next street. The two guards stood at the doorway of the guardhouse with drawn weapons and looked alertly about them.

Tomyra and her two warrior maidens watched silently from the shadows by the gate, their spirits sinking. Time dragged on, the women shifting uncomfortably and the horses becoming increasingly restless.

"We must do something," whispered Bithyia. "Sarmatia and I could rush them."

"Across open ground?" Tomyra shook her head. "You would die without accomplishing anything." She pointed to the far side of the gate. "See, the shadows run along the wall and to those buildings. One of us could hide within those shadows and create a diversion."

Sarmatia tapped Tomyra's wrist. "Forgive me, my lady, but we would have to cross the open space in front of the gate to reach it. And what about the horses? The shadows will not hide them."

"What sort of diversion?" asked Bithyia. "They will not hear any noise we could make, and if they did, would just think it was the searchers returning."

Tomyra thought. "Fire. It will have to be fire."

Bithyia nodded. "I have iron and flint, my lady. I will find something to light."

"Go with the Goddess, Bithyia." Tomyra bent and scrabbled in the snow at her feet for a few moments then held out a rock to Sarmatia. "Your arm is good. Throw this past the guards at that building."

Sarmatia took the rock and hefted it, her teeth glinting in the faint light. "Be ready, Bithyia." She threw, the stone thumping against wood. The guard's heads turned and one stepped out of the doorway and moved a few paces down the street. Bithyia flitted forward, across the lighted open snow and into the deep shadow along the outer wall.

"We must prepare," said Tomyra softly. She took her dagger out and felt her way to the gate crossbeam and the half-severed rope. "Watch, and tell me if they hear me." She started sawing at the frozen hemp fibres.

Sarmatia peered out of the darkness at the two guards leaning against the doorposts of the guardhouse, talking quietly to each other. The sound of the sawing behind her was loud but the noise of the storm effectively drowned it. At last the sawing stopped and Sarmatia crept back to see why.

"It is cut," whispered Tomyra. She tested the weight of the beam, pushing upward with both hands. "Two of us should be able to remove it." She restrained Sarmatia as the young woman pressed forward. "Not yet. It will make a noise when it falls and besides, the force of the wind is likely to throw the gate wide. We must wait for Bithyia."

Time passed again. The guards stamped their feet and slapped their arms together as the chill bit through their leathers. Gradually they eased back inside the comparative warmth of the guardhouse, though always one of them remained staring out toward the gate.

"What is keeping her?" whispered Sarmatia. "Perhaps something has gone wrong."

"We cannot leave without her. One of us must go and find her."

Sarmatia nodded and dropped to her knees, searching for another rock. "I will go, my lady." She rose and hefted the rock in her hand, choosing her target.

A faint glimmer of light tickled Tomyra's eyes. She blinked and stared into the night. "Wait." Tomyra put out a restraining hand just as Sarmatia drew her arm back to throw.

"What is it?"

"Over there, to the right. Do you see it?"

"No, my lady. What do you see?"

"I thought I saw...yes, there!" Tomyra's voice rose excitedly and she stepped back hurriedly. "See, a light," she went on in a loud whisper. "Flames. I am sure of it."

The glow grew stronger, building in strength and size until flames could be seen ascending in a column through the falling snow. The sound of crackling and spitting timbers could be heard over the wind and billows of smoke poured over the town.

"Why do they not see it?" hissed Sarmatia. "Are they blind? And deaf?"

"Throw the rock, Sarmatia. Bring them out."

Sarmatia threw, the stone cracking against the guardhouse. The man in the doorway swore, ducking back reflexively before jumping out, his weapon lifted. He swept his eyes round and saw the conflagration. For a moment he stood paralysed, his sword drooping. Then he gave a great shout and pointed as his fellow guard ran out to join him. They raced off down the street, shouting at the tops of their voices, hammering on doors. Lights appeared as the inhabitants of the surrounding streets woke to their peril. People poured out into the streets.

Tomyra turned back to the gate. "Quickly. Help me lift the beam."

The two women struggled to raise the thick piece of timber barring the gate. It moved sideways, slipping through the angled supports then, just as it seemed as if it would fall free, it jammed. Sarmatia swore colourfully and pounded her fist on the beam.

Tomyra gave a small cry of anguish and slumped against the gate. Snow crunched behind her and she turned in alarm. Bithyia ran across the open space and collapsed against the timbers. She grinned at the other women, wiping her soot-grimed face with a blackened hand.

"By the Mother, that fire spread fast," she panted. "I didn't think I was going to get out of there."

Tomyra looked round at the scene in the town. The fire was rapidly spreading, jumping from one house to another, sending a ruddy glow over the whole area. Already the shadows around the gate were vanishing, leaving the three women exposed to the gaze of any who might look in their direction. "Speaking of which, dear friend," smiled Tomyra. "That fire will also bring people upon us. We must leave immediately."

"Then let us do so." Bithyia looked up at the gate and the jammed crossbeam. "Ah!" She studied it for a moment then nodded. "My lady, if you and Sarmatia would pull down on the beam at this end, I will try to free it here."

Tomyra took a grip on the rough wood and put her weight on it, swinging her legs off the ground. Beside her Sarmatia pulled and heaved downward, grunting with exertion. Bithyia walked to the other end and drew her sword. She swung it experimentally; measuring the distance then set her feet firmly, grinding them through the snow. Her sword arced in an underhand blow, biting deep into the underside of the beam. Splinters of wood showered the ground as she wrestled the blade free. She swung again, the chunk of her blow echoing around the gate well. Again, and the beam shivered and moved upward a finger width.

Bithyia stepped back and caught her breath. "Once more, I think." She nodded at the others. "All your weight now." She swept her sword up again and the beam shook then with a squeal of wood, lifted from the bracket and toppled. Sarmatia fell clear but Tomyra landed awkwardly, feeling a flare of pain in her ankle. She limped to the side and was promptly knocked off her feet as the wind caught the gate and slammed it open.

The horses, standing calmly to one side throughout, their reins tied to a stanchion, bucked and shied as the gate flew open. Bithyia sheathed her sword and hurried over, calming the nervous animals. Sarmatia bent over and lifted Tomyra to her feet, supporting her as the priestess gave a small cry of pain.

"You are hurt, my lady?"

"My ankle. It will pass. Help me onto my horse, Sarmatia. We must go."

Tomyra scrambled onto her mare with a helping push. She swung the horse's head around and looked back down the street toward the blazing conflagration as her companions mounted. The three women on their horses were in full view. A shout rose from the men milling around in the street and faces turned toward the gate.

"Time to leave," said Tomyra grimly. She wheeled her horse and urged it through the gate, followed by Bithyia and Sarmatia. They increased their speed as they moved out onto the drifted road, angling down to the river. Their flickering shadows sped ahead of them. Something hit Bithyia gently on the back then another fell into the snow alongside her. She looked down in surprise at the arrow sticking out of the snow then back at the town. Men crowded round the open gate, backlit by the mounting flames of burning

Zarmet. A number had armed themselves with bows. Several archers shot arrows at them while she watched but the arrows fell short. She grinned and moved on.

They clattered down to the shallow river, the darkness falling in around them once more as the town receded. They slowed, the horses picking their way carefully over the icy rocks. As they clambered up the inclined road on the far side of the river, Tomyra turned to her companions. "Pray that the others have reached safety too. We will find them in the herder's hut."

"And if they are not there?" asked Sarmatia quietly.

"Then we wait for them." Tomyra dug her uninjured heel into her mare's flanks and it broke into a reluctant trot.

Chapter 23

The herder's hut lay off the main road leading south from Zarmet, its rough stone walls and thatched roof mellowed by the blown drifts of snow against its walls. Tomyra reined her horse in and looked across the pristine white fields to the hut, searching for signs of occupancy. Nothing stirred in the darkness, the hut itself squatting cold and lonely in the open plain. She looked up at the sky and smiled to see great rents in the cloud cover, the stars blazing through in the icy air. The snow died as she watched, the only flakes being the myriad of fallen particles driven by the strong wind. Faint patches of moonlight flitted across the landscape, dancing between the shredding clouds.

"Smoke!" Tomyra cried. "They are here." She pointed across at the hut and the faint smudge of white wood smoke oozing through the thatched roof. She nudged her mare into motion, off the road. The animal stumbled across the open ground, sinking up to its fetlocks in the drifting snow.

Bithyia and Sarmatia followed. Bithyia leaned across to the other woman and whispered, "At least someone is here. Be prepared." She drew her sword and laid it across the horse blanket in front of her.

The trio crunched through the snow to the front of the hut and halted there, looking at the shut door. A faint glimmer of light shone through a crack but apart from that there was no sign of life. Sarmatia slid off her horse and rapped on the door with the hilt of her sword.

A few moments passed then the door opened a crack and a face appeared, shadowed by the light behind it.

"Who is it?" asked a coarse voice in the Serratae tongue.

"Travellers," said Sarmatia. "We ask shelter."

Tomyra hesitated then spoke quietly, "Tomyra."

The face disappeared abruptly and the door slammed open. A flood of light poured across the snow and the three riders. A burly figure filled the doorway, staring at the two women on horseback.

"Bithyia!" roared Timon. He strode out and plucked the woman off her horse, enveloping her in his strong arms. She laughed delightedly and flung her arms about him, kissing his face.

"My Timon," she cried. "At last!"

Other figures now crowded out of the hut. Prithia ran over to Sarmatia and hugged her then started dragging her toward the hut, chattering. Certes and Parasades looked at each other then helped Tomyra from her horse.

"My lady," said Parasades simply. "I am overjoyed to see you safe."

"Thank you, Parasades," replied Tomyra, her eyes drifting toward the door. "Niko? Where is he? Is his wound serious?"

Certes looked away, busying himself gathering up the reins of the horses. Parasades coughed and stood aside. "See for yourself, my lady. I fear his spirit stands ready to cross the barrier."

"No. That cannot be. The Mother..."

Timon disengaged himself from Bithyia's enthusiastic welcome and turned toward Tomyra, his features showing his concern. "My lady..." His voice cracked.

Tomyra paled and limped into the hut, supported by Bithyia. Timon and Parasades followed them in while Certes led the horses around the hut to a solidly built lean-to. Here he fed and groomed them, stabling them with the others.

Tomyra stopped inside the hut and looked round. The small one-room structure was crowded. A roaring fire blazed in a stone circle close to the middle of the room, sending pulses of heat across her. Despite this, the stone walls of the hut remained damp and cold, thin blasts of icy air whistling through chinks in the stonework. A rickety table stood in one corner, with the remains of a meal scattered over it. Stools sat or lay beside the table on the bare earth floor. Crouched beside the table, fumbling through bags and bundles, an old woman clothed in rags looked up at her.

Beside the woman sat the man who had opened the door to them. He looked away as Tomyra met his eyes, an expression of fear on his face. On the far side of the fire lay a pile of ragged skins and fleeces, arranged as a bed in the warmth. On it lay a still figure, covered with a torn wool blanket.

"Niko!" Tomyra ran over to the bed and dropped to her knees beside it. She scanned his pallid face and arms with a look of horror, her hands reaching out then drawing back in indecision. At last, she rested her hands lightly on his brow, his cheeks then took his right hand. The skin was icy. She ran her hands up his arm and across his throat, feeling a searing heat beneath his skin. Trembling, she drew back the old blanket and gasped at the wound in his left shoulder.

The ragged wound stretched from his collarbone to his armpit, a raging red rupture that seemed to pulse with its own heat. The skin across his chest and down his arm was inflamed, streaked with red blotches. A thin yellow fluid dripped from the wound, soaking the cloth beneath him. Within the fluid were streaks of creamy white pus. Tomyra bent over her lover, her nose wrinkling involuntarily.

"How long ago did this happen?" she whispered.

Timon came and crouched beside her. "About a day ago. The fever struck quickly and he has been like this since nightfall."

Tomyra probed the wound gently with her fingers. "What caused it?"

"An arrow. The head broke off and remained in him till an hour ago. We removed it when we reached this hut."

"An arrow should not do this," said Tomyra, her voice trembling. "Not within a day."

"The Serratae have been known to put things on their arrows," commented Parasades. "They sometimes smear faeces on the point. They did with this one." He shrugged. "I always thought it was designed to insult their foes. Why should it cause a wound to go bad?"

"Can you help him, lady?" asked Timon quietly.

Tomyra stared down at Nikometros, watching his chest rise and fall with his shallow, shaky breaths. "If we were home," she said dully. "Here I have none of my herbs."

"Can't you find them?" Timon turned and gripped Tomyra by her shoulder, shaking her. "By the Mother you hold so dear, do something! Find the herbs! He'll die if you don't help him."

Bithyia leapt forward to restrain Timon. Prithia cried out in horror. "My lord, you must not lay hands on the priestess."

"Hush, Prithia." Tomyra gently disengaged Timon's hand and stood up. "He's right, though." She looked around her at the squalid hut and its contents. Her gaze ran over the old woman and the bags and bundles scattered around her. She walked over and knelt by the old woman. "Do you worship the Mother?" she asked gently.

The woman's gnarled face looked up suspiciously. She nodded slowly, hunkering back into her ragged clothes.

"I am Tomyra, a priestess of the Mother. What is your name?"

The old woman stared at Tomyra then at the other people in the room.

"It's true," growled Parasades in the Serratae dialect. "She speaks for the Mother."

The old woman bobbed her head. "Millpa. H...how may I serve?" she quavered.

"You have medicines, Millpa? Or the herbs to prepare them?" asked Tomyra. "I need cattle-tongue, Mother's cloak and hoof-plant if you have them, also..."

Millpa shook her head. "I do not know this cattle-tongue."

"It grows in moist places. It has a ring of leaves at the base, soft like a cow's tongue, and a tall spike of drooping yellow flowers."

"Ah! You mean deer's lip. I know it." The old woman nodded and gave Tomyra a gap-toothed smile. "It's good for wounds."

"Also, I need Polemonion and myrtle," went on Tomyra. "You have them?"

Millpa shrugged. "Possibly Polemonion." She got up and hobbled over to a small wooden chest in a corner of the room. She lifted it with a groan and staggered back to the fire with it. Timon stepped forward to help her, grabbing the box. The old woman screeched and wrestled the box away from him then kicked him in the shins. "Keep your hands to yourself," she mumbled, turning her back on him and sitting herself down by the fire, the box in her lap.

Timon retreated in confusion. He sat down and rubbed his leg. Bithyia came over with a laugh and put her arm around him. Together they watched the old woman as she dug into her box of herbs.

"So," muttered Millpa, sorting through bundles of dried herbs tied with twine and small cloth bags. "We have Mother's cloak, yes indeed. And Polemonion. Also...where is it? Ah, here...deer's lip. What else, lady?"

"Hoofplant, myrtle, gead would be useful."

"No hoofplant. We are too far from the woods," whined Millpa. "I cannot move well these days." Timon snorted softly, earning him a leer from the old woman. "I have a few leaves of myrtle," she said, holding up a withered branch, "But no gead unless I know it by another name."

"May I see?" asked Tomyra, holding out her hand toward the herb box.

Millpa pursed her lips in thought then nodded, holding out the box. Prithia leaned forward eagerly, peering at the contents. "Not you!" screeched the old woman, snatching the box back, "Only her."

Tomyra smiled, waving Prithia away. "No one shall see but myself, Millpa." She knelt and lifted dried bundles to the side, digging down through the dusty bags. A rich and heady scent of summer herbs filled the small room. Tomyra nodded to herself as she picked out bags, opening them and peering at their contents. Some she sniffed, with a few she crushed a leaf between her fingers and tasted it carefully. Others she rejected with a look of distaste. At last she leaned back on her heels, her eyes on the small pile of dried vegetation beside the box. "It will do," she muttered. "It will have to do."

Tomyra turned to the group standing about her. "Agarus," she said crisply. "Boil two pans of water. Make sure the pans are clean and that you use clean water." She picked out three bags and tossed them at Bithyia. "Grind these very fine then add a few drops of water when Agarus has boiled it. Make a thick paste." Tomyra weighed another bag carefully then passed it to Prithia. "Poppy gum. Pick out only as much as will sit on the tip of your dagger. Dissolve it in some wine."

The old man, Millpa's husband, snorted softly. "Wine? You think I have wine? Look around you. Does it look like I have wine?"

"Watch your tongue, old man," growled Parasades.

"Never mind him," quavered Millpa. "Trorax is a fool, but a kindly fool."

"My apologies," said Tomyra softly. "I didn't mean to draw attention to your poverty." She turned to Parasades. "You have a coin?" she asked.

Parasades grunted and unfastened a small leather bag from his waist. He weighed it in his hand then passed it over. Tomyra picked out a silver coin and handed it to the man.

"We are grateful for your hospitality and wish to pay you for your trouble."

Trorax gaped and held the coin in the light, examining it closely. He grinned and slipped the coin into his tunic. "I have some koumiss, lady, and a little ale. Will they do?"

"Thank you, Trorax. Perhaps the ale."

The old man rummaged around beneath a pile of old skins and pulled out a flask made from badly cured goatskin. The contents sloshed as he gave it to Parasades. The warrior unstoppered the flask and sniffed.

"Gods! What an evil odour." Parasades wrinkled his nose in disgust. He passed it to Prithia with a grimace.

While the herbs and water were being prepared, Tomyra went back to Nikometros' side and held his cold hands, rubbing them to get some warmth into them. She dabbed a cloth at the weeping wound, wiping away the pus and clear yellow fluid. A few small fragments of wood and cloth came with it. "We must clean the wound," she murmured.

Agarus poured some of the hot water into a rough earthenware pot and brought it to the bedside. Tomyra picked out a few wilted stems of soapwort and whisked them in the water. A scanty lather scummed the surface of the pot. She dipped a rag into the hot water and began cleaning away the debris from the ragged wound. Nikometros stirred and cried out, feebly trying to push her hand away.

"Is this going to take long?" asked Parasades.

"As long as it takes," replied Tomyra calmly. "Unless his wound is treated, he'll die."

"Treated or not, he'll die if the Serratae find us," growled Parasades. "And the rest of us with him. We must be away from here before dawn."

"Perhaps not," grinned Sarmatia. "They'll have their hands full putting out the fire."

"Fool!" snarled Parasades. "We've just shamed and insulted the Serratae as a whole and Sparses in particular. Do you really think they'll just sit at home and allow us to show their weakness to the world?"

"We'll leave by dawn, my lord." Tomyra held out her hands for the now boiling water. "Boil up these bear-dock leaves, Agarus, and add some wild garlic. When the water changes colour add these rags and take it off the heat. Let them steep."

"Those rags, lady?" queried Timon. "I can probably find cleaner ones. The healers in Macedon swear by cleanliness."

"Dirt doesn't matter, Timon, as long as the herbs are there to counteract the evil in the wound. Besides, this way we have all the elements working to cure him. We have earth on the rags, the water heated by fire, and open to the air. Now, Prithia, you have the poppy?"

Prithia handed the small bowl of ale to Tomyra. She propped Nikometros up and dribbled the ale into his mouth. He gagged and spat, moving his head aside. She wiped his mouth and poured more in, until Nikometros swallowed, and again. "Good. Bithyia, you have the paste?"

Tomyra removed the hot rags from the bear-dock and garlic steep, wrung them out and smeared them liberally with the herb paste. She laid the rags gently over the wound and pressed them down firmly, working the paste deep into the ragged flesh. Nikometros groaned and thrashed weakly for a few moments before collapsing back onto the bed, soaked in sweat. Tomyra bound the poultice in place with strips of cleaner rag then pulled the blanket up over him.

"Will he be all right, my lady?" asked Prithia.

"It is in the hands of the Goddess."

"How long before we can move him?" queried Timon.

"He should rest until he regains consciousness," replied Tomyra. "It would be better if we could remain here for a few days."

"Impossible!" Parasades pushed away from where he had been looking out through a gap in the door. "The moon is setting and dawn will not be far behind. Search parties will arrive here before the sun is halfway to noon. We must be far from here by then."

"We won't be able to travel fast, my lord," commented Certes. "Can we outrun them?"

"No." Parasades slammed a fist into his open hand. "We cannot outrun them, therefore we must evade them."

Timon nodded. "Something tells me you have a plan already."

Parasades squatted and picked up a piece of wood. Clearing the ground of debris he quickly drew a few lines on the dirt floor. "Zarmet is here, with the river here." He drew a wavy line near the town. Our goal is to reach the Oxus River about five days travel to the east." He stretched his hand out. "Over here. Now, tracking us will be easy. Snow covers the ground and the storm has stopped. Our trail will be obvious even to a blind man, so how do we do it?" He sat back on his heels and grinned at his audience.

Timon shrugged and looked at Bithyia. The others looked equally nonplussed.

"We will leave tracks in the snow, so we must avoid the snow." Parasades chuckled. "Come, it is not hard. Where is there no snow?"

Prithia stared at the rough sketch on the ground. "The river," she said slowly.

"Excellent. And how do we use the river?"

"We ride along it, in the water..." went on Prithia.

"...until we reach the Oxus," completed Certes excitedly.

Parasades groaned. "Five days ride to the east, I said. Even if the river went all the way, they would find us within a day or two. No, we ride upstream, to the west."

Timon furrowed his brow in thought. "West? We would add many stadia to our already long journey."

"Half a day, maybe. No more. Then we angle north around Zarmet and head for the northern tribes along the Oxus. Perhaps seven days. The Serratae will expect us to head for home the shortest way. With luck we can evade their pursuit altogether."

Tomyra thought it through and nodded. "It may work. I cannot think of a more reasonable plan." She looked around at the others enquiringly. The others looked away or shook their heads. "Then we shall follow your plan, my lord."

Parasades got to his feet and brushed the dirt from his clothes. "Good. We leave within the hour." He beckoned to Agarus. "Find the largest hide sack among this pile of rubbish." He kicked the bags and bundles lying on the floor. We shall put our Greek in it and sling him on his horse. Counterbalance him with what food you can find."

Agarus nodded and immediately started throwing the bags aside looking for a sack, or at least a good-sized hide with which to make one. The others started gathering their things together.

"My lord," said Certes quietly. "What about them?" He jerked a thumb at Trorax and Millpa, sitting quietly by the fire. Parasades turned and stared at them. Trorax flinched and pulled back. "Won't they tell our plans?"

Parasades nodded slowly and drew his dagger. "I should have considered that. Still, no matter. I'll silence them now." He stepped rapidly across the room toward the old man and woman.

Trorax let out a screech of alarm and bolted toward the door where he struggled ineffectually in Certes' grip. His wife made a dive for the pile of skins and burrowed into them, wailing.

Tomyra leapt up from where she knelt by the bed and rapidly interposed herself. She grabbed Parasades by the arm. "No, my lord. You will not do this."

Parasades glanced at Tomyra then at the struggling man near the door. "If we do not silence them, we may as well wait here for our pursuers."

"No. We do not kill if there is another way."

Parasades shook his arm free and glared at Tomyra. "These people are dogs of the Serratae," he hissed. "What other way is there?"

"I speak for the Mother Goddess." Tomyra drew herself up and tossed back her hair. "Would you openly defy the Mother?" She waited a few moments for Parasades to reply then continued. "No, I thought not. These people also worship the Mother. If I bind them with an oath on the Great Goddess, will you let them live?"

Parasades sighed and sheathed his dagger. "Do as you see fit, Tomyra." He turned away, shaking his head. "You will tie my hands once too often, woman."

Tomyra smiled and turned to her women. "Bithyia, please fetch Millpa out from under those skins before she suffocates. Certes, bring Trorax over here...gently. We have an oath to administer."

Chapter 24

Eight riders splashed through the ford below the town of Zarmet in the darkness between moonset and dawn. Wind blew briskly from the north, carrying the stench of wood ash and smoke to their nostrils. A fine flurry of snow, whipped up by the wind from the drifts that blanketed the landscape stung the legs of their horses. Above, the last remnants of storm cloud shredded in the wind, revealing a blaze of stars strewn across the cold heavens.

Silently, the lead rider pointed up-river, motioning for the others to precede him. He counted off the riders as they passed, the horses treading carefully over the water-worn stones in the shallows. Certes led, his young face eagerly searching the riverbanks ahead of him, his dark eyes glinting in the starlight. Close beside him rode Prithia, her eyes fixed on the young warrior. Next rode Tomyra and Sarmatia, abreast, and bundled against the cold. On their heels came Bithyia, torn between her duty to her mistress and her lover, Timon. The object of her passion followed, carefully leading the stallion Diomede, who appeared rider less, though burdened by two huge hide sacks, counterbalanced and secured by leather thongs. Agarus, the crippled

Massegetae, rode beside the burdened stallion, his eyes never leaving the right-hand bundle, nor the pale face of Nikometros curled within it.

Parasades nodded, watching the horses pick their way up the shingle banks and through the shallow water, keeping well clear of any snowdrifts. He glanced across at the low hill that rose from the river to the north. Hidden still by the night, the town of Zarmet revealed its presence by the fires still burning within it. A pall of smoke hid the top of the hill, lying close like cloud though the wind scattered rifts and rents of grey toward the river.

Dawn spread a thin coating of crimson on the eastern horizon. Parasades removed a ripped and torn tunic from a bag across his horse's back and tossed it into the river, watching as it tumbled and sank, caught by the current flowing swiftly over the rocks. He turned his horse and splashed his way upstream.

Agarus waited for him by a gravel bank. He looked at the Massegetae war chief suspiciously. "What was that you threw away?"

Parasades grunted and moved his horse past. "Your lord's old tunic." He rode on, feeling the query in the other man's silence. "The Serratae will know we took the river route soon enough. If they find the Greek's tunic down river, with luck they'll think we went that way. It may buy us time."

The river wound slowly west and north, curving around the bluff dominated by Zarmet. The riders pushed through the shallow water riffling over gravel banks and boulder beaches, wading through the deeper pools. Parasades turned and looked back toward the ford as the other members of his group rode around a bend in the river. Far back he glimpsed a large body of horsemen splashing through the river, heading south. He waited motionless until the last of the Serratae vanished from view before wheeling his horse and riding off upriver.

The sun rose, sending coruscations of light dancing across the unbroken fields of white along the riverbanks. The landscape was deserted save for a handful of deer that broke for the woods, startled by the presence of humans and horses in the riverbed. Parasades drew in great breaths of the crystal-sharp air, blowing billows of white over his horse's neck. He grinned. "By all the gods," he muttered, "It is a great day to be alive." He kicked his horse into motion again, splashing through the river shallows as he caught up then passed, the other riders.

"We must leave the river." Parasades pointed to the north, across the open plains of snow. "If we follow the river any further we only lengthen our journey."

Certes watched from the riverbank as the other riders urged their mounts up the steep sides, floundering in the snowdrifts. He frowned at the great slashes their passage wrought on the pristine whiteness. "It will be obvious we left the river here," he commented.

"We have to leave somewhere and wherever we do, we leave signs," replied Parasades calmly. "If the gods are with us...and those fornicating peasants have not betrayed us," he growled. "We may yet be far from here before they pick up our trail."

Parasades forced his horse up the slope and into the lead. He led the small group over the plains to the north, slowly angling their route to the east as the day wore on. They stopped at noon in the cover of a small copse of leafless alder to rest the horses. They dismounted and stretched aching muscles.

Tomyra immediately went to attend to Nikometros. With Timon and Agarus, she extricated the unconscious man from the leather bag and gently laid him on calfskin on the frozen ground. She bent over the wound in his shoulder, peeling back the poultice and probing gently with her fingers. "Still inflamed and hot," Tomyra murmured. Leaning close, she sniffed at the wound. "It does not putrefy at least. The herbs are working."

Timon knelt beside them, his great body hunched and his face downcast. "Why has he not woken then? He barely clings to life." A slim hand pressed down on his shoulder and he looked up.

"He will recover, my lord," said Bithyia softly, as Timon's hand found hers. "The Mother has a purpose for this man and will guard him from death."

After resettling Nikometros in his great leather bag they resumed their journey, eating small quantities of coarse bread and baked roots as they rode. The sun dropped slowly through the afternoon sky, their shadows now lengthening before them as they turned to the eastern horizon.

Parasades, who had been leading the file of riders along the low outcrops and ridges of the undulating plains, now led them down into the shallow valleys. Within minutes, their pace slowed as the horses stumbled and floundered their way through deeper snow.

"This is pointless," grumbled Prithia. "We must go back to the tops again."

"We are visible on the skyline," observed Parasades.

"Then why have we been on them all day?" asked Certes. "Have we not always been visible?"

Parasades reined in his horse and swivelled round to face the others. "Had there been any to see, yes. Think for a moment." He looked around the little group. "It appears you scared those peasants properly, my lady." He nodded at Tomyra. "However, by now the Serratae will know we didn't go downstream. They'll have found no trace of us. So they'll search upstream. How long before they find our trail?"

Agarus glanced over his shoulder. "Then they follow us already?"

Parasades nodded. "If they must follow our trail they move almost as slowly. If they caught sight of us..." He left his conclusion unanswered. Instead, he turned and urged his horse onward.

"But if they follow faster then shouldn't we make as good time as possible?" called out Timon.

Parasades called back over his shoulder. "Maybe. On the other hand, if we can remain undiscovered till nightfall we may make the relative safety of the pine forests. They'll find it harder to track us through them."

Timon grunted and shrugged. He kicked at his horse's side, forcing the unwilling animal to push into the deep snow. Slowly, the others followed, stumbling in the tracks forged by the lead horses.

Fear of discovery grew as the sun sank. Agarus, at the tail of the little column, remained watchful, his head continually turning to scan the valley behind them and the valley rims on either side. His shoulders ached from the tension in his muscles, braced against the momentary expectation of the killing arrow, or the shout of triumph from their pursuers. Not until the gloom of approaching night hid the horses in front of him, reducing them to no more than vague silhouettes, did he dare to relax.

When the moon rose ahead of them, glowing on the eastern horizon and casting a pearly light over the frozen landscape, Parasades led the group out of the valley and onto the ridges again. The pace picked up as the horses made better going in the exposed grass where wind had scoured the surface of snow.

By midnight the horses had slowed once more despite the easier going. Exhaustion, following on the tension of the past days made the riders reel, fighting to retain control over animals that sought only to stop and rest. Certes drummed his heels into the sides of his unwilling mount, forcing it to catch up with Parasades.

"My lord, we must rest," he called out urgently.

Parasades turned a bleary face toward the younger man, the harsh shadows of the moonlight hiding his expression. He reined in his horse and pointed back toward the southwest. "Look," he said softly.

Certes turned and scrutinised the pale landscape, the hillocks and valleys disappearing into the silvery distance like a roiling ocean. "What am I looking for?"

"To the right a bit, at the horizon. Do you see it?"

"A star?" said Certes doubtfully. "A reddish star...or a torch."

The other horses trudged up and stopped around Certes and Parasades. Their heads drooped and their breath came noisily in great white clouds. Timon swivelled round to stare back in the direction the other men looked. After a moment he stiffened and leaned closer to Bithyia, his arm outstretched.

"So, they come at last," he breathed.

"How far away are they, Timon?" asked Bithyia.

Timon shrugged. "Two hours, maybe three. See, another torch. They are close enough that we can detect their motion." He swung round on Parasades. "How far to these pine forests of yours?"

Parasades bared his teeth in a grimace. "Two hours, maybe three." He chuckled grimly. "It will be a close-run thing. We have made better time than I dared hope but they have been faster than I feared." He spurred his horse into reluctant motion again, the others falling into a straggling line behind him.

Tomyra stared back at the far-off brands, twinkling in the icy air. Sarmatia plucked at her mistress' cloak, urging her onward. Tomyra sighed and turned away. "They will not take me again," she whispered. "Neither I nor my lord shall be at their mercy." She fingered her dagger beneath her cloak.

The first fingers of the pine forest crept toward them as the moon set behind the moving points of light to the southwest. Black shadows sprawled out from the stygian blackness ahead of them, starkly contrasted with the white glimmer from the snowfields. Parasades turned off the ridge toward a finger of trees.

The light reflected off the snow faltered and died beneath the first of the trees, the dense, overhanging branches laden with ice but the ground beneath bare except for a covering of pine needles. The horse's hooves crunched softly in the needles as they passed from the lit stage of the plains into the shadowed depths of the forest. Behind them the torches of their Serratae pursuers burned brightly, flickering and moving in their relentless pursuit.

Less than an hour passed before the first of the warriors rode into the fringes of the forest. Light glinted redly off drawn weapons as the riders spread out, searching the ground for a sign of their quarry's passing. Anger flared and men shouted; their rage boiling over into frustrated blows before the leader reasserted his control. The men spread out into a line, hundreds of feet across. They moved slowly into the forest, scanning the ground, alert for the presence of their enemies.

Chapter 25

The Oxus River flowed swiftly over its bed of boulders, the waters swollen by the unseasonably warm rains of the past few days. The snowstorms and cold clear interludes passed with a southerly turn in the winds, the white covering of the plains and forests disappearing almost overnight. The frozen earth turned muddy, making the footing treacherous in the approaches to the river valley. Winter would no doubt reassert itself, but for now the warmth in the air spoke of the turning of the seasons.

Parasades led his small troupe of riders down from the forests on the western bank just before sunset. He agonised over this decision, weighing the advantages. Cross in daylight and any enemy nearby would see them: cross at night and risk losing people in the dark and swollen waters. In the end he compromised, hurrying them down to the water's edge with the last of the day. Though they had not seen any clear sign of their pursuers since the previous day, Parasades felt their proximity and feared discovery while they were most vulnerable.

Positioning himself at the rear of the group, Parasades watched as Certes coaxed his horse into the boisterous current. The animal was reluctant, shying at the swirling and foaming turbulence. With a firm hand, the young man eased his horse forward until the water broke over its withers. At his urging, the horse plunged forward and began swimming, angling across the flow. Behind him, her hands gripping the reins of her horse tightly, rode Prithia. Sarmatia and Bithyia rode in close attendance of their mistress Tomyra, followed by Agarus and Timon. Timon led Diomede with the great hide bag containing the unconscious body of Nikometros.

Timon coaxed his horse into the shallows, the icy water leaping around its legs. Diomede followed reluctantly.

"Will somebody let me out of this bag?" quavered a weak voice.

Timon drew rein and turned so abruptly he slipped from his horse's back. He splashed through the water until he reached the hide bag, now moving feebly in the weak light. Ripping open the restraining cords, Timon grinned incredulously.

"Niko! By the gods, you've awoken!"

Nikometros struggled to focus his bleary eyes, fighting his way out of the constricting bag. "Timon? Where are we? What's happened?" He peered out at the rushing river and the circle of grinning riders. "Gods, I feel as weak as a newborn pup," he muttered.

A look of concern flitted across Timon's face. "Perhaps you should rest some more, Niko."

Nikometros shook his head gingerly. "No, I need to be up." He stared at the river for a long moment. "We're crossing it?" he asked. "Then I should be on my horse, not slung over one. Help me out, Timon."

For the river crossing, Nikometros sat swaying on the back of Timon's horse, tightly gripping the old soldier's tunic. Diomede, allowing no other person on his back, followed Timon's horse closely, nuzzling his master's leg.

Parasades plunged into the river at the rear. He half expected at least one of the groups to be swept away by the current and steeled himself for the necessary rescue. The river was wide at this point, deep and slow moving on the surface, though terrifying in its power. The horses battled to prevent themselves being swept downriver, the icy water, augmented by snow melt, sapping their strength.

The first of the riders stumbled into the shallows on the eastern bank. Certes looked back in the twilight to wave the others onward when a tree trunk, waterlogged and heavy, nudged Agarus' horse. The animal screamed and plunged away, upsetting its rider who disappeared into the frigid water. Timon looked around, hesitated then made a vague movement to follow the unfortunate man. He felt Nikometros clutching at him as his horse changed course and Timon recollected his primary duty, reluctantly leaving Agarus to his fate.

The crippled Massegetae rose to the surface, sputtering and coughing, only to sink again. The current swept him away from the horses, toward the swifter motion of the rapids. Parasades dug his heels into his horse's sides and pulled the animal's head downriver.

Agarus broke the surface again as the water burst over a submerged shingle bank, erupting over large boulders in a flurry of spray. Parasades' horse stumbled after him, surging through the water toward the drowning man. Parasades bent low and swept his arm through the water, his fingers gripping and pulling. His fingers hooked in the man's long black hair, Parasades urged his horse toward the bank, pulling Agarus behind him. Within minutes, the two reached a low gravel bank, the horse standing shivering as Parasades dropped the limp man and stretched, flexing his cramped fingers.

Upstream, the others in the group came splashing through the river's edge toward him.

"By the gods, my lord," laughed Certes, "I thought we had lost the cripple." He looked down at the sodden supine form on the gravel with some concern. "Is he alive?" he asked.

Parasades slipped off his horse and with a grunt, turned Agarus over with the toe of his boot. The man coughed and groaned, making weak pawing motions at the air. "He'll live," snorted Parasades. He turned away and surveyed the dark rim of the eastern valley wall. "We must find shelter."

Sarmatia and Prithia dismounted and helped Agarus to his feet. The man coughed and sneezed then blew his nose loudly on his sleeve. "Those fornicating river demons had me," he muttered. "I could feel them dragging me down."

"Well, you're safe from them now," said Prithia primly. "And you have my lord Parasades to thank for saving you."

Agarus felt his scalp gingerly, smoothing his soaked hair. "Pity he couldn't do it without tearing my hair off." He spat to one side and cleared his throat. "My thanks, lord," he called.

Parasades waved a hand dismissively as he consulted with Certes and Timon. Nikometros slid to the ground and, with considerable effort, hauled himself up onto Diomede again. Parasades pointed a way up the steep slopes. Remounting, he moved away from the river, his horse slipping on the slick ground. With difficulty, they emerged onto the plains above the river.

Parasades grunted with satisfaction and pointed at a low hill standing black against the night sky. "Wolf's Rock." He grinned and turned to Timon and Tomyra. "Six days across trackless enemy territory, pursued and harried, and I still lead you exactly where I intended."

"And just where is that?" asked Timon sourly.

"The southern border of the Jartai, my friend. Now I have a decision to make but I will hear your counsel first."

"What gives you the right to decide?" grated Timon. "My lord Nikometros outranks you among the Massegetae, he was blood-brother to their chief, and war-leader."

Nikometros reached over and tugged at Timon's arm. "Hush, Timon," he chided weakly. "Parasades knows what he's doing."

"Indeed," commented Parasades. "In case you hadn't noticed, Timon, we're not among the Massegetae. The chief is dead," he inclined his head toward Tomyra. "Forgive me, lady...severing all ties of brotherhood and Areipithes leads the tribe as king and war-leader. Your lord is a leader without a people."

"Not quite," said Tomyra softly. "As long as I live there will be those who will follow his lead."

"Just so," added Bithyia. Sarmatia, Prithia and Agarus nodded, murmuring support. Certes looked uncomfortable, avoiding Prithia's questioning eyes.

"Where do your loyalties lie, my lord?" asked Tomyra quietly. "Perhaps it is time for you to declare them."

Parasades sat silently, staring out over the plains. "I?" he said slowly. "You question my loyalty?" He stirred and swung round suddenly, making his horse whinny and sidestep. "My loyalty lies with the People. With our chief dead and his power usurped I will fight to restore law to the Massegetae." He guided his horse close to Tomyra. "What I won't do," he said, "Is hand over my people to an outlander, a foreigner." His hand gripped his sword hilt and he half drew the blade. "I would kill him now rather than allow that."

Timon gave a roar of rage and swung his horse around, interposing his bulk between Parasades and Nikometros. Nikometros called weakly for calm but his voice was lost among the confusion. The others milled uncertainly and Tomyra had to raise her voice to be heard.

"It won't come to that, my lord," she called. "The Mother has a purpose for him but it lies elsewhere. The People are not his concern." She pushed closer, forcing her way between the two men. "Do you hear me? His fate lies elsewhere."

Parasades glared at Timon and the reeling figure of Nikometros on his great stallion. He rammed his sword back into its sheath. "Very well," he snarled. "I shall hold you...and the Mother, to that promise."

Silence fell over the small group of riders, and into the silence intruded a calm voice.

"Please make no sudden moves. My men have arrows aimed at every one of you."

For a long moment no one moved. Then with a flurry of motion Timon leapt from his horse, bearing Nikometros to the ground, shielding him with his body. His sword rasped from its sheath and he peered into the darkness, searching for the source of the voice. At the same time, Tomyra and her women pushed their horses forward, blocking the two men on the ground from immediate danger. Tomyra's hand leapt to her dagger and she fingered it beneath her robe, her breath coming fast.

Parasades gave a wry smile, masked by the night, and barked out an order to Certes and Agarus as they drew their weapons, wildly looking around. "Hold, you fools!" He held up a hand in the darkness and called out. "Who seeks to challenge us?"

A low chuckle answered him, picked up by other voices around them. "More to the point, traveller," came the voice again. "Who is it that dares trespass on our lands?"

"Your lands?" asked Parasades quietly. "You are Jartai?"

"Who wants to know?" enquired the voice curiously. "You don't have the sound of the western tribes, though you ford the river at night. You speak the Massegetae tongue." The voice flattened and became colder. "Are you loyal to Areipithes or do you defy him?"

Parasades pursed his lips, drawing out the silence. At length, he spoke matter-of-factly. "The Jartai once swore allegiance to the Massegetae, when the Wolf was defeated. Do the Jartai hold true to their oath?"

"We're not oath-breakers," growled the voice. The unseen horsemen around the little group shifted, leather creaking as they realigned their weapons. A feeling of menace washed over Parasades.

"So you're followers of Areipithes." Parasades made his hand move slowly toward his sword, feeling the bitter taste of defeat and death creep over him. *We have no chance,* he thought, *yet I cannot just surrender.* He muttered a swift prayer to the Great Goddess, gathering himself for his last battle.

"We follow no one but Lugartes, our chief," rasped the voice. "Where he goes, we go."

"Lugartes?" quavered a weak voice from the darkness near the Massegetae warrior. "How is my friend Lugartes? Does Ket still live with him?"

"Who calls Lugartes, friend? Stand forth and declare yourself."

Nikometros pushed himself up and shoved Timon to one side. He stumbled out from behind Tomyra's horse and stood shakily in the open. "I call him friend."

"And who are you?"

"My name is Nikometros, son of Leonnatos. I count Lugartes among my friends."

"Niko...? Nikomayros? The Lion?" The voice sounded doubtful. Movement in the shadows and the form of a horseman loomed over the thin figure of the Greek. "You're the one they call the Lion?"

Timon pushed his way to stand beside Nikometros. "Aye, he's the Lion, and my lord. If you seek to harm him you must pass by me first."

"I shall not harm him, loyal one." The rider paused. "Neither shall I let you pass though. Lugartes himself must decide your fate." He turned and snapped out a series of commands. The unseen riders moved closer, surrounding the small huddled group, weapons openly displayed. "Please give up your weapons," the rider went on. "You are now under the protection of the Jartai, within our lands. No harm will come to you from others."

Parasades drew his sword slowly and passed it over, with obvious reluctance. The others followed suit, though Tomyra kept her dagger out of sight beneath her cloak. When one of the Jartai warriors tried to search her, she hissed at him. "I am a priestess of the Mother Goddess. You touch me at your peril." The warrior drew back in confusion and the leader signed him away.

"A priestess?" he said. "With the Lion? Curious." He ordered his men into a column and they started out across the plains, away from the river, into the rising moon. "I regret we cannot spend time feeding you or getting you dry after your swim. Wait until morning and you will have all the time you need...should Lugartes grant you life."

"You are kind," said Parasades dryly. "What's your name, that I may commend you to your chief?"

"I am Jaxes, first of his commanders," said the man. "Now, be silent. We ride."

Chapter 26

T he Jartai village lay at the confluence of two small rivers, the Spagus and the Purul, which joined to become a tributary of the Oxus, about a day's travel east of the main river. The village itself was fortified, a double barrier of sharpened stakes extending across the narrow spit of land, broken only by a single gate. The rivers, at the point where they joined, were deep and slow moving. Steep banks prevented access by any save the most determined invaders. A resolute attacker though, would have been extremely vulnerable as he struggled up those slippery banks.

The village was crowded, the wooden buildings forming huge sprawling edifices with many families sharing a single structure. The Jartai, unlike many other Scythian tribes, were only semi-nomadic, spending most of the year within a few days travel of their village.

Timon reined in his horse and stared down at the village from a low hill overlooking the rivers. His recent travels gave him now a broader perspective of Scythian ways. Many of the northern tribes were wholly nomadic, wandering where the grazing was best. The Massegetae and Serratae, he knew, lived in towns or cities, but only over the winter months. When the flush of spring growth swept over the plains, the tribesmen gathered their vast herds of horses and cattle and moved north in a great meandering migration. In the autumn months, as the weather cooled, they wandered back to their winter quarters to spend the snow months making and repairing weapons, fashioning complex jewellery from the alluvial gold of their rivers and generally relaxing.

The cities were not wholly abandoned during the months of migration. A separate grouping of tribes-people had split off over time. No longer content to wander the plains, one part settled more or less permanently in the towns, trading in goods, farming and providing a variety of services for the true nomads. As with people everywhere, each group now regarded itself as the true Scythian people and the others as barely tolerated semi-barbarians.

The Jartai patrol of Jaxes trotted down the hill toward the village, the strangers carefully shielded in their midst. They forded the southern river at a guarded shallow where a well-worn road indicated considerable intercourse between town and country. The news of the capture sped from post to post as they advanced, and by the time they walked their horses through the open gate, a large crowd had gathered to gawk.

Jaxes ushered his prisoners into the town and ordered them to dismount in the central public square. Their horses were led aside and they stood uncertainly, staring back at the crowd that surrounded them. Here and there, voices rose above the general hubbub, most raised in incredulous recognition. People called out Nikometros' name, waving to attract his attention.

"I don't see anyone I recognise," muttered Nikometros to Timon. "I thought I would."

"Let us hope their chief still counts you as a friend, my lord," growled Timon. "Where in Hades is he anyway?"

The crowd parted as he spoke and a small body of men pushed their way through. A burly man dressed in fine embroidered clothing led the group. He pushed out into the open and stopped, looking at the captives with his head cocked on one side.

"Nikomayros? Is it truly you?" he asked.

Nikometros stepped forward shakily, holding onto Timon's arm for support. "Lugartes, my friend. It's good to see you."

Lugartes nodded and frowned. "You are changed, Lion. These past months haven't been kind to you." His eyes flicked over Niko's companions. "Nor to those who follow you."

"In adversity, one knows one's true friends," said Nikometros in a soft voice.

Lugartes looked away, his eyes moving restlessly over the crowd of Jartai. "These are indeed difficult times," he murmured. He coughed and turned back to Nikometros, raising his voice so all could hear. "Come to my tent, all of you. Let me refresh you with food and drink and you can give me the news." Lugartes turned and moved resolutely off into the crowd, which parted before him.

Jaxes and his men formed a cordon around the Massegetae and Greeks and hurriedly ushered them along in their leader's wake. The procession, with a large part of the crowd following, ended at a richly appointed tent on the north side of the village. Jaxes formed his men outside as a guard and led the others into the tent.

Inside, the tent boasted a thick, warm carpet and heavy drapes that wrapped the interior in a heavy gloom. Several smouldering braziers gave off a wash of heat and oil lamps shed a soft yellow light, revealing a trestle table, a bench and several stools. Piles of cushions and rugs in a far corner served as bedding. A young girl, nestled in the rugs, hurriedly threw on a shift and scrambled out of the tent as they entered.

Timon half-carried Nikometros to the bench and seated him, sitting down beside him with an arm around him for support. Tomyra crossed to his other side and sat down too, her eyes bright with concern. She straightened the dressing on his shoulder, noting with dismay blossoms of fresh blood on the cloth. Nikometros panted heavily, sweat beading his pale forehead. The women gathered behind and beside their mistress, looking alert and watchful. Parasades and Certes moved off to one side and squatted, staring at Lugartes. Agarus moved uncertainly then rapidly hobbled forward and slumped to the carpet by Nikometros' feet.

Jaxes busied himself at the trestle table as servants brought in food and drink. He poured out cups of koumiss and passed around platters of meat and bread. Parasades and Certes immediately started eating, while Tomyra sipped at her cup, her eyes on Lugartes.

Nikometros waved the food and drink away. "Lugartes," he asked softly. "Has our friendship died?"

Lugartes looked uncomfortable. "It is not a simple matter."

"That is exactly what it is for me," replied Nikometros. "What has complicated it for you?"

"You have powerful enemies, Lion."

Nikometros nodded slowly but did not speak. After a long pause, Lugartes resumed.

"Areipithes now leads the Massegetae. He demands the Jartai remember their oath of fealty. He demands the surrender, to him, of his enemies. He names you, Lion, and," Lugartes nodded in the direction of Parasades, "This one."

"And how have you answered him?"

Lugartes shrugged. "I denied all knowledge of your whereabouts. It was the truth." He took a deep breath and started pacing, his agitation showing. "Now he'll learn of your...capture. He has spies even in my village. He'll demand I hand you over."

"And you'll do this? Our friendship means nothing to you?"

Lugartes stopped in front of Nikometros, his hands moving restlessly over each other. "The Jartai are a weak people. How can we stand against Areipithes? I must consider my people." His voice trembled and he looked at his audience beseechingly. He flinched from Timon's expression and stumbled on. "I'm ashamed, Nikomayros, but how can I fight Areipithes? He's too strong."

"Have you forgotten it was this man here who defeated your people less than a year ago?" demanded Parasades. "Nikomayros led the charge that routed the Wolf and led to you becoming chief."

Lugartes shook his head. "I haven't forgotten. Why do you think I have delayed sending word south?" He wrung his hands, his face taking on an agonised expression. "I want to stand with you against Areipithes but how can I? Look at him! Look at this Lion of Scythia. He cannot even stand by himself but must be helped by a woman. He has no army, no force of inspired young men to fight for him." Lugartes buried his face in his hands. "If I openly support the Lion, my days as chief are numbered."

"Perhaps it would be better if they were, my lord," rumbled Jaxes. "Better we all die as honourable men than live in shame because we fear the usurper. Would you return us to the days of the Wolf?"

Lugartes gaped at his lieutenant. "You would turn on me, Jaxes?"

"No, lord. I've given you my oath and I will not forswear myself. But lord, consider. Will any hold the Jartai name in honour if this friend, this supplicant, is betrayed?" The man shook his head. "Better an honourable death."

"You cannot be serious, Jaxes." Lugartes backed away from his subordinate, a look of puzzled horror on his face. "You would destroy our people for one man?"

"Not for one man," said Jaxes. "Not for any man, lord. But for the honour of our people, yes, I would risk all. If you won't take my word, ask of your councillors."

Lugartes gulped and opened his mouth, croaking out "Guards!" He swallowed then straightened and called out again, more loudly. "Guards!" A warrior ducked his head into the tent, a spear at the ready.

"Send for my council of elders," barked Lugartes, "Hurry!"

"My lord," stammered the guard. "They're outside already...at least some are, my lord...I..." The guard ducked out again, flushing in confusion. A minute later a group of five men, burly and well fed, dressed in brightly coloured embroidered felts pushed into the tent. Three of them pressed forward, questioning expressions on their faces.

"Ah, Sopartos, Lucos, Teraxes." Lugartes beckoned them over and waved a hand at the men and women in his tent. "We have a problem and I need your counsel."

Lucos nodded solemnly. "That is our function, my lord. What is the nature of the problem?"

"It's to do with the Lion, isn't it my lord?" grinned Sopartos. "The town is aflame with news of his coming." He smiled broadly at Nikometros. "Welcome, Lion. It's good to see you once more."

"No, no!" cried Lugartes in agitation. "He'll bring about our ruin unless we act carefully."

Sopartos frowned. "How?"

"A serious matter," conceded Teraxes. "But he's a friend of the Jartai, isn't he?"

"Our chief believes we must hand over the Lion to the usurper," growled Jaxes. "He won't listen to my pleas for honour. Counsel him, brothers."

"Your comments border on disrespect, Jaxes," said Sopartos disapprovingly. He turned to Lugartes and bowed. "Please lord, honour us with your thoughts that we may weigh them."

Lugartes flashed a bitter look at Jaxes then advanced toward his three councillors, arms outstretched. "My friends, hear me. You all know of our situation. Since the Massegetae defeated us in battle, freeing us from the tyranny of the Wolf, we have lived quietly, peacefully. We have been able to do this because Spargises, chief of the Massegetae, treated us with honour and welcomed us as brothers." He started pacing up and down in front of his councillors. The other two junior officers who had entered the tent drew nearer, exchanging worried looks.

"Now Spargises lies dead and his son Areipithes holds the power. He makes demands of us and backs his demands with his army. He asks for this man," Lugartes pointed at Nikometros, "To be handed over to him." He paused and looked around the group. Lugartes caught Jaxes' glowering eyes and dropped his gaze, flushing beneath his beard. "You know we are not strong enough to defy Areipithes. We must preserve our people by acquiescing to his demands, distasteful though they be."

Parasades snorted softly in the silence that followed the chief's speech. The others sat or stood quietly, waiting for the response of the councillors. It was not long coming.

"I have made my view plain," growled Jaxes. "We cannot in honour hand over the Lion to his enemy. We must defy Areipithes."

"Softly, Jaxes," said Lucos. "We must discuss this fully."

Teraxes nodded. "Yes, decisions should not be made hastily."

"You would betray the Lion, a proven friend of the Jartai, to our common enemy?"

Teraxes scowled. "I lost a son in that battle, Jaxes. Was that the act of a friend?"

"You know as well as I do that your son fell in defence of the Wolf, as did many of our people," replied Jaxes. "Blame their deaths on him rather than the Lion. He--and Spargises--have treated our people with justice and generosity."

"That is true." Lucos nodded slowly. "The Lion has shown himself a friend of the Jartai. Perhaps friend enough to sacrifice himself for our common good?"

"I cannot believe I am hearing this!" Tomyra stood, white-faced, and pushed between the arguing men. "Since when do any of the horse-people betray their friends?"

"And who in Hades are you, girl?" rasped Lugartes.

Tomyra took a deep breath and drew herself up straight. "I am Tomyra, daughter of Spargises and priestess of the Great Goddess. This man Nikomayros, known to all of you as Lion of Scythia, enjoys the favour of the Goddess. How dare you treat him..."

"Enjoys the favour of the priestess by all accounts," snickered one of the junior officers.

Timon leapt to his feet, crossed the tent in three huge strides and crashed his fist into the young man's face. The officer reeled backward and collapsed, blood spurting from his nose. Timon stood over him, red with rage, his fists clenched. The other officer drew his sword and held it at Timon's throat, the point wavering uncertainly.

Parasades uncoiled himself and stood up. He walked casually over and put his hand on Timon's shoulder. "Youth is ever quick to speak and slow to think, eh, my friend? You have taught him a lesson." He turned to the other officer and pushed the sword blade to one side. "Put that away, that's a good fellow. Get your friend cleaned up, eh?"

The officer looked at his chief then at the councillors. Sopartos nodded and the young man slipped his sword back into its scabbard and lifted the fallen man to his feet, helping him out of the tent.

"Come, friend." Parasades eased Timon back toward Nikometros. "Hot heads will get us nowhere. Let our hosts make up their minds through cool reasoning."

Lugartes looked appraisingly at the tall young woman in front of him. "This is true...er...my lady? You are truly daughter of Spargises and holy priestess of the Massegetae?"

Tomyra inclined her head. "The Mother has told me that this man, Nikomayros, is under her protection. If you hand him over to Areipithes you will feel the anger of the Goddess."

The councillors muttered among themselves, shuffling their feet. Lucos cleared his throat. "This puts a new perspective on the problem."

"Yes," agreed Teraxes. "Loyalty to friends is one thing but to disobey the Mother..."

Lugartes frowned. "I agree in principle, we must not anger the Mother, but..." his voice trailed off and he flushed, looking down at the ground. "Er, forgive me, lady, but perhaps there is some truth...I mean, we have all heard stories." He gulped and glanced up at Tomyra's impassive face in desperation. "Is it...is it the Mother who speaks, or is it her priestess?"

Timon got to his feet again with a growl of anger. Nikometros placed a hand on his arm in restraint and Tomyra held out her arm toward him.

"My lord," interjected Lucos anxiously. "Take care. If she speaks truth you slander the Goddess." He held his palm out flat to the ground in supplication to the Earth Mother. He looked at the other councillors for assistance. "Sopartos, you've been silent. Tell us what you think we should do."

Sopartos looked up from where he was apparently scrutinising the complex patterns on the flooring rug. "I have listened to you all, and to my heart. It is shameful to betray a friend though I can understand why one might be tempted. It is, however, folly to betray a friend if that same action will bring down the curse of the Great Goddess." He held up a hand as Lugartes made as if to speak. "Hear me out, my lord, I beg." Sopartos pursed his lips and thought for a moment. "If the Mother supports this man then no enemy can stand against him. If he opposes Areipithes then so should we. The Mother will be at our sides."

"Providing the Mother truly does support him," muttered Teraxes.

"How can we be sure?" asked Lucos. "Forgive me lady, but we have only your word for that..."

"The word of a priestess is enough for any man," hissed Bithyia.

"...And there is a suspicion...only a suspicion," Lucos went on hurriedly, "Of self-interest."

"Are you all bereft of your senses?" asked Sopartos impatiently. "We have the means to test her at hand."

Jaxes grinned and slapped a meaty fist into his other hand. "Lynna. Of course. We have our own priestess."

"Just so," nodded Sopartos. "Send for her. Let her pronounce whether the Lion has the protection of the Goddess."

Lugartes' face lit up. "Yes. That is what we must do. Send for Lynna at once."

Jaxes strode to the tent entrance and bellowed to the guards outside to carry a message to the priestess. He ducked outside. Lugartes beckoned to his other councillors and led them into a corner of the tent where he conferred with them in whispers, leaving the others alone by the trestle table.

Certes got up and picked over the platters of meat and bread, washing hunks of the food down with draughts of warm koumiss. He belched and looked apologetically at Prithia. "I am hungry. It does us no good to weaken ourselves." Prithia smiled and picked up a plate, offering it to Tomyra and Sarmatia. Bithyia squatted beside Timon and spoke to him softly.

"My lord, thank you."

Timon looked puzzled. "For what, my love?"

"For defending my mistress' honour."

Timon shook his head. "The man was a foul-mouthed whore-son." He jerked his head toward the tent entrance. "Will their priestess support our priestess?"

Bithyia gaped. "How not? It is the Mother's will, not any man's...or woman's."

Tomyra sat down again beside Nikometros. She pushed the plate at him. "Eat, Niko," she said. "You must build your strength."

Nikometros smiled weakly and wiped the sweat away from his face. He picked up a piece of cold meat and nibbled at it. After a few moments he dropped it and closed his eyes, leaning back against the table. "I am tired," he whispered.

Jaxes coughed from the tent entrance and stood aside to let a young girl, only barely past puberty, step inside. The young girl advanced toward the knot of Jartai elders and inclined her head. She looked round with a keen interest at the strange faces, frowned when she saw Nikometros and Parasades then turned back to Lugartes.

"You have need of me, lord?" Lynna asked in a clear voice.

"Yes, Lynna." Lugartes pointed at Nikometros. "You know this man?"

"Indeed, my lord. I administered the oath of brotherhood when you became chief." Lynna smiled. "This man is your brother in blood, the man we call the Lion."

Lugartes coughed and hurried on. "Yes, yes. Who he is, isn't in dispute. This woman here," he indicated Tomyra, "Claims to be a priestess and further, that the man enjoys the favour of the Goddess."

"And you want me to verify these claims?"

"Yes, Lynna. That's it exactly."

Lynna looked at Tomyra, running her eyes over the tall slim woman dressed in plain but well-fitting woollen robes. She noted the confidence and air of authority with which she carried herself. With a light, almost dancing step she circled Tomyra, humming softly to herself. After completely circling the woman, Lynna dipped into a pouch attached to her waistband and drew out a bundle of stripped willow sticks. She smiled and handed them to Tomyra.

"Please throw down the sticks, lady," murmured Lynna.

Tomyra weighed the sticks in her hand and stared into Lynna's cheerful but plain face. She nodded and bending over the richly patterned carpet, threw the sticks in a sweeping curve.

Lynna dropped to her knees, scrutinising the pattern of the willow sticks, picking up one here, shifting another to study the way the ones underneath lay. She grinned and turned to Lugartes. "She is who she says she is, my lord." Lynna swept up the scattered sticks and rose, turning back to Tomyra. "Welcome elder sister."

"And the man?" asked Lugartes. "What of him?"

Lynna danced over to where Nikometros sat with his eyes closed, panting in the close warmth of the room. Sweat stood out on his pallid face and a bloom of fresh blood stained his tunic. She dropped to her knees in front of him. "My lord Nik...Nikam...Lion." She laughed, a clear tinkling laugh, and handed Nikometros the willow sticks. "Please, my lord, throw the sticks on the ground."

Nikometros opened his eyes and blinked, his gaze wandering weakly over the face of the girl in front of him. He looked down blankly at her hand for a moment then accepted the sticks. Nikometros nodded and stretched his hand out to scatter the sticks but a tremor ran through his body and his hand shook as droplets of blood fell from his tunic. Some of the sticks fell, spattered with blood and then he gathered his strength and tossed the others down.

Tomyra gasped and her eyes widened but she kept silent, watching Lynna as the girl trod carefully between the widely scattered twigs, her face frozen in concentration, the tip of her tongue curling up over her top lip.

"Well?" rasped Lugartes.

Lynna closed her eyes and concentrated. Her breathing slowed and she swayed on her feet. Her breath puffed out, visible as a bloom of white in the suddenly frigid air.

"Three lives shall this man lose, one is past, one is now and one comes at life's end. Each is greater than the last yet shall he live long in the land of the Golden King. Death is all around him yet shall this man conquer. The Mother's hand is with him for he shall protect mother and daughter."

Lynna's voice died away into a whisper. The air gradually warmed again and the watching men and women coughed and shuffled their feet, unconsciously drawing back from the young girl.

"Mother and daughter?" muttered Timon. "What mother and daughter?"

"There we have it," rumbled Jaxes in satisfaction. "Could it be plainer, my lord? The Great Goddess protects the Lion. We must stand by him and oppose Areipithes."

Teraxes nodded and Lucos muttered his agreement. Sopartos turned to Lugartes with a questioning look. "My lord? Surely you have no further doubts?"

Lugartes bit his lip and shook his head. "No," he muttered. "No. The Goddess has spoken, so shall it be." He forced a smile to his face and opened his arms wide in welcome. "Welcome, indeed, my friends. The hospitality of the tribe is open to you."

Parasades shook his head, a wry smile on his face as he stepped forward to embrace the Jartai chief. "I thank you for your generosity, brother, on behalf of my companions," he intoned formally. "May the Mother give you long life and large herds."

Chapter 27

The hut buzzed with muted conversation, the drone rising and falling as if a cloud of unseasonable flies had invaded the warm room. Outside, snow lay once more over the village of the Jartai and the surrounding countryside. Inside the hut was warmth and life, men moving from trestle tables loaded with smoking meats, freshly baked bread and roasted roots, and flagons of koumiss, back to the central table and their cliques. The odours of cooking mingled with the herbal scents of the Scythian body perfumes. The murmur of conversation covered topics as diverse as the coming war, the hunting along the Oxus River, a newly acquired piece of jewellery, a young wife, a new horse and an old wound.

The men filling the hut kept themselves in two groups, talking in slightly different dialects, with scarcely any communion between the groups. One, the larger and older group, appeared to be typical Scythian tribesmen, heavyset, with long locks and abundant facial hair. Their dark brown eyes wandered to the others in the hut, eyeing them with a certain amount of suspicion. Lugartes, chief of the Jartai, stood in one corner, locked in conversation with his councillors Lucos, Teraxes and a handful of minor officials, discussing the general day-to-day affairs of the tribe. Jaxes and Sopartos stood apart, hovering near the central table, bending over a large scroll of parchment laid upon it. They shook their heads and argued. A small number of other Jartai tribesmen lounged near the food trestles, laughing and joking, directing coarse comments at the second group of men in the hut.

This group was younger, and while still obviously Scythian in their dress and mannerisms, their faces were clean-shaven for the most part, though a few still sported luxuriant moustaches. They gathered in an amorphous knot to one side of the hut and spoke softly to one another, though occasionally darting suspicious glances around them. Holding a central position in the group was a young man called Tirses. A Massegetae, the others in the group deferred to him, recognising his authority. A gold ornament in the shape of a woman, whose lower body flowed into the coils of a snake, circled his arm. All the men in the group knew that ornament, with the bright slash of iron showing through the gold overlay. The antique circlet belonged to Nikometros, the famed Lion of Scythia, their leader. Nikometros had bestowed it on Tirses as a token of authority before he pursued the priestess Tomyra into the lands of the Serratae.

Heads turned and the conversation died away as two men pushed through the hide curtain over the doorway. Nikometros entered, thin and wan after his long illness, but the fire of life blazed in his eyes once more. At his side strode Timon, his hand, as ever, firmly set on the hilt of his sword. His eyes darted from man to man, warily weighing the dangers before moving on. A man moved suddenly, recovering his fallen cup, and Timon subtly interposed his bulk, protecting his lord from possible danger.

Lugartes silenced his still muttering councillors and walked across the carpet to Nikometros, forcing a welcoming smile to his lips.

"Welcome, Nikomayros. May I offer you some refreshment before we get down to business?" Lugartes waved in the general direction of the provisions.

"Thank you, Lugartes, old friend," murmured Nikometros. "Maybe later." He looked around the room at the other men. He nodded and smiled at Jaxes and Sopartos, nodded politely to the other Jartai then turned his attention to the young Massegetae warriors. A big grin creased Nikometros' face and he strode forward to embrace Tirses.

"Tirses. Thanks be to all the gods. You are alive!" Nikometros looked at the other young men. "And you have brought me men."

The others crowded round, pressing their hands against their leader, smiling and chattering. Timon hovered anxiously. Voices rose in a babble of query and comment all about him.

"Remember me, lord? Pallos."

"We are here for you..."

"...to kill the usurper..."

"Gods, he looks thin!"

"Paraxes, lord. Welcome!"

Tirses nodded solemnly and stepping back, saluted gravely. "More than you see here, my lord. Every single one of your Lions awaits your command, and many others besides. Two hundred men are camped outside the town." Pride burst from the young man.

"You've done well, Tirses." Nikometros said, keeping his face impassive though the news tempted him to delight. "I can see I was right to make you my senior officer. You are confirmed in that position."

Tirses grinned delightedly then slipped off the gold armband. "Here, my lord. Take back your token."

Nikometros held up a hand. "Keep it safe for me for now, Tirses. It is a symbol of your authority to act for me."

Behind him, Lugartes coughed. "My lord Nikomayros. If we might start this meeting?"

"Of course, my friend." Nikometros walked slowly up to the table and leaned on it. Timon watched him carefully, moving up alongside his commander, steadying him.

Lugartes straightened his tunic nervously and coughed again. "Friends and...er..." He flushed beneath his beard and started again. "Friends. We are gathered here to decide on actions that could spell victory or utter ruin. I enjoin you all, in the Mother's name, to consider what you say carefully. Don't be led astray by the bravado of young men..."

"Nor the fear of old women," muttered Jaxes softly.

"...into throwing away everything we've gained in recent months," went on Lugartes. "The council of elders of the Jartai people has voted to oppose our neighbour to the south, King Areipithes of the Massegetae. As you all know, Areipithes assumed power through the murder of his father, a god-cursed action if ever there was one. We can rely, thus, on the favour of the gods. Let us pray that we can resolve this matter speedily and with a minimum of bloodshed."

There was a long silence following the chief's words then a subdued murmuring broke out as pairs and groups started discussions. After a few moments Jaxes called for quiet and addressed the room.

"The decision of the council was war," said Jaxes bluntly. "You cannot make war without spilling blood, nor will our foe hesitate to spill ours, so let us not delude ourselves. Either we are determined to win this war or we may as well give in to the usurper now."

"Agreed." Sopartos nodded vehemently. "Let no man hang back on this venture."

Lucos had a pained expression on his face. "You are talking as if some of us are afraid to fight. That is offensive."

"No offence was intended, Lucos," replied Sopartos. "I wished merely to point out that war calls for resolve. If any have misgivings, let them air them now." He looked around at his audience. "Do any here have doubts?"

Lugartes smiled ingratiatingly. "Spoken like a true Jartai warrior, Sopartos. Let no man doubt that the Jartai will fight valiantly to overcome all odds."

Someone in the Massegetae throng snickered and Lugartes wheeled round, his face working in anger. Seeing no one to accuse, he gestured toward the clean-shaven young men. "Come," he sneered. "We have heard nothing from our young Massegetae allies. What say you? Will you fight against your brothers or will you hang back from war?"

"We are Massegetae and we are loyal to our oaths," stated Tirses coldly. "Our loyalty lies with our dead chief Spargises and his legitimate successors, his daughter Tomyra and our elected war-leader Nikomayros. We will never recognise the usurper and parricide, Areipithes." A growl of assent rose from the throats of the other Massegetae.

"I thank you, Tirses, and all of you loyal men," said Nikometros softly. "I also thank Lugartes and his loyal Jartai for their stand. However, to successfully oppose Areipithes we must be united. Decide who is to lead our armies."

"There is only one choice," growled Timon. "I nominate Nikometros, Lion of Scythia, as war-leader of our combined armies."

"Aye!" shouted a dozen throats, all Massegetae.

The Jartai nobles stood silently then Jaxes stirred. "Are there any other nominations?" he asked.

"The Jartai chief has always led our army," protested Lucos. "And this will be a Jartai army will it not? How many Massegetae will stand alongside us?" He shrugged. "Two hundred will not prevail."

"There will be others," broke in Tirses. "Even now Parasades and Certes are raising loyal forces to help us."

"Even so, the Massegetae contribution will be small. A Jartai should lead. I nominate our chief Lugartes." A murmur of agreement rose from a number of Jartai officers.

"Lugartes is our chief," agreed Sopartos. "However, we face a strong army and one whose tactics the Jartai have not stood against successfully. We should have a leader who is conversant with the way their army works."

Teraxes snorted. "And who did you have in mind? Let me guess, your friend Nikomayros?"

"Actually, no," retorted Sopartos. "I believe the Massegetae would more readily follow Parasades, however, he is not here and we need a leader now."

"Many Massegetae would follow the Lion," grated Tirses, amid a chorus of agreement.

"We could send for Lynna and let the Goddess decide," put in Lucos.

"No," replied Sopartos. "Warfare is men's business. We can decide this. I say we choose now: Lugartes or Nikomayros."

Jaxes drew his dagger and raised it. "I vote for the Lion." He passed the dagger to Sopartos.

"In the absence of Parasades, I too." Sopartos passed the dagger on.

Teraxes shook his head. "The Greek has ability, but I choose Lugartes. What say you, Lucos?"

Lucos opened his mouth to speak, closed it again and looked hesitantly round the room. He glanced at his chief's glowering face and flushed in embarrassment. "Lugartes," he squeaked.

"Nikometros," growled Timon. "Who else?"

"Nikometros," agreed Tirses.

The dagger passed on around the junior officers and councillors. Jaxes and Teraxes counted as the men declared themselves. By the time the dagger returned to Jaxes, twenty-seven votes had been cast, fifteen for Nikometros and twelve for Lugartes.

"It is done," said Jaxes in satisfaction. "Nikomayros is war-leader against the usurper Areipithes." He nodded deferentially at his scowling chief. "This decision in no way affects the leadership of the Jartai as a tribe. Nikomayros' word is supreme only in matters of war."

Nikometros nodded and moved slowly around the table, aided by Timon, until he stood next to Lugartes. "Thank you," he said quietly. "My first decision is that my friend Lugartes is to be regarded as joint war-leader, responsible whenever I am not present." He turned and embraced a surprised Lugartes. "Now," he went on. "To business. We have a war to plan."

"Perhaps you could first explain the meaning of this parchment," said Jaxes, indicating the scroll spread out on the main table, the edges pinned down by smooth river rocks. "Timon tells me it is our lands, but that does not make sense."

"It is what we call in Greece a carta, or map," explained Nikometros. "The lines you see upon it represent things like roads and rivers, towns and hills. We use them to plan our campaigns."

Teraxes laughed, spittle flying as he doubled over with mirth. "What? You have tiny horsemen riding on these roads and little tents and huts?" He lifted the edge of the map and peered underneath it. "Perhaps herds of tiny cattle are hiding under it?" Several of the Jartai nobles also laughed and even some of the young Massegetae smiled at the words.

"No," smiled Nikometros. "Just as this line here," he traced a finger across the map, "Represents the River Oxus, so we can use little things like these breadcrumbs," he scattered a few on the parchment. "To take the place of riders."

Teraxes still shook with merriment as he shook his head. "To what point, Nikomayros?" he gasped. "We all know where the river is, it is over there." He pointed unerringly to the west. "Why do we need lines on a piece of paper to tell us that?"

"Perhaps our war-leader wishes us to play games," Lucos sneered.

"What if you were in a strange land and did not know the landmarks? Or wished to communicate your position to others who did not know it?"

Teraxes shrugged. "I would have to make sure I knew where I was."

"My lords, allow me to make a small demonstration of the use of this map." Nikometros turned to Lugartes, who peered at the lines on the parchment without the least sign of comprehension. "My friend, pick a place where you think Areipithes might seek to fight us. Devise a means for us to attack him. Now whisper this plan in my ear."

Lugartes frowned. "Why do I not just tell everybody my plan?"

"I will tell Timon, who can read a map such as this, your plan without speaking a word."

Lugartes raised his eyebrows. "Without speaking?" He snorted. "It cannot be done." He thought a moment then pulled the taller Nikometros down by the arm and rasped a few short sentences into his ear. "Go on then," he said loudly. "Use your map."

Nikometros leaned over the table and studied the parchment for a few moments. He picked up a fragment of charcoal and wrote a tiny 'alpha' on the map. He then stabbed his finger down at another place and traced a curving path across the paper, coming to a halt near the charcoal letter. Looking up at Timon, Nikometros cocked his head inquiringly.

Timon smiled. "Areipithes waits for us with his army at," he peered closely at the map. "Double Rock. We move west from here to the Oxus near Wolf Rock then south to the swampy ground then skirting the hills, move around to take him in the rear."

All eyes turned to Lugartes. The chief nodded slowly, sucking his lower lip pensively as he stared at the path traced by Nikometros down to the tiny charcoal smear. He put his finger down on the paper. "This is Wolf Rock?" he asked.

"Yes. Here is the Oxus River, here the swamp, hills along here and here, and Double Rock here." Nikometros looked round at the assembled men. "We can draw up complex battle plans on maps like this," he said. "Study them then turn them into actions where every man, every battle group knows his exact place, knows exactly what he must do, even if he cannot see his commanders. The Great King Alexander wins his battles by using maps to plan his campaigns. We can too."

"We have fought wars since the gods first walked the plains," growled Lucos. "We still fight them, and without maps. I cannot see how they will help us fight better."

"I have watched Scythian leaders in action," went on Nikometros. "As long as the battle can be seen, their generalship is unsurpassed. But if they lose sight of their men, or of the enemy, the action becomes confused."

"Interesting," commented Sopartos. "But this map of yours still looks like a lot of lines to me."

Timon grunted and tapped the table with his knuckle. "Every young officer in the Greek army thinks the same when he first sees one of the King's campaign maps. Give me a few days with men willing to learn and I will have them using maps. I even have a skilled scribe ready to make as many copies as we require."

Lugartes looked doubtful. "We are Scythian warriors," he said. "Not bookish clerks from barbarian lands. This is something new." He shrugged. "Perhaps this is not something for Scythians."

"Nor is fighting in disciplined horse columns," murmured Tirses. "It took the ideas of a man from Outland to introduce that to the Massegetae." He bared his teeth in a fierce smile. "Yet I seem to remember that innovation had a devastating effect on the Jartai army."

Several young Jartai rounded on the speaker with expressions of anger. One forced his way toward Tirses, only to be restrained by Jaxes. Lugartes scowled but waved his young men back.

"Yes, I remember," grated the Jartai chief. "Though some may consider it impolite to brag about it."

Tirses inclined his head. "Then forgive my impetuous words, my lord. I wished merely to point out that innovation is not necessarily a thing to be avoided."

Jaxes moved to the table and gestured down at the map. "I think this map may be useful," he said. "If Timon can teach us to use it by the time the campaign starts then we should make use of it."

"Very well," agreed Lugartes. "But we have more urgent matters to discuss. Where is Areipithes now and what is he doing?" He looked around at a thin, colourless man hovering near the edge of his councillors. "Dilactos is my spy-master. He has just returned from the south with disturbing news."

Dilactos moved reluctantly to the table. He stood with his shoulders hunched and stared at his feet. When he spoke, it was only as a low murmur, a breathy whisper, the ends of his sentences often dying away into inaudibility.

"Areipithes is still in Urul. The usurper has united most of the Massegetae into a considerable...He has opened negotiations with the Dahai to the west for mutual...The combined army will probably number at least..."

"Speak up!" growled a voice from the rear.

"Yes," cried another. "How many did you say?"

"Five thousand. He said five thousand," called a voice nearer the front.

A babble of noise erupted, as men turned on one another in loud argument. Lugartes called for quiet unsuccessfully. Jaxes finally managed to restore order with a series of stentorian bellows.

As the disruption died away, Tirses interjected. "I dispute these facts," he said quietly. "I have my own sources, especially one who was a lot closer to the enemy than your man."

"Who is he, Tirses?" asked Nikometros.

"This man, here," replied Tirses. He urged a slim bearded Scythian to the fore, patting him reassuringly on the shoulder. "Scolices once worked for Areipithes as a personal servant. He has recently defected to our ranks. The story he paints is very different."

Nikometros frowned. "Scolices? The name sounds familiar." After a moment he shook his head. "Go on, man. Tell us what you know."

Scolices smiled, and walked slowly up to the table. "Areipithes is indeed in Urul," he agreed, "But that is as accurate as this man gets." He jerked a thumb at Dilactos. "The father-killer has talked to Tellos, chief of the Dahai, but was refused aid. Men are deserting his army daily and he fights incursions of the Serratae continually. At the moment he could put maybe three thousand men in the field but in a month's time when the weather breaks, perhaps half of that."

Jaxes pursed his lips. "Fifteen hundred men? Still a sizeable army but manageable." He looked across at Tirses. "How accurate is this information?"

Tirses shrugged. "It agrees loosely with some reports, is at variance with others. However, Scolices is the only source from close to the usurper."

"And how trustworthy is he, I wonder?" growled Timon. "He betrays his one-time master yet seeks our trust."

Scolices shrugged and smiled diffidently. "My oath was to my chief, Spargises," he stated. "Not his son. When Areipithes killed his own father I could not in conscience remain with him."

"Yet you waited until now to leave him?" asked Nikometros.

"There was much confusion," replied Scolices. "Areipithes killed men who questioned his right to lead. I deemed it better to keep out of sight but keep my ears open and wait for an opportunity to escape."

Jaxes grunted. "Seems reasonable. So, Scolices, what does the usurper plan to do?"

"I cannot be sure," Scolices said, spreading his hands out. "I was not on his council. I heard, though, that he intends to march north to crush the Jartai around the spring equinox."

"That late?" queried Sopartos. "The weather is good enough for fighting weeks before that. Why should he wait if his army is disintegrating?"

"He has sent word north to the Dumae," said Scolices softly. "He has an offer of support from them but he must wait until after the feast of the New Herds at the equinox."

"Nemathres? Support Areipithes? I don't believe it!" Nikometros slammed his fist down on the table, his eyes blazing.

"I have heard nothing of this," complained Dilactos. "If this were so, my men would have heard something."

"Out of his own mouth," murmured Tirses. "If his information is so bad, why should we listen to the rest of his talk?"

"You're sure of your facts?" Nikometros leaned over the table, staring at the slim Massegetae defector.

"I cannot say, I wasn't there when the promise was made, my lord," smiled Scolices. "I only know that Areipithes makes his plans as if it were fact."

"This is serious news." Lugartes muttered. "Fifteen hundred Massegetae are one thing. With luck we could win there, but to have the Dumae attack us from the rear? How many are they, Sopartos, do we know?"

"A thousand, twelve hundred if they leave their lands defenceless."

"And how many can we put in the field?" queried Lucos timidly.

"If we take every man who can bear arms, strip the village of the merchants and farmers, use every youth and boy who can use a bow...eight, nine hundred." Sopartos spoke quietly but his voice carried in the silence.

"Do not forget the loyal Massegetae," put in Tirses. "We number two hundred already and more join every day."

"And Parasades," chipped in another warrior. "He's recruiting even as we speak. No doubt he'll find hundreds more."

Lugartes looked gloomy. "So, our total army may nearly equal the usurpers in size, if his continues to decrease and if the Dumae don't join him?"

"The outlook is not good," agreed Sopartos.

"Perhaps we should ask what terms Areipithes will give us," muttered one of the junior councillors.

"Yes," said another, more loudly. "If his terms are honourable..."

"Silence!" roared Jaxes. "There will be no talk of surrender. We know already what the usurper wants of us and we have rejected it."

"But what are we to do?" whined Lucos. "We cannot fight Areipithes and Nemathres together. We would be slaughtered."

"So, fight them separately," interposed Nikometros softly. "This man here, Scolices, says that they cannot meet up before the equinox. I'm not sure I believe him." He held up a hand as Tirses opened his mouth, and turned toward the slim defector. "If I wrong you, Scolices, I will beg your pardon, but I cannot accept the unsupported word of one man. I do not believe Nemathres would betray me." Nikometros paused, letting the silence grow around him. "I will send word to Nemathres myself. In the meantime, let us march an army south immediately and face Areipithes alone."

"Nikomayros is right," nodded Sopartos. "Face a single foe. Once Areipithes is defeated there is no reason for Nemathres to take the field."

Lugartes smiled then a look of concern came over his face. "But Areipithes' army is larger now, maybe as large as both armies combined after the equinox."

"My lords," interrupted Scolices with a grin. "The usurper is relying on the Dumae to bolster his flagging support. If the Jartai show up with the Lion as their leader, most of his army will desert at once." He chuckled. "You may not even have to fight a battle."

Lugartes smiled again. "Now that sounds like a plan. What think you, my lords?"

The Jartai councillors looked thoughtful and nodded, as did most of the Massegetae warriors. Jaxes spoke briefly with Sopartos and Teraxes in a quiet voice then turned to his chief.

"I agree with the intent, my lord, but I must stress this is far from a plan. We must move carefully and swiftly if we are to succeed."

"Then draw up one." Lugartes waved his hands dismissively. "We have elected a war-leader, let him plan a strategy with his officers. Play with your maps, decide on your route, do whatever you must." He gathered his cloak around him and strode to the entrance to the hut, most of the Jartai councillors following him. He turned in the entrance and looked back. "Just remember that I am chief of the Jartai. Any move you make that affects the tribe, any supplies you desire, horses, cattle, whatever, must be cleared by me."

Nikometros watched Lugartes leave. "He has changed," he sighed. He turned back to the others. "Timon, make sure Ket has supplies of parchment for the maps. Jaxes, Sopartos, Teraxes. You will speak for the Jartai on the war council?"

Sopartos nodded. "For now, my lord. Others may be required later." He looked at the Massegetae warriors. "And who speaks for the Massegetae?"

"Timon of course, and Tirses. He leads the Lions now." Nikometros smiled. "When Parasades returns, he too."

"Then we had best get started, my lord. Time is running out."

Chapter 28

Tomyra lay on soft cushions looking out at the rain. Winter had given way to the first signs of an early spring; the moisture-laden westerly winds sending sheets of cold rain sluicing over the Scythian plains. The rivers bordering the Jartai village grew to surging brown torrents, the topsoil washing down in leaping torrents from a land denuded of grass and churned up by the herds. A cool gust lifted the flaps of the heavy hide tent, sending a spray of water over the fine rugs. Sarmatia and another young maiden of the priestess, Dolra, hurried to secure the tent entrance, cursing as their feet splashed into an icy puddle on the floor.

Tomyra shifted and winced as a stab of pain arced through her pelvis. Bithyia noted the fleeting pain and leaned closer, holding a horn cup.

"Drink, my lady," Bithyia murmured. "It will ease the pain."

Tomyra waved the cup aside and struggled to sit up. "I am not an invalid," she snapped. Instantly contrite, she put a hand out and touched the young woman gently on the arm. "I am sorry, Bithyia. I never expected to feel like this." She forced a small laugh. "It is a wonder any woman bears children."

"You must not make light of it, my lady," said Prithia. She straightened the cushions behind Tomyra and drew up a soft goatskin around her mistress' legs. "Most girls feel sickness in the morning, it's true, but that passes. What worries me are the pains you continue to have. I fear that...that beast did you some damage inside."

"It is in the Goddess' hands," said Tomyra. "If it is my lot to bear the child, I shall. If She chooses to take it from me, I shall not be sorry to see it go."

"My lady!" Sarmatia gaped at the young priestess. "How can you say that? It's your child."

"But not my lord's," rejoined Tomyra, her face carefully neutral. "My pregnancy does not yet show and you will see to it that my lord Nikomayros does not find out."

Prithia screwed up her face in anguish. "He must find out eventually, lady."

"If I do not lose it I shall tell him before it shows. Now fetch me some koumiss, Prithia, and stop fussing. You too, Sarmatia. Dolra, fetch me another cushion please."

Prithia and Sarmatia sniffed and drew their cloaks over their heads before lifting the tent flap and ducking out into the rain. Bithyia looked askance at her mistress as she shifted uncomfortably, settling onto the cushion proffered by Dolra.

"Why haven't you told him, dear one?"

Tomyra scowled then relented, stroking Bithyia's face. "I am afraid," she said simply. "I fear that he will leave me when he finds I bear another man's child, or if he does not, that he will grow away from me."

"You could tell him it is his. He is a man and will readily believe you."

"I will not lie to him. Yet I fear he will draw away from the truth."

"He would not," affirmed Bithyia fiercely. "He loves you too much. Timon has often spoken of the great love he has for you." She gripped Tomyra's hand and squeezed it hard. "Oh, I dare say he will be shocked at first. He is a man after all." Bithyia snorted. "Men seem to think women are their property and that another man's attention somehow taints us. Never fear, mistress, he will stop and think. He knows Dimurthes forced you..."

"Do not name that man," snarled Tomyra, her eyes flashing. "I would that all parts of him might die from this world." Her hands crept over her belly as she spoke.

"Anyway, lord Nikomayros knows your heart is his alone. He risked death to find you; he will not turn you away."

Tomyra smiled wanly. "You are probably right, Bithyia. It is just the fear of a young girl thrust into womanhood before the time of her choosing."

"So tell him, my lady. Put your mind at rest."

Tomyra shook her head. "He has enough to worry him. He works so hard, planning and training the army, consulting with his generals, talking to spies. He comes to bed late and rises before I wake. I do not want to put an extra burden on him."

"Timon says the plans are going well."

"Yes. The army will set out within five days if the rain lets up. They plan to force my half-brother to battle within ten more. Then it's in the hands of the gods."

"They will prevail, Tomyra. I know it. You can take your place in the tribe once more, with your lord by your side."

"As what, Bithyia? As the secret lover of the priestess? As a kept man? He has too much pride."

"Why, as war-leader. Perhaps as chief of the tribe. The people love him. They will accept you as his wife when they see he has the favour of the Mother."

"Yes, they love him but as a talisman, as the luck-bringer. If they stopped to think about it they would not accept him as their leader. He is not of the People. Besides, some would dispute his elevation. Parasades, for one."

Tomyra shivered and drew the goatskin tightly about her. "What is it about that man, Bithyia? I thought he was a friend. He is strong, capable, well liked but there is a thread of violence and treachery within him. Remember how he tried to leave Niko behind?"

"He's being watched, dear one. I have instructed Prithia to keep her ears and eyes open. She is seeing a lot of Certes these days." Bithyia laughed. "The poor man is besotted with her."

"Speaking of Prithia," said Tomyra. "Where is that girl? I am thirsty."

Bithyia got to her feet and sauntered over to the tent entrance. She looked out into the rain for a few minutes before ducking back in again. "She is coming," Bithyia said, shaking the water from her long black hair. "And she has company."

"Oh? Who?"

"Your Egyptian friend with the unpronounceable name," laughed Bithyia. "At least I know you will be in a good mood for the rest of the day."

Dolra looked up from where she sat carving on a piece of bone. "An Egyptian? Who is he?" she asked.

Bithyia grinned. "That's right; you haven't met Ket, have you?" She laughed at the puzzled expression on the young girl's face. "He is an old slave of the Jartai, but apparently he saw the lord Nikomayros in Egypt many years ago. We met him last year, just after we defeated the Jartai."

Dolra gaped. "Lord Nikomayros has been to Egypt?"

"Of course he has," snapped Bithyia impatiently. "Nikomayros was a lord in the Macedonian army. He has been everywhere. Anyway, this old man Ket saw him there and prophesied he was of the blood of kings."

"Kings..." breathed Dolra, her eyes wide.

"Our lady here dotes on the old man and has missed him almost as much as she missed her lord," interrupted Bithyia, a mischievous twinkle in her eye. "Although I dare say, for different reasons."

Tomyra stuck out her tongue at the other woman and hefted the cushion at her. Bithyia ducked and laughed again as the tent flap opened. Prithia staggered in, breathing heavily. She placed a large hide flask of koumiss on the floor and straightened, massaging the small of her back. A young Scythian boy followed her, carrying a large wicker basket. He placed the basket on the ground near Tomyra, bowed, and quickly edged out of the tent as Sarmatia entered, along with a very old man.

Tomyra scrambled to her feet and bobbed her head courteously, giving the newcomer a broad smile. "Ketherennoferptah, you are welcome," she said, speaking slowly and with great care. She grinned. "There! I managed it without a slip. I have been practicing."

The old man blinked and turned his ancient rheumy eyes at the young girl. His already profoundly wrinkled forehead furrowed further in concentration and he cleared his throat. "Where is Bubis?" he asked querulously. "I have been looking for him all day. I am sure this rain has made him run away."

Behind him, Sarmatia and Prithia dissolved into fits of giggles. Dolra stared at them then at the old man in wonder. Bithyia stifled a grin and pointed at the basket. "He is here Ket-herongfer..." She shook her head and smiled. "He is here, Ket, in the basket. See?" She bent and took the lid off the basket.

A deep rumble echoed from the depths of the basket and a large black cat raised its head above the rim. It looked at the women standing around and yawned widely, unconcerned. Then with a lithe fluidity it leapt out and butted itself against the legs of the old man, its purring reaching a crescendo.

"Ah, Bubis!" exclaimed Ket. "There you are. You have been hiding in this tent with this young girl, have you?" He stared vacantly at Tomyra. "I have seen you before, girl."

"I am Tomyra, dear Ketherennoferptah. I am happy that you have come to see me again."

Ket's dreamy stare suddenly focused and he straightened, adjusting his robes. "Well, of course you are, Tomyra, honoured priestess of the Massegetae." He bowed and smiled around at the other women. "Bithyia too, and Sarmatia and...Prithia is it not? This other young lady I do not know."

"Dolra," whispered the young girl.

"Will you be seated, Ket?" asked Tomyra. "Your presence and your conversation is a delight on such a dreary day."

"Thank you, Tomyra. You do an old slave much honour." Ket folded himself carefully into a cross-legged sitting position and lowered himself to the ground.

Tomyra sat down beside him and took one of his wrinkled hands in hers. "You are no longer a slave, dear Ket. I have told you this before. You are an honoured guest until such time as you can return to your own land."

A dreamy look overtook Ket once more and the muscles of his face relaxed, his gaze becoming unfocussed again. "Ah, the sunny climes of the glorious Double Kingdom," he muttered. "Will I ever see thy face again?"

"Curses!" whispered Bithyia. "Just when I thought he had a hold on things. You never know what is going to set him off."

Bubis walked over to Tomyra, tail cocked firmly upright and pushed his way into the young woman's lap. He butted her in the belly with his great black head and yowled softly. Pummelling her thigh briefly with his front feet, he settled down and closed his eyes, purring loudly. The old man looked across at Tomyra, his eyes wide open in shock.

"He has never done that before," he muttered. "What is it he sees that I do not?" He stared at the cat asleep on Tomyra then up to her smiling face. "Ahh!" he nodded, his whole scrawny body rocking as his eyes drifted, unfocused.

"It almost never rains in my land, you know," said Ket in a sing-song voice. "Yet the river rises just the same. The god Khnum raises the Nile and spreads his seed over the land, making everything fertile once more." Ket looked up at Tomyra with a sudden smile. "It seems other seed has been spread."

Tomyra flushed, her knuckles whitening as she gripped her koumiss cup. Her hand shook as she set it carefully on the ground. She took a deep breath and forced herself to speak calmly. "What do you mean, Ket?"

"The field has been planted, has it not, child?"

"Who has been speaking out of turn?" Tomyra's eyes flashed as she looked round at her companions.

Ket shook his head, his straggly white locks falling over his face. "No one, child." He brushed his hair aside. "It is obvious if you know what to look for. My Bubis here spotted it immediately." He smiled and shrugged. "I am an old man and slower. Do you deny it?"

Tomyra sat in silence for a long time. Finally, she whispered "No," in a small voice.

Ket nodded solemnly. He scratched the carpet with a long fingernail. Bubis opened his eyes and stared at Ket's finger. His tail twitched and his feet bunched up under him. The reverberating purring grew louder. "You are not happy, Tomyra. Why, I wonder?"

The silence drew out, the drumming of the rain on the taut hide tent and the thunder of the black cat filling the hollow between words. Finally, Tomyra stirred and looked Ket in the eye, a defiant look in her eye.

"The child is not my lord's," Tomyra said quietly. "When I was carried off I was raped."

"Aaah..." Ket nodded sagely. "And Lord Nikometros takes this amiss?"

Tomyra blinked in surprise. "He doesn't know, but if he did then...yes, I fear he might."

Ket started rocking gently backward and forward, humming softly to himself as he did so. A tiny thread of saliva trickled from the corner of his mouth and his hand stopped scratching the carpet.

Bubis' eyes flicked up at the old man and he stared up at him with obvious disapproval. He got up, stretching and bared his sharp teeth and pink tongue in a wide yawn before settling back down to sleep.

"Lost him again," muttered Bithyia. "Shall I fetch his servant?"

"Most men treat women as property," Ket said suddenly. "Yet in any civilised land a woman is regarded as the equal of a man. My own people are quite civilised in this regard. The Sauromantians and other tribes of Pontus have even reduced men to a lower status, using them to father children when the women desire them."

Tomyra frowned. "I know this, Ket, my mother was of the..."

"The Trocmi of Cappadocia..." interrupted Ket, "...allow a woman to take a lover provided she is discreet. If she is not, they put her and her lover to death. On the other hand, the Mtelabi of Nubia encourages women to have relations with any man if it will produce a baby. All children are held in common regard and treated equally." A smile flitted across the old man's face and he winked at Tomyra. "Many men are narrow in thought but some are worth the effort. I think you misjudge your man, Tomyra."

Tomyra smiled wanly. "Few men will accept another man's bastard."

"We shall see, child. Your Nikometros deserves the title of 'Golden'."

Bithyia gasped and pressed forward, gripping Tomyra's shoulder as she peered into Ket's face. "You think Nikomayros is the Golden King of your prophecy?"

Tomyra kept her face expressionless, though her hands clasped each other tightly in her lap. "I never named him the one," she whispered.

"No," agreed Ket amiably. He looked around at Prithia and held out his cup. "Pour me some more of that sour milk, my dear. I must admit the flavour does improve with experience." He waited while she sloshed koumiss from the skin flask into his cup, spilling as much as she poured. Ket raised the milk to his mouth and drank thirstily, the thin nutty-tasting fluid dribbling from the corners of his mouth as he gulped. His hand shook as he set the cup down.

"My hand is cramped," he complained, massaging it with his other hand. "Too many maps to draw."

Bubis opened his eyes again and leapt down from Tomyra's lap. He leaned forward to investigate the drops pattering down on the old man's stained tunic. He sniffed delicately then drew back with a faint look of disdain on his face, turning to stare at the tent entrance hide flapping in the breeze.

"You never did like koumiss, did you Bubis," chortled Ket. "Though you like milk well enough before it sours." He looked up at the young women and adopted an air of pedantic seriousness. "My Bubis likes cow's milk better than mare's milk you know. He will not drink goat's milk though. I have often wondered why." He cocked his head on one side as if listening and nodded. "Perhaps it is because the cow is sacred to my people. What do you think?"

Tomyra sighed. "Yes, Ket. That sounds right."

Sarmatia edged forward and plucked at her mistress' sleeve. "Do you think he's right, my lady?" she asked. "Could Nikomayros be the Golden one?"

"Oh, it would be wonderful if he was," breathed Prithia with a dreamy expression. "He would be king and rule over the plains bringing riches and gold to our people."

Tomyra gave her a sharp look and slapped her arm lightly. "Stop that, Prithia. I never saw my lord as the one, only that he is bound to the Golden One somehow."

"I have given this much thought," mused Ket, his eyes still unfocused. He picked up Bubis and settled him on his own lap. "And I must admit I am undecided. A case could be made for Nikometros actually being the Golden King. His hair is gold, a colour strange in these lands. He rides a great stallion, the colour of gold. Further, the Jartai described him as flaming as he led the charge against them last year. He has power, and with it riches if he desires."

"A real king," breathed Dolra.

"Then you do think he's the one," cried Prithia excitedly.

"No." Ket smiled and set down his cup. He patted his damp chin and tunic with a scrap of cloth then went back to stroking Bubis. "There are other possibilities much more likely."

Tomyra and her women waited, but Ket's attention remained riveted on his cat, his fingers seeking out the animal's pleasure spots behind its ears and under the chin. Bubis resumed his thunderous purring. At last Tomyra could bear the silence no longer.

"Well?" she demanded. "What are these possibilities?"

"Eh?" Ket looked up, startled. "Oh, just that you should consider the words you actually prophesied." He patted his tunic and drew out a small scrap of parchment. Ket unfolded it slowly and scrutinised it, his brow furrowed in concentration.

Prithia peered over Ket's shoulder at the scrap of parchment. "What are all those little lines and squiggles?" she asked.

"Writing," muttered Ket. "Have you not seen writing before?"

"Of course I have seen writing before," retorted Prithia. "But none of it looked like little pictures of eyes and hands and ducks and...what is that one?" She pointed at a symbol on the parchment.

"It is a uraeus, child. A symbol of royalty. Now be quiet and let me remember exactly how the prophecy was uttered." Ket's lips moved as his finger traced over the symbols. "Ah, yes...'*From the blood of kings comes a warrior of the People. Great glory. A golden king lies in his future. Death, and...*'

"And what?" asked Sarmatia.

"You must ask Tomyra that," said Ket. "She ended the prophecy there, though from what I have heard from those who were present, there was more."

"My lady?" asked Dolra. "Was there more? What else did the Mother say?"

"Dolra!" snapped Bithyia. "Remember your place. It is between the Goddess and her priestess. If she feels others should know, you will hear it."

Tomyra nodded. "Those were the words, Ket. How do you interpret them?"

"Nikometros is descended from royalty, we know that." Ket smiled. "You really should remember that your lord is a bastard son of a bastard son, grandson of Philip of Macedon and nephew of the Great King Alexander."

"You are joking?" Dolra gaped at Ket. "Nikomayros is related to Alexander?"

"He will not be acknowledged," said Tomyra, waving her hand dismissively. "Go on, Ket."

"Not only will Nikometros not be acknowledged," added Ket, "But he could be in danger should Alexander die. He could be used by others. Courts are full of power-hungry men."

"That is not likely, though," put in Bithyia. "Alexander is only some thirty years old and by all accounts loved by his people."

"Enough!" said Tomyra impatiently. "Go on, Ket. Tell us who the Golden King is."

Ket chuckled. "Think about the wording of the prophecy. *'From the blood of kings comes a warrior of the people.'* This is obviously Nikometros himself. He is royal and he became a great warrior in your tribe."

Bithyia nodded. "Yes, and *'Great glory'* came next!" she cried. "It came true. Nikomayros brought great glory to the Massegetae."

"Which brings us to *'A golden king lies in his future'*," said Tomyra.

"And *'Death'*," added Prithia with a shudder.

Bithyia shrugged. "Death is always with us, Prithia. He is a warrior and fights battles. Of course, death will follow him."

"What about the deaths Lynna foretold when she cast the sticks for Nikomayros?" Prithia said. "She talked about three deaths for Nikomayros and death being all around him."

"That part is easily understood," replied Tomyra quietly. "She talked rather of the three lives my lord will lose, meaning times of great danger." Tomyra counted off on the fingers of her hand. "One life was 'lost' in the past, when Nikomayros first came to us. He died to his former life and was reborn as a Massegetae warrior. The second is now. He almost died from the wound received in Serrata. There will be a third, I am sure, but that is the death all men come to."

"And her next words confirmed he is not the Golden King." Ket stretched his arms over his head then pushed one scrawny leg out straight, massaging his thigh muscle. "A cramp," he muttered. "This rain and cold is making me old before my time."

Bubis slid off his lap and landed on the rug. His eyes flew open and he turned an aggrieved stare at the old man. Seeing no apology forthcoming the cat stretched and stalked over to Tomyra and settled down on the ends of her robe.

"What did she say next?" asked Prithia. "I could not make it out as Certes was making some comment about the three lives."

"I think it was *'yet shall he live long in the land of the Golden King.'*" Tomyra looked at Ket inquiringly.

"Just so," nodded Ket. "He will live in the lands of this king, not be him."

"So if Nikomayros is not the Golden King then who is?" demanded Prithia.

"I have communed with my gods and I believe him to be Alexander," stated Ket firmly. "It is possible that the prophecy talks of a man yet unknown, or a Scythian king, but I think it unlikely."

"Why not?" blurted Dolra.

"Of course," sighed Bithyia.

Ket laughed. "To answer you first, Dolra. Scythia is indeed known as a land of gold. All around me are ornaments and jewellery fashioned from the gold found in your streams, yet how are the Scythians to find a king? Your tribes are too independent to be ruled by one man."

"Areipithes calls himself king."

"He calls himself king, yet is he? I think not. There is more to kingship than holding a people in fear. No, the king of gold is not Scythian. Nor is he likely to be a man yet unknown. In the year since the prophecy was first uttered there has been no hint of such a one. No," Ket shook his head, "It is Alexander."

"Why Alexander?" asked Bithyia.

"He is king of much of the known world already, though still a young man. He has riches beyond measuring. His hair shines like gold and the fire of his spirit burns like gold." Ket's voice dropped to a hoarse whisper. "Why, when he came out from the oracle of the God Ammon-Ra at Siwah after visiting his heavenly father's temple, his face shone as if lit from within. If any king can be called 'golden' it is he."

"Does this mean Alexander will invade us?" squeaked Prithia.

"No," replied Ket. "He will stay in the south, which means our Nikometros must leave the Scythian plains and go to meet him. It is his prophesied destiny. Only after he leaves Scythia will he find his Golden King."

"So my lord Nikomayros will leave here to live in the land of the Golden King?" Tomyra's gentle voice caught and she turned away. Bithyia put her arm around the young girl's shoulder and gently wiped away a tear from her cheek.

"Do not fear, my lady. He won't leave you."

"I won't try to stop him, Bithyia. He'll return to his people and his king and leave me behind on these now empty plains." Tomyra sniffed and rubbed her nose with the back of her hand. She smiled weakly up at Bithyia's concerned face. "It's all right, dear one. As long as I have friends like you I'll survive."

"My lady, I..." Bithyia paused, uncertain. "My lady, he loves you. He won't leave you."

Sarmatia and Prithia reached out to comfort their mistress, stroking her hair and murmuring reassurances. The cat, Bubis, ousted from his position on Tomyra's cloak by the crowding women, stalked off, his tail erect. After pausing for a short while in the middle of the tent, he sauntered slowly back to Ket and rubbed against the old man, butting his head against Ket's leg.

Ket reached down and picked up the cat, cradling him against his thin chest, nuzzling his thick fur. "Come, beloved Bubis," he murmured. "You have disturbed these dear girls enough for today." He looked up and called out in a loud voice. "Excuse me, miss. Would you happen to have some fish for my cat? It is past his dinnertime and..." A loud clamour from outside caught his attention and his voice trailed off in surprise.

The noise increased, with the sound of horses galloping through the muddy streets and men shouting excitedly. Sarmatia dashed to the tent entrance and pushed out into the rain. A few moments later she ducked back in, her face aglow with excitement. She wiped her rain-streaked face and grimaced.

"Areipithes!" she exclaimed. "He's marching north at the head of a large force. The army is called out."

Bithyia, together with Dolra and Prithia helped their mistress to her feet and together the five women hurried from the tent, leaving Ket and Bubis sitting quietly. Ket remained silent, listening to the rain and the rising clamour of the town, his hand rhythmically stroking the soft black fur of his cat. After many minutes he nodded, his hand pausing on the cat's back. Bubis opened his eyes and looked up into the old man's wrinkled face.

"So, Bubis," Ket whispered. "It starts at last. The journey south to the Golden King."

Chapter 29

Nikometros turned, calming Diomede's impatient prancing as he looked back along the column of horsemen trudging through the mud and sleeting rain. Two days of continuous travel in the inclement weather had sapped the strength and spirit from his men despite the encouragement of his officers.

At least my Lions look halfway prepared, he thought. *Not like the Jartai force.* Nikometros brushed the rain from his face and stared through the curtains of drizzle at the main army. Nearly a thousand riders plodded dispiritedly along, even the semblance of order lost as the columns of men and horses disintegrated into a slowly shifting mob.

Moving through the advancing swarm, Nikometros saw his Jartai officers, Jaxes, Sopartos and others vainly trying to restore order. In their presence, the men shuffled their mounts into vague lines, stepping out with purpose. As soon as the officers passed on to another group, however, the disorder reasserted itself.

Nikometros cursed and kicked his horse into motion, galloping forward along the column of Lions. The men raised their heads as he passed and gave a ragged cheer, sheets of water cascading from their sodden clothes. Nikometros gave a wave of terse acknowledgement and splashed through the puddles to the front of the column where Timon and Tirses rode side by side.

"This venture is lost before we even meet the enemy," Nikometros fumed. "Look at this rabble." He gesticulated at the Jartai army. "Do you expect them to fight?"

Tirses gave Nikometros a mildly reproving look. "My lord, you have nothing to fear from your loyal Massegetae," he said. "They will fight, even if those Jartai women do not."

"Aye, Niko," growled Timon. "We've trained them well."

"You're right, Tirses, my apologies," muttered Nikometros. "But what can we do with only two hundred men?"

"There are Parasades and his troops too," reminded Timon. "His men are almost as well trained. That's another two hundred."

"Speaking of Parasades, where in Hades is he?" Nikometros scanned the muddy plains ahead of them, searching for any sign of life in the misty rain. "If he's going to scout the way ahead, he ought at least to report back from time to time," he grumbled. "It's dawn since we saw him."

A rider detached himself from the rambling Jartai army and galloped across the mud, sending sprays of water into the air. As the rider approached, the trio at the head of the Massegetae column could make out the burly form of Jaxes whipping his mount along. He brought his horse to a sliding stop beside Nikometros, spattering him with mud then guided it into a slow walk alongside his commander.

"Jaxes," greeted Nikometros. "What brings you here so urgently?"

"My lord," growled Jaxes. "Lugartes has received word that a small group of Massegetae are nearby. He intends to turn and fall upon them."

"What?"

"Outriders saw a body of Massegetae encamped in the valley of Ubul-tagarn. Lugartes is determined to attack them."

"Where is this Ubul-tagarn?" asked Nikometros. "I haven't heard of it."

Jaxes shrugged, sending water showering from his broad shoulders. "A small valley to the east. It's flat ground, suitable for horses."

Nikometros shook his head. "He must not attack," he snapped. "Certainly not until the enemy position has been reconnoitred."

"I fear it's too late, my lord," growled Jaxes. "See, even now he turns the army."

The ragged columns of Jartai horsemen turned to the east in disorganised groups, the mob streaming across the soaking plains toward a low line of hills. In the lead, Nikometros could make out a small group of figures beneath a colourful pennant, the personal standard of Lugartes.

"Who does the fornicating fool think he is, Niko?" grated Timon. "You were voted war-leader, not he. He has no business leading the army off like that."

"No, but my lord Nikomayros insisted on making Lugartes joint war-leader," reminded Jaxes. "Forgive me my plain speaking, lord, but that was ill advised. The power has gone to Lugartes' head and he is determined to assume full command. He thinks a quick and easy victory will give him the support he needs."

"Curse the man," fumed Nikometros. "We must restrain him. Tirses," he turned to the Massegetae officer beside him. "Bring your men on the double, we must..."

"My lord," interrupted Tirses. "I think the scouts return." He pointed southwest, toward the river.

Moving slowly through the swamped fields spreading out from the flooding Oxus River came a large body of riders. For a long time the column of approaching horsemen remained indistinct, the only noteworthy fact that could be deduced being the discipline of the riders. As they neared, pennants flying from tall lances identified the column as being Parasades men. A tight group at the front of the column was recognised as the Leopards, the spotted hide of their titular beast encircling the spear hafts. Behind them rode a less disciplined body of men, sporting a rag-tag of emblems and pennants.

Parasades drew his column of riders up alongside the Lions, and rode across to where Nikometros awaited him. He nodded at Jaxes politely then jerked his head in the direction of the Jartai. "Where in Hades are they going?"

"Lugartes has decided to attack a small enemy encampment," replied Nikometros.

"That man has the brains of an ox," observed Parasades. "Where does he think he is? Areipithes lies not half a day's travel south of here."

"You found him?" asked Nikometros sharply.

"Camped near the river, in full sight." Parasades grinned, the humour never touching his eyes. "Settled down for a long stay too. He has put up fortifications."

"Why in all the gods' names would he do that?" queried Timon in a puzzled voice. "He marched out to meet us. Now he hides behind walls?"

"Perhaps he's lost his nerve," laughed Tirses.

"How many men does he have?" asked Jaxes. "Has his army deserted him?"

Parasades nodded. "His army is smaller than we . thought. Barely a thousand men if the number of tents is anything to go by. Their morale is poor too, they barely noticed us when we rode up."

"They saw you?" queried Nikometros. "Was that wise?"

"We were in no danger, barely a dozen men bothered to fire arrows at us." Parasades grinned again. "I tell you, I was tempted to attack them and end this war immediately."

Nikometros frowned. "You have alerted them to our presence, though."

"Do you think he hasn't had his spies reporting back our every move anyway? I left fifty of my men to watch them until we could bring the army up."

"What do we do, Nikometros?" queried Timon. "The army is getting further away by the minute."

"We ride to stop Lugartes attacking until we ascertain the strength of the enemy," replied Nikometros crisply. "With Areipithes close we must move cautiously." He waved his command forward and picked up the pace to a measured gallop, splashing off across the water-soaked plain in pursuit of his allies. Parasades waved his own command into a parallel course. Slowly the disciplined squads of warriors overtook the plodding masses of Jartai.

Lugartes looked round at the noise of horses thundering up behind him. He scowled as he recognised Nikometros and reined in his horse. "Why have you left your station on the right flank, Nikomayros?"

Nikometros ignored the question and posed one of his own. "Why have you turned aside, Lugartes?"

"I'm about to win the first victory against the enemy," said Lugartes, satisfaction oozing like rancid oil over his beard. "My scouts tell me there's an enemy camp in the next valley, in Ubul-tagarn. I will destroy this camp and every man in it."

"Must I remind you that I am war-leader," said Nikometros softly. "You can take no independent action."

"I am joint war-leader," replied Lugartes. "By your own mouth. I make my own decisions regarding *my* Jartai army." He sneered and gestured at the men behind Nikometros. "You play with your own small force. I will exercise my skills with the main army."

Nikometros bit back his anger and put out an arm to restrain Timon whose face darkened at the insult. "It seems we must clarify this position later.

However, for now, I assume you have reconnoitred the enemy camp properly?"

"And alert them to our presence? I will sweep over the crest of the hill there," He pointed ahead of the trudging army, "And crush them like an avalanche." Lugartes smiled. "If you wish to partake of the victory and the spoils, you can join my army," he added magnanimously.

Nikometros inclined his head. "I will be there, at the head of my men."

Lugartes barked out a short laugh and galloped up to the front of the straggling army, now nearing the crest of the valley of Ubul-tagarn. He drew his sword, waving it above his head and rode over the crest, out of sight. With a half-hearted roar, the Jartai army followed him, the mounted warriors spilling over the edge into the long descent.

Nikometros met Parasades' eyes with a look of resignation tinged with anger. He turned and shouted out orders to Tirses who passed them along to the men in his command. The Lions, with the Leopards alongside, galloped up the low hill and into Ubul-tagarn.

Below them, the first of the Jartai warriors reached the enemy camp, Lugartes now hanging back exhorting his men forward. Nikometros started to give the command for a cavalry charge but the words died in his throat. He drew rein and sat staring down at the developing melee.

"Where are the horses?" Nikometros rasped.

"What do you mean, my lord? What horses?"

Nikometros pointed. "How did the enemy get here? Where are their horses?"

The enemy camp stood stark on the empty valley floor, a scattering of tents off to one side, scarcely sufficient to house even the few soldiers present. There was no trace of horse lines or baggage, as if the enemy had magically appeared out of thin air.

The soldiers below them, numbering only some hundred or so men, stood stolidly in a square, facing outward in all directions. The men held long sarissae, or jabbing spears, and sheltered behind large hide shields. A shower of arrows arced toward them, spending its force on the shield wall. Only a handful of men fell, the wounded being dragged back to the shelter of the middle of the square.

"Where did they learn that manoeuvre," mused Parasades.

The first Jartai horsemen arrived, swerving to avoid the long spears and stumbling into other riders, throwing the line into confusion. More arrived and began circling just beyond reach of the spears, firing arrows at the defenders and screaming insults.

"Cowards!" grated Timon. "One good charge and they could split that line."

"Those Jartai women have not got the stomach for it," crowed Tirses.

"Control yourself, Tirses," said Nikometros softly. "Remember they are our allies." He sighed and adjusted the sword at his side. "I do not like this situation but we must make the charge for them," he added.

"Wait," cried Tirses. "There, Jaxes leads them."

A small group of Jartai riders gathered itself about one of their number and hurled themselves at the defenders. The line buckled but held, the attacking horsemen withdrawing, leaving several bodies on the ground. Another group tried, with no greater success.

"Too few," stormed Timon. "The fools! How can a few break the line? It must be a massed charge."

"The leadership is divided," commented Parasades quietly. "None can agree, hence nothing useful is accomplished."

"What do we do, Niko?" queried Timon.

"There is something wrong here but we cannot abandon our friends." Nikometros turned to Tirses. "Signal a charge. We shall break that square for them." He kicked his stallion into motion, the column of his men forming up behind him. Their speed increased as they broke into a gallop down the long slope of the valley.

Behind, on the crest, Parasades controlled his fidgety mount and stared after Nikometros. Certes looked at his commander then at the fast-moving column of men.

"My lord? Do we not join them?" he asked anxiously.

"In good time," drawled Parasades. "His men are quite capable of breaking the line without us. We shall follow on behind." He urged his horse into a walk, sitting relaxed as it ambled down toward the fighting, his warriors laughing and joking behind him.

Nikometros leaned forward over the neck of Diomede, working his feet under the leather strap in front of him. His thighs gripped the horse firmly and he took a tight grip on the reins, winding them about his left hand. He glanced to his left and was glad to see that Timon had already braced himself for the impact with the enemy. He drew his sword and held it out in front of him, the thundering vibration of the charge making the point dance in front of his eyes. Blood pulsed in the veins of his forehead as the excitement built.

The fighting drew nearer. Jartai warriors cast worried looks over their shoulders and moved aside, parting as gauze before a sharp dagger. Ahead was the enemy line, the soldiers in it suddenly visible as individuals. Niko's eye caught that of a tall, thin man in the front rank of defenders. Hidden behind a large shield and long facial hair, the dark brown eyes appeared vacant, as if dreaming of home and family. Blue eyes, fair hair and gleaming armour atop a foaming horse ripped at his attention. The man's eyes widened then shifted, looking for an escape. His lance wavered, drooped then disappeared as the fast-moving avalanche of horses and men burst into and through the line. The thunder of the collision contrasted with the brittle snapping of lances and bones, and the high-pitched squealing screams of horses.

Nikometros' eye caught a flash of steel arcing beside him and the man with the vacant eyes dropped, his head split open. Around him rose a cacophony of shouts and screams as men died, fled or found a purpose for living in the destruction of their fellows.

The line of men opposite the point of impact, their backs turned against the charge, disintegrated as the momentum hurled the column out the other side of the square. In the trampled ruin of the battlefield, the Jartai warriors raised a cry of triumph and fell upon the scattered remnants of the Massegetae defenders.

Nikometros found himself in an open space beyond the battle, surrounded by his men. Faces distorted, the young warriors of his command grinned or grimaced as the fact of victory and survival overtook them. They milled, turning to stare back with interest at the heaving mob of Jartai warriors consigning the last of the defenders to an ignominious death.

A horn sounded, far off, seemingly unconnected to the events of the past minutes. One or two of the Lions looked around, curiosity rather than anxiety moulding their features. A distant storm rumble, now comfortingly familiar in the early spring rains, grew and swelled as the thundering became more than just a noise. A vibration shook the ground, the puddles on the water-soaked valley floor shivered. Men ceased their killing and looked up, looked round.

Down the far side of the valley poured a flood of horsemen. Massegetae horsemen, bred to the horse's back, clinging with muscular legs leaving arms free to wield lethal hunting bows, raced toward the disorganised throng of Jartai tribesmen. In the lead, at the front of a disciplined wedge of warriors, rode Areipithes. His bulky body leaned forward into the charge, the wind of his passage whipping his long black hair and beard free from his exultant face. He roared a challenge as he came, a formless paean of hate and triumph.

The Massegetae horde, over three thousand strong, swept through the milling Jartai, brushing them aside and trampling them underfoot, reddening the mud with their life. Many, on the outskirts of the flood, hammered at their horses' sides, desperate, panic stricken, forcing their way from the valley floor. Arrows, released in sky-darkening swarms, cut down those who fled. Lugartes, his weapons discarded, fleeing for his life, fell impaled.

Nikometros, off to one side of the initial battle, sized up the situation with a glance as the first of Areipithes' army tore into his own army. He swore, loudly and colourfully then signalled his Lions to wheel about and flee the field. Riding fast, he led his men down the valley, racing westward toward the main river.

Parasades, following far behind Nikometros' charge, wheeled his command at the first sight of the enemy and galloped back over the valley rim, turning westward parallel to the flight of the other survivors.

Chapter 30

Areipithes, at the head of his triumphant army, rode into the Jartai village at the confluence of the Spagus and Purul rivers in the light of the late afternoon sun, three days after the battle at Ubul-tagarn. His first order was the massacre of any male inhabitant capable of bearing arms. The bodies, mostly those of children and old men, were thrown down the steep banks of the rivers to carry a message of despair far downstream.

The conqueror of Ubul-tagarn regarded the huddled mass of women and young children now gathered into the village square by armed soldiers. A smile quirked his lips as his eyes slipped over the faces, tear-streaked, and bodies, begrimed, of the younger women. He nodded and rasped out commands to his officers.

"Let the men choose whom they will," he said. Raising his voice, Areipithes called out to the squads near him. "Breed good Massegetae sons off them, men." To the officer nearest him he added in a low voice. "See to the disposal of the rest, Scolices. Then join me in..." Areipithes looked around the square, his eyes settling on the largest, most imposing structure. "...In there. Bring Thoas and Arxes. I will hear your reports." He turned and walked his horse over to the house, dismounting and handing the reins to one of his men.

Behind him, the soldiers moved in, laughing and joking coarsely, lust rising like a miasma over the village. In the wake of lust followed death; squads pushing the older women and infants toward the rivers, swords silencing the wailing and screaming that ripped the dying day.

Areipithes sighed and stripped his cloak from his shoulders, running his fingers through his lustrous hair. He looked around the room, noting the rich fabrics and well-made furniture. He walked over to a table and rummaged through the pots and flasks on it, eventually finding a flask of wine. Pouring himself a drink he wandered over to the low fire and sat down, sipping his wine as he stared into the embers.

A sharp knock at the door preceded the arrival of three men. Scolices, thin but well-muscled, moved fluidly into the room. He took up a position near his king and nodded at the other two men.

"My lord," said Scolices softly. "Thoas and Arxes have prepared their reports for you."

Areipithes grunted and turned from his contemplation of the dying fire. "So, Thoas, you first. What of the army? How are we placed?"

A thickset man, slow of body and mind though an efficient soldier, Thoas thought for a moment before replying. "Men are still deserting, my lord, but nowhere near as many as before. The battle gave them confidence in their ability to face the Greek."

"Yes, we shall get to him in a moment. Continue, Thoas."

"We are well provisioned," continued Thoas. "The march north has been rapid but the men's morale is high." He flashed a quick grin. "Now their appetites are being satiated, they will welcome further opportunities for conquest."

Areipithes nodded. "Good. They shall have it. Scolices, make sure the Jartai cattle and horses are divided fairly. Keep only a twentieth part for my herd."

Scolices raised his eyebrows. "A twentieth, my lord? The chief's share is more commonly a fifth."

Areipithes waved his hand in casual dismissal. "The men will fight harder if they have more at stake." He turned back to the army officer. "How many casualties?"

"Less than fifty, my lord." Thoas shrugged. "Except for the bait. They were wiped out."

"A small loss," grinned Areipithes. "I doubted their loyalty anyway and they thought, right up to the end, that they would earn their freedom by fighting for me."

"The army currently numbers thirty-two hundred, my lord. They are well armed and have sufficient horses. I doubt there is another army within a month's travel that can match us."

"And what of the Jartai?" asked Areipithes. "Do they still represent a threat? Arxes?"

Arxes turned startlingly pale eyes on his chief. Despite his swarthy skin and stocky build, the Massegetae spymaster's features betrayed the Caucasian origins of his mother. An aura of cruelty hung about the man as he slid forward into his chief's sight.

"They do not," he whispered hoarsely. "The Jartai have effectively ceased to exist as a tribe. Perhaps a hundred or so still live but they are scattered. Their chief, Lugartes, died as he fled the battle, as did several of his advisors."

"And the Greek?" grated Areipithes.

"He fled early but he kept his force intact," went on Arxes. "The Macedonian is dangerous but with a mere two hundred men he is no real threat."

"Good. Now Scolices, your mission was obviously a success. Tell me..."

"I haven't finished," interrupted Arxes. The man's eyes flashed with anger. "There's still one real threat to your safety."

Areipithes' face flushed at the interruption. He turned back to face his spymaster, making an effort to control his temper. "And what threat is that?"

"Parasades. He is Massegetae and commands a small but disciplined force of men loyal to him and your father."

Areipithes frowned. "I didn't see Parasades at the battle."

"He never committed himself," commented Thoas. "He hung back and rode away with his men when he saw what was happening."

"Interesting," mused Areipithes. "What are your thoughts, Arxes?"

The spymaster's pale eyes hooded over. "Parasades is no coward. Nor is he overly cautious. I believe he's not fully committed to their cause, though whether because he supports you or because he wishes the power for himself, I cannot say."

"Find out." Areipithes flashed a questioning look at Arxes. "Can you?"

"I have a man who can gain access to him," conceded Arxes in a sibilant whisper. "He might need persuasion though. What can I offer as incentive?"

"Anything you have to, short of sole power." Areipithes laughed harshly. "I can always change my mind." He nodded at the spymaster. "See to it, as quickly as you can." Dismissing the man with a gesture, Areipithes turned to Scolices, waiting patiently by the fire. "Back to your mission then. Tell me about it."

Scolices stretched and cracked his knuckles. He gestured toward the table inquiringly. When Areipithes nodded, he walked over and poured himself a cup of wine, ignoring the hopeful expression on Thoas' face. He drained the cup, belched and set it down on the table.

"It was easy." Scolices grinned broadly. "The trusting fools were only too willing to believe anyone who said they fled from your tyrannical rule." He noticed the thunderous expression on his chief's face and hurried on. "My apologies, lord, but I had to blacken your name to gain their trust."

"Naturally. Go on," growled Areipithes.

"They believed everything I said. They fell over themselves in their hurry to meet you before you could meet up with your ally Nemathres of the Dumae."

Areipithes laughed and slapped his thigh. "They believed that?" He frowned and nodded, thinking to himself. "I must attend to that one later," he muttered. "So, what other disinformation did you sow?"

"I said the Dahai were your allies, that men were deserting your army and that the Serratae raided your lands continually."

"The Dahai are too cautious," spat Areipithes. "The best I could get them to agree to was not to interfere. Still, they have served their purpose."

"There are fewer desertions now, my lord," repeated Thoas. "The bulk of your army is loyal."

Areipithes nodded and looked around the room. He walked over to a clutter of boxes in one corner and started rummaging through them. "You have done well, Scolices. You too, Thoas," he added. Finding a parchment he scanned the writing on it then ripped off a corner. Further search revealed a sharpened feather and a container of rather lumpy ink. He scratched a few words on the fragment of parchment and handed it to Scolices.

"Take this to the herd-master. Select a hundred cattle and twenty horses each."

Scolices bowed obsequiously and smiled. "You are generous, my lord."

Thoas saluted, pleasure suffusing his swarthy face. "Thank you, lord." Together the two men backed out of the room.

Areipithes carried the damaged parchment back to the fire and, pulling up a stool, sat down. He tilted the parchment to the light and struggled to make sense of the writing. His lips moved silently as his finger traced the lines.

"Poetry!" snorted Areipithes. Abruptly he threw the scroll into the fire, watching as flames flared up around the blackening parchment. "Useless words," he muttered. "The sort of thing my bitch sister would enjoy." He fell silent and stared at the ashes of the poetry.

My sister still lives, he thought. *And as long as she lives, she and her Greek lover will be a danger, no matter what that fool Arxes says.* Areipithes bent and threw a few pieces of wood, lying next to the fireplace, onto the glowing ashes. He stirred them with a stick until flames flickered and caught. *Why do men follow him? Why have so many otherwise sensible Massegetae gone over to his side?*

Lifting the stick from the flames Areipithes waved it through the air. The flames died, leaving smoke as their legacy. *The excitement of the exotic,* he decided. *Young men cannot be trusted to stick with the old ways, the ways that served our ancestors well.* He poked the stick back into the flames, watching the wood leap into life again. *So, do I send out patrols hoping to find the Greek and my sister, or do I let them try to raise another army?*

Areipithes stretched and got up, wandering back to the table for another cup of wine. From outside, the screams of the female Jartai survivors faded into muted sobs and wails as his army turned from killing to the more pleasurable pursuits--for men--of victorious armies everywhere.

That bitch Tomyra, he reflected. *Without her and her subversion of the true worship of the Mother, none of this would have happened. Like mother, like daughter...*Areipithes swore and hurled the cup from him, spattering his arm with the dregs of the wine. *Just as her whore mother turned the love of my father from me, so did Tomyra turn his respect by whoring after the Greek barbarian. Bitch!* He wiped the wine from his sleeve and picked up another cup, filling it with more wine. He sipped. *That fool Dimurthes let her escape...*Areipithes snorted derisively. *And got himself killed! No wonder the Serratae are upset.* He walked back to the fire and kicked another log into the flames, feeling the welcome heat wash out into the room. *So why do they attack me? She is as much my enemy as theirs.*

Areipithes raised his voice and called out to the guards he knew waited outside the house. When they entered he ordered food and koumiss then dismissed them. Within minutes, servants carried in a rich beef stew, bubbling in an iron pot, and freshly baked bread. Koumiss sloshed in a skin flask, the sour, nutty smell filling the room as the servant unstoppered it and poured out a generous serving.

Replete and feeling truly warm for the first time since setting out on this campaign, Areipithes eventually pushed his bowl away and sipped at his koumiss, the tartness cleansing the fatty stew from his palate. He called out again and a guard put his head around the doorjamb.

"Ah, Tyros," he said. "Come in." He beckoned him in and sat smiling encouragingly at the man. "You have eaten?"

"Yes, lord," said Tyros, fidgeting nervously in the presence of his king.

"And sampled the delights of this poxed village, no doubt?"

"Er, yes lord."

"Find a young one for me, Tyros. I feel like being entertained."

"A...young one, my lord?"

"A woman, Tyros. Better still a girl. Find me a pretty one."

Tyros saluted and ducked out of the room. A few minutes later he pushed open the door, dragging an apathetic young girl behind him. The soldier pushed her forward roughly, grinning as she collapsed on the ground by the fire. "Here, lord. Best I could find at short notice." He shrugged. "There're a couple of others but they're being used at the moment. This one's untouched, so far."

"She will do," drawled Areipithes. He waved Tyros away. "Leave us." He waited until the door closed behind the man then nudged the girl with the toe of his boot. "Get up."

The girl stirred and, her eyes hooded, face averted, struggled to her feet. She stood, head down and swaying slightly, in front of the Massegetae king.

Areipithes ran his eyes over the girl, noting with satisfaction the clear unblemished skin showing through rents in her dress and the swelling curves of her body. *Fifteen,* he judged. *Young enough to be a virgin, old enough to know what to do.* Lust stirred in his groin.

"Come here," he breathed.

The girl raised her head and looked at him for the first time. She shivered but stepped closer. Areipithes smiled, his eyes alight with a savage delight and, putting his hands at the neck of her dress, ripped it apart. The girl reacted instantly, her right hand swinging up and across, fingers extended and nails reaching for the man's eyes.

Areipithes jerked his head back, the nails scoring his cheek. He bellowed with rage and backhanded the girl, knocking her across the room. She collapsed into a moaning heap near the table, her dress in tatters round her waist. Areipithes looked at her, one hand raised to the bloody scratches on his face. He licked his lips, staring at her ripe breasts. "You shall pay for that," he muttered.

Striding over to the supine girl, Areipithes dug his fingers into her hair and pulled her upright. The girl moaned, her hands gripping his, desperately trying to relieve the agony in her scalp. He reached down and stripped the dress from her body, grinning at her nakedness. Pulling her after him, Areipithes walked over to a soft rug in a corner, loosening his trouser cords with his free hand. The girl stumbled against him, almost falling, and he let go of her hair, supporting her. She moved sideways and slammed her knee upward, aiming for his groin. Her knee connected with his thigh and Areipithes grunted from the pain then reached across and slapped her, hard. Before she could recover he hurled her to the floor and collapsed on top of her, forcing her legs apart.

The girl screamed, piercingly, her nails once more seeking his eyes. Areipithes grunted again, grappling with her and gripped her wrists, forcing them over her head.

"Enough, bitch!" he rasped.

A frantic hammering on the door pulled his attention from the girl. He looked up then back down at the struggling girl. "Go away!" he bellowed. The hammering came again, more insistent, followed by muffled shouting. With a roar of anger, Areipithes rose to his feet, the girl frantically scrabbling away into a corner, covering herself with her hands. He looked at the girl; half moved after her then with a curse strode to the door, his hands clutching his loose trousers.

Areipithes slammed the door open. "You had better have a very good reason for disturbing me," he snarled.

Thoas stared wide-eyed at his king; his eyes flicking to the sobbing girl in the corner then back to Areipithes' angry face. "My...my apologies, lord. A courier from Urul...I thought you should hear..." Thoas gulped. "Er, I can go away..."

Areipithes stared at his army commander then with an effort controlled his anger. "A courier?" Abruptly, he wheeled and strode back to the fire, doing up his dishevelled clothing. "Send him in. I will hear his news." He looked back over his shoulder. "Thoas," he said softly. "This had better be important."

The courier stumbled in and saluted. His exhaustion was evident and he swayed on his feet, his eyes hollow and staring in a sallow face. His clothing was sodden and caked with mud. "My lord," he whispered. "News from Urul."

Areipithes signalled Thoas to fetch the man a cup of koumiss. He nodded at the stool and waited while the courier drank and collected his thoughts. At length the man looked up.

"My lord, the Serratae has crossed the river in force. They move inland, toward Urul, burning and killing." The courier faltered at his king's stony expression. "My lord," he continued. "When I left Urul they were but three days from the city."

"Then they'll have burned the city and moved on by now," grated Areipithes. "Who knows where they will be."

"No, my lord. They won't be there yet. There is still time..."

"When did you leave Urul?" snapped Areipithes.

"At daybreak, yesterday, my lord. The city defences marched out to meet them. With luck they will delay them long enough for you...er, should you wish..." The courier's voice trailed off uncertainly.

"You travelled fast." Areipithes turned and paced, thinking. He looked up at Thoas, who snapped his attention back from his interested contemplation of the naked girl. "Find this man a hot meal and a soft bed. Then send your officers out into the town. Gather your men together. We march south at daybreak."

As Thoas hustled the courier out of the door, Areipithes called him back. "Take this girl out too." He noticed Thoas' expression and grinned cruelly. "You won't have the time, Thoas. Give her to your men instead; she may be the last they get for a while." He listened and smiled as the door closed on the appreciative cries of the guards outside then dismissing everything else from his mind, Areipithes started pacing, his mind grappling with the logistical problems of fighting two wars at the same time.

Chapter 31

Despondency hung over the encampment like the acrid pall of wood smoke that guttered from the damp wood. Several hundred men and women gathered in groups of ten or twenty on the loose shale slopes below the river bluffs. Campfires burned in the night, the darkness hardly alleviated by the reluctant flames, the gloom deepened by dense smoke. Meat heated slowly on spits, turned by slow moving men in wet clothing. Horses whickered and stamped in groups, hobbled against wandering, feeding on sparse grasses and the occasional handful of hay or grain scraped from the bottom of empty supply bags.

Close up against the cliffs, sheltered by a concavity so slight the westerly wind scarcely paused in its play with the plumes of smoke, sat Nikometros, head bowed and forehead furrowed in thought. Around him, staring moodily at the fire sat or stood his friends and leaders of the army so recently routed by Areipithes.

After two days of traveling west to the Oxus River then north along its banks, their numbers swelled by refugees, the Jartai survivors of the debacle halted at last. Many of the men were too weary to run farther, others were just too uncaring. If the enemy found them now then so be it, the gods had spoken, and here they would die.

A day later Nikometros and Parasades arrived, nearly four hundred strong, their men still alert and eager for battle. After the flight from the valley of Ubul-tagarn, Nikometros and Parasades galloped north, swinging east of the Jartai village to pick up Tomyra and her warrior maidens from their station guarding the Jartai herds. Moving north and west of the village, they sent word of the defeat and the imminent arrival of the Massegetae army. Some fled into the countryside but most stayed, not believing the foreigners. They would, they declared; await the arrival of their own Jartai men folk. Unable to convince them, Nikomayros moved away in front of the oncoming army, bitter at his failure to convince his Jartai friends.

North and west they rode, toward the river, eventually picking up the tracks of many horsemen. Now they camped, depressed and uncomfortable, to decide the future.

"At least they will give us some respite," growled Timon, his arm around Bithyia. He leaned over and kissed her damp hair, eliciting a weary smile from the young woman. "Gods, but these Jartai look like whipped dogs." He tossed his head in the general direction of the encampment.

"Not all of us," rumbled Jaxes. "Though I will admit I have seen morale higher." A wry smile tugged at the corner of his mouth.

A loud sneeze erupted from a bundle of rags hard against the cliff wall. It was followed by a sniffling mutter and the answering cry of a cat.

"Poor Ket," sighed Tomyra. "He cannot abide the wet and cold. He needs his hot lands and the sun."

"Better here in the wet than dry in the Jartai village," commented Parasades dryly. "If those reports are accurate, Areipithes has shown his true self for all to see." He snorted. "It will make our task the easier."

"That's my people you are talking about," said Jaxes. He shook his head. "I'm thankful now my wife died last year. I could not have borne it had she lived to suffer as so many others have. I grieve for my fellow tribesmen. Many have lost their families."

"I cannot believe even my brother would do such a thing," whispered Tomyra. She sat close to Nikometros but not touching. The small but definite distance between the man and woman drew concerned looks from those about them. If either Nikometros or Tomyra noticed the looks, however, they ignored them.

"It's war," stated Nikometros. "In the aftermath of battle, men's minds turn to other things. A disciplined army can be controlled. Alexander never allowed his men to pillage unless the enemy had proved themselves to be without honour." He poked at the smouldering embers with a bent stick, listening to the sizzle of drying wood. "In all my life I have only seen such things once. When Tyre fell, Alexander razed the city to the ground and crucified the survivors. He allowed the soldiers to do what they willed." Nikometros shook his head, his damp bronze locks tossing. "Maybe the Tyrian soldiers deserved it; certainly the women and children did not. I think Alexander lost his innocence at Tyre. Before that he saw war as a noble venture, after that only as a necessity."

"All of this is very interesting, Nikomayros," drawled Parasades, "But how does it help our situation? We know only too well Areipithes is a conqueror. Winning does give him certain rights."

"He has no right to slaughter and rape innocent women and children," hissed Tomyra. "Only barbarians act like that."

Parasades smiled and stretched out. His clothing steamed as the growing heat of the fire slowly drove the water out. "Barbarians, eh? Like our Greek friends from the west?" He lazily waved his hand in the direction of

Nikometros and Timon. One of his men approached and coughed, waiting discreetly for his lord to notice him.

Parasades waved him forward and listened as the man bent and whispered in his ear. He raised an eyebrow and waved the man away. "I will see him later," he muttered.

"Not all of us act like that," replied Nikometros softly.

"I was forgetting," grinned Parasades. "We have a tame Greek. We should thank the civilising influence of our own dear priestess for that."

"Your words are offensive, Parasades," declared Tomyra. "My lord Nikomayros is his own man."

"And I find them offensive too," grated Timon. He rose and stared through the billows of smoke at Parasades. "You accuse Niko of dishonourable behaviour, yet your own conduct is less than honourable."

Parasades' smile vanished and he tensed, sitting up from his sprawl. "What do you mean?"

"You were less than enthusiastic in rescuing Niko from the Serratae, despite declaring him your friend. You wanted to betray him to save your own skin."

"And yours, Timon. Not to mention our priestess who is precious to all of us." Parasades shrugged and yawned. "Besides, we all thought he was dying." He glanced over at Nikometros. "Sorry, my friend, but it's true. I wouldn't have bet even a broken-down nag on you living."

"I did not forsake him, but I have no doubt the lady Tomyra is much more important to you," went on Timon, his face turning red as his anger grew. "You seek power, not honour."

"What would you know of honour?" sneered Parasades. "You are but a common dirt soldier whereas I am a Scythian noble. My forefathers were chiefs."

"How did they get to be chiefs?" taunted Timon. "By betraying their masters?"

"Timon! Please! Settle down," pleaded Nikometros. "None of us gain by this."

"Aye, Timon. Don't rise to him," growled Tirses.

Timon ignored them, shaking off the restraining arm of Bithyia as well. "Nearly worked again at that Ubul place, did it not? Now I know why you were so slow to follow. Hoping Areipithes would do your work for you?"

"Be careful what you say, Greek," snarled Parasades, leaping to his feet.

"Timon! Enough!" roared Nikometros, also rising.

Timon strode around the fire, his face suffused with blood. "I say you deliberately hung back. You refused to join battle, hoping Niko would be killed."

"Are you calling me a traitor?" yelled Parasades. He drew his sword and swung at Timon with it, his face livid.

Timon dragged his own sword from his belt and leapt back, parrying the other man's blow. He stepped back again, retreating before Parasades' furious attack. Parasades slipped and almost fell on the loose shale of the hillside, allowing Timon to counterattack. The uproar and clash of steel brought men running from nearby campfires. They ringed the fighters, calling out encouragement to one or the other, inquiring of the cause of the fight.

Nikometros struggled through the cordon of watchers, yelling for Timon and Parasades to desist. Bithyia stood white-faced in the open circle, her hands clenching her bow, an arrow half strung. She raised and lowered it again uncertainly as the fighters circled and lunged. Tomyra stood beside her, calling to the fighters, pleading with them. Certes and Prithia swayed in the jostling crowd, agonised uncertainty washing over their faces.

Tirses watched avidly, excitement glowing in his eyes. "Take him, Timon," he muttered.

Timon lunged, passing close to Nikometros, who stepped out, deflecting Timon's sword arm upward and parrying Parasades' answering blow on his own blade.

"Enough!" yelled Nikometros. "Parasades, I will not allow this." He deliberately turned his back on Parasades and glared at Timon. "Put up your sword, Timon," he snapped.

Parasades, his face twitching with anger, hesitated. He half raised his sword at Nikometros' back then thought better of it. He swore and shoved his sword back in his belt and turned on his heel, pushing through the circle of soldiers.

Nikometros, having calmed Timon, called after the Scythian noble. "Parasades, come and sit with me. Do not let this misunderstanding come between us."

Parasades whirled. "Misunderstanding, Nikomayros? When he calls me a traitor? I think not." He tossed his head at the glowering figure of Timon, with Bithyia and Tomyra standing beside him at the fire's edge. "Will he apologise? Beg my forgiveness?" He waited several moments then snorted derisively. "I thought not." He turned and stalked into the darkness, Certes and several of his men hurrying after him.

"Where are you going, Parasades?" called Nikometros. "I have need of you here. There is much to plan."

"Then plan it yourself, Greek," called back Parasades from where he stood in the darkness, removing the hobble from his horse. "I will not stay with those who question my honour." He leapt upon his horse's back and jerked its head around, facing downhill. "I will therefore remove myself...and my men, from your untrusting presence." With a shout he spurred his horse down the rocky slope, followed a few moments later by Certes then swelling numbers of his men.

The surrounding soldiers wandered back to their fires, shaking their heads and muttering. Nikometros swore, kicking moodily at the loose rocks then sat down on a boulder near the fire and put his head in his hands. Tomyra consoled a weeping Prithia, quietly dissuading her from riding after her man.

Timon spat into the fire. "No great loss," he growled. "I never did trust the man and it seems I was right not to."

Nikometros raised his head and gave him a bleak look. "He has just taken a quarter of our forces and left. Do you think we can oppose Areipithes without him?"

"We are better off without him," said Timon stubbornly.

"We are, my lord," added Tirses.

Jaxes walked up, with two of his Jartai officers. "Nikomayros, I would talk with you."

Nikometros smiled and waved toward the strewn boulders. "Take your pick of a seat, my friend. I can only offer you a meagre hospitality I fear."

Jaxes nodded, unsmiling. He seated himself, as did his officers. After a short pause, Jaxes coughed and stared into the smoky fire. "He has left with one hundred of his men and rides south."

"He'll be back," replied Nikometros calmly. "When his anger cools he'll realise he acted hastily."

"I hope so." Jaxes paused again. "There's other news, my friend. I beg you not to show any alarm for the remains of my army are poised on the edge of despair." He caught the quizzical uplift of the other man's eyebrows and hurried on. "Yes, my army, Nikomayros. With Lugartes and Sopartos dead I have taken command of the Jartai. I will lead them into battle under your leadership."

Nikometros nodded wearily. "I know, my friend. I don't doubt you. But you spoke of other news?"

"The Dumae. You remember how Scolices..."

"That pile of turds?" snarled Timon. "A spy, straight from the side of his whore-master Areipithes." Tirses clenched his teeth and looked away, embarrassed.

"...told us his master and Nemathres were allies?" continued Jaxes. "He may have lied. Nemathres is camped less than half a day's travel north of here with his army. He comes in answer, he says, 'to an unasked-for favour'." Jaxes frowned. "Whose side is he on, Nikomayros? Whose favour is he answering? His men do not march as if prepared for battle."

Nikometros smiled uncertainly. "Nemathres? I would like to believe he wouldn't betray us. Yet I thought Lugartes a trusted friend. Even Parasades..." He broke off, shaking his head. "So he comes in response to an unspoken request? Let us pray to the gods it's our request he answers." He grimaced at Jaxes. "Pray he comes to help us. How many men does he have?"

"Nearly a thousand, I am told, though I have not seen them for myself."

"Gods! We must send envoys immediately, Jaxes. We must know whose side he fights on. Then we must decide how best we are to oppose our enemy, whether he be one or two."

"You must talk to the men, Nikomayros. They need to hear from your lips that their cause is not yet lost."

"I will," said Nikometros grimly. "At daybreak. Let them rest and eat for now, Jaxes, though do not neglect safety. Have sentries posted. And send those envoys to the Dumae now. I need to know by first light."

"I have already set sentries, my lord. I will see to the envoys now." Jaxes turned away, gesturing to his officers.

"So, my friends." Nikometros looked around the vaguely seen faces in the dimly lit campsite. "What are we to do? Give me your counsel."

The men and women around the fire sat silently, looking at one another for a few minutes. As the silence grew to an uncomfortable length, Tomyra coughed, partly due to the billowing smoke and said softly.

"We will do whatever you decide, Niko. You were elected war-leader to depose my brother from his throne. We will follow you in this."

Timon grunted. "Smash the bastard son of a whore," he growled. "If we cannot then leave these fornicating savages to it and go home."

Bithyia dropped her arm from Timon's shoulder. "Am I a savage too, Timon?" she asked in an angry voice. "These are my people. I am home already."

"Oh, turds!" muttered Timon. "I'm sorry, Bithyia. I was talking from anger. That traitor Parasades..."

"Anyone else?" inquired Nikometros. "Now is the time. Say whatever you're thinking, I need to know."

"Keep on fighting," said Tirses. "What else?"

"Whatever you decide," stated Jaxes calmly, "I will lead my Jartai against Areipithes. He has slaughtered my people and I will not rest until he is dead or we are."

Sarmatia nodded. "Yes, Nikomayros. We swore to avenge ourselves on the parricide. We'll follow you against him."

Nikometros looked around the circle, noting the determined looks on their faces. Prithia wiped tears from her face with the back of her hand and nodded. Agarus tapped his hand with the point of his dagger and grinned.

Ket shrugged. "I am no warrior but I will implore the gods for their favour. I am lost in a cold, wet land far away from their sunny homes but maybe they can still hear me."

Nikometros nodded. "Very well then. We continue to fight. Next question: how are we to do this?" He stood and raised a hand. "Our position isn't good. We have an army of uncertain enthusiasm numbering perhaps six hundred, seven if Parasades returns." Timon hawked and spat into the fire. "A thousand more if Nemathres joins us," Nikometros went on, ticking off the points on his fingers. "Together we still fall well short of Areipithes' army."

"We can take him," called Tirses confidently.

Nikometros shook his head. "If we face Areipithes head on, we'll lose. We have achieved a lot in a short time but the men are not disciplined enough for complex manoeuvres. We must find a way to draw him into a trap, to put him at a disadvantage then make good use of it. Any ideas?"

Jaxes thought for a moment then said slowly. "If we are to set a trap we must bait it. What is irresistible to Areipithes? What is it he wants?"

"Power, riches," grunted Timon. "What any Scythian noble wants."

"Yes," agreed Jaxes equably. "And time will give him that if he outlasts us. What does he want in the short term?"

"Me," said Tomyra simply, "And Niko. My brother will not rest easy until we are dead."

Nikometros nodded. "We are the only things that will draw Areipithes into a trap. So we must give him what he wants." He looked around the circle of faces. "I must put myself into a position where he feels he can take me."

"You joke with us, Niko!" exploded Timon. "There is no way you are baiting a trap with yourself."

"You cannot, my lord," added Tirses. "Who would lead our armies against the usurper whilst you are acting as bait?" He turned apologetically to the de facto Jartai chief. "Forgive me, Jaxes, but only the Jartai would follow you. And would any Jartai follow Timon or me? And what of the Dumae? Will they follow either of us?"

Jaxes nodded. "He is right, Nikomayros. Only one man holds this coalition of tribes together. You cannot be the bait in the trap."

Nikometros slumped down on his rock again and ran his fingers through his damp bronze hair. "Then how do we bait it?"

"There is but one way," Tomyra said.

Nikometros looked up at her set face. "No," he whispered.

"There is no other way," she repeated. "My brother desires our deaths. We cannot risk you, Niko. I am the only other choice."

"I won't risk you."

"You must. My brother will shy from anything that looks like a trap unless he reacts to the bait instantly, without thought. He'll do that if he thinks he can kill me or capture me."

Bithyia frowned. "My lady, there will be great danger."

Tomyra nodded. "Indeed. We mustn't underestimate Areipithes. Yet I will feel safe knowing my Niko is able to come to my rescue." She laughed nervously. "I wouldn't be able to rescue him were the roles reversed."

"No! I won't let you do this. I forbid it," snapped Nikometros.

Tomyra raised an eyebrow. "Forbid it?" she asked coolly. "I am a priestess of the People, my lord, and my own woman besides. You do not forbid me."

Nikometros ground his teeth in frustration. "Tomyra, for pity's sake. I didn't mean to command you but, think...I mean, for the love we..." His voice trailed off as he flushed. He stared round the circle of faces wildly. "Tell her. Surely you can see the folly..."

"She is right," said Jaxes. "One of you must do it and it cannot be you." He shrugged. "Therefore, my friend..."

Timon nodded soberly. "You know I would do anything to save her from harm, Niko, but she's right. Areipithes will go after her without a second thought. With his guard down, you can spring the trap and finish him once and for all."

"It will be all right, Niko." Tomyra rose and crossed to Nikometros, falling on her knees beside him. She looked up into his troubled face, a slight smile tweaking her lips. "Don't you believe the Mother Goddess holds me in her hands? She won't allow me to come to harm."

Nikometros stared into her dark eyes then slowly nodded. "I don't like it but I suppose you're right, my love," he whispered. "If anyone enjoys the protection of the Goddess, you do."

"So how do we set this trap?" asked Tirses. "How is the usurper to find the bait alone and seemingly defenceless?"

"And where?" queried Jaxes. "His suspicions will be aroused if he has to come into our territory."

"Wherever it is, it must be in a place that is favourable for our cavalry charge." Timon gave a savage bark of humour. "The charge is our strongest weapon. I would hate not to show that bastard how it is properly carried out."

"The plains around Urul," said Nikometros slowly. "But how to get him there? And how to surprise him? He'll see our army half a day's travel away."

"I know!" squeaked Prithia, in great excitement. "There is a place, my lady. Remember, three years ago, during the drought..."

"Yes," nodded Bithyia, with a grin. "The shrine of the Mother at Marsil-tagal."

Nikometros looked from one young woman to the other. "What is this place and why might it be the place?"

"Marsil-tagal is a shrine to the Great Goddess in the foothills south of Urul, not far in fact from where you were captured, Niko." Tomyra smiled and squeezed Nikometros' knee. "We pray to the Mother there in times of direst need, such as during the drought three years ago." She rocked back on her heels, her voice rising in pitch as excitement gripped her. "Areipithes will think nothing of my going there. We're in dire need. He'll half expect it."

"I'll have Timon and a squad of Lions ride with you. I won't put you in unnecessary danger."

"You cannot," said Tomyra simply. "It would immediately arouse his suspicions if my brother saw any man ride toward Marsil-tagal. Only women go there."

Nikometros kept silent, biting his lip. At last, he sighed deeply. "Very well. At least you'll be armed and ready for him."

"That neither, my lord," smiled Tomyra. "No priestess or her maidens would go to Marsil-tagal dressed for war. We must wear our priestly robes, though we shall have our bows. They are sacred."

Nikometros grunted. "What is the ground like?"

"The shrine itself is in a rocky cleft in the hills, my lord," broke in Prithia. 'Tagal' is the word for a woman's er...female parts...I mean..." She blushed and stuttered to a stop.

Bithyia raised her eyes with a look of exasperation. "The shrine is hidden, my lord, but two low rolling hills stretch out into the plains. The ground between them is flat and hard."

"With squadrons hidden behind both the hills..."

"...We can sweep out and surprise him."

"Our lady will never be in any danger," said Bithyia triumphantly.

"Divide our forces?" queried Jaxes. "Not a good idea."

Nikometros grinned, feeling his mood lighten. "That is where my maps come in. By the time I have finished, every commander will know his place, where everyone else is, when to move and precisely where to."

Shouting erupted from the Jartai camp; interrupting Nikometros and making everyone crane their necks to see what was happening. Several Jartai soldiers hurried over, jabbering excitedly.

"He comes, lords, he comes!" cried one.

"Met our envoys, he did," said another.

Jaxes strode out and grabbed one of the soldiers and shook him. "Who?" he barked. "Who is coming?"

"The Dumae chief," crowed the first man. "He's here with his army. He comes to aid us against the Massegetae beasts."

"Nemathres?" grinned Nikometros. "He is here?"

The shouting in the Jartai camp changed to cheers as a small column of riders appeared in the flickering light of the numerous campfires. Banners flew proudly from spears and the men carried themselves with assurance.

"I knew he would not betray me," said Nikometros softly. He grabbed a wine skin lying on the ground near the fire. He unstoppered it and held it up then poured some onto the ground, where it splashed and pooled like blood.

"Gods and goddesses of Greece and Scythia," Nikometros cried. "Accept this offering and hear our prayer. Grant us victory over the parricide and usurper." He lifted the skin to his lips and drank, the liquid pouring over his chin and chest. Passing it on to Tomyra he urged her to drink.

One by one the others drank from the flask and passed it on, each lifting it to the skies beforehand with a cry of 'Victory!'

Chapter 32

A reipithes sat astride his horse in the vast rolling plains to the west of Urul staring into the setting sun. Two days of forced marches, riding day and night from the Jartai hills, brought his tired army to within sight of the city defences. Around it, and within the city walls, waited the remnants of the force that marched out barely three days before, to meet the Serratae invaders. Now bloodied and defeated, the survivors still streamed back to the city, determined to fight one last battle for their homes and families. Behind them marched the Serratae army, inexorably, spreading like a stain over the land, looting and defiling.

Looking around him at his exhausted men, Areipithes felt the first wash of doubt. He clenched his teeth and kicked his horse into a gallop, riding along the ranks of his army as it spread out like a thin earth wall in front of the approaching flood of Serratae.

"Men!" he cried. "Remember who we are. We are Massegetae warriors and no other tribe can stand against us, certainly not these Serratae curs. Our enemies thought they could use the Jartai to defeat us but look where that got them. I tell you, the gods are with us. Even now, our priestess in Urul is praying to the Mother for our victory. She will not let Her People down." Areipithes reined in his horse and sat silent in front of his troops for long moments.

"Remember your training and wait for the word from your officers. Fight for your honour, my friends. Show these dogs what we are made of. Victory is ours!"

Areipithes rode back through the ranks toward the knot of officers around his black and grey wolverine standard. The men raised a thin cheer as he passed, the cries fading as the situation gripped their attention once more. They settled down to wait for battle, grasping each moment of life as if it was their last.

The Serratae tide halted a long bowshot from the thin line of Massegetae defenders and milled indecisively. A horse squadron galloped out from the invading mass, passing close along the strung-out line of their opponents. A cloud of arrows rose, hid in the eye of the sun for a long moment then fell, dispensing death. The Massegetae drew their dead and wounded to the rear and readied themselves once more. The horsemen galloped back to cheers from their fellows. A few minutes later another squadron sallied forth and repeated the manoeuvre.

Thoas fidgeted on his horse, his fear and anxiety communicating itself to his mount. The beast squealed and kicked, trying to pull away from its fellows. "How long must we wait, my lord?" Thoas muttered.

"Control your horse, Thoas," replied Areipithes calmly. He raised his hand and two young men drew deep breaths and blew a deep quavering note on their horns. They sounded again and, with a roar that quickly rose to scream of excitement and rage, the Massegetae army surged forward.

Arrows hurtled skyward, falling now behind the defender's lines as the two forces crashed together, all order disappearing in a welter of fighting men and horses. The line swayed back and forth, the men behind the fighting striving to get to grips with the enemy, those exchanging blows ready to step back. The rage and determination of the Massegetae defenders balanced the superior numbers of Serratae invaders forced to fight far from their homes and loved ones. It could not last, though the sun dipped toward the horizon before the Serratae forced Areipithes' army back.

At the rear, from his vantage point on a low swell of land, Areipithes saw the first faltering backward steps and knew them for an indicator of panic and defeat.

"We cannot wait any longer," he stated. "Prepare yourselves." Areipithes signalled the horn-bearers and a series of high notes rang out, repeated then again. The Massegetae line shivered, split and pulled back, horsemen wheeling their mounts, foot soldiers stumbling as they disengaged with the enemy. A cry of triumph rose from Serratae throats and a horde broke through into the gap.

"Wait!" cried Areipithes. "Wait!" He watched the invaders closely, judging their distance, knowing if he moved too soon his success would be limited, move too late and his army died. *I have but one chance, one throw of the dice.*

His arm chopped down and a long note rang out. Areipithes spurred his horse forward, down from the swell, hearing the gathering thunder of hooves behind him as his 'Wolverines', his trained troop of personal guards, three hundred strong, surged behind him. The arrowhead of riders galloped straight into the gap between the tattered remnants of his army, scarcely faltering as they battered aside the first ranks of Serratae horsemen, trampling them under. Onward, excitement and a cleansing terror lifting their hearts and spirits as they sped like a thrown spear into the bowels of the enemy.

Areipithes slashed and cut, his sword arm sodden with blood. Behind him then beside him and all around men screamed and thrust and died as the momentum of the charge faltered and died. "Not enough!" he groaned. Areipithes squinted through eyelashes sticky with men's blood and saw the

Serratae leader, his plumes and standards flying, beating back his force. He turned toward him, urging his horse to a last effort. Cutting and slashing, the Massegetae king forced his way through the melee. The Serratae chief stared at the approaching blood-soaked warrior and looked into the eyes of his fate. He spurred forward to meet him, a cry of defiance bubbling from his throat.

The leaders clashed as around them lesser men drew back in deference. The two men circled, swords drawn, each waiting for the other to move.

"Where is Dimurthes?" rasped Areipithes.

"Dead. Slain by your tribesmen. Now you shall die."

Areipithes laughed. "What is your name, Serratae, that I may offer a sacrifice for your ghost?"

"Sparses," said the other man, spurring his horse forward.

Sparses' horse collided with Areipithes' and the two men swung their swords in a clash and grate of steel. Breath became ragged as they clutched their opponent and strove to connect metal with flesh. Areipithes gave a cry and whipped back, clutching his side, his sword dipping. Sparses leaned forward eagerly, overextending himself. Too late he saw the rising blade and the triumphant smile. The sword bit deeply, life billowing from the wound.

Areipithes raised a paean of victory as around him the invaders drew back, fear in their faces. The Massegetae army pressed forward again and suddenly the Serratae turned and fled the field, streaming back toward the setting sun. Areipithes let his army course after them, calling to Thoas and his officers to keep control of their men.

Watching his army triumphant, Areipithes leaned back on his horse and stretched, the dried blood caking his face and beard cracking as he broke into a broad grin. *We won!* He thought. *By all the gods, and against all odds, we won!*

301

Chapter 33

Raucous laughter and drunken singing rose into the star-strewn skies along with the pungent smells of roasting meat and wood smoke. Areipithes, wineskin in one hand and a haunch of half-cooked goat in the other, staggered from one fire to the next, bellowing out a bawdy soldier's song. Massegetae tribesmen, drunk with wine, koumiss and the unexpected lease on life deriving from their victory, bellowed along with their king, slapping him on the back in an orgy of comradeship.

The roaring fires lit the night sky, painting the stone and wooden walls of Urul's habitations in fiery colours, black shadows dancing over the ground. The whole city shuddered and jumped as if the life force of the hundreds of dead men strewn about the countryside gathered to innervate the inanimate structures. On this night the warriors of the tribe forgot their natural superiority over the grasping merchants of Urul and celebrated a common victory. The merchants and craftsmen likewise, eschewed their normal feelings of disdain for the uncouth rider of the plains and hailed him as a brother and a friend.

Hundreds of tribesmen lay dead, either in makeshift graves or lying cold in the arms of the Mother. Surviving them, suddenly bereft of husbands and fathers, the women and young girls of Urul put aside their grief and pragmatically sought solace and a future in the homes and beds of other men. The night descended into an orgy of rutting, grief and despair sublimating into the one activity that would assure both men and women of a future purpose in life.

Into this bacchanalia rode a single man, reeling from exhaustion on a horse that staggered and fell, its heart bursting with the effort of its long journey. The man hit the ground and rolled, rising to his feet with a whimper, only to stand swaying as he stared in disbelief at the drunken scene.

"The king," he croaked, doubling over in a paroxysm of coughing. He lurched toward a group of men and women frantically coupling on the bare earth. "Take me to the king."

A tall man pulled free of his woman and stood, hands on hips, staring at the dirty, dishevelled stranger and past him at his dead horse. He made no effort to hide his tumescent genitalia. "Who are you, stranger?" The tall man grinned suddenly and gestured at his woman, still lying in wanton abandon on the ground. "Join us, friend. Have some wine," he belched suddenly, "A woman, whatever you want." The woman smiled up at the stranger, beckoning him.

The stranger drew back, his face pulling into a rictus of horror. "Have you no shame?" he muttered, pushing past the half-naked man. He raised his voice above the laughter and drunken singing. "Where is the king? I must speak with Areipithes immediately."

"Who wants him?" called a voice from the dancing shadows. "Declare yourself or..." the speaker dissolved into high-pitched giggles. "...Or have a drink. You're spoiling the mood."

"I must see the king at once. It is a matter of great urgency."

A chorus of groans and laughter answered the stranger. A short fat man barrelled up and fell over. He pointed back the way he had come. "Over there," he tittered. "But he won't like being disturbed." He gave the stranger an exaggerated wink and fell over again.

The stranger moved away, hurrying past the hordes of men and women, drinking and gorging on roasted meats. The rich cooking odours mingled with the stench of vomit and the heavy musk of unrestrained sex, making his head swim. Face averted, he stumbled on until he fell prostrate over a man engaged in the common pursuit.

The man gave a bellow of rage and rose, clutching his clothes about him. He spotted the stranger lying on the ground and nudged him with an ungentle toe. "What in Hades are you playing at? Have you no regard for your king?"

Rolling over and clutching his bruised side, the stranger stared aghast at the figure of Areipithes swaying above him. "My lord king?" he gasped. "I must speak with you."

"Speak on then," growled Areipithes, tucking himself into his clothes. "Who are you and where have you come from?"

"My lord." The stranger rose slowly to his feet and looked about him at the gathering crowd of interested revellers. "I must talk to you in private. I bear news from the north."

"The north?" Areipithes looked at the stranger sharply, his eyes taking in the man's dirty and stained clothing, his sagging exhausted features. He nodded incisively and turned on his heel. "Come with me," he said crisply. He pushed through the crowd and led the way to a hide tent, sagging on one side where the supporting ropes hung loose. Areipithes grabbed the comatose occupants, a naked man and woman, by the feet and dragged them outside to ribald cheers from the crowd. Gesturing the stranger inside the tent, he closed the flap behind them.

"Right!" snapped Areipithes. "Who are you and what is your news?"

"My lord," muttered the stranger, swaying on his feet. "My name is Scytogages. I am an Erimathean in the employ of your man Scolices." He staggered and almost fell. He squinted at Areipithes, rubbing his face tiredly with one filthy hand. "May I sit, my lord," he murmured. "I have killed two horses beneath me to bring you this news." Scytogages grimaced. "It would be a pity if I died before I could deliver it."

Areipithes nodded. "Sit!" he grunted. He looked around the meagre contents of the tent and picked up a badly cured skin flask. He sniffed at the contents then passed the flask to Scytogages. "Drink. Take your time. If you've spent as long as you say you have on the road, another few moments won't kill us."

Scytogages swallowed feverishly, his throat working convulsively and the thin wine spilling down his front. The liquid cut runnels in the dust coating his tunic. He lowered the flask and belched long and hard. "By the gods, that was good, my lord. Thank you."

"Your news, man. Out with it."

"The rebels, my lord. They've regrouped and..."

Areipithes snorted. "A handful of whipped dogs. They won't trouble us."

"They march south my lord...with the Dumae."

"The Dumae? Nemathres? He dares challenge me?"

Scytogages nodded slowly. "Together with the rebels, lord, they number almost as many as the former Jartai army. And most of them are fresh and rested. Whereas..." He hesitated a moment. "My lord, the Serratae?"

Areipithes grinned ferally. "The Serratae are dead or running back to their mothers. Why else do you think my army celebrates?"

"Then you will march to meet this new force?"

"A night to feast, a day to recover." Areipithes laughed out loud. "Yes, indeed. I will take my battle-hardened warriors north and smash these rebels once and for all."

The army took longer to assemble than anticipated and it was closer to noon on the second day before the Massegetae forces started sluggishly for the north. A cool wind blew from the west and a warm sun slowly dried the rich dark Scythian earth beneath the hooves of their horses. Areipithes rode with his 'Wolverines' far ahead of the main army, scouting out the best routes, searching for the best new grasses for the horses and revelling in the sensation of being a king, a conqueror and a man on such a beautiful spring day.

A steady stream of riders crossed the gap between scouts and main army, conveying information as to routes, the disposition of the army and rates of progress. One such rider from the army brought an old Jartai man, crippled in some forgotten war, who had sought out the Massegetae army.

Areipithes looked the old man up and down as he sat astride the army horse, clutching its mane. He noted the wasted muscle of the man's right leg and his dirt-covered features. The sunny day soothed Areipithes mind and he easily rejected his first impulse to make the old man grovel on the ground at his feet.

"Why have you come, old man?" asked Areipithes jovially. "Have you not heard I killed all your people?"

"Not all, lord," quavered the old man. "Though all the kind ones are gone." His face twisted with emotion. "They have no time for an old warrior now. No food either." The man's voice quivered with anger. "Once they would not have dared to insult me to my face. Once I would have..."

"Yes, I'm sure you were once a redoubtable warrior," drawled Areipithes. "However, I have better things to do than listen to you reminisce. Do you have anything worthwhile to say or shall I just have you killed?"

Fear flashed across the old man's face and he cringed. "I have news my lord would be willing to pay for, I think," he whined.

"Really? I doubt it. What could you possibly know that warrants my wasting any more time on you?" Areipithes raised a finger toward one of his men and nodded. The warrior smiled and drew his sword.

"Your sister, lord. The priestess. She rides south, alone," babbled the old man, staring wide-eyed at his approaching executioner.

Areipithes raised a hand, stopping his man. "My sister? What do you mean?"

"The Jartai lords and that foreigner, the Greek, my lord. They grow desperate." The old man grinned at Areipithes, gap-toothed. "You would not begrudge an old man a coin or two? Perhaps some small gold trinket?"

Areipithes removed a ring from his finger and tossed it to the man, who pocketed it at once. "They seek the favour of the Mother Goddess, lord." He made a placatory sign with his hand. "The priestess, your sister, rides to invoke the Goddess at a shrine near here. I forget the name, my lord, but it's an important one, nearby. Marsil something, I think."

"Marsil-tagal?" queried Areipithes quietly.

The old man nodded vigorously. "Yes, lord. That is it."

"You said she rides alone. You mean with the Greek?"

"No, lord. He commands the army. I think he wanted to accompany her," the old man winked and leered, "But the others insisted he stay behind. They believe you still to be in the north, my lord, else they would not have let her come alone. Only a few of her maidens go with her." He chuckled. "Some nice-looking young women too, if you know what I mean."

"When did she leave?"

"Three days ago. They plan for her to be there by daybreak tomorrow. The spring equinox, my lord."

Areipithes sat in thought. A single finger tapped out a repetitive rhythm on his thigh. "How is it you know all this, old man?"

The old man shrugged, his bony shoulders bobbing under his threadbare tunic. "No one pays any attention to an old crippled man, my lord, save to kick him or make him the butt of their jokes. I hear things," he spat. "I remember!"

Areipithes nodded and signalled to a rider. "Rejoin the army. Tell Thoas to keep moving northward. When he sights the enemy he is to wait. He is not to attack, make that plain."

The rider saluted. "Yes, lord." He half-turned his horse toward the distant army then hesitated. "What do you do, lord?"

"I ride to Marsil-tagal with my Wolverines," Areipithes snarled. "I think I shall pay my bitch-sister a visit."

The rider nodded and jerked a hand at the old man. "What of him?"

"Let him go." Areipithes stared at the old man. "Ride south to Urul, old man. Spend your gold and tell them I bring my sister's head to grace my tent pole." He barked out a laugh and dug his heels into his horse's sides.

Followed by his troop, Areipithes wheeled and headed south again. The old man watched them go then shifted his eyes to the distant courier heading for the Massegetae army. He grinned and straightened his back. "I think I shall put off visiting Urul for a while. At least until my lord Nikomayros triumphs." Agarus grinned again and started trotting north toward his friends.

Chapter 34

The hills above the shrine of the Mother at Marsil-tagal loomed black in the dark spring night. Cold stars, the colour of ice, winked silently in the still clear air, accentuating the unrelieved inkiness of the hunched land. Areipithes drew rein where the wide expanse of the southern grasslands narrowed between the spread 'thighs' of the sacred hills. Behind him, his command sat silently, even the restless horses cowed by the spirit of the place.

Areipithes sat and stared into the darkness, a niggling worm of unease disturbing his poise. Beside him, a voice spoke in hushed tones. "My lord," whispered the voice. "Why do we wait?"

"Something is wrong, Scolices," muttered Areipithes. "I feel it as surely as I feel this horse beneath me."

"I can see nothing amiss, lord," replied Scolices, staring into the night. "Only the dark hills and the stars."

Areipithes ignored him, waiting. His hunches seldom led him astray and he could afford to be patient. If Tomyra were already here, she would have to ride past them to safety; if not, they would have to wait anyway.

Slowly the stars wheeled across the Scythian night. Areipithes sat patiently, growing uneasy as the night wore on. At last, he shifted his weight and stretched. He flicked his horse's reins and slowly began to walk his mount around the flank of the western 'thigh'. His command followed, the only sound to be heard above the gentle sough of the wind being the muffled hoof tread on soft earth.

Areipithes drew rein once more and stared at the altered perspective of the hills. "There!" he sighed, pointing.

Scolices scratched his beard, peering into the blackness. "What, my lord? I can only see the hills and the stars."

"Follow the line of hills from the point nearest us...third hump. See the star, the little orange one?"

"Yes," said Scolices, puzzled. "What of it, my lord?"

"It is below the crest of the hill."

"Ah! It is not a star, it is a fire."

"Yes, I was right, they have set a trap for me and my beloved sister is the bait."

"One fire?" queried Scolices. "It could just be a herder or a hunter."

"Perhaps, but my gut tells me differently."

Scolices scratched again and looked at his king. "So, we ride back to the army, my lord?" he said hopefully.

Areipithes snorted. "No. We end this here at Marsil-tagal. If my sister acts as bait you can be certain her Greek whore-master is up there waiting and watching."

"My lord," said Scolices with an anxious undercurrent to his voice. "We are but three hundred. The rebels are sure to be stronger. Why not fetch the army here to root them out? I would willingly ride to get them."

The king laughed, short and sharp. "Not necessary, my fearful friend. I shall turn this trap upon them and snare myself the prize." Areipithes started his horse westward again, passing in a great curve around the promontory of hills. The rising land fell away to a smudge on the horizon and Areipithes picked up the pace, his command strung out behind him as they galloped through the night.

Judging the passing of time by the stars, Areipithes started angling back, south and east, picking up the main line of hills, working up the lower slopes, losing himself in the swales and gullies that scored the hillsides. When at last the riders paused in the darkness before first light, they saw to their north and beneath them a dark and sombre valley, bordered by two out flung ranges of hills. On the hidden sides of both ranges a handful of tiny fires flared, scattered pinpoints of light.

Areipithes grinned and looked to the east. "Dawn soon. Time to move down into the cleft. No doubt my sister will be there, ready to offer up her prayers at sunrise."

The Massegetae warriors set off down the steep slope in the darkness, guiding their horses carefully over the rough terrain. Rapidly, the flat slope turned into a gentle concavity, deepened and became the female cleft of the shrine to the Mother Goddess. In almost complete silence, hooves softly impacting on springy turf, Areipithes led his men in single file past the altar stone with its crude statue and scattered offerings. Several of the men uttered soft mutterings of respect and fear as they passed.

Below the altar lay a small glade, sheltered from the north wind by several scrubby willows eking out an existence in the shallow soil by a tiny rivulet. Five horses stood, heads down and dozing, by the trees. A small fire burned by a large rock and figures, swaddled against the dawn chill, lay or sat beside it. As dawn spread, delicately pink, the figures stirred and rose, stretching out their stiffened muscles. One stumbled into the lee of a rock and lifted her skirts, squatting. Another threw a stick onto the fire, yawned and looked up toward the shrine.

The woman froze, her hand over her open mouth, her eyes widening in shock at the sight of the massed riders sitting patiently at the head of the glade. Her hand dropped slowly to her side and her mouth closed, her eyes darting from side to side. Abruptly, with a flurry of priestly robes, she turned, a cry on her lips and arm stretching for the bow lying unstrung by the fire.

Areipithes moved his hand and the woman died, arrows thumping into her body, forcing an inarticulate scream from her already dead lips. The other women leapt to their feet, clutching for weapons as the warriors rode down on them, throwing them to the ground and binding them. Areipithes dismounted and sauntered over to the bound women, nudging them with his boot.

"Ah! Dear sister!" grinned Areipithes. "What a surprise finding you here." He looked around at the hillside with exaggerated gestures. "And where might your lover be? I don't see him."

"You...you're treading on dangerous ground, brother. You have killed a maiden of the Mother Goddess on holy soil." She looked over at the arrow-riddled body of Sarmatia, her teeth clenched in a feral snarl.

Areipithes ignored her. "Perhaps he's hiding somewhere? Maybe behind the hills with his men?"

Tomyra paled and Areipithes dropped to one knee beside his sister. "Did you really think you could fool me so easily, bitch? That I would be so overwhelmed with anger I would throw away caution?" he hissed. "I know he hides behind those hills waiting to ambush me. Well, we mustn't disappoint him, must we?" He got up and dusted his knee off, smiling.

"Gag her. Set her and her sister whores on horses, Scolices, but guard them well. Set them to ride within a cordon of warriors. I don't want her lover to see her until it's too late." Areipithes watched as his men tied grimy rags around the women. "I was going to kill you immediately I found you, sister, but I think I'll kill your Greek lover in front of you first." He roared with laughter and mounted his horse, waiting until his men were mounted and ready before setting off into the widening plain in the gathering light of the new day.

The plain and the surrounding hills crouched in shadow though the first rays of new light lit the crests. A thin mist hung heavy in the still air between the hills. Areipithes' men rode out into the open space, their bodies tensed and alert, weapons at the ready. The mist swirled with their passing, rising and obscuring them. Areipithes stared into the rolling vapours, searching for an early sign of his enemies.

Ahead the mist churned, parting as something moved arrow-like through it from the wide plains beyond the hills. Areipithes reined in his horse, sending riders off to each side with quick movements of his hands. He looked intently at the disturbance, smiling as it resolved into a small body of men, approaching at a canter. *Why so few, Nikomayros? I hoped you would bring your whole army to watch your death.*

The approaching body of men slowed as they caught sight of the waiting riders, slowed then stopped within bowshot. After a brief pause, a rider detached from the group and trotted slowly toward Areipithes, a leopard skin band tied below the blade of a long spear held aloft.

Areipithes gaped as the rider came to a halt a few paces from him. "Parasades!" he barked. "Have you taken leave of your senses?"

Parasades smiled and raised a hand in salute. "I greet you, Areipithes, chief of the Massegetae."

"Do you wish to die?" snarled Areipithes. "If so I can oblige you." He raised a hand and a dozen bows trained arrows at the other man's chest.

"Now what sort of a welcome is that?" drawled Parasades. "Your man came to me with an offer of friendship. I, in turn, come to you with a promise of fealty and you threaten to kill me."

"You're friend of the Greek. That's reason enough."

A shadow passed over the other man's face. "He's no friend of mine," Parasades stated flatly. "I seek only stability and a peaceful succession for the tribe. I have no wish to see a foreign barbarian in power. Only Massegetae should rule Massegetae."

"How did you know I was here if you aren't one of the Greek's jackals?"

"Thoas. He told me at once where you were. You know, Areipithes, he really is only marginally competent. I'm surprised you keep him in command of your army."

Areipithes snorted. "I suppose you're looking for his position."

"Maybe." Parasades grinned. "Is that an offer?"

"Why should I trust you?"

Parasades shrugged. "Why not? You asked for my support once before but I declined. Perhaps I've just changed my mind. Certainly, if the choice is between a Massegetae or a Greek I will choose the Massegetae."

"You offer fealty to me?"

"At Urul, at the proper time, I'll swear my loyalty for all to witness. For now, I'm at your side with a hundred of my men."

Areipithes pursed his lips and thought hard. After a minute he nodded. "Very well. Your presence could be useful when I confront the Greek. He should be here soon."

Parasades looked startled. "He's here?"

"He thought to set a trap for me, using his bitch as bait." Areipithes laughed and signalled Tomyra to be brought forward. "Instead, I have her and shall use her to bring her lover to his death."

Parasades stared at Tomyra, bound and gagged on her horse. Her eyes burned brightly as she stared mutely back at him. Parasades inclined his head, his expression impassive. "My lady," he intoned. "I grieve to see you in this state." He turned back to Areipithes. "She should be treated with respect, even in captivity. She is a priestess."

"Not for long," barked Areipithes. "Now bring your men over, Parasades. I think I can see our enemy's response."

As the sun rose in the bright morning sky, the heat began to bake the mist away and the shadows fled for the cover of rocks and trees. Around the ends of the hills rode two large bodies of men, pennants flying as they wheeled and met, blocking the entrance of the valley with a thin line of riders. They halted then at an unseen signal formed up into a wedge, the point glowing bronze in the morning light.

"He is so predictable," murmured Areipithes. "He does so love his massed cavalry charge."

"Effective though," replied Parasades dryly. He shaded his eyes and studied the opposing forces. "Fewer than us, but not by much. If it comes to a fight it could go either way."

Areipithes forced a laugh. "Only a few are Massegetae rebels. The bulk is Jartai women. We'll have no trouble with them."

Parasades shook his head. "Those Jartai are the ones that fought free of your army at Ubul-tagarn, under the leadership of Jaxes. Don't underestimate them."

Areipithes pondered this information then shrugged. "It doesn't matter. I didn't come here to fight, just to finish my enemies. I have one," he jerked his head at Tomyra, "Neutralized another," staring at Parasades, "and will soon kill the last of them. Come, let us finish it." He beckoned to Scolices and galloped out into the open field between the opposing forces.

After a moment's hesitation, Parasades followed. Three riders detached themselves from the opposing group and approached rapidly. Areipithes drew rein at the midpoint and sat relaxed as he waited for the others.

Nikometros slowed Diomede to a walk, his brightly burnished steel armour scintillating diamond-bright in the sunlight, a warmer glow arising from the bronze ornamentation on helmet and breastplate. His stallion stepped high and proud beneath him, eager for the battle charge. Timon rode beside him, dressed in Scythian fashion but with a Macedonian army helmet and shield. Jaxes accompanied them, his fine quality garments adorned with gold and enamel ornaments.

"Still trying to impress us with your shiny armour, barbarian?" sneered Areipithes.

Nikometros stared at Areipithes then his eyes flicked across to Parasades. He opened his mouth to speak to Parasades, hesitated then changed his mind.

Instead, he turned to the Massegetae king. "Surrender, Areipithes. You must answer for your crimes."

Areipithes laughed. "I choose not to, Greek. How about yourself? Will you surrender to me?"

"Must I force you? Too many Massegetae have died already."

"They are my people, not yours," Areipithes said. "Don't pretend concern for them." He narrowed his eyes. "And don't think you can shatter my men as you did the Jartai or those poor fools at Ubul-tagarn. I have with me my Wolverines. They're more skilled and disciplined than even your Lions."

Nikometros shrugged. "As you wish." He jerked on his horse's reins, turning the beast back to his troops.

"How is my sister?" asked Areipithes quietly.

Nikometros stopped and looked back at the other man.

"Have you not wondered how I got past your ambush? How is it I ride out of Marsil-tagal instead of into your trap?"

Nikometros stared at Areipithes in silence then glanced at Timon and Jaxes.

"He plays with your mind, Niko," growled Timon. "Finish the bastard and be done with it."

"Good, honest Timon," sneered Areipithes. "How is that bitch of yours, Timon?" He threw back his head and roared with laughter. "At least she is alive like my sister, not riddled with arrows like...what *is* her name...Sama...ah, yes, Sarmatia."

Nikometros paled and Timon reddened. With a growl, the old Macedonian soldier started forward, his hand scrabbling at the sword at his side.

Areipithes grinned. "Come on then. I'm sure your woman would enjoy seeing you cut down by my archers."

Nikometros grabbed Timon's arm as he passed. "Control yourself, Timon," he said. "Don't rise to his baiting." Louder, he asked, "Where are Tomyra and Bithyia?"

"Oh, quite well, if a bit uncomfortable," remarked the Massegetae king affably. "See?" He raised a hand and the riders behind him parted, revealing four young women on horses, bound and gagged. Warriors trained arrows on them, holding their threatening poses despite the strain from the taut bows.

Timon growled deep in his throat, his jaw clenching in fury. Nikometros glared across at Areipithes, his eyes cold. "What do you intend?" he grated.

Areipithes scratched his beard and yawned. "I could just kill them all. The problem with that is that you would just fight the harder." He smiled across at Nikometros. "Believe me, I have no wish to compliment you, but you have been a considerable nuisance." Areipithes shook his head and waved vaguely in the direction of the two groups of armed men. "Massegetae fighting Massegetae. I want the war to end, Greek, so I offer you good terms. Your life for my sister's...and her women's of course."

Jaxes erupted into a snarl of curses, consigning the Massegetae king to the foulest of fates. Timon, too, swore and cursed, his face pale and set hard as he gazed across at his woman. Nikometros stared at Areipithes, holding the other man's eye.

"Very well," he said coldly.

"No, Niko!" grated Timon. "Not even for...for..." The Macedonian's voice broke with anger and frustration. "He won't honour his promise, Niko. He's god-cursed. Of what value is his word?"

"Timon's right," said Jaxes. "My friend, don't even consider this thing. With you gone, none can hope to stand against him. Don't sacrifice yourself."

Nikometros ignored his companions. "Areipithes," he said quietly. "The Jartai are to be spared. You will offer a general amnesty for all who fought against you. You will not harm, or cause to be harmed, Tomyra, Timon or Bithyia. Swear this on all your gods."

"Of course," replied Areipithes smoothly. "I do so swear. Come now," he added, impatience creeping into his voice, "Throw away your sword and surrender to me."

"Not until the women are freed."

Areipithes murmured to Scolices, who galloped back to the Wolverines. A few minutes later the four women rode up, still bound and guarded by men with drawn bows. They stared, wide-eyed at the men, straining against their bonds and gags. At a nod from Areipithes, his guards cut the ropes binding the young women.

"Say your farewells, bitch-sister," laughed Areipithes. "I'll allow you a few moments together."

Tomyra ripped the gag from her mouth, working her jaws to moisten her lips. "What?" she croaked. "What does he mean? Niko, my love. I'm sorry, my guard was down."

Nikometros shook his head. "No matter, Tomyra. Listen, I want you to go with Timon now, he'll take you to a place of safety..."

"Niko! What's happening? Why aren't you coming?"

Areipithes laughed. "I really don't know what he sees in you, sister. I can only think it is lust, but if that were so, why not leave you to your fate and find another woman?"

"You wouldn't understand love, Areipithes," said Nikometros quietly.

"You think not?" spat Areipithes, his lips curling into a snarl. "I loved my father and was loved by him until this whore of a sister poisoned his mind against me."

"And so, you killed him," growled Timon. "True love indeed."

"Enough!" snapped Areipithes. "I won't stay here and argue with barbarians. Say your farewells and be done with it."

Bithyia sidled her mare alongside Timon. "What is happening, love?"

Timon dragged his eyes from Tomyra and Niko as they sat alongside, holding hands and whispering. "Niko has chosen to trade his life for Tomyra's...and yours."

Bithyia shuddered. "He cannot! Timon, you must persuade him. If he is lost we all die."

Timon shook his head. "He is adamant. He will do this thing."

Areipithes shouted and forced his horse between Tomyra and Nikometros. For a moment, Nikometros' face flashed red, his jaw clenching in anger. He nodded, and with a last word to the weeping girl, walked his horse over to Timon. Ignoring the look in his companion's eyes, Nikometros drew his short sword and placed it carefully in his friend's hand. Then with a smile and a nod to Jaxes he dismounted, giving Diomede's reins to Timon. He turned and walked toward the Wolverine patrol.

As Nikometros passed near Parasades, he slowed. "Why, Parasades? He's your enemy too."

Parasades shrugged. "At least he is of the People. I could not stand by and see you become king."

"Me?" asked Nikometros. "I have no desire to be a king."

"Nonsense, Nikomayros. No man turns down power when it is offered him."

"Nevertheless. I only wanted to live with Tomyra and return to my own people."

Nikometros walked on into the lines of Massegetae warriors. They closed about him. Areipithes wore a huge grin as he turned to Timon and Jaxes. "Go then. Disband your army. The war is over. I shall expect you to come to Urul within the month to swear allegiance." He turned and trotted after his men, not deigning to look back at his enemies.

Areipithes, his captive and his ally moved out of the narrow valley of Marsil-tagal, past the confused and uncertain Jartai and rebel Massegetae tribesmen. He rode north, moving quickly after his army. After a while, Timon and Jaxes brought some order to their men and slowly followed the other group, though falling ever farther behind.

As the following group disappeared from sight, Areipithes veered to the east, away from Urul, and picked up the pace. His men rode close guard on Nikometros, now mounted on a rangy plains horse. Their short double-curved bows with arrows at the ready remained always pointed at his heart. Parasades followed, his men keeping their distance from him. Certes along rode close by, a murderous expression on his face. At last he could not contain himself.

"That was ill done, my lord," Certes snapped. "Seldom have I seen an action more dishonourable."

Parasades raised an eyebrow. "Oh? You think being in thrall to a foreigner is the proper station for one of the People?"

"No, of course not. But to betray him to his sworn enemy? It would sit better with my conscience if you'd just killed him."

"Perhaps I should have just let him die in Zarmet?"

"Aye, better that, my lord." Certes slowed his horse and pulled back to the other men in his command, where he rode in a glowering silence.

Areipithes halted at noon near a small rivulet to let the horses rest and for a meal. He ordered his men to strip Nikometros of his armour and to bind his arms firmly. Certes remonstrated with Areipithes but was ignored. Parasades watched silently, his face impassive as Nikometros remounted, with much ribald comment and assistance and was led off again at a slow gallop.

Parasades and his men followed, again hanging back from Areipithes and his prey. Toward nightfall, Areipithes ordered his men to camp. After they set watch fires and sentries, they slaughtered Nikometros' horse and butchered it.

Parasades sauntered up to the cooking fires where the rich odours of sizzling horse flesh mingled with the stench of blood and intestines.

"What is Nikomayros to ride tomorrow?" he asked.

"He rides nowhere," grinned Areipithes. "Tonight, he dies."

Parasades nodded sombrely. "Good. It is best done quickly."

"Quickly? I think not. I've waited a long time for this moment. I promise you, the Greek will scream like a raped virgin by the time I've finished with him." Areipithes laughed, his men joining in with lewd comments and suggestions.

Parasades shook his head but said nothing. He hacked off a slab of half-cooked meat and took it back to his own fire where he sat alone and ate his evening meal.

Around the main fire, the hubbub of the meal died away. Coarse laughter erupted as the men drew aside, leaving a large open space around the fire. Areipithes signalled and two men dragged Nikometros close to the fire and threw him to the ground. The Massegetae king squatted beside the Macedonian officer and gripping his head, tilted it up.

"Greek," he whispered. "Prepare for death. When it comes you will welcome it as a friend."

Areipithes took out a small dagger and rested the tip in the corner of Nikometros' right eye, dimpling the skin. He pushed gently and a ruby tear appeared. Nikometros stared back at his tormentor in silence, not even acknowledging his presence. Areipithes pursed his lips, considering. "Not yet," he tittered. "I want you to see what happens to you, as well as feel it."

Parasades sat by his own fire, casting concerned looks at the circle of Massegetae warriors and the deadly game taking place in their midst. His own men kept their distance and he heard mutterings of discontent drifting across the still night air. Abruptly he grimaced and stood up, brushing the dirt from his clothes. Parasades glanced at his men then wandered casually over to the larger circle.

He pushed his way through the sweating cordon, feeling blood lust rising like a miasma from so many cruel and avaricious minds. Within the circle lay Nikometros, stripped naked and covered with blood. Two burly warriors held him down while Areipithes worked on him with his little dagger.

As he watched, Parasades saw Areipithes delicately draw the tip of the dagger down the helpless man's arm, leaving a red-beaded trail in its wake. Areipithes giggled, the tip of his tongue resting on his upper lip. "Can you feel it, Greek?" he whispered. "No? Well, you will. In a moment I'll start to flay the skin from your arm. I promise you the pain will be extreme."

"Areipithes," rumbled Parasades from the inner edge of the cordon. "Don't do this. It lessens you. Kill him and be done with it."

The Massegetae king looked round, his dark eyes glinting red in the firelight. "If you don't have the stomach for it, go away." Areipithes grinned and Parasades was horrified to see blood staining his beard and teeth.

Areipithes turned back to his victim and carefully lifting a detached piece of skin, drew it back, peeling it wetly from his arm. Nikometros drew in a ragged breath and shuddered, sweat starting from his forehead. The wounded flesh gleamed in the fire glow.

"Ah! A reaction at last," whispered Areipithes. "Soon you will be screaming like a girl."

Parasades swallowed, tasting bile in the back of his throat. He hawked and spat, moving a few steps closer. "Don't do this, Areipithes," he repeated.

"You're getting tiresome, Parasades. Go away if you don't wish to see his death."

"His death is one thing," growled Parasades. "I've often wished for that, but torture dishonours us all. When have the Massegetae done such things?"

Areipithes shrugged then dropped his head forward on his chest, the blood-soaked dagger trailing in the dirt by his side. "I think I was wrong about you. I don't want men beside me who are slaves to an old-fashioned moral code."

"No more than do I." Parasades stepped quickly across the intervening space and kicked the dagger from Areipithes' hand. With a swift motion he drew his own dagger and held it at the king's throat, his other hand firmly gripping the other man's long hair.

The two men holding Nikometros down leapt to their feet and drew their swords. Around them, warriors leapt for their weapons, dozens of arrows aimed in their direction.

"Call your men off," snarled Parasades. "Or die. Your choice."

Areipithes swallowed uncomfortably, his head tilted back painfully. "You're a fool, Parasades. My men will cut you down where you stand."

"Then why haven't they already?" Parasades moved, altering his grip swiftly. He put one arm around Areipithes' neck, choking him and holding him close while the tip of his knife continued to threaten his throat. "If I die, you die. Without you, your war ends and your sister Tomyra will rule in your place."

Areipithes squatted awkwardly, his head thrown back and his hands vainly seeking to alleviate his choking by pulling at Parasades' arm. "All right," he whispered hoarsely. "What do you want?"

"I want to trade. Your life for mine...and that of Nikomayros too."

Areipithes nodded and gurgled. Parasades let up on the pressure of his arm and the king whooped for breath. "Go ahead," he croaked. "See how far you get."

Parasades quickly slipped his blade between the ropes binding Nikometros and cut them. For the first time Nikometros cried out as the ropes brushed past his savaged arm. Parasades slipped the knife back into place against the king's throat and stood up, dragging the other man with him. He nudged Nikometros with his boot. "Get up!" he said. "Get up or die in the dirt."

Nikometros rolled over onto his knees and stood up, shaking with the effort. Blood cascaded down his arm and over his hip, pooling on the ground beneath him. He said nothing but looked at Parasades quizzically.

"Now what?" grunted Areipithes. "Kill me and you die. Move and you die."

"Perhaps not." A cool voice spoke from outside the ring of warriors. Immediately heads turned, bows lowering involuntarily. The firelight flickered indistinctly on Certes and his hundred men, standing with their double-curved bows strained. Despite being outnumbered more than three to one, no one doubted that the Leopards controlled the situation.

Parasades grinned. "Good man! I was getting worried there for a moment."

Certes nodded humourlessly. "I am glad to see you found your honour at last, my lord."

Parasades moved crabwise out of the circle, trying to keep his eyes on every armed warrior. He kept Areipithes in front of him as a shield. Nikometros walked unsteadily after them, his head high. Outside the circle, half the bowmen slipped away and brought the horses. They mounted and covered the enemy while the rest joined them. One man edged cautiously into the circle and picked up Nikometros' armour and helmet.

Certes helped a now-shivering Nikometros onto a horse, throwing a cloak about him. "To hide your nakedness, my lord," he whispered.

Nikometros forced a smile and wrapped the cloak tightly about him. "We Greeks feel quite comfortable in our nakedness, my friend. But I thank you, the wind is somewhat cool."

Parasades stood beside his horse, still clutching Areipithes, undecided. "What do we do with this bastard? Take him with us or kill him?"

"Neither," replied Nikometros. He shifted uncomfortably on the horse's back, his wounds stiffening in the cool night air. "Let him go. We'll meet again very soon on more equal terms."

"You always were a fool, Nikomayros, but as you wish." Parasades shoved Areipithes away and turning, vaulted onto his horse. The troop immediately wheeled and galloped off into the night, Areipithes' men belatedly sending a ragged volley of arrows after them.

"Where to, my lord Nikomayros?" yelled Certes as the riders thundered over the plain.

"North, of course," Nikometros replied. "We must get to Nemathres' army before he attacks Thoas. We have a battle to win."

Chapter 35

A murmur as of the encircling Ocean rose and fell on the morning breeze, accompanied by a distant clangour as if Hephaestus, smithy to the gods of Olympus, strove to create anew the enormous sword of the war-god Ares.

Nikometros gave a savage grin as he recognised the familiar sounds of battle. He and Parasades, along with the hundred warriors of the Massegetae leader, trotted slowly over the rolling plains toward the sounds. The long night passed into day and at last they pulled their tired horses to a halt on a long, winding ridge looking down into a flat, fertile valley. Below them swayed two mighty armies, locked in a fatal embrace, dancing drunkenly to the tune of five thousand swords and shields.

Even as they watched, the larger army, drilled and disciplined, achieved an ascendancy over the other. The Massegetae, under the command of Thoas, slowly pushed the Dumae army backward up the valley. The northern tribesmen fought stubbornly, contesting every reluctant foot of ground, but still they retreated.

"Not a moment too soon," said Nikometros grimly. He twitched his horse's reins and started it slowly down into the valley, his heels drumming into the horse, encouraging it onward. Dressed once more in his burnished armour, donned during a break in their long journey, his wound covered with soothing ointments and bandages, Nikometros drew his sword and uttered the war-paean of his family. Parasades, along with Certes and his men, fell in behind Nikometros in a tight column. They swept down on the struggling mass of bodies that parted before them, men pulling exhausted horses aside, or stumbling back on foot.

Nikometros' column impacted the front line of the Massegetae. It shuddered all along its length and splintered in the face of Nikometros as he wielded his short sword, stabbing and slashing. Behind him, the Dumae rallied, pushing forward again, heaving the other army back. An overjoyed cry pierced the air, turning heads.

"Nikometros! My lord, it is you! How?" Timon galloped up, brushing warriors aside and jumped from his horse, throwing himself at Nikometros, hugging and kissing his foot. Parasades men closed about them, affording them protection as they embraced.

Timon caught sight of Parasades. "What is that traitor doing here?" he screamed, tearing his sword out of his belt. He lunged forward, even as Nikometros sought to restrain him.

"He saved me, Timon," said Nikometros urgently. "He fights for us...or we for him. Leave it, man, we have a battle to fight."

Timon reluctantly turned away and helped Nikometros to remount, being jostled himself by the surrounding fighters as he also mounted. "I've sent for Diomede. We never thought to see you alive, my lord."

"Where is Tomyra?"

"On the right wing," grinned Timon. "She fights as if she would single-handedly kill all her brother's men."

Nikometros smiled and clapped the other man on the shoulder. "You have the map, the battle plan?"

Timon passed over a scrap of parchment, creased and stained, and watched Nikometros as he perused the scratchings on it. Nikometros looked up at the line of struggling men then back down at the plan. He nodded. "The other commanders have copies? Good. The old Egyptian has done well. Let us hope Nemathres can follow this. It's a good plan and could work but it requires captains to follow orders without seeming reason."

"We have capable commanders, Niko. Jaxes leads the remnants of his Jartai too." Timon looked around as a small group of men galloped up. "Ah, here is Diomede."

Nikometros grinned and nodded again. He slid off his mount and vaulted onto his stallion's back. Diomede whickered a greeting to his master, pawing the soft earth and tossing his great golden head.

"Now, take me to Tomyra." Nikometros raised his voice and yelled out to Parasades, "I go to rally the right wing. Keep up the pressure here."

Parasades nodded and turned back to the fighting. The line surged and rallied as the Massegetae warriors slowly gave before the pressure. Nikometros and Timon pushed their way along the line toward the right wing. Their way was hampered by Dumae tribesmen hurrying to close with the enemy and by struggling knots of men vying for each other's lives. At length, bloodied and aching, they reached a dense body of riders, the press of horses and men so close that weapons thrust and cut impotently. Every few moments the mass heaved and moved a few paces forward or back and men fell dying or dead. Others hurried to fill their places and died in their turn.

At the front of the Dumae tribesmen, surrounded on three sides by slim, leather clad young warriors, fought Tomyra. Her pale face, framed by her raven hair and splashed with blood, was set and lined, her eyes red but dry as she stabbed and parried grimly. A man screamed and died beneath her blade and she urged her horse forward into the tiny gap, immediately encountering another man. Beside her fought Bithyia, her face taut with concern for her mistress.

A vibration rippled through the mass of fighters as Timon and Nikometros pushed their way forward. Bithyia looked round and her face creased in delight as she recognised Timon then in astonishment and excitement at Nikometros.

"My lady!" she screamed, pointing. Tomyra glanced around and froze. A warrior sensed his chance and drove at the young woman, his blade seeking her life. Bithyia yelled and launched herself at her mistress, the two of them disappearing into the maelstrom of horses together with the warrior.

Nikometros gave an incoherent yell of horror and forced his way through, hacking and slashing at any who refused to get out of his way, Timon at his heels. Diomede kicked and bit at the other horses, forcing them away. For long moments the battlefield remained empty of either woman then suddenly both were there, upright but staggering, covered in mud and blood. Nikometros reached down and plucked Tomyra up, setting her down on a rider-less horse. Timon helped Bithyia up behind him.

Tomyra, grinning with joy, threw her arms about Nikometros and kissed him. "My lord," she breathed, between kisses. "You have escaped!"

Timon, also grinning, leaned close, his blade flicking out to the side as he did so. A Massegetae warrior howled with pain and fell back. "Perhaps we might put this reunion off for the moment?" he inquired.

"Indeed," replied Nikometros. He gave Tomyra another quick kiss then released her. He raised himself high and lifted his arm, waving his bloodied sword as his great golden stallion reared. "To me!" he shouted. "Lions, to me!"

Heads turned. Recognition and hope flared within the Dumae army; recognition and apprehension skittered over Thoas' men. The men and women around Nikometros gathered and threw themselves at the enemy.

Slowly the right wing forged ahead, swinging round behind Thoas' force. From the centre too, the sounds of battle strengthened as Parasades and his men, disciplined and eager, forced their way deep into the breast of the opposing army.

Thoas, guiding the battle from the rear, saw his left wing forced back. He recognised the danger and, to stave off a collapse, bled men from his centre and his right wing to shore up his crumbling flank. The whole battle lurched to one side. A look of worry fled across Thoas' craggy face. He sought for some way to establish his former supremacy, sending small bodies of men scurrying over the battlefield, strengthening first one place then another. Despite all his efforts, his army continued to retreat slowly before the relentless attack of the Dumae.

Then came the thunder of hooves from the rear. Almost afraid to see this new threat, Thoas forced himself to turn, his look of dread turning to muscle-sagging relief as Areipithes raced up with nearly four hundred men.

The tide of the battle turned again, the Massegetae retreat hesitating and reversing. The battle lines heaved and swayed again as men died, the fighting breaking up into struggling knots of riders and men on foot. Areipithes forced his way to Thoas' side.

"You fool," Areipithes snarled. "You outnumber this rabble. How is it you retreat before them?"

"My...my lord," stammered Thoas. "It's not just the Dumae. Your sister fights on our left and now Nikomayros the Lion has joined her. Parasades attacks our centre."

Areipithes slitted his eyes and stared into the dust of battle, shading his eyes against the glare. He surveyed the whole battle scene then pointed to the centre where the Massegetae had stopped the oncoming surge of Parasades, men. "Scolices, go with Thoas. Take my Wolverines and fold up their centre. I will deal with my sister and her barbarian." He drummed heels into his horse and pushed into the throng.

Tomyra saw her brother coming, saw the Massegetae tribesmen parting in front of him like sheep before the leopard then reforming behind him in his drive forward. She spurred her horse into his path, her face alive with excitement and loathing in her heart.

Father, Tomyra cried inside herself, *I will avenge you now.* She raised her sword and swept it down at his head. As her blow fell, her mount shuddered and stumbled beneath her, knocking her from her horse's back. She lay half-stunned on the ground, legs of horses and men trampling the ground around her. Running her hands over her limbs and body, she held her breath, expecting to find some dreadful wound. She rolled to avoid a flying hoof, sprawled over a bloody corpse and staggered to her feet. Tomyra stared through the melee at Areipithes who, apparently unaware of his sister's presence, had ridden her down in his hunger to get to grips with Nikometros.

Areipithes swung at Nikometros with a savage oath, missed and barely avoided the return stroke. He fought to control his mount, circling then driving forward again, hacking at a rider who came between them. His next stroke clanged on Nikometros' sword, rasping along its edge as the horses parted.

Nikometros circled, feeling the stiffness in his shoulder and the wave of fire coursing over his partially skinned left arm. He flexed his right arm and swung his blade back and forth, looking for an opening in the other's guard. Flicking a look to the area where Tomyra had disappeared beneath the horses, relief swept through him when he saw her face again. He snatched his eyes back just in time to avoid another frenzied attack. Nikometros parried and aimed a blow of his own.

"I will have you," panted Areipithes, droplets of saliva speckling his beard. "You escaped me last night because I wanted to hurt you. Now I'll just kill you, then my bitch-sister."

A knot of five battling horsemen burst in upon them, three onto two, hacking and stabbing, sweeping Areipithes and Nikometros apart. Areipithes pushed back into the fray, stabbed one of the three in the back then rode past as another man fell. He closed with Nikometros again, shaking his hair free of muddy sweat.

"Settle this with just me," called Nikometros. "Spare your men."

Areipithes slashed again, the jar of the swords connecting sending shivers up his arm. He parried a blow that put Nikometros off balance and smashed his fist into the other man's face. Nikometros reeled and slipped backward off Diomede. Areipithes yelled in triumph and spurred his horse forward, attempting to trample his enemy underfoot. Nikometros dodged and aimed a blow at Areipithes as he passed, the sword ripping a shallow wound in the king's thigh and a deeper one in the flank of his horse. The animal squealed in agony, sending a fine spray of blood over Nikometros then bolted.

Areipithes vainly tried to control his mount as the beast snorted and bucked, trying to rid itself of the stinging wound in its side. Other horsemen swept into the gaps around him, cutting him off from Nikometros. He forced his way back into the fray but could not locate his enemy. With a curse he turned away, searching for Thoas and Scolices in the seething centre of his army.

Nikometros rubbed his jaw and looked about him. He dodged a spear thrust from a Massegetae and parried a blow from a yelling Dumae, ducking under a wounded horse to escape. Diomede whickered and pressed forward, nudging Nikometros forcefully from behind. He swung up onto its back and set off in the direction he last saw Tomyra.

～✦～

Tomyra ran through the jostling crowd of animal and human bodies toward Nikometros and Areipithes. She clutched the broken haft of a spear, her sword lost in her fall. She pushed past two men fighting on foot, just as one ran the other through with a sword. The victor turned on her with a gap-toothed roar, his eyes staring wildly and the upper half of his body covered in a drizzle of blood. He slashed down, just missing Tomyra who leapt back, swinging her spear haft ineffectually. The man followed through with a wild sideways slash, almost overbalancing. Tomyra cracked him behind one knee and he fell, holding himself up on one hand. She hit him again with the ashen spear, splitting his scalp open. He roared with rage and staggered to his feet, swinging blindly. Tomyra dodged, backpedalling, jabbing the broken end of the wood in the man's face.

The fighting pressed close about Tomyra and she looked around desperately for a weapon. The man grinned and stepped closer, forcing her between two dead horses. She stumbled backward then stood still, her weapon trailing in the dirt and her shoulders slumped. The man sensed victory and strode forward eagerly. As he came close, Tomyra pushed forward with the spear haft, gripped it in both hands and swung viciously up, catching the man hard between the legs. The man's scrotum split from the force of the blow,

333

sending a pulse of blood into his trousers and fiery agony through his whole body. His face turned a congested purple as his eyes bulged and he dropped to his knees, breath escaping from his throat in a tortured whistle and clutching the wreckage of his crushed testicles.

Tomyra whipped the haft round and rammed the splintered end deep into the man's throat, leaning on the end of it and twisting. The sword dropped from his fingers and his hands scrabbled briefly at his throat. He collapsed backward, his heels kicking up a spray of mud as they drummed on the churned-up earth. Tomyra scooped up the man's sword and set off again, dodging between the horses.

⌇⌇⌇

Areipithes fought his horse to a standstill then withdrew from the fighting. He sat on a small hillock, a wall of dead bodies providing a measure of protection, and looked out over the seething battlefield. A tremor ran through his army. He watched, a stony expression on his face, as his left wing collapsed, men streaming back in disarray. The centre still held though and his own right wing advanced slowly against the enemy. The battle teetered in the balance and Areipithes knew the next minutes would hold his future. He felt torn between a desire for personal vengeance and a need to strengthen his hold on his kingship.

Ride back and I can find the Greek, he mused. *I can kill the bastard but unless I help Thoas, the centre will collapse and I lose the battle. Then I lose all.*

With a sigh, Areipithes made his decision. He rode down from the hillock and, rallying a squadron of horsemen retreating before the Dumae tribesmen, led them back into battle, searching for Thoas.

He found him, on foot, hard-pressed and bloodied, breathing hard and holding a wound in his side. Thoas looked up at his king and grimaced.

334

"The battle is lost, my lord," he panted. "Unless you can think up a plan."

"How in Hades did you let it get this far?" rasped Areipithes. "You outnumbered them and had more disciplined men."

Thoas shook his head and coughed. "I don't know, lord. Their army units showed incredible coordination. No orders passed between them, I swear, yet each knew exactly what the others were going to do before they did it."

"What are they? Mind readers?"

"I don't know." Thoas passed a bloody hand over his brow. "Unless you can come up with a good plan soon, we're all dead."

Areipithes swore, thinking hard. He looked back at his disintegrating left wing then at the centre, now slowly giving way before a renewed offensive. He abruptly spurred his horse and hurled it forward into the ranks of the Dumae.

"Parasades!" he screamed. "Parasades! Answer me!" He galloped into the small space between the two armies, his own pulling back slightly faster than the Dumae advanced. Arrows leapt out at Areipithes as he passed, tugging at his clothes.

"I hear you," came an answering call. The Dumae line parted and Parasades, with Nemathres and Jaxes close behind, rode out into the area littered with bodies, some still moving, and others lying motionless. Men on both sides ceased fighting, pulling back and resting on their weapons, watching their leaders.

"What do you want, Areipithes?" asked Parasades coolly.

Areipithes turned his horse back and trotted up to Parasades. "I want to stop this bloodshed."

Jaxes laughed and Parasades raised an eyebrow. "Since when have you cared about men's lives?"

Areipithes shrugged. "Meet me in battle, single combat."

Parasades considered the offer, hand stroking his moustaches. "And if I win?"

"Then my army is yours. If I win I will send the Dumae and the Jartai back to their own lands."

"Let me kill him," grated Jaxes. "The blood of my slaughtered tribe calls for his life."

Areipithes spat. "You don't lead an army, merely a rabble. I disdain to fight you."

"You arrogant bastard. Do not think to leave this field alive."

Areipithes shrugged and turned back to Parasades. "Well?"

"If you win I'll fight you myself," growled Nemathres. "Enough of my men have died this day."

"And I," snarled Jaxes.

Areipithes waved a dismissive hand. "If you wish."

"General amnesty for all?" asked Parasades. "On both sides?"

"If you wish it."

"You swear? On the gods?"

"Of course," said Areipithes smoothly. "By any or all of them."

"The ease with which you swear doesn't fill me with confidence," replied Parasades sourly. "Still, I'll agree. Have your heralds sound a truce."

Presently the mournful sounds of long horns resounded over the battlefield. Fighting slowly died away, the clash of swords replaced by moaning and the laboured bubbling breathing of mortally wounded men. A space opened up between the two armies, spreading into a wide circle. Men jostled and pushed, eager to be in the front row, Dumae and Massegetae, quarrels forgotten in the excitement of the moment.

Nikometros and Timon arrived, with Tomyra and her Owl maidens close behind. They moved around the circle to where Jaxes, Nemathres and Parasades stood, preparing for battle.

"I should be the one to fight him," declared Nikometros. "It is I he hates."

Tomyra looked troubled, caught between her desire to see her brother dead and her concern for the safety of her Niko. "Let the Mother decide," she said. "If Parasades doesn't succeed then my lord should fight him."

"He'll have to wait in line," growled Nemathres. "Too many of my men have died today for me to hang back and let others fight my battles. If Parasades falls, I'll kill him."

"Or I," snarled Jaxes. "Whatever that piece of dung says, I will fight him."

"I'm delighted by your confidence in me," Parasades scowled. "I would like to point out that I'm a true-born Massegetae and it's my right to fight Areipithes."

Timon frowned. "What do you mean it's your right?"

"He formally challenges the chief to combat," explained Tomyra hesitantly. "If he wins he will ask for challenges from all comers. If none come forth, he'll be acclaimed chief of the Massegetae."

Nikometros chewed his lip in silence, casting a speculative look at Parasades as he stripped off his worn and slashed tunic and donned a new one. Timon looked at his commander quizzically. "Will you?" he whispered. "If he wins?" Nikometros did not reply.

Across the circle, now cleared of bodies, stood Areipithes. As he changed into new clothing and selected his weapons, he engaged his companions Thoas and Scolices in earnest conversation.

"Be prepared. If I win..."

"You will, my lord," interrupted Scolices.

"If I win," repeated Areipithes, "You are to lead an immediate attack on the rebels, before they can recover. I want the Greek, my sister and Nemathres the Dumae dead immediately. Jaxes too."

"But my lord," protested Thoas. "We're under truce. We dare not break..."

"You will do as I say."

Thoas and Scolices nodded glumly. "Of course, my lord," murmured Scolices. "Er, what if...I mean if just by chance..."

"If I fall?" Areipithes grimaced. "It's possible. Should it happen, I want you, Thoas, to challenge him. I do not want that traitor Parasades to become chief after me."

Thoas nodded, a grim expression on his face. Scolices looked put out. "What about me?" he said indignantly.

Areipithes gave a bark of laughter that made heads turn. "Single combat isn't your style, Scolices. No, you take advantage of their honour and escape to the south. If Thoas fails in his task I want you to kill the Greek for me later."

"I thought your Persian friend the Scorpion was going to do that?"

"Perhaps. I don't trust him. Will you do it?"

Scolices grinned. "A pleasure."

Areipithes turned away, swinging his sword, feeling the balance. He fitted the straps of the small round shield more snugly to his left forearm and flexed his limbs, feeling for any catches in his clothing. "Ready!" he called out.

Parasades stepped out from the other side of the circle, still fitting his own shield. The watching armies fell silent, all eyes on the two men advancing into the centre of the ring. The protagonists stopped about five paces apart and glared at each other. Areipithes dropped into a crouch and started moving to his right, circling the other man. Parasades edged around also, carefully watching his foe.

"Wait!" cried Tomyra. Parasades' eyes flicked toward her and Areipithes lunged, his sword slicing through the other man's tunic as Parasades twisted away.

"Wait!" called Tomyra again. "This is a holy ritual, not a simple fight. The Mother must be invoked."

Parasades moved back, his eyes never leaving his enemy. "She's right, Areipithes. I have formally challenged you. The priestess must invoke the Goddess."

Areipithes gave out a bark of derision. "What priestess? This bitch is forsworn. She cannot invoke the Goddess and no priestess is closer than Urul." He leapt forward, his sword clanging on Parasades' shield.

Parasades fell back, circling, his feet feeling the uneven ground behind him. "The priestess at Mora declared her holy still." A murmur ran through the watching armies and Areipithes faltered in his advance. Then he shrugged and lifted his weapon again.

"I only have the word of my enemy for that. You must think me mad if you believe I would ask a blessing from the Mother through my sister. She would bring down a curse on me." Areipithes laughed, his eyes icy.

"Then let the loser go to his grave unblessed," said Parasades softly. He stepped forward as he spoke, feinted to his left and swept his blade across the face of Areipithes. The king lifted his shield, momentarily blocking his sight, and Parasades punched the edge of his own shield into the other man's belly.

Areipithes grunted, his own sword arcing across and into emptiness as Parasades danced back. Areipithes followed, his sword weaving a complex pattern in front of him. He lunged, caught a sweep on his shield and thrust again, jarring his arm as his sword tip connected with the brassbound leather shield of his opponent. He wrenched it free, blocking a series of blows with his own shield.

The fighters fell apart, circling slowly and cautiously on the broken ground. Areipithes stumbled slightly, his foot catching on some obstruction and he glanced down involuntarily. Parasades jumped in close, his sword thrusting toward his opponent's eyes. As Areipithes stepped back hurriedly, Parasades hooked his foot around the other man's, colliding with him, swords locking. Areipithes fell backward, his sword arm flinging wide. Parasades grinned, stabbing downward.

Areipithes rolled, and rolled again as Parasades stabbed his sword into the ground. He scrambled to his feet and ran a few paces then turned to catch his breath. A sigh went up from the watchers. Parasades ran in pursuit, his weapon held low, arcing upward and clashing on the other sword. Areipithes fell back a pace, parried, desperately holding his shield across his body. A sword flashed at his head and he fell to one knee, slashing out wildly. Parasades stepped back to avoid the blow then forward again, his sword high above the king's unprotected head.

Areipithes, his arm still outstretched from his previous, unsuccessful attempt, swept his fist back, the hilt of his sword hammering into Parasades' side. Parasades uttered a cry of agony and fell sideways. He stumbled and fell as Areipithes gripped his sword two-handed and, still on one knee, hacked downward with all his strength. Sword met shield, hacking through leather and bronze fittings in the ferocity of the blow. Parasades cried out again as the shock raced through his arm, numbing it. He pushed himself away, feet scrabbling at the earth, sword raised in a desperate attempt to block the next blow.

The blow came, at the limit of Areipithes' reach, swords clashing. The king overbalanced and he flailed his arms, trying to break his fall. For a moment, both men lay on the ground within a pace of each other, breathing hard and feeling hearts pounding with exhaustion.

With groans, Parasades and Areipithes pushed themselves to their feet again. They stood swaying, only a few feet between them and traded blows, swords hammering down on upraised shields or meeting in ringing clashes of steel, sparks showering them with silver. The men's movements slowed, the effort necessary to lift a sword, let alone aim and deliver a cut or a thrust becoming too great. Bruised and weary they sank simultaneously to their knees a few paces apart then leaned on hands, panting.

At the edge of the circle, Tomyra looked with growing concern at the circling fighters. She dreaded the thought of her brother winning but remained unsure about what the survival of Parasades would mean. "This is not right," she muttered. "The Goddess must decide who becomes chief of Her People."

"Mistress?" murmured Bithyia. "What would you have us do?"

Tomyra shook her head. "I couldn't force them to pay me heed before the duel, but I can invoke the Mother nonetheless." She beckoned over Prithia and three of her Owl Patrol. "Prithia, you have the sacred drum, or the flute?" Prithia withdrew a small drum from her cloak, evoking a smile from her mistress.

"I have a flute, my lady," said one of the Owls.

Tomyra nodded. "Binara, is it not? Good. If my brother refuses the rite of blessing we shall perform another rite. Let the Mother speak through her holy drum." She turned back to face the fighters just as Areipithes collapsed forward onto the ground in front of the supine body of Parasades.

The drum started throbbing like a low, insistent roll of thunder, the flute breaking in with high-pitched squeals that set teeth on edge even as the drum set fingers tapping. Around the circle of men, soldiers recognised the ritual, even though few remembered the last time it was enacted, when Spargises, father of Areipithes successfully contested for the leadership. Hands twitched and beat, softly at first, in time to the staccato drum, on shield or thigh.

Tomyra lifted her arms and broke into a clear melodic song. The words were strange, unlike the Scythian tongue of those parts, archaic in form, harking back to a day when the Earth Mother ruled all men and none lived or died save by Her will. The song rose and fell, dragging the drum beat with it, the flute wailing like shades condemned to wander the earth with none to say the rites for them. Men shivered, the hair rising on their forearms, the pulse

341

in their chest rising and falling in time with the song, their breath gushing noisily.

In the centre of the circle, Areipithes and Parasades heard the drum, the flute and the song. For a long moment they lay and listened, hearing the breathing of the Great Goddess within the susurration that rose from a thousand lungs. Areipithes stirred first. He got slowly to his feet and stared blankly at the armies beating steadily on their shields. A smile flitted across his face, as if a stray memory from a happier time broke over him. Parasades joined him after a moment, standing a few paces away, his sword hanging by his side. Neither moved, just stood, watched their inner thoughts and listened to the will of the Mother Goddess.

The wailing died away, fading into a measureless distance, the flute following in its wake, leaving only the low, muted rumbles of the drum. The beat slowed, paused and settled into a double beat, the vibrations permeating the air and ground as if the heart of some great beast or demon pulsed in the earth beneath them.

Areipithes twitched, his arms jerking spasmodically as he surfaced from the dream that surrounded him. He stared at the circle of men as if seeing them for the first time. His eyes flicked over Nikometros and Tomyra then settled on Parasades. Areipithes growled, the insistent heartbeat working on him, feeding his anger.

Parasades too, felt the passion rising in him. He hefted his sword and moved slowly toward the Massegetae king. "Areipithes!" he called. "Make your peace with the Mother. I will kill you."

Areipithes yawned and stretched then started whipping his blade back and forth. "You think so? Come and try it then." He strode forward with a laugh, his sword flashing as he ducked and weaved, carrying the fight to Parasades, pressuring him and pushing him backward. Parasades moved in a desultory fashion, barely blocking his enemy's blows and retreating before him.

Nikometros, closely watching the battle from the circle rim, leant toward Tomyra. "What was the purpose of that singing?" he whispered. "Your brother has had his strength renewed."

"As the Mother wills," Tomyra replied quietly. "Watch." She nodded at Prithia and the drumbeat sped up slightly. All around the circle men gasped and swayed forward as the rhythm gripped them anew.

Areipithes laughed again. He stopped his forward motion, letting Parasades flex his still-aching arm. Looking at the small knot of men standing near his sister he yelled, "Get ready, Nemathres! You're next!" He unbuckled his shield straps and shook his arm, sending the small battered leather buckler spinning to the ground. Gripping his short sword in both hands, Areipithes leapt forward and delivered a smashing overhead blow.

Parasades blocked the blow on his already shattered shield, feeling his knees tremble beneath the force of it. He stumbled as Areipithes came at him again, hammering him backward. The drumbeat increased its tempo and Parasades felt himself stir within, the blood rushing faster in his veins as his heart sped to keep up with the beat.

Areipithes blinked, the pressure in his head from the insistent pulse making his eyes water. His breath came in great whooping gusts as he swung his weapon, pounding the other man backward, ever backward. Sweat burst out, slicking his skin, running in rivulets down his face. He stopped again and thrust his sword into the muddy earth. Fumbling with thongs and clasps he ripped his leather tunic off, tearing his undershirt and throwing it from him.

Areipithes roared, the veins on his neck standing out on his molten skin. Snatching up his sword he stumbled forward, slashing and cutting wildly, two hands gripping his weapon. Around him the pulsing quickened. Areipithes breathed faster, the cold air raw in his throat and the sweat stinging his eyes, cascading over his body, making his hands slippery. Still, he hammered at his enemy and still his enemy retreated before him.

Parasades too, felt the wild rhythm within his body. It beat around him, rising up from the earth through his feet, strengthening his weary muscles. He felt a strange mirth bubble up inside, energizing him. Either the blows raining down on shield and sword weakened or else he himself gained in strength. More often now he turned the strokes with the edge of his sword. He still moved back but firmly, giving way rather than being forced.

Areipithes panted and cursed the man in front of him. He swung wildly and missed, recovered and missed again. The other man's sword flicked forward and Areipithes stopped dead, staring down at a welling cut on his left bicep. He roared with rage and delivered a whirlwind series of blows before stepping back, purple in the face and struggling for breath. Two more cuts dripped blood down his arms.

Parasades felt a cool wind on his body, refreshing him. He frowned at the swaying figure in front of him, puzzled by the stress evident on the king's body. Increasingly, Areipithes' blows failed to connect. He smiled then, recognising the balance of the duel turning in his favour. For the first time in many minutes, Parasades moved forward, his blade dancing.

Areipithes fell back before the onslaught, his arms leaden. The flashing steel in front of him weaved mesmerically, flicking effortlessly through his guard. His sweat flowed red over a body laced with stinging lines. Strength washed from him and the bitterness of defeat soured his dry mouth. He glanced across at his sister, feeling another slash across his naked chest as he did so. He caught a quick look of triumph strangely mixed with compassion in her eyes. Rage boiled again and Areipithes leapt forward, his sword raised above his head, roaring his defiance.

Pain ripped redly in his belly and Areipithes halted abruptly, leaning up against his opponent. He stared into Parasades' face, eyes wide, seemingly fascinated by the fine lines in the corners of his enemy's eyes. Glancing up at his upraised arms, he saw steel glinting in the afternoon sun. He opened his sticky fingers and watched the sword fall slowly to the ground. A smile creased his lips and he opened his mouth. "Where is my father?" he whispered.

"Go to him," answered Parasades and pushed Areipithes back, wrenching his sword out as the Massegetae king fell to the ground, blood flooding over his ripped abdomen. Areipithes cried out, then whimpered and drew his legs up, curling around his dreadful wound. Parasades stared down at him for a moment then raised his bloody sword toward Tomyra. The drum fell silent and Parasades spoke clearly into the hiatus. "I claim the tribe by right of combat." Turning, Parasades positioned himself and hacked downward, twice. He stooped and curled his fingers into blood-spattered hair and lifted the head of Areipithes aloft.

Parasades turned slowly on his heel, watching the now silent armies. He tossed the head into the middle of the circle. "I claim the leadership of the Massegetae by right of combat. Do any here dispute my claim?" He waited, listening to the shuffle and creak of armour and the high, distant call of a lark somewhere in the blue sky above him.

Turning toward the Massegetae army, he sought out Areipithes' commanders. "Thoas," he called. "Do you challenge me?" Thoas stared down at his feet then shook his head.

"No. I recognise your claim, Parasades."

"Scolices. Do you dispute me?" The thin man scowled and, turning, pushed back through the packed ranks of warriors and disappeared.

Parasades frowned, then dismissing Scolices from his mind, turned across the circle to the Dumae forces. "Nemathres? Do the Dumae continue to feel enmity for the Massegetae?"

Nemathres shook his head. "We fought the usurper Areipithes. He lies dead and the Dumae remember the bonds of friendship we had with the Massegetae."

"And what of the Jartai? Jaxes, do you challenge me?"

"I do not," declared Jaxes. "Though your people and mine can no longer be friends. Too much has passed between us."

"What do you intend?" asked Parasades.

"I will take the scattered remnants of my people and leave this place. I will seek a place for them in the northwest."

Parasades nodded. He looked across at Nikometros, standing tensely beside the rugged figure of his friend Timon. "And what of you, Nikomayros the Greek, whom men style Lion of Scythia? Do you challenge my right to lead the Massegetae?"

Nikometros sighed and glanced across at Tomyra. He smiled at her, striving to read her thoughts in her dark eyes. "There is only one thing I want," he muttered. Raising his voice to carry across the gathered armies, he addressed the new chief of the Massegetae. "I do not dispute your right to lead the Massegetae, Parasades. You have won that right before us all."

Parasades nodded solemnly. "The tribe has suffered enough in recent months," he said. "I offer a full amnesty to all who will acknowledge me as chief." He turned back to the Massegetae warriors, now noisy with speculation and chatter. "Thoas. Form up your army and proceed to Urul." To Nemathres, "You are welcome to join us, my friend and ally, though I deem it best if you took your army home now and joined us later."

Nemathres nodded and turned to his commanders, issuing terse orders. He clasped Nikometros' arm wordlessly in passing then strode off among his men. Thoas, too, marshalled his troops and led them off the field of battle.

Certes, a huge grin on his face and his chest puffed up, swaggered across to Parasades. "A wonderful victory, my lord. I never doubted you."

"I seem to remember a few occasions," remarked Parasades sourly. "However, I confirm you as my deputy for now." He gestured around him at the carnage of the battlefield. "Take a hundred men, more if you need them, and arrange a decent burial for all the fallen. All," he added sharply. "They are all one People now."

Parasades sauntered slowly across to the group around Nikometros. "Now what do I do about you?" he asked softly. He held up a hand as Nikometros opened his mouth to reply. "No. I must think on this. Go back to Urul, all of you. I will consult with my advisors and the priestess...no, not you, Tomyra...before I reach a decision." Parasades nodded dismissively and walked over to where Certes was gathering loyal men about him.

Chapter 36

U rul glowed in the darkness like a jewelled crown, the fires that sprinkled the city and surrounding countryside casting a warm flush over the myriads of people who swarmed through the city. The faces of the people reflected a muted festivity. The deaths of so many of their men, only a week past, dampened the normal ardour of the Scythian spirit, though pragmatically, life went on. The natural optimism of the plains people encouraged them to happiness. And they had reason for joy. A new chief led them, one whom the Mother Goddess blessed, one who did not carry the stain of parricide. As if awakening from a nightmare, the tribe put the past behind them and stirred itself into a happy anticipation of times to come.

For several days, Parasades held court under a vast felted tent erected in the great square in the centre of the city. Officially confirmed as chief--having denied the title of king--he met openly before his people, organising and deliberating. The great tent remained open on three sides, day and night, despite the residual winter chill. Fires warmed all who came to see the new chief and the slaughtered bodies of a hundred cattle fed the multitudes.

Parasades sat on the great chief's chair, set up in the back of the tent, surrounded by his advisors. If he tended to pick his advisors and commanders from among those who had remained loyal to him in the times of trouble, none saw anything amiss in this. If his decisions favoured his friends, well, that was his right as chief. Any of them would do the same. The common man rejoiced in the newfound peace and promise of prosperity. What did it matter if others, self-styled leaders, now wore glum expressions, passed over for promotions by the new chief?

The crowds at the front of the tent stirred and parted. Parasades looked up from a discussion of his plans, the animation in his face fading to careful neutrality. He watched as Nikometros, with Tomyra by his side, walked up the aisle of people and stopped before him.

"You are welcome, Nikomayros," Parasades said clearly. "And you too, Tomyra."

Nikometros inclined his head and Tomyra smiled, remaining silent.

"I summoned you to make my decisions known to you. They affect the tribe so I deemed it proper to inform you before all." Parasades waved his hand toward two padded stools. "Please, be seated." He beckoned a servant forward with cups of fresh koumiss and waited until they drank. Rising from his seat he addressed the pair in formal tones, pitching his voice for all to hear.

"We owe a debt of gratitude to you, Nikomayros, styled Lion of Scythia." A smattering of applause and cheering broke out. Parasades waited for it to die away before continuing. "Nevertheless, you came to us in a time of trouble and that trouble has now passed away. It would be selfish to ask you to remain in the lands of the Massegetae any longer."

Muttering rippled through the crowd. A voice near the back called out, "Ask him!" evoking cheers and laughter.

"Instead, I would ask you to perform one last service for the People. Will you do it, Nikomayros?"

Nikometros inclined his head again. "If I can, my lord Parasades."

"I do not seek to extend the boundaries of the Massegetae beyond the newly vacated lands of the Jartai. The tribe will still make its annual journey to the Mother Sea but if the gods are willing we shall live in peace with those around us." Nods and cheers of agreement met this statement.

"However," Parasades went on, "There are peoples around us who do not live peacefully, who may threaten our security. To the east lie many small tribes, none of whom pose any credible threat as yet. To the west lie the Serratae..." Jeers of derision erupted from the listeners. "...The Serratae, who no longer are a problem. But to the south lies the realm of Alexander of Macedon, the conqueror from the west who continues to look farther afield for new lands to invade. I do not want him to cast greedy eyes upon the wealth of Scythia."

Parasades paused and looked at Nikometros. "Nikomayros, will you go to the court of Alexander, as envoy from the Massegetae, with an offer of friendship between our peoples?"

Nikometros started, his mouth open. He shut it firmly and rose to his feet. Facing Parasades, he smiled briefly and nodded. "I am honoured to be chosen for this task, my lord...but..." He hesitated then stopped, looking flustered.

"Go on, Nikomayros," said Parasades, frowning. "Why do you object to this task?"

"I don't object, my lord. It's just that I'm Macedonian, not Massegetae. Such an offer of friendship should come from one of the People."

"There is truth in what you say, Nikomayros. Yet you know the mind of Alexander and the ways of the Greeks. This is why I chose you."

"Then let me accompany your envoy as advisor. I will be able to help him through the intricacies of protocol and advise him as to how he should gauge the offers made to him. He will need an interpreter too," Nikometros added.

Parasades stared hard at Nikometros before nodding. "Very well. Your argument makes sense, Nikomayros." He turned back to the audience of tribesmen listening outside the tent. "Men and women of the Massegetae," he said, "You have witnessed the decision to send the lord Nikomayros to speak with Alexander on our behalf. We trust Nikomayros with our very lives but aspects of this mission must now be discussed in private. I ask that you withdraw from here so that I might deliberate with my advisors. Eat well, all of you, for there is much meat. Drink, for koumiss has been prepared. Rejoice, for our sorrows are past."

Cheers and shouting erupted from the crowd as they jostled and streamed away, chattering and laughing. Parasades turned back to the small group within the tent. He beckoned to the waiting servants. "Bring meat and drink." Turning to one of his advisors he muttered softly to the man before sending him running off into the night. Parasades crossed to a trestle table and picked up a chunk of roasted meat, carrying it back to his chair. He proceeded to gnaw at the tough meat, ignoring the others.

Nikometros sat down again and pondered his mission. After a few minutes, Tomyra broke in on his thoughts.

"Whom will you take to the south?" she asked quietly.

Nikometros shook his head. "I don't know. It'll be up to Parasades, but Timon will go with me of course."

"What of Bithyia?" asked Tomyra. "He won't want to leave her."

"No, but he's a soldier. He knows his duty."

"And you, my lord? Do you know your duty?"

"Of course, I..." Nikometros flushed and looked away.

"Will you come back to Scythia, my lord?"

"Tomyra, you know I..." Nikometros stuttered to a halt. Drawing a deep breath he faced the young woman. "Tomyra, my place is with my king. You know that. I'll help the Massegetae as much as I can, for I recognise my debt, but I must remain in the south."

Tomyra lowered her eyes and folded her hands in her lap, withdrawing into herself. "I shall rejoice for you, my lord," she whispered. "But Scythia will seem very empty."

Nikometros frowned. "I cannot stay, Tomyra. Even your goddess foretold that I would follow the Golden King, whoever he may be. Remember, Ket thinks he is Alexander."

"Then you must go, Nikomayros."

Nikometros sat silently, not sure what to say. He watched, aghast, as a tear slowly trickled down Tomyra's cheek. "Tomyra," he started awkwardly. "Why do you...?" He reached out and gripped Tomyra's hand. "Tomyra, there's nothing to hold you here, is there? I mean, do you...er...will you come with me?"

Tomyra looked up, eyes glistening. "Do you want me to?" she asked in a small voice.

"Of course I do."

"Why?"

"Why?" repeated Nikometros. "Because I...because you..." He looked away, into the night where the cooking fires blazed. He flushed red then steeling himself, turned back to Tomyra and took her hands in his again. He gazed into her eyes for a long moment.

"Because, Tomyra, when I first saw you, in the dust of battle, there before me on the ground, I knew our souls were joined. Before ever I knew your goddess had a purpose for us, I dared hope. When we're together, my heart sings and I feel I can do anything. When we're apart, I count the hours to your return. You're a part of me. I would sooner give up a limb than give you up. I cannot live without you, Tomyra, daughter of Spargises. You mean everything to me. I love you."

Tomyra burst into tears and threw her arms around him. Through her sniffles and sobs, she asked, "Why did you not say, my lord? Didn't you know that I feel this way too? Why else would I risk my life to give myself to you if I didn't love you?"

Nikometros grimaced, stroking Tomyra's long black hair. "I'm sorry, Tomyra. I couldn't be certain. I thought...I don't know what I thought."

Tomyra pulled away and wiped her eyes on the hem of her cloak. "There is something I must tell you, Nikomayros. Though I fear when I tell..."

The tramp of approaching feet and cries of greeting interrupted her. Into the tent marched a small group of clean-shaven Scythians, Tirses in the lead. Behind him walked Timon, arm in arm with Bithyia and a handful of other Owls.

"Ho, Nikometros," cried Timon. "What is happening? We were rousted out of a most enjoyable drinking party with no word of explanation. What's going on?"

"We ride south!" grinned Nikometros. "We're going home, Timon."

"Home?" yelled Timon. He let out an exultant whoop and punched the air. "By all the gods, how? And when?"

Bithyia stared at her man then at Nikometros and Tomyra. She saw the fresh tears in her mistress' eyes and frowned. "What is it, my lady?"

Tomyra smiled. "My lord Nikomayros and I travel to his country and his people in the south, Bithyia. Will you come too?"

Bithyia looked to where Timon and Nikometros talked together animatedly. "If my Timon wishes it, yes."

A cough sounded behind them and all four turned to see Parasades rise from his chief's chair. He looked gravely at them then glanced at Tirses and the young shaven men.

"I have gathered you here," Parasades said abruptly, addressing the young Scythian officer, "To tell you of your mission. I have decided that you, Tirses, will carry an offer of friendship from the Massegetae to Alexander of Macedon at Ekbatana in Persia. He resides there, having returned from his conquests in the east. These young men, 'Lions' I believe they style themselves, will accompany you as your honour guard." He turned back to Nikometros. "The lord Nikomayros will act as interpreter and advisor. Pay heed to him, Tirses. Nikomayros will be accompanied by his man, Timon." Parasades nodded toward the women. "Tomyra, as a holy priestess, will go as a token of our good intentions, and to make sacrifice as necessary, for the success of the mission. Such of her maidens as wish to accompany her as guards, may do so."

Timon's grin faded as he listened. "Getting rid of us, more like," he muttered. "Every single one of us knows of his actions of late and his weaknesses."

Parasades glared at Timon. "Yes, Timon," he said coldly. "But not from any desire on my part to get you out of my lands. However, there are those, in my late predecessors' employ I believe, who wish you harm. I wouldn't forgive myself if anything happened to you." Timon snorted softly and opened his mouth to retort. Nikometros put out a hand to restrain him.

"We shall, of course, be honoured to represent the Massegetae in this important mission," said Nikometros. "We'll start preparing immediately. I'm sure we can be ready to start out within a month."

Parasades smiled thinly. "All is prepared. You leave at dawn tomorrow."

"Tomorrow!" exclaimed Timon. "How can we possibly be ready?"

Parasades narrowed his eyes, his nostrils flaring. "A word with you, Nikomayros. In private." He turned and stalked away from the group. In the shadows at the back of the tent he turned and hissed at Nikometros. "Explain to your man that he is not to question my decisions. Let him remember his place."

"He's right though, isn't he, Parasades? You're hurrying us out of here with unseemly haste. Even I ask myself, why?"

"You have to ask? My tribe is still divided, now when healing is most needed. The young men follow you. Look at those 'Lions'." Parasades gestured at the young shaven warriors, standing around awkwardly, listening to the animated discussions between Timon and the women. "Aping Greek customs instead of honouring the traditions of their fathers. No, if you remain, there will be trouble." Parasades sighed and ran his fingers through his hair. "I don't want to have to kill you, Nikomayros, so I'm sending you away. Take your young men and such women as will follow you and make a life for yourselves far from my lands."

"So this task, this diplomatic mission, is but a fiction?"

"Not entirely. I do desire peace with Alexander. Present him with gifts-- I'll send gold with you--and make a treaty if you can."

"You would trust me with this?"

Parasades raised an eyebrow. "You're an honourable man, my lord Nikomayros. If you undertake to do it, you will, to the best of your ability."

Nikometros held the other man's gaze for a long time before he nodded. "I will do as you wish, my lord Parasades. You haven't been an easy man to understand, but I don't doubt you have the good of the Massegetae at heart. I will do what I can for you at Alexander's court."

"Good enough! Now let us rejoin the others," smiled Parasades. "A drink in celebration then I'll let you go. You have much to do before dawn."

Chapter 37

Twenty riders sat looking south over mountains, folded and twisted, falling slowly to distant plains, lost in a haze of dust and smoke. The borders of Scythia, long disputed by those who lived on them, were generally accepted to lie where the plains of the horsemen abutted on the mountainous regions of the hill tribes of northern Persia. Here, on the crest of the first range, peering down the great cleft in the rock walls that was styled the Persian Gates, the entrance to the rich lands of the south, the terrain was already strange.

The Scythians in the little group looked around at the up-thrust rock and shivered then turned to the figure on the great stallion for comfort. Nikometros stared down into Persia, remembering when he first rode north through this mountain pass, young and inexperienced. Now less than two years later, he rode back, a leader and a general, a newfound confidence swelling his chest and the woman he loved beside him.

Nikometros looked around at the other riders and smiled encouragingly. "Persia!" he exclaimed with a sweeping gesture. "Our future."

A richly dressed Scythian, clad in expensive clothes and adorned with gold and enamelled ornaments, smiled at him. "I will leave you now, Nikomayros. I do not look to see you again."

"Had to be sure we left, eh Parasades?" grinned Nikometros. "Do not fear. We won't return. Go back to your tribe and rule them wisely."

Parasades nodded. "Time to take them back to the old ways, I think. And heal the wounds. Your life cord is a strong one, Nikomayros. You hurt those close to you."

A shadow passed over Nikometros' eyes. "We are all in the hands of the gods." He nudged his stallion and it started forward down the rocky trail into Persia. Behind him, Timon nodded silently at the Massegetae chief as he passed, following his commander. Tomyra and Bithyia clattered past, Agarus leading two heavily laden packhorses in their wake, and Ket, astride an old placid mare. A wicker basket slung over the mare's withers uttered disgusted yowls at each step. Tirses rode at the head of a dozen young horsemen, grinning and chattering as they left the land of their ancestors without a backward glance.

Parasades watched them go, disappearing already into the cloud of dust kicked up by the horses. "May the gods be with you, Lion of Scythia," he murmured, "In your quest for your Golden King." He wheeled his horse and galloped back down the slope toward his waiting entourage and the open plains of Scythia.

Behind him, on the crest of the mountain ridge, the dust settled as the sun rose high into the crisp new spring day. Silence returned to the mountain pass. In the distance, riding on the still air, came the cawing of a pair of crows, following the riders south on their long journey to a new destiny.

The story of Nikometros and Tomyra will be concluded in 'Funeral in Babylon'

If you enjoyed this author's book, then please place a review up at the site of purchase, and any social media sites you frequent!

You can find ALL our books up on our website at:
https://www.writers-exchange.com

All our Historical Novels:
https://www.writers-exchange.com/category/genres/historical/

All Max's Books:
https://www.writers-exchange.com/max-overton/

About the Author

Max Overton has travelled extensively and lived in many places around the world--including Malaysia, India, Germany, England, Jamaica, New Zealand, USA and Australia. Trained in the biological sciences in New Zealand and Australia, he has worked within the scientific field for many years, but now concentrates on writing. While predominantly a writer of historical fiction (Scarab: Books 1 - 6 of the Amarnan Kings; the Scythian Trilogy; the Demon Series; Ascension), he also writes in other genres (A Cry of Shadows, the Glass Trilogy, Haunted Trail, Sequestered) and draws on true life (Adventures of a Small Game Hunter in Jamaica, We Came From Königsberg). Max also maintains an interest in butterflies, photography, the paranormal and other aspects of Fortean Studies.

Most of his other published books are available at Writers Exchange E-Publishing, https://www.writers-exchange.com/Max-Overton/ and all his books may be viewed on his website: http://www.maxovertonauthor.com/

Max's book covers are all designed and created by Julie Napier, and other examples of her art and photography may be viewed at www.julienapier.com

If you want to read more about books by this author, they are listed on the following pages...

A Cry of Shadows

{Paranormal Murder Mystery}

Australian Professor Ian Delaney is single-minded in his determination to prove his theory that one can discover the moment that the life force leaves the body. After succumbing to the temptation to kill a girl under scientifically controlled conditions, he takes an offer of work in St Louis, hoping to leave the undiscovered crime behind him.

In America, Wayne Richardson seeks revenge by killing his ex-girlfriend, believing it will give him the upper hand, a means to seize control following their breakup. Wayne quickly discovers that he enjoys killing and begins to seek out young women who resemble his dead ex-girlfriend.

Ian and Wayne meet and, when Ian recognizes the symptoms of violent delusion, he employs Wayne to help him further his research. Despite the police closing in, the two killers manage to evade identification time and time again as the death toll rises in their wake.

The detective in charge of the case, John Barnes, is frantic, willing to try anything to catch his killer. With time running out, he searches desperately for answers before another body is found...or the culprit slips into the woodwork for good.

Publisher: https://www.writers-exchange.com/a-cry-of-shadows/

Adventures of a Small Game Hunter in Jamaica
{Biography}

An eleven-year-old boy is plucked from boarding school in England and transported to the tropical paradise of Jamaica where he's free to study his one great love--butterflies. He discovers that Jamaica has a wealth of these wonderful insects and sets about making a collection of as many as he can find. Along the way, he has adventures with other creatures, from hummingbirds to vultures, from iguanas to black widow spiders. Through it all runs the promise of the legendary Homerus swallowtail, Jamaica's national butterfly.

Other activities intrude, like school, boxing and swimming lessons, but he manages to inveigle his parents into taking him to strange and sometimes dangerous places, all in the name of butterfly collecting. He meets scientists and Rastafarians, teachers, small boys and the ordinary people living on the tropical isle, and even discovers butterflies that shouldn't exist in Jamaica.

Author Max Overton was that young boy. He counted himself fortunate to have lived in Jamaica in an age very different from the present one. Max still has some of the butterflies he collected half a century or more ago, and each one releases a flood of memories whenever he opens the box and gazes at their tattered and fading wings. These memories have become stories-- stories of the Adventures of a Small Game Hunter in Jamaica.

Publisher: https://www.writers-exchange.com/adventures-of-a-small-game-hunter/

Ascension Series, A Novel of Nazi Germany
{Historical: Holocaust}

Before he fully realized the diabolical cruelties of the National Socialist German Worker's Party, Konrad Wengler had committed atrocities against his own people, the Jews, out of fear of both his faith and his heritage. But after he witnesses firsthand the concentration camps, the corruption, the inhuman malevolence of the Nazi war machine and the propaganda aimed at annihilating an entire race, he knows he must find a way to turn the tide and become the savior his people desperately need.

Book 1: Ascension

Being a Jew in Germany can be a dangerous thing...

Fear prompts Konrad Wengler to put his faith aside and try desperately to forget his heritage. After fighting in the Great War, he's wounded and turns instead to law enforcement in his tiny Bavarian hometown. There, he falls under the spell of the fledgling Nazi Party. He joins the Party in patriotic fervour and becomes a Lieutenant of Police and Schutzstaffel (SS).

In the course of his duties as policeman, Konrad offends a powerful Nazi official who starts an SS investigation. War breaks out. When he joins the Police Battalions, he's sent to Poland and witnesses there firsthand the atrocities being committed upon his fellow Jews.

Unknown to Konrad, the SS investigators have discovered his origins and follow him into Poland. Arrested and sent to Mauthausen Concentration Camp, Konrad is forced to face what it means to be a Jew and fight for survival. Will his friends on the outside, his wife and lawyer, be enough to counter the might of the Nazi machine?

Publisher: https://www.writers-exchange.com/ascension/

363

Book 2: Maelstrom

Never underestimate the enemy...

Konrad Wengler survived his brush with the death camps of Nazi Germany. Now, reinstated as a police officer in his Bavarian hometown despite being a Jew, he throws himself back into his work, seeking to uncover evidence that will remove a corrupt Nazi party official.

The Gestapo have their own agenda and, despite orders from above to eliminate this troublesome Jewish policeman, they hide Konrad in the Totenkopf (Death's Head) Division of the Waffen-SS. In a fight to survive in the snowy wastes of Russia while the tide of war turns against Germany, Konrad experiences tank battles, ghetto clearances, partisans, and death camps (this time as a guard), as well as the fierce battles where his Division is badly outnumbered and on the defence.

Through it all, Konrad strives to live by his conscience and resist taking part in the atrocities happening all around him. He still thinks of himself as a policeman, but his desire to bring the corrupt Nazi official to justice seems far removed from his present reality. If he is to find the necessary evidence against his enemy, he must first *survive...*

Publisher: https://www.writers-exchange.com/maelstrom/

Book 3: Dämmerung

Konrad Wengler is captured and sent from one Soviet prison camp to another. Even hearing the war has come to an end makes no difference until he's arrested as a Nazi Party member. In jail, Konrad refuses to defend himself for things he's guilty and should be punished for. Will his be an eye-for-an-eye life sentence, or leniency in regard of the good he tried to do once he learned the truth?

Publisher: https://www.writers-exchange.com/dammerung/

Fall of the House of Ramesses Series,
A Novel of Ancient Egypt

{Historical: Ancient Egypt}

Egypt was at the height of its powers in the days of Ramesses the Great, a young king who confidently predicted his House would last for a Thousand Years. Sixty years later, he was still on the throne. One by one, his heirs had died and the survivors had become old men. When Ramesses at last died, he left a stagnant kingdom and his throne to an old man-- Merenptah. What followed laid the groundwork for a nation ripped apart by civil war.

Book 1: Merenptah

The House of Ramesses is in the hands of an old man. King Merenptah wants to leave the kingdom to his younger son, Seti, but northern tribes in Egypt rebel and join forces with the Sea Peoples, invading from the north. In the south, the king's eldest son Messuwy is angered at being passed over in favour of the younger son...and plots to rid himself of his father and brother. Publisher: https://www.writers-exchange.com/merenptah/

Book 2: Seti

After only nine years on the throne, Merenptah is dead and his son Seti is king in his place. He rules from the northern city of Men-nefer, while his elder brother Messuwy, convinced the throne is his by right, plots rebellion in the south.

The kingdoms are tipped into bloody civil war, with brother fighting against brother for the throne of a united Egypt. On one side is Messuwy, now crowned as King Amenmesse and his ruthless General Sethi; on the other, young King Seti and his wife Tausret. But other men are weighing up the chances of wresting the throne from both brothers and becoming king in their place. Under the onslaught of conflict, the House of Ramesses begins to crumble...

Publisher: https://www.writers-exchange.com/seti/

Book 3: Tausret

The House of Ramesses falters as Tausret relinquishes the throne upon the death of her husband, King Seti. Amenmesse's young son Siptah will become king until her infant son is old enough to rule. Tausret, as Regent, and the king's uncle, Chancellor Bay, hold tight to the reins of power and vie for complete control of the kingdoms. Assassination changes the balance of power, and, seeing his chance, Chancellor Bay attempts a coup...

Tausret's troubles mount as she also faces a challenge from Setnakhte, an aging son of the Great Ramesses who believes Seti was the last legitimate king. If Setnakhte gets his way, he will destroy the House of Ramesses and set up his own dynasty of kings.

Publisher: https://www.writers-exchange.com/tausret/

Glass Trilogy
{Paranormal Thriller}

Delve deep into the mysteries of Aboriginal mythology, present day UFO activity and pure science that surround the continent of Australia, from its barren deserts to the depths of its rainforest and even deeper into its mysterious mountains. Along the way, love, greed, murder, and mystery abound while the secrets of mankind and the ultimate answer to 'what happens now?' just might be answered.

GLASS HOUSE, Book 1: The mysteries of Australia may just hold the answers mankind has been searching for millennium to find. When Doctor James Hay, a university scientist who studies the paranormal mysteries in Australia, finds an obelisk of carved volcanic rock on sacred Aboriginal land in northern Queensland, he realizes it may hold the answers he's been seeking. A respected elder of the Aboriginal people instructs James to take up the gauntlet and follow his heart. Along with his old friend and award-winning writer Spencer, Samantha Louis, her cameraman, and two of James' Aboriginal students, James embarks on a life-changing quest for the truth.
Publisher: https://www.writers-exchange.com/glass-house/

A GLASS DARKLY, Book 2: A dead volcano called Glass Mountain in Northern California seems harmless...but is it really?

Andromeda Jones, a physicist, knows her missing sister Samantha is somehow tied up with the new job Andromeda herself has been offered to work with a team in constructing Vox Dei, a machine that's been ostensibly built to eliminate wars. But what is its true nature, and who's pulling the strings?

When the experiment spins out of control, dark powers are unleashed and the danger to mankind unfolds relentlessly. Strange, evil shadows are using the Vox Dei and Andromeda's sister Samantha to get through to our world, knowing the time is near when Earth's final destiny will be decided.

Federal forces are aware of something amiss, so, to rescue her sibling, Andromeda agrees to go on a dangerous mission and soon finds herself entangled in a web of professional jealousy, political betrayal, and flat-out greed.

Publisher: https://www.writers-exchange.com/a-glass-darkly/

LOOKING GLASS, Book 3: Samantha and James Hay have been advised that their missing daughter Gaia have been located in ancient Australia. Dr. Xanatuo, an alien scientist who, along with a lost tribe of Neanderthals and other beings working to help mankind, has discovered a way to send them back in time to be reunited with Gaia. Ernie, the old Aboriginal tracker and leader of the Neanderthals, along with friends Ratana and Nathan and characters from the first two books of the trilogy, will accompany them. This team of intrepid adventurers have another mission for the journey, along with aiding the Hayes' quest, which is paramount to changing a terrible wrong which exists in the present time.

Publisher: https://www.writers-exchange.com/looking-glass/

Haunted Trail A Tale of Wickedness & Moral Turpitude

{Western: Paranormal}

Ned Abernathy is a hot-tempered young cowboy in the small town of Hammond's Bluff in 1876. In a drunken argument with his best friend Billy over a girl, he guns him down. Ned flees and wanders the plains, forests and hills of the Dakota Territories, certain that every man's hand is against him.

Horse rustlers, marauding Indians, killers, gold prospectors and French trappers cross his path and lead to complications, as do persistent apparitions of what Ned believes is the ghost of his friend Billy, come to accuse him of murder. He finds love and loses it. Determined not to do the same when he discovers gold in the Black Hills, he ruthlessly defends his newfound wealth against greedy men. In the process, he comes to terms with who he is and what he's done. But there are other ghosts in his past that he needs to confront. Returning to Hammond's Bluff, Ned stumbles into a shocking surprise awaiting him at the end of his haunted trail.

Publisher: https://www.writers-exchange.com/haunted-trail/

Hyksos Series, A Novel of Ancient Egypt

The power of the kings of the Middle Kingdom have been failing for some time, having lost control of the Nile Delta to a series of Canaanite kings who ruled from the northern city of Avaris.

Into this mix came the Kings of Amurri, Lebanon and Syria bent on subduing the whole of Egypt. These kings were known as the Hyksos, and they dealt a devastating blow to the peoples of the Nile Delta and Valley.

Book 1: Avaris

When Arimawat and his son Harrubaal fled from Urubek, the king of Hattush, to the court of the King of Avaris, King Sheshi welcomed the refugees. One of Arimawat's first tasks for King Shesi is to sail south to the Land of Kush and fetch Princess Tati, who will become Sheshi's queen. Arimawat and Harrubaal perform creditably, but their actions have far-reaching consequences.

On the return journey, Harrubaal falls in love with Kemi, the daughter of the Southern Egyptian king. As a reward for Harrubaal's work, Sheshi secures the hand of the princess for the young Canaanite prince. Unfortunately for the peace of the realm, Sheshi lusts after Princess Kemi too, and his actions threaten the stability of his kingdom...

Publisher: https://www.writers-exchange.com/avaris/

Book 2: Conquest

The Hyksos invade the Delta using the new weapons of bronze and chariots, things of which the Egyptians have no knowledge. They rout the Delta forces, and in the south, the unconquered kings ready their armies to defend their lands. Meanwhile in Avaris, Merybaal, the son of Harrubaal and Kemi, strives to defend his family in a city conquered by the Hyksos.

Elements of the Delta army that refuse to surrender continue the fight for their homeland, and new kings proclaim themselves as the inheritors of the failed kings of Avaris. One of these is Amenre, grandson of Merybaal, but he is forced into hiding as the Hyksos sweep all before them, bringing their terror to the kingdom of the Nile valley. Driven south in disarray, the survivors of the Egyptian army seek leaders who can resist the enemy...

Publisher: https://www.writers-exchange.com/conquest/

Book 3: Two Cities

The Hyksos drive south into the Nile Valley, sweeping all resistance aside. Bebi and Sobekhotep, grandsons of Harrubaal, assume command of the loyal Egyptian army and strive to stem the flood of Hyksos conquest. But even the cities of the south are divided against themselves.

Abdju, an old capital city of Egypt reasserts itself, putting forward a line of kings of its own, and soon the city is at war with Waset, the southern capital of the Nile Valley, as the two cities fight for supremacy in the face of the advancing northern enemy. Caught up in the turmoil of warring nations, the ordinary people of Egypt must fight for their own survival as well as that of their kingdom.

Publisher: https://www.writers-exchange.com/two-cities/

Book 4: Possessor of All

The Hyksos, themselves beset by intrigue and division, push down into southern Egypt. The short-lived kingdom of Abdju collapses, leaving Nebiryraw the undisputed king of the south ruling from the city of Waset. An uneasy truce between north and south enables both sides to strengthen their positions.

Khayan seizes power over the Hyksos kingdom and turns his gaze toward Waset, determined to conquer Egypt finally. Meanwhile, the family of King Nebiryraw looks to the future and starts securing their own advantage, weakening the southern kingdom. In the face of renewed tensions, the delicate peace cannot last...

Publisher: https://www.writers-exchange.com/possessor-of-all/

Book 5: War in the South

Intrigue and rebellion rule in Egypt's southern kingdom as the house of King Nebiryraw tears itself apart. King succeeds king, but none of them look capable of defending the south, let alone reclaiming the north. Taking advantage of this, King Khayan of the Hyksos launches his assault on Waset, but rebellions in the north delay his victory.

The fall of Waset brings about a change of leadership. Apophis takes command of the Hyksos forces, and Rahotep brings together a small army to challenge the might of the Hyksos, knowing that the fate of Egypt hangs on the coming battle.

Publisher: https://www.writers-exchange.com/war-in-the-south/

Book 6: Between the Wars

Rahotep leads his Egyptian army to victory, and Apophis withdraws the Hyksos army northward. An uneasy peace settles over the Nile valley. Rebellions in the north keep the Hyksos king from striking back at Rahotep, while internal strife between the Hyksos nobility and generals threatens to rip their empire apart.

War is coming to Egypt once more, and the successors of Rahotep start preparing for it, using the very weapons that the Hyksos introduced--bronze weapons and the war chariot. King Ahmose repudiates the peace treaty, and

Apophis of the Hyksos prepares to destroy his enemies at last. Bloody warfare returns to Egypt...

Publisher: https://www.writers-exchange.com/between-the-wars/

Book 7: Sons of Tao

War breaks out between the Hyksos invaders and native Egyptians determined to rid themselves of their presence. King Seqenenre Tao launches an attack on King Apophis but the Hyksos strike back savagely. It is only when his sons Kamose and Ahmose carry the war to the Hyksos that the Egyptians really start to hope they can succeed.

Kamose battles fiercely, but only when his younger brother Ahmose assumes the throne is there real success. Faced with an ignominious defeat, a Hyksos general overthrows Apophis and becomes king, but then he faces a resurgent Egyptian king determined to rid his land of the Hyksos invader...

Publisher: https://www.writers-exchange.com/sons-of-tao/

Kadesh, A Novel of Ancient Egypt

Holding the key to strategic military advantage, Kadesh is a jewel city that distant lands covet. Ramesses II of Egypt and Muwatalli II of Hatti believe they're chosen by the gods to claim ascendancy to Kadesh. When the two meet in the largest chariot battle ever fought, not just the fate of empires will be decided but also the lives of citizens helplessly caught up in the greedy ambition of kings.

Publisher: https://www.writers-exchange.com/kadesh/

Scythian Trilogy
{Historical}

Captured by the warlike, tribal Scythians who bicker amongst themselves and bitterly resent outside interference, a fiercely loyal captain in Alexander the Great's Companion Cavalry Nikometros and his men are to be sacrificed to the Mother Goddess. Lucky chance--and the timely intervention of Tomyra, priestess and daughter of the Massegetae chieftain--allows him to defeat the Champion. With their immediate survival secured, acceptance into the tribe...and escape...is complicated by the captain's growing feelings for Tomyra--death to any who touch her--and the chief's son Areipithes who not only detests Nikometros and wants to have him killed or banished but intends to murder his own father and take over the tribe.

LION OF SCYTHIA, Book 1: Alexander the Great has conquered the Persian Empire and is marching eastward to India. In his wake he leaves small groups of soldiers to govern great tracts of land and diverse peoples. Nikometros is one young cavalry captain left behind in the lands of the fierce, nomadic Scythian horsemen. Captured after an ambush, Nikometros must fight for his life and the lives of his surviving men. Even as he seeks an opportunity to escape, he finds himself bound by a debt of loyalty to the chief...and his own developing love for the young priestess.
Publisher: https://www.writers-exchange.com/lion-of-scythia/

THE GOLDEN KING, Book 2: The chief of the tribe of nomadic Scythian horsemen is dead, killed by his son's treachery. The priestess, lover of the young cavalry officer, Nikometros, is carried off into the mountains. Nikometros and his friends set off in hard pursuit.

Death rides with them. By the time they return, the tribes are at war. Nikometros must choose between attempting to become chief himself or leaving the people he's come to love and respect to return to his duty as an army officer in the Empire of Alexander.

Winner of the 2005 EPIC Ebook Awards.

Publisher: https://www.writers-exchange.com/the-golden-king/

FUNERAL IN BABYLON, Book 3: Alexander the Great has returned from India and set up his court in Babylon. Nikometros and a band of loyal Scythians journey deep into the heart of Persia to join the Royal court. Nikometros finds himself embroiled in the intrigues and wars of kings, generals, and merchant adventurers as he strives to provide a safe haven for his lover and friends. With the fate of an Empire hanging in the balance, Death walks beside Nikometros as events precipitate a Funeral in Babylon...

Winner of the 2006 EPIC Ebook Awards.

Publisher: https://www.writers-exchange.com/funeral-in-babylon/

Sequestered
By Max Overton and Jim Darley
{Action/Thriller}

Storing carbon dioxide underground as a means of removing a greenhouse gas responsible for global warming has made James Matternicht a fabulously wealthy man. For 15 years, the Carbon Capture and Sequestration Facility at Rushing River in Oregon's hinterland has been operating without a problem...or has it?

When mysterious documents arrive on her desk that purport to show the Facility is leaking, reporter Annaliese Winton investigates. Together with a government geologist, Matt Morrison, she uncovers a morass of corruption and deceit that now threatens the safety of her community and the entire northwest coast of America.

Liquid carbon dioxide, stored at the critical point under great pressure, is a tremendously dangerous substance, and millions of tonnes of it are sequestered in the rock strata below Rushing River. All it would take is a crack in the overlying rock and the whole pressurized mass could erupt with disastrous consequences. And that crack has always existed there...

Recipient of the Life Award (Literature for the Environment):

"There are only two kinds of people: conservationists and suicides. To qualify for this Award, your book needs to value the wonderful world of nature, to recognize that we are merely one species out of millions, and that we have a responsibility to cherish and maintain our small planet."

Awarded from http://bobswriting.com/life/

Publisher: https://www.writers-exchange.com/sequestered/

Strong is the Ma'at of Re, A Novel of Ancient Egypt

{Historical: Ancient Egypt}

In Ancient Egypt, C1200 BCE, bitter contention and resentment, secret coups and assassination attempts may decide the fate of those who would become legends...by any means necessary.

Book 1: The King

That *he* is descended from Ramesses the Great fills Ramesses III with obscene pride. Elevated to the throne following a coup led by his father Setnakhte during the troubled days of Queen Tausret, Ramesses III sets about creating an Egypt that reflects the glory days of Ramesses the Great. He takes on his predecessor's throne name, names his sons after the sons of Ramesses and pushes them toward similar duties. Most of all, he thirsts after conquests like those of his hero grandfather.

Ramesses III assumes the throne name of Usermaatre, translated as "Strong is the Ma'at of Re" and endeavours to live up to the sentiment. He fights foreign foes, as had Ramesses the Great; he builds temples throughout the Two Lands, as had Ramesses the Great, and he looks forward to a long, illustrious life on the throne of Egypt, as had Ramesses the Great.

Alas, his reign is not meant to be. Ramesses III faces troubles at home-- troubles that threaten the stability of Egypt and his own throne. The struggles for power between his wives, his sons, and even the priests of Amun, together with a treasury drained of its wealth, all force Ramesses III to question his success as the scion of a legend.

Publisher: https://www.writers-exchange.com/the-king/

Book 2: The Heirs

Tiye, the first wife of Ramesses III, has grown so used to being the mother of the Heir she can no longer bear to see that prized title pass to the son of a rival wife. Her eldest sons have died and the one left wants to step down and devote his life to the priesthood. Then the son of the king's sister/wife, also named Ramesses, will become Crown Prince and all Tiye's ambitions will lie in ruins.

Ramesses III struggles to enrich Egypt by seeking the wealth of the Land of Punt. He dispatches an expedition to the fabled southern land but years pass before the expedition returns. In the meantime, Tiye has a new hope: A last son she dotes on. Plague sweeps through Egypt, killing princes and princesses alike and lessening her options, and now Tiye must undergo the added indignity of having her daughter married off to the hated Crown Prince.

All Tiye's hopes are pinned on this last son of hers, but Ramesses III refuses to consider him as a potential successor, despite the Crown Prince's failing health. Unless Tiye can change the king's mind through charm or coercion, her sons will forever be excluded from the throne of Egypt.

Publisher: https://www.writers-exchange.com/the-heirs/

Book 3: Taweret

The reign of Ramesses III is failing and even the gods seem to be turning their eyes away from Egypt. When the sun hides its face, crops suffer, throwing the country into famine. Tomb workers go on strike. To avert further disaster, Crown Prince Ramesses acts on his father's behalf.

The rivalry between Ramesses III's wives--commoner Tiye and sister/wife Queen Tyti--also comes to a head. Tiye resents not being made queen and can't abide that her sons have been passed over. She plots to put her own spoiled son Pentaweret on the throne.

The eventual strength of the Ma'at of Re hangs in the balance. Will the rule of Egypt be decided by fate, gods...or treason?

Publisher: https://www.writers-exchange.com/the-one-of-taweret/

The Amarnan Kings Series, A Novel of Ancient Egypt

{Historical: Ancient Egypt}

Set in Egypt of the 14th century B.C.E. and piecing together a mosaic of the reigns of the five Amarnan kings, threaded through by the memories of princess Beketaten-Scarab, a tapestry unfolds of the royal figures lost in the mists of antiquity.

SCARAB - AKHENATEN, Book 1: A chance discovery in Syria reveals answers to the mystery of the ancient Egyptian sun-king, the heretic Akhenaten and his beautiful wife Nefertiti. Inscriptions in the tomb of his sister Beketaten, otherwise known as Scarab, tell a story of life and death, intrigue and warfare, in and around the golden court of the kings of the glorious 18th dynasty.

The narrative of a young girl growing up at the centre of momentous events--the abolition of the gods, foreign invasion, and the fall of a once-great family--reveals who Tutankhamen's parents really were, what happened to Nefertiti, and other events lost to history in the great destruction that followed the fall of the Aten heresy.

Publisher: https://www.writers-exchange.com/scarab/

SCARAB- SMENKHKARE, Book 2: King Akhenaten, distraught at the rebellion and exile of his beloved wife Nefertiti, withdraws from public life, content to leave the affairs of Egypt in the hands of his younger half-brother Smenkhkare. When Smenkhkare disappears on a hunting expedition, his sister Beketaten, known as Scarab, is forced to flee for her life.

Finding refuge among her mother's people, the Khabiru, Scarab has resigned herself to a life in exile...until she hears that her brother Smenkhkare is still alive. He is raising an army in Nubia to overthrow Ay and reclaim his throne. Scarab hurries south to join him as he confronts Ay and General Horemheb outside the gates of Thebes.

Publisher: https://www.writers-exchange.com/scarab2/

SCARAB - TUTANKHAMEN, Book 3: Scarab and her brother Smenkhkare are in exile in Nubia but are gathering an army to wrest control of Egypt from the boy king Tutankhamen and his controlling uncle, Ay. Meanwhile, the kingdoms are beset by internal troubles while the Amorites are pressing hard against the northern borders. Generals Horemheb and Paramessu must fight a war on two fronts while deciding where their loyalties lie--with the former king Smenkhkare or with the new young king in Thebes.

Smenkhkare and Scarab march on Thebes with their native army to meet the legions of Tutankhamen on the plains outside the city gates. As two brothers battle for supremacy and the throne of the Two Kingdoms, the fate of Egypt and the 18th dynasty hangs in the balance.

Finalist in 2013's Eppie Awards.

Congratulations
Max Overton
EPIC's eBook Awards Competition™ commends
you on being a
2013 EPIC eBook Awards™ finalist
in the category
Historical Fiction
with the entry
**Scarab
Tutankhamen**
Publisher:
**Writers Exchange
Epublishing**

Publisher: https://www.writers-exchange.com/scarab3/

SCARAB - AY, Book 4: Tutankhamen is dead and his grieving widow tries to rule alone, but her grandfather Ay has not destroyed the former kings just so he can be pushed aside. Presenting the Queen and General Horemheb with a fait accompli, the old Vizier assumes the throne of Egypt and rules with a hand of hardened bronze. His adopted son, Nakhtmin, will rule after him and stamp out the last remnants of loyalty to the former kings.

Scarab was sister to three kings and will not give in to the usurper and his son. She battles against Ay and his legions under the command of General Horemheb and aided by desert tribesmen and the gods of Egypt themselves. The final confrontation will come in the rich lands of the Nile delta where the future of Egypt will at last be decided.

Publisher: https://www.writers-exchange.com/scarab4/

SCARAB - HOREMHEB, Book 5: General Horemheb has taken control after the death of Ay and Nakhtmin. Forcing Scarab to marry him, he ascends the throne of Egypt. The Two Kingdoms settle into an uneasy peace as Horemheb proceeds to stamp out all traces of the former kings. He also persecutes the Khabiru tribesmen who were reluctant to help him seize power. Scarab escapes into the desert, where she is content to wait until Egypt needs her.

A holy man emerges from the desert and demands that Horemheb release the Khabiru so they may worship his god. Scarab recognises the holy man and supports him in his efforts to free his people. The gods of Egypt and of the Khabiru are invoked and disaster sweeps down on the Two Kingdoms as the Khabiru flee with Scarab and the holy man. Horemheb and his army pursue them to the shores of the Great Sea, where a natural event...or the very hand of God...alters the course of Egyptian history.

Publisher: https://www.writers-exchange.com/scarab5/

SCARAB - DESCENDANT, Book 6: Three thousand years after the reigns of the Amarnan Kings, the archaeologists who discovered the inscriptions in Syria journey to Egypt to find the tomb of Smenkhkare and his sister Scarab and the fabulous treasure they believe is there. Unscrupulous men and religious fanatics also seek the tomb, either to plunder it or to destroy it. Can the gods of Egypt protect their own, or will the ancients rely on modern day men and women of science?

Publisher: https://www.writers-exchange.com/scarab6/

The Pyramid Builders, A Novel of Ancient Egypt
{Historical: Ancient Egypt}

The third dynasty of the Old Kingdom of Egypt saw an extraordinary development of building techniques, from the simple structures of mud brick at the end of the second dynasty to the towering pyramids of the fourth dynasty. Just how these massive structures were built has long been a matter of conjecture, but history is made up of the lives and actions of individuals; kings and architects, scribes and priests, soldiers and artisans, even common labourers, and so the story of the Pyramid Builders unfolded over the course of more than a century. This is that story...

Book 1: Djoser

King Khasekhemwy has two sons, Djoser and Imhotep, but their destinies are very different. One will become king and the other his architect and the power behind the throne. Together, they plan to build something new, a great tomb that will be the wonder of the world. But not all is peaceful within the kingdoms of Egypt. Djoser's son Sekhemkhet will inherit the throne, but there are others that seek power and set their plans in motion, and they care nothing for the architectural ambitions of their king.

Ordinary men and women inhabit Djoser's Egypt too, living their own lives, dreaming of power or simple happiness, but sometimes these dreams do not harmonise with the plans of kings...

Publisher: https://www.writers-exchange.com/djoser/

Book 2: Sekhemkhet

Sekhemkhet faces the daunting prospect of following on from the glories of his father's achievement. He desires an even bigger pyramid than that of Djoser and orders Imhotep and Den to build it. However, the king finds it easier to build a tomb than to raise heirs to follow him on the throne, and a cousin seeks to take advantage of Sekhemkhet's precarious position and challenge the king.

Not all is well within Den's family. He is married, but love from an unexpected source threatens to destroy the success he has so laboriously built up. Will he sacrifice love for ambition, or can he find a way to have both?
Publisher: https://www.writers-exchange.com/sekhemkhet/

Book 3: Khaba

The throne of Egypt has passed to Khaba, an old man who seeks only to secure his family's position. Construction of a pyramid tomb is a secondary consideration, and the fortunes of those who desire to build them languish as he refuses further innovations. It is left to his grandson and heir, Huni, to dream of greater architectural glories.

Architect Den has achieved love, but at the cost of ambition. He and his burgeoning family struggle to survive, his relatives seeking out love of their own even as they look for opportunities to further their careers. The promise of a return to fulfilment is offered, but will they be able to grasp it?
Publisher: https://www.writers-exchange.com/khaba/

Book 4: Huni

Like a breath of fresh air after a generation of stagnation, Huni becomes king and sets about reorganising Egypt. He divides the land into administrative regions under governors and devises a way to bring the blessings of the gods to all men--he will build small pyramids up and down the length of the river, reserving a simple tomb for himself.

Even as Den and his sons build for the king, his twin daughters threaten to tear down the king's future. One falls in love with the heir to the throne, while the other seeks the heir's death. Which one succeeds will determine the fortunes of their extended family.

Publisher: https://www.writers-exchange.com/huni/

Book 5: Sneferu

The kings of Egypt are turning from the worship of all gods to raising the sun god Re above them all. Rather than a stepped pyramid for the spirit of the king to ascend to the undying stars, they seek a representation of the beneficent rays of the sun in a smooth-sided pyramid. This brings with it a host of new problems to be overcome by the king's architects. Meanwhile, the king takes several wives and has many sons who vie for power, using murder to achieve their ends.

Den is old and passes the title of architect on to his son Khepankh and grandson Djer, but they make mistakes as they try to learn new techniques of building massive pyramids. Their mistakes threaten to be their undoing, but they find a way to build true and strong, and a new talent arises from a union between Den's family and the heir to the throne.

Publisher: https://www.writers-exchange.com/sneferu/

Book 6: Khufu

Khufu is excited by the pyramids of his father Sneferu and wants to build a great one that will eclipse everything else ever built. The Great Pyramid presents unique challenges that must be overcome if the pyramid is to be built. Architect Hemiunu finds solutions, but even he relies on help from Rait, a woman of great talent. She must battle prejudice even from her own father if she is to achieve ultimate success.

The sons of Khufu vie for power. Their actions will lead to wars between nations, and call into question who has the right to sit on the throne of Egypt.

Meanwhile, the family of Den have taken to sailing and trade and find the fabled land of Punt where discoveries will affect the lives of kings yet unborn.
Publisher: https://www.writers-exchange.com/khufu/

Book 7: Djedefre

Djedefre becomes king, with his brother Hordjedef his principal adviser. Breaking with tradition, the king appoints Rait as his architect, gambling that she will be up to the task of building a pyramid. An earthquake damages the Sphinx, and is seen as an omen of the gods' disfavour, but the king makes a decision that might avert disaster, though many view it as added blasphemy. Concerned for the future, those close to the king plot to remove him.

The king's heir is put aside, and a struggle for power breaks out, leading to deadly strife between the brothers Baka and Setka. Death and exile follow, with consequences that threaten Egypt's future.
Publisher: https://www.writers-exchange.com/djedefre/

Book 8: Khafre

Khafre seizes control and takes the throne of his brother, while his nephew Baka flees to Amurru with his uncle Hordjedef. The new king wants a pyramid as big as his father's, appointing a conventional male architect. However, he has cause to regret his decision, bringing back Rait when things go wrong. Others passed over for the position seek to hurt Rait and violate her daughter Neferit.

The head of the Sphinx is rebuilt, with Khafre's features replacing the damaged face of the god Inpu. Hordjedef quarrels with exiled Baka and returns to Egypt, pleading for forgiveness, but as Khafre sickens, Baka seeks revenge. The heir, Menkaure, must battle for the throne of Egypt when his father Khafre dies.
Publisher: https://www.writers-exchange.com/khafre/

Book 9: Menkaure

Menkaure meets Baka in battle and defeats him. Baka returns to Amurru, but Menkaure's reign is beset by troubles at home and abroad. Although Menkaure's pyramid is rising swiftly, the king falls sick with the 'shaking fever', for which there is no cure. Only a medicine brought back from Punt seems to hold out hope, but Shepseskaf assumes the power of regent, ruling in place of his sick father.

An ambitious army officer by the name of Userkaf takes command of the northern army, and he is deeply devoted to the god Re, allying his family with the priests of Iunu. Neferit's daughter Peseshet strives to become a physician in the face of opposition from the medical fraternity.

Book 10: Shepseskaf

Menkaure's health continues to decline and Shepseskaf must now become king. He strives to finish his father's pyramid, but desires something simpler for himself, forsaking the pyramid form. Others desire power in Egypt--the king's sister Khentkaus wants to be king; Userkaf, now a General, dares to think of greater things; and even the priests of Re and Ptah look to increase their status. Shepseskaf's heir dies, and the king must not only rescue his family's future but must fight off Egypt's enemies at home and abroad.

In Amurru, Baka dies, and his son Bauefre desires the throne of Egypt. He leads an army south against Shepseskaf and Userkaf in a final battle.

TULPA
{Paranormal Thriller}

From the rainforests of tropical Australia to the cane fields and communities of the North Queensland coastal strip, a horror is unleashed by those foolishly playing with unknown forces...

A fairy story to amuse small children leads four bored teenagers and a young university student in a North Queensland town to becoming interested in an ancient Tibetan technique for creating a life form. When their seemingly harmless experiment sets free terror and death, the teenagers are soon fighting to contain a menace that reproduces exponentially.

The police are helpless to end the horror. Aided by two old game hunters, a student of the paranormal and a few small children, the teenagers must find a way of destroying what they unintentionally released. But how can they stop beings that can escape into an alternate reality when threatened?

Publisher: https://www.writers-exchange.com/TULPA/

We Came From Konigsberg
{Historical: Holocaust}

Based on a true story gleaned from the memories of family members sixty years after the events, from photographs and documents, and from published works of nonfiction describing the times and events described in the narrative, *We Came From Konigsberg* is set in January 1945.

The Soviet Army is poised for the final push through East Prussia and Poland to Berlin. Elisabet Daeker and her five young sons are in Königsberg, East Prussia and have heard the shocking stories of Russian atrocities. They're desperate to escape to the perceived safety of Germany. To survive, Elisabet faces hardships endured at the hands of Nazi hardliners, of Soviet troops bent on rape, pillage and murder, and of Allied cruelty in the Occupied Zones of post-war Germany.

Winner of the 2014 EPIC Ebook Awards.

Publisher: https://www.writers-exchange.com/we-came-from-konigsberg/

You can find ALL our books up on our website at:

https://www.writers-exchange.com

All our Historical Novels:

https://www.writers-exchange.com/category/genres/historical/

All Max's Books:

https://www.writers-exchange.com/max-overton/